Hester Browne is the author of numerous bestselling novels including *The Little Lady Agency in the Big Apple*, *The Finishing Touches* and *Swept Off Her Feet*. She divides her time between London and Herefordshire.

'Hester Browne writes with such wit and polish.
I love it!' Sophie Kinsella

'Gorgeous writing' Jill Mansell

'Deliciously addictive' *Cosmopolitan*

'Funny and flirty' *Glamour*

# THE RUNAWAY
# PRINCESS

Hester Browne

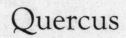

Quercus

First published in the USA in 2012 by Gallery Books,
a division of Simon and Schuster, Inc.

First published in Great Britain in 2013 by

Quercus
55 Baker Street
7th Floor, South Block
London
W1U 8EW

A CIP catalogue record for this book is available
from the British Library

PB ISBN 978 1 78206 567 8
EBOOK ISBN 978 1 78206 568 5

10 9 8 7 6 5 4 3 2 1

Printed and bound in Great Britain by Clays Ltd, St Ives plc

Typeset by Ellipsis Books Limited, Glasgow

For Her Majesty Queen Elizabeth II,
who can teach all of us a thing or two about
grace, determination, and a signature handbag

# PROLOGUE

Like most little girls raised on a diet of glass slippers and royal weddings, I used to believe that princesses were born, not made.

I mean, that was the whole point, surely? You either had the tiara-wearing, crowd-charming, prince-captivating, good-deed-doing, swishy hair genes or you didn't. Even Cinderella – not the greatest prospect, on the face of it – had the Daintiest Feet in the Land as a big flashing sign, just in case we missed the gracious humility and dazzling beauty.

Personally, I never saw myself as a long-lost princess. I was more interested in the magic beans, for a start. My feet weren't exactly dainty, and after a hard day's gardening, you could have put a *marrow* under my mattress and I'd have snored away quite happily. In fact, the only remotely princess-like trait in my family was a bad habit of making a run for it when things looked like they might go pumpkin-shaped.

(You could also argue that I had an ugly sister — but then my sister, Kelly, would say the same thing, so that probably doesn't count.)

Luckily, I never had to worry about any of this . . . until I fell in love with a prince.

Once I'd got over the shock of discovering that princes do

exist outside of Disney films, I realized very quickly that a girl isn't automatically transformed into a princess once he's wedged on the glass slipper. Oh no. No, that's just the *start* of it.

What marks out a true princess is how she handles the bit that comes after Happily Ever After. And for that you need more than a set of hair extensions and a ballgown that changes color. You need to know exactly who you are, underneath that tiara. And you need to realize that princesses don't run away. Not even in glass slippers.

# CHAPTER ONE

'Imagine I'm Max Barclay,' said Jo. 'I've just got you a drink. I'm coming over to have an uncomplicated, no-pressure party chat with you.'

To make it more real, she began to swagger across the balcony toward me as if wearing a pair of invisible leather chaps, a takeaway cup of coffee standing in for the cheap white wine.

'Well, if it isn't the lovely Amy Wilde, Chelsea's very own Queen of Spades,' she drawled in Max's confident Sloaney tones. '*Hoe's* it hanging, Amy? Ha-ha.'

Then she did a startling impression of Max's wink, and paused for me to respond, as rehearsed. Right on cue, my brain emptied of all thoughts, leaving only a faint background buzz of panic, and the sinking knowledge that I was about to say something stupid. I always did. That was why I spent 90 percent of all parties in the kitchen by the sausage rolls.

I groaned inwardly. I wasn't even at the party yet. We weren't even in a *room*. I couldn't even claim Jo had Max Barclay's disconcerting Roman nose to put me off. This party would be the third time Jo had tried to matchmake me with Max, and on both previous occasions the famous Barclay nose had robbed me of all coherent thought; it was supposed to 'prove' some familial indiscretion with the Duke of Wellington but all my brain could see was a golden eagle in red trousers. I'd virtually had to hold my jaw shut to stop myself mentioning it, which hadn't exactly made for sparkling conversation.

I took a deep breath and made an effort to remember the inoffensive conversational underhand serves we'd been practicing. There were some advantages to sharing a flat with the woman who put the *art* into *party*. Jo put lots of other things into parties too, like vodka melon pops and undetectable guest-mingling, but for the last year or so her considerable attentions had been focused on coaching me out of what she called my 'party paralysis.'

'Um . . .'

'No!' Jo dropped Max's swagger and pointed at me. 'That's where you always go wrong. Stop thinking about what you *shouldn't* say and let the conversation *flow*.' She made a graceful gesture with her free hand. 'Let the inoffensive small talk about the weather and the shooting and what you got for Christmas ripple forth until you find a mutually interesting topic—'

'Jo, I keep telling you — I'm from Yorkshire,' I interrupted. 'We don't *do* small talk in Yorkshire. We don't do *any* talk, if we can help it. Our menfolk play cricket, a game conducted in respectful silence by both spectators and players, and our womenfolk hold entire conversations using only their eyebrows and their bosoms. If in doubt, say nowt. It's practically the county motto.'

'But how do you *meet* anyone?' Jo looked bewildered. The concept of not talking for more than ten seconds was something she found incomprehensible; she was constantly yakking away on the phone at home, even while she was in the *bath*, usually to someone called Tilly, Milly, or Lily. Sometimes Billy.

'We move to London. Can I have that coffee now, please?' I asked, holding out a hand. I'd been digging flowerbeds over since 9 a.m.; I needed the caffeine.

Jo lifted it just out of my grasp and raised her eyebrows expectantly, so I sighed, and delivered the line she wanted. 'Everything in the garden's rosy, Max, thanks for asking.'

She handed over the cappuccino with a proud smile. 'See? You're funny. You just need a prompt.'

'I have one. It's called standing in the kitchen asking people what they'd like to drink. It's been working for me for years.'

'You are *not* spending another party lurking around in there with the dishcloths and vol-au-vents. I want you out in the action. Mingling. Meeting people. Showing them the light you keep hiding under that portable bushel of yours.'

'You want me to show them my bushel now?'

Jo ignored that, and pounced on another hot topic while I was busy sugaring my coffee. 'Now, do you need any help with your costume? The brilliant thing about a heaven and hell theme is that it gives everyone enough scope to come up with something flattering *or* icebreaking or even—'

'Yes, I've been thinking about that,' I said swiftly. 'Why don't I go as a mime artist? They're pretty hellish. *Or* Ted suggested that he and I could go as a pantomime horse; then you wouldn't have to worry about *either* of us putting our feet in it. We could just do party chitchat by fluttering our eyelashes. Or nodding our horsey head.'

Jo leaned back against the balcony (not a safe thing to do,

several hundred feet above Chelsea, given the balcony owner's lackadaisical approach to maintenance), and inhaled deeply through her nose. She did that so she wouldn't have to pause to take a breath and so allow me to interrupt her.

'*One*,' she said, counting off on a gloved finger, 'you are the cohost of this party and, as such, you can't spend it miming "Here are the drinks" and "Please don't be sick on the sofa." *Two*: if you spend the evening in a *horse costume* with Ted Botham's nose shoved up in your business, everyone will think you and Ted are a couple, not work partners with a common fear of conversation. Which leads me to *three*: the whole point of this party is for you to meet at least one of the lovely men I have lined up for you. It's in your horoscope for this month. You're irresistible from January the ninth. Just let Max talk about his car. I do. Ask him about fuel consumption and nod every time you hear the word *torque*, and you'll be fine.'

I stared at her. Jo had been going to parties since she was knee-high to a cocktail sausage. She'd probably been match-making at them from that age too.

Before I could protest she slung an arm around my shoulders and squeezed. 'Amy, you're far too much fun to waste good mingling time trapped by the fridge with the sobbing drunk girls and the weirdos. You should be out there *sparkling*. You're fantastic company. You make me laugh all the time.'

'That's because you can't understand my accent,' I pointed out.

'Your accent is fine,' she said darkly. 'It's your weird suspicion of an honest compliment that I can't understand.'

You wouldn't take me and Jo for flatmates. When I first met

her, she was flicking through a copy of *Tatler* and sipping a mineral water, and I thought she'd be one of those glossy posh girls who'd never had a job and screamed at the sight of bread — which goes to show how wrong you can be. (The 'mineral water' was a vodka and tonic, for a start. And she could demolish a white loaf quicker than you could say 'carb hangover.')

But the glossiness was real. Jo de Vere had a few princess genes in her, I could tell. Everything about her was glossy, from her long brown hair to her crimson pedicure and her *divine* pearls-and-Labradors accent. She knew everyone — reliable builders, unreliable baronets, taxidermists, tax accountants, taxi drivers — and she was never, *never* lost for words, even when everyone else was rigid with embarrassment or shock. She claimed it was down to a combination of her constantly remarrying parents and moving house a lot as a child but she had the happy knack of putting people at ease, and then getting them to do exactly what she wanted.

I, on the other hand, was a newly qualified gardener from one of Yorkshire's sleepiest villages, with the ragged nails of a serial killer and corkscrew blond hair only a troll could love. I'd been known to deliver a one-liner or two, but usually after I'd rehearsed it for three days while doing someone's pruning. My sole claim to fame was that my mum had baked the Eccles cake that Princess Anne sampled on her visit to the Great Yorkshire Show ('Deliciously moist, Mrs Wilde'), and although I had plans to stun London with my wildflower balcony designs, at the moment I was London's most thorough hedge trimmer and lawn mower.

What Jo and I did have in common, to begin with at least, was Ted Botham. Ted and I shared a house while I was studying to be a garden designer and he was studying estate management, but mainly spending his days irritating local farmers with his metal detector. He was also one of Jo's oldest friends from boarding school. The summer we graduated, Ted needed someone to help him with a couple of gardening holiday jobs he'd blagged in London, and I, apparently, was his first choice, thanks to my first-class degree in horticultural design and, coincidentally, my van. I was full of plans for my own business, but I needed work and a place to live. And it just happened that Jo needed a lodger for the spare room in her flat near Buckingham Palace, and *really* didn't want that lodger to be Ted, something I could understand after having shared a bathroom with him myself for the previous year.

Despite Jo's demure appearance, I had an inkling that she and I might get on when my 'interview' consisted of her dragging me and Ted off to her friend's karaoke bar in Battersea. After our fourth Cher duet in a row, delivered with an impromptu dance routine and genuine tears of emotion, I realized that Jo had somehow managed to get me to sing in public, something that had never happened before, not to mention dance. The interview ended twelve hours later back at her house, with me frying up a full English breakfast for our hangovers, which she said was the best she'd ever had. (True. My fried eggs are my calling card.)

I'd been there nearly two and a half years now. That added up to about twenty parties, one roomful of 'eligible men' in red trousers whom I'd so far failed to click with, dozens of full English breakfasts, and seven houseplants that Jo had killed off with loving neglect.

'Costume,' she repeated, with the same knee tap and urgent stare she used on her dilatory workmen. 'We need to get it sorted out before Ted borrows that horse costume from whichever idiot friend of his wore it to Hattie's wedding in Wiltshire last year.'

'What?' So Ted hadn't been joking when he suggested it.

'Never mind. Chop-chop. What's your idea of heaven? Or hell? I don't mind which, so long as it can be accessorized with a feather boa.'

'Hell would be going on *Britain's Got Talent*, making a fool of myself in front of millions of people,' I said at once. 'So I suppose I could maybe just wear my normal clothes and carry Badger under my arm? There's always someone with a performing dog.'

Badger was my dog. Well, sort of my dog — I'd inherited him from my grandmother, so his tricks were limited to sitting for a mint imperial and bringing a remote control. He came to work with me or Ted, depending on which location had the more interesting digging opportunities.

'Reality shows — good idea!' Jo gave me her best encouraging smile. 'But we need to think *hot* reality shows. We need a costume where we can really trowel on the makeup. Make the most of your beautiful eyes.' She squinched her nose up in thought — not her best look. 'What about *Strictly Come Dancing*?'

'Yup. That's hell,' I confirmed. 'Fake tan is hell. Low-cut dresses held on with sticky tape are hell. Public voting is hell. People having to do sexy tangos with washed-up soap stars is—'

'Okay, okay. I've got the perfect dress for you,' said Jo.

'Oh, come on! I'd look *ridiculous* in one of your dresses.' I laughed without thinking, then realized that hadn't come out the way I'd meant it to. 'Um, not that you wear ridiculous dresses, just that they're much smaller than . . . I mean, *you're* so much smaller than me, not that your dresses are too small, I mean, they're very nice, but you do that low-cut thing better than me . . .' I starfished my hands in horror as my mouth carried on running long after my brain stopped and sat down.

This was my problem, basically. Imagine that, at a party. With guys you were trying to impress. That's what comes of growing up somewhere chat-less.

Jo opened her eyes so wide I could see where her mascara started. 'Amy. *Stop thinking so hard.* Fill the silence with a choking fit if you have to.'

'Oi? How long has this tea break been going on?'

We both swiveled round to see Ted Botham's broad frame looming tweedily from Grace's minimalist Scandinavian loft kitchen. He'd managed to trail mud from somewhere, although that could have come from Badger, who galloped across the balcony toward us, a stick in his bearded jaws, and made straight for Jo's immaculate black pencil skirt.

'Badger!' squeaked Jo, holding out her arms for him to jump up on her.

One of the little things that had made me warm to Jo was that despite her meticulous dress sense — today: leopard-skin swing coat, pencil skirt, black patent leather boots for kicking her client's slow-moving decorators back onto schedule — she could never see a dog without stopping to pat it. When I'd moved in, she'd worried more about where Badger wanted to sleep than whether I had references.

'Hello, Jo,' said Ted. I guessed he'd been digging borders, because his curly brown hair was even curlier with the damp, and his cheeks were as red as his trousers. I didn't know what it was with Jo's male friends and their red trousers. 'What is it today?' he added in the gently horrible tone so beloved of old school friends. 'Bullying builders, or voice-overs for washing-up liquid?'

'Builders.' She checked her watch. 'In fact, I should be getting back to Callie Hamilton's — her electricians have been fitting those dimmer switches so long now she should start charging them rent.'

Although Jo was officially an actress and had appeared in two television ads for washing-up liquid (which was nearly a series, we reckoned), she had a far more lucrative sideline managing building projects for friends of friends who were either too busy or too scared to chivvy workmen along. Between her charming manners and her refusal to hear the word *no*, Jo saved her clients thousands in overtime.

'You could start by cracking a whip here,' Ted observed, nodding at my packed lunch, then tapping his watch. 'We need to get to Fulham by two.'

'No, I think you'll find that's your job.' I reached into my rucksack for our diary, glad of the chance to steer us away from the rocky subject of the party. I was in charge of bookings, as well as driving, invoicing, design, and plant purchasing. Ted chopped things and mowed things. 'You were supposed to be in Fulham this morning.'

Ted looked sheepish. 'I thought we could go together. I've, ah, had to move that job in Eltham Avenue. Mrs Matthews wasn't ready for me when I called round.'

'What? Wasn't she back from the gym?'

He flushed. 'Um, she hadn't quite . . . got up.'

'What on earth do you mean?' I asked, even though I had a good idea what was coming. 'Was she ill?'

'She will be if she thinks a dressing gown like that's appropriate for *January*,' he went on. 'Seriously, I could see her . . . She should look into pajamas.'

'She was in her negligee!' Jo hooted with glee, making Badger wriggle in her lap. 'Ted! She wanted you to *refresh her beds*!'

'Stop it.'

'Or was she after some *hoeing*? Or . . .' Jo tapped my arm impatiently. 'Help me, Amy, I'm running out of double entendres.'

I put a finger on my chin. 'Did she want you to harden off her perennials? Um, *something something* her ranunculus?'

Ted gave us a baleful look, and I couldn't go on. It was like poking fun at a big cow. A big Hereford cow in a sweater.

A significant number of our clients had seen too many TV adaptations of *Lady Chatterley's Lover* and fancied having their own Mellors popping round once a week to trim the borders — it certainly kept our coffers full over the summer. Ted, with his broad shoulders and habit of turning up for work in his old rugby kit, was the perfect garden accessory, especially in hot weather when he liked to work in a white undershirt (he wasn't the type to work topless, not even in a heatwave, not even with encouragement from his swooning employers).

'You'll just have to be less irresistible,' said Jo. 'Dig less, talk more. Start giving her your wildflower meadow lecture. God knows I love you both, but if I have to listen to the pair of you droning on about the plight of the honeybee for one more dinner, I'm going to boycott honey altogether.'

'You won't be saying that when I've put a beehive on the roof of Leominster Place and we're making our own honey,' I started.

Ted tossed his head as much as a six-foot bloke could. 'If you understood the first thing about the basic biomechanics of—'

'Buzz off,' said Jo, meaningfully. 'With the emphasis on zzzzzz.'

'So you just came round here to pick up your chaperone for the afternoon job?' I asked. I didn't want Jo puncturing our business dream for the year, just a few days in.

'Actually, no,' he retorted airily. 'I wanted to see what you've been doing with the famous feng shui cottage garden balcony. And, ah, to see if Grace's famous Dream Seeds are surviving without her while she's away skiing?'

I was pretty sure this was a convenient lie — he'd almost certainly come to 'bump into' Jo — but I humored him, and pointed to five artisan-crafted terracotta pots lined up along the far railing, showing precisely arranged compost and not much else. 'They're probably quite glad of the break. She chants over them, you know.'

Grace — a twenty-six-year-old Trustafarian who'd spent more time being life-coached than most people did in full-time employment, and one of our most regular clients — had been given the seeds at the end of her latest course, and planting them 'with faith and love and self-belief' was supposed to make both the plants and her secret dreams spring forth. She planted and chanted; I tended. And mended.

Jo looked deeply cynical. 'What are they supposed to be bringing her again?'

'Serenity, prosperity, stability in the foreign bond market, and for Richard to seal the Palace View deal, then propose by Valentine's Day. With a ring from Asprey.'

Ted and I also wanted Richard, a property developer, to buy Palace View, a huge development with even huger possibilities for gardening contracts. Not just the hundred or so balconies, but also the land around the site, and the rooftop. I had a bit of a bee in my bonnet — yes, ho ho — about wildflower meadows, the sort that brought butterflies and bees and insects into the heart of the city; it had been my final year project. I had a plan to create localized wildflower meadows and then set up local beehives — but first I needed the space to plant meadows.

As a side order, some serenity for Grace would be a bonus for me. I'd redesigned her balcony twice in a year already, once for feng shui, once for color therapy.

Jo and Ted were both staring at the pots, their faces strained with the effort of finding something positive to say.

'Nothing so far?' asked Jo. 'I mean, should there be? I don't blame the plants for not wanting to get out of bed in this weather.'

Ted did a deliberate double take, from me to the pots and

back again. 'Well, duh! They're probably *designed* not to sprout so she'll have to sign up for another session. That's how these people get gullible women hooked.'

'You're so right,' said Jo, deadpan. 'Before you know it poor Grace'll be on the hard stuff, like bulbs. And boracics.'

'Brassicas.' Ted's ears went red.

'Ooh, Ted, no need for that!' She swiped him playfully. 'So, when's Grace back from skiing?'

'Next week.'

'Can you speed them up a bit?' She peered into a pot, but there was nothing to see. 'Or just put in something that's actually growing?'

'Not allowed, apparently. Only *her* energies will awaken the magic seeds.' I made woo-woo gestures over it.

Jo put the pot down. 'Then she's doomed. Grace has all the energy of a three-day-old salad.'

'Ah, now.' I raised a hold-up-a-second finger. 'I had a feeling she'd manage to kill them off by feeding them Red Bull or leaving them under her sunbed, so I nicked the rest of the packet while she was planting these pots and took the spare seeds home. I've planted my own set. For her, not for me,' I added when they both looked blank. 'I haven't completely lost it.'

To be honest, I'd felt so sorry for flaky Grace, putting what little self-esteem she had into this latest nonsense, that I'd wanted to make sure she got the boost she was hoping for. Even if she didn't get the ring from Asprey, she might get a buzz from making the seedlings appear. I was just . . . helping.

Jo caught on first. 'Forward planning — I like it! So, how's her future looking?'

'Or should I say ours?' added Ted. 'Not that I'm being mercenary here, but we could do with that contract.'

I thought of the row of pea-green seedlings on the kitchen windowsill. With careful feeding and overnights in the airing cupboard, they weren't looking too bad. 'She's okay for the bond market, the health, and the proposal, but serenity's looking dodgy. Still, if you've got the first three . . .'

'Do we know what they are, these magic seeds?' Ted didn't normally get too involved in the horticultural side of things, but he could sense a business opportunity when he saw one. 'Could we be selling them? To other hippie weirdos who need backups?'

'No idea.' I'd done a bit of trawling, but so far hadn't been able to work them out. Not even my dad, a walking plant encyclopedia, had any idea. 'They look like some sort of—'

'Sorry as I am to leave this episode of *Gardeners' Question Time*, I should be making tracks.' Jo got up and rearranged her huge scarf. 'Callie Hamilton, the world's neediest client, will be wanting to quiz me about this party, and I'll have to think of reasons why I can't invite her.' She pointed at each of us in turn, fixing us with her sharp brown eyes. 'Keep thinking about your party outfits. I want glitter and conversation pieces, from both of you. And no pantomime horses.'

'If I wear those jeweled washing-up gloves you gave me for Christmas, can I stay in the kitchen?' I asked. 'Ted can wear his undershirt and bring his best rake — that seems to be most people's idea of heaven round here.'

'I'm not wearing an *undershirt* to a party in January,' said

Ted, horrified.

Jo laughed, a full-bodied cackle that was always a surprise to hear bursting out of her rosebud mouth, and with a final affectionate ear scratch for Badger, she clip-clopped off in her patent leather boots, waving a hand behind her.

Ted watched her leave with an expression of longing I usually only saw him direct toward takeaway curries. When he turned back and saw me and Badger staring at him, it vanished at once, to be replaced by faint embarrassment. He pinched what was left of my egg sandwich and stuffed it in his mouth before I could stop him.

'So, what's the plan with Amazing Grace's plants? When are you going to swap them over?' he asked through a mouthful of crust.

'I'll take these ones home with me tonight, then bring back the five pots I've managed to grow when she's back next week. If I put my plants into her special pots, she'll think these are the ones she grew herself.'

'These are special pots?' Ted peered at the handmade terracotta containers. 'Look pretty bog-standard to me.'

I sighed. Grace had had them shipped over from Italy specially. 'How little you know your female clientèle, Ted.'

'And that's what I keep you on board for,' he said, stretching out his hand for the last of my crisps.

I took enormous pleasure in swiping them out of his reach and feeding them to Badger.

# CHAPTER TWO

The airy flat in Leominster Place that I shared with Jo had belonged to her family since 1865.

Once upon a time, the de Veres owned the whole house, four elegant stories of it, with a squad of servants below stairs and a view, if you leaned out of an attic window, of Buckingham Palace. After the war, it had been divided into apartments and sold off to pay death duties, all except the flat Jo now lived in, which had once been the de Veres' living quarters, and a tiny garden flat in the basement where her mother, Marigold, stayed when she needed to escape whatever her domestic crisis was that month. Jo insisted on keeping at least two full floors between them, 'for everyone's sanity.'

I'd seen prewar photographs of 17 Leominster Place when it was a society-party hot spot, with uniformed staff lined up the sweeping front staircase and potted palms everywhere, but those days were long gone. A mail table full of pizza leaflets and Dickon from upstairs's mountain bike now stood where housemaids had once bobbed curtsies, and the parquet they'd polished was covered by durable carpet. Not every trace of opulence had vanished, though. Our flat might have been the smallest, but it contained the jewel of the old house: the master bathroom. Faced with the depressing task of dividing his family home up into apartments, Jo's grandfather drew the line at ripping out the marble-tiled main bathroom, with its magnificent clunking mahogany loo and Art Nouveau stained-glass window.

'Showers are for the French. If an Englishman can't have a decent bath, he might as well give up,' he'd said, and I couldn't have agreed more. During the border-digging and bulb-planting months, the thought of a long soak in Montgomery de Vere's rolltop bath, wineglass propped against the metal rack, a sneaky dollop of Jo's Penhaligon's bath oil soothing my weary muscles, was the only thing that kept me going through the backbreaking working day.

I loved living with the ghosts of the old house. From my bed, I could see one half of the plaster ceiling rose that had supported a magnificent brass light fitting, and there were two wrought-iron balconies outside the long French windows in our sitting room, where it didn't take much to imagine blushing debutantes stepping out to cool their cheeks after a vigorous Viennese waltz with men in starched evening dress.

That was what I liked to imagine anyway. Jo had a whole array of other, more outrageous stories.

The balconies made excellent window boxes for the various cuttings and seedlings I always had on the go, and gave Badger somewhere to sunbathe. There wasn't room for a human to lie down and the rusty ledge didn't look strong enough to support a modern human being anyway, so I kept them full of blowsy red geraniums and pots of Mediterranean herbs, and on warm summer nights, the soft fragrance of wallflowers drifted through the flat along with the rumble of London traffic.

This Saturday morning, I was moving all the houseplants, including Grace Wright's Dream Seeds, onto the balcony, which we'd agreed would remain firmly out of bounds throughout the party. I wedged the seedlings safely behind a window box and sat back on my heels, oddly proud of the seven brave green shoots and the beginnings of tightly furled leaves.

Even without Grace's guru business, seeds always felt magical to me. I hadn't mentioned it to Jo — she had an allergy to anything remotely mystical — but ever since my dad had first helped my fat little fingers to shove a tomato seed into a pot, I'd been spellbound by them. You opened up the packet with impossibly tall and colorful flowers on the front to find these ordinary brown chips of nothing. But then you covered them with a blanket of warm soil, watered them, fed them, and — as if by magic — something woke up inside the seed and it knew when to grow, and where to find the light, and how high to reach. Add in all the amazing natural magic with bees dancing pollen around on their wings, from flower to orchard to flower, and who needed fairy tales?

Okay, so I'd nicked a couple of Grace's seeds for my own dreams.

One for the Palace View contract, so I could unveil my plans for a whole building's worth of cottage garden balconies, and so Ted could have a really big lawn to mow into the perfect stripes – his goal in life.

And another to wish for something . . . new. Didn't matter what. A surprise. I shivered at the thought of inviting the unknown into my life. As a rule, I didn't like surprises. I liked to know exactly where I was. But lately, I'd felt ready. I could handle something new.

Just moving to London had been a massive leap of faith for me, and I'd been incredibly lucky so far. To have found an affordable flat right in the middle of town, and a brilliant flatmate like Jo, and a job straight out of college — sometimes I looked back and couldn't believe it had slotted into place like that. My sister Kelly had always said (not very nicely) I was one of those lucky people who fell on their feet, but the luckier I felt, the harder I worked to make sure it wasn't just luck.

I closed my eyes and let anticipation ripple through me.

*Just not a surprise in red trousers,* I added quickly, in case some invisible force was listening in.

'Are those Grace's seedlings?' Jo asked, appearing by my side with a clipboard.

'Yup.' I glanced upward. 'We're going to lock the balcony windows this time. Aren't we? After what happened at Christmas?'

We both grimaced.

At our Christmas party, the fire brigade had come round to rescue a guest clinging to the edge of our balcony by his fingertips. We never found out if he'd been climbing up or had fallen off. He was wearing a Santa hat, so we guessed he'd been planning a big entrance and missed the chimney. He ended up getting a date with one of Jo's actress friends who'd strapped up his sprained wrist, and Jo had drinks with a fireman, so, as Jo pointed out, it wasn't entirely for nothing.

She nodded. 'Strictly out of bounds. Much as I'd like a visit from those *divine* fire brigade men again, I don't think it's worth the risk. And I promised Mrs Mainwaring there would be no danger of inebriated young men trying to climb in through hers by mistake.'

'Are you sure she wasn't hoping you'd say exactly the opposite? She was the one trying to get them to unjam her sticky window last time.'

Irene Mainwaring, and her supercilious tomcat Elvis, had the flat below ours. She was a retired piano teacher with pale blue hair, and although she frequently complained about being 'driven to derangement' by Jo's parties, she nearly always appeared at the end of them herself and could very easily be persuaded to demonstrate variations on the twist. She undermined her outrage by holding a raucous fortnightly date with her bridge club, after which we'd see her staggering out with a clanking recycling box while wearing diamante-studded dark glasses. Elvis made himself scarce for those.

'Well, I've invited her, to be on the safe side. She can't moan once she's here. And Dickon from upstairs. The Harrises are on holiday, and Marigold is in the country. Thank God.' Jo looked up from her clipboard. 'Hell *is* a party with your own mother chatting up the handsomest specimens and getting tiddled on cherry brandy cocktails.' She shuddered theatrically.

'Did you tell Mrs Mainwaring and Dickon it was a heaven and hell party?' I asked. 'Or is Dickon going to come in his usual costume?'

Dickon in the attic was a portrait painter. Not, as I'd initially thought, a painter and decorator. That had caused an awkward misunderstanding when I'd asked him if he could paint my bedroom, but we were over that now. More or less. He drifted around the house in a series of big shirts and tight jeans, and you'd never guess that his dad was actually a senior policeman from the smells that emerged from his studio.

Jo sighed. 'I think he got the message. It's so hard to talk to Dickon when you can see him eyeing up your proportions. Anyway, he's the heaven/hell expert right now. Have you seen his latest work in progress?'

'How can I miss it? It's a seven-foot canvas and he leaves it on the landing to dry. Just because he gave the angel green hair doesn't make it look any less like you in a big pair of wings.'

'Oh!' Jo looked surprised. 'I thought it was you.'

'Me? Why would I pose for him?' I turned red. 'I don't even like having my passport photos done! And this angel's . . . how can I put it? Somewhat challenged in the robe department.'

Jo squinted at me. Jo's squints were the sort that cut right through to the heart of the matter. 'So what if Dickon's based this angel on you? It's not a cardinal sin to acknowledge your own good points,' she informed me. 'In fact, it's a weird form of inverse vanity, pretending you're some kind of wild-haired yokel when in fact you're perfectly presentable, bordering on very attractive. And you can't keep playing the country bumpkin card when you've been living here long enough to cut up the black cab drivers round Hyde Park Corner. You're cute! Men fancy you! Embrace it! Although,' she added, 'you might want to clean under your nails first.'

My cheeks felt hot. 'Is this about Max Barclay? Because the thing is, I know he's your friend, but I honestly don't have any amusing stories about ski lifts, and he makes me feel—'

'That's exactly what I mean.' Jo turned up her palms in despair. 'You're so *resistant* to being set up. Have you got a secret celebrity boyfriend you're not telling me about? Are you in love with Ted?'

'No!' I unbuckled a bit under her gaze. 'It's just . . .'

'What?' she implored. 'What do I have to do to get you up on the dating horse?'

'Don't laugh, but I've always thought the right guy will turn up on his own. And I'm not *unhappy* being single, you know. If I'm not working, I'm asleep.'

'Sure there's no handsome farmer back home? No honest-faced country vet drinking tea with your parents and waiting for you to return?'

Jo read a lot of romantic fiction.

I nearly choked. 'Definitely not. I wouldn't take any boyfriend home until I'd got a ring on my finger — my dad makes the Spanish Inquisition look like a bunch of kindly aunts. No one's good enough for his princess.'

'Dickon's got a degree from the Royal College of Art.' Jo nodded significantly. 'Stick *that* on your allotment.'

I allowed myself a tiny glow of pride at the thought of inspiring a real artist to paint, then remembered just how detailed the painting had been, particularly in the décolletage region. My head spun round to Jo. 'Did you see where the *freckles* were on that angel?'

'That's it,' said Jo grimly, scribbling on her clipboard. 'If you refuse to let me find you a boyfriend, then I will devote tonight to finding Dickon a muse. A really foxy one who doesn't mind taking her kit off.'

I'd seen the guest list. Four of Jo's friends were burlesque dancers and most of the rest could easily be mistaken for one. 'That shouldn't be hard.'

'I like a party with a *purpose*.' She jangled my van keys at me. 'Are you ready? Lots to do! We need to take Badger to his safe house and go to the supermarket for enough crisps to stuff a donkey, and then I'm going to throw open my wardrobe and transform you into something so gorgeous Mr Right will gravitate into your orbit from hundreds of miles away, all of his own accord and with no reference to skiing or tennis or any other posh topic that activates your defensive chip.'

I opened my mouth to disagree, but Jo did her Pointy Finger of Silence and I shut up.

We'd said eight o'clock on the invites, and at quarter past, Jo and I were sitting in an empty, dust-sheeted flat surrounded by dishes of stuffed olives while Jo had her usual panic that everyone was having the best night of their lives round at some other friend's flat.

'I bet it's that cow Emma Harley-Wright!' She glared at her unusually silent phone. 'She's always throwing guerrilla pop-up parties, just to *ruin other people's nights!*'

Secretly, a tiny part of me was hoping maybe we *had* chosen the wrong day. I wasn't totally convinced about my costume, which was making me yearn for a DVD box set and a pizza, rather than a night's carousing. After some heated discussion about turning me into Eve (Jo's theater-school body stocking, loose hair, and an apple), we'd compromised on her pink silk pajamas and smudgy eye makeup. I was a heavenly long lie-in.

I was worried I looked more like Satan's unironed laundry basket.

Jo had opted for heaven too, but she did look heavenly: her neat curves were poured into a gold velvet evening dress, with her granny's fake diamonds round her neck, gold foil in her hair, and a lavish amount of glittery body lotion on the rest of her. She was, obviously, a glass of champagne.

'No one's going to come, and we've massively overcatered.' Jo paced up and down, trailing bits of body glitter as she went. 'It looks like we're hosting some sort of snack convention!'

That was my fault. Whereas Jo's mum had drilled cocktail recipes into her from an early age, my mum had taught me that it was bad manners to let a guest leave a party without a small rucksack of food for tomorrow's tea. I think when Mum met Princess Anne, she'd even tried to slip her an Eccles cake for later.

I eyed the décor. We'd put all the Christmas stars back up and tacked fairy lights round everything. Every spare sheet we owned was covered in gold stars, while the red lightbulbs in the hall and Jo's bedroom were probably making the flat look highly dubious from the outside.

'Right.' Jo stopped pacing and fixed me with a look. 'It's time to break open the emergency bottle.'

Party rules were that if guests hadn't arrived by half past, we could open the best bottle of wine to cheer ourselves up. Just as I was fiddling with the foil, the doorbell rang, at which point the cork exploded and prosecco gushed all over our makeshift confessional (the sofa).

'I'll get it.' Jo dashed out and left me to mop up the wine

as best I could with one of the 'clouds' (cushions encased in bubble wrap). I wasn't presenting the best view of myself when Jo reappeared, plus guests.

'Look who's here!' she said, shepherding in our first party-goers while doing her 'whoa, Nelly!' expression behind their backs. I had to struggle to keep a straight face.

It was hard to say what Mrs Mainwaring and Dickon had come as. Her chartreuse evening blouse clashed violently with Dickon's red velvet jacket. He was looming over her, his hair all wild and artisty. My mind went blank, but Jo was making vigorous 'say something' gestures over their heads. Nothing we'd rehearsed had prepared me for this, though.

'Um . . . wow!' I blurted out. 'Have you come as one of those spooky ventriloquist acts? Ha-ha! Dickon, are you working Mrs Mainwaring from behind?'

'No!' they both said, equally horrified. Jo clapped a hand over her eyes. But it was too late; we were all embarrassed.

'I am His Satanic Majesty,' said Dickon, hurt.

'And I'm Liza Minnelli,' said Mrs Mainwaring, as if it were completely obvious from the blouse.

'Of course! So clever! I should have known from the . . . false eyelashes? Not false. Okay. Now, listen, Amy has made the most marvelous punch,' said Jo, shoving me toward the kitchen. 'Dickon, you must try some. Mrs Mainwaring? Can we get you a sherry?'

I felt better once I was safely behind a plate of sausage rolls and Dickon immediately launched into a long story of how he'd been using egg-white paint mix in his quest for artistic authenticity and was, as a result, eating a lot of custard with the leftover yolks. I got about four words in over the course of twenty minutes, but while I was nodding sympathetically I put away about three cups of St. Peter's Punch, a cocktail Jo had found in a vintage party guide (heavenly ingredient: Benedictine and brandy, plenty of it). I had a very effective Party Listening expression, honed over many years, and before long Dickon was confessing that he'd actually based all the tiny demons in his painting on everyone who'd ever made fun of his name over the years. (There were a lot.)

Meanwhile, the doorbell buzzed again and again, shrieks of delight heralded each fresh arrival, and gradually Dickon and I were forced farther into the kitchen by the wave of newcomers, all in the weirdest outfits. I'd assumed most guests would just wear normal clothes with horns or a halo, but Jo's friends never wore normal clothes if they could wear sequined hot pants and a pig mask instead. There was a golfer, a butcher, a man dressed as a pole dancer (I think it was his idea of heaven, but coincidentally a little glimpse of hell for everyone else), three Britney Spearses at various ages, and a Bono.

At ten, Jo fought her way through the Three Ages of Britney Spears girls clogging the doorway, with a desperate look on her face and her mobile in her hand. I could barely hear her over the noise of pop music and theatrical flirting.

'I've got to nip out,' she yelled, pointing at the phone. 'Maternal crisis. Marigold's saying she thinks she might have left the gas on in the flat downstairs.'

'What? You're kidding!' My mouth went dry. 'Should we call the—?'

Jo shook her head. 'Don't panic — probably just one of her

ploys to get me to go down there ASAP. You know Marigold. Such a drama farmer. Bet you anything that once I'm in there she'll suddenly "remember" some handbag she needs couriering to wherever she is this weekend. Listen, I won't be long. Get out there and do some hosting. Ted's just arrived. He's come as a Mafia don or Don Draper from *Mad Men*, I can't tell which.'

I wasn't sure which was making me feel more panicky — Marigold 'probably' turning the house into a giant bomb, or having to take charge of the heaving throng in our sitting room.

'Is everything okay in there? It sounds quite loud,' I said anxiously.

'That's what a great party sounds like, you plank.' Jo flapped her hand. 'Get in there and mingle! See if Max's here yet! That'll make you look more confident.'

And she was gone.

*Come on, Amy,* I told myself sternly. *You've met most of these people before. You're the hostess. You've got to get out there, for the sausage rolls' sake, if nothing else.*

I nudged my way out between Schoolgirl Britney and Saucy Cabin Crew Britney, canapé platter ahead of me like a shield. I'd managed to get rid of three sausage rolls and had sighted Ted by the big window, being chatted up by a miniskirted nun, when there was a loud commotion by the door. My head spun to take it in and I nearly dropped the tray in shock.

A ridiculously handsome man was striking a magazine pose in the doorway, his hands braced against the doorframe and his head thrown back as if caught in a strong gust of wind, all the better for his mane of brown hair to fall away from his face. I say ridiculously handsome: his face was *so* tanned and symmetrical and model-perfect that he didn't look quite real. He was wearing a striped shirt that reminded me of hard candies, and a pair of tight red jeans. Very tight red jeans. Too tight, actually.

Behind him were three tall blond girls in black bandage dresses who'd clearly come from at least one other party, because when he stopped to pose in the doorway, they carried on marching in their heels and collided into his back in a tipsy jumble of golden limbs.

'Steady on, ladies!' he drawled — if you can drawl at the top of your voice. 'Let's wait till we get into the party, at least!'

Everyone's attention was now trained on the door, and the blood drained from my body.

A gatecrasher. My worst nightmare. And Jo wasn't even here to see him off the premises. She was *excellent* with gate-crashers; she usually ended up going on to a different party with them.

'Who the hell invited him?' muttered Ted, who had made his way through the throng to my side.

'I don't even know who he is,' I squeaked back. 'I mean, what's he come as?'

It was supposed to be a whisper, but because I'd been holding my breath it came out a bit louder than I'd meant, plus it coincided with an unfortunate break in the music, which one of the blond girls was now fiddling with.

Everyone turned to look at me and I shrank down behind Ted as far as I could.

The man didn't seem to mind. In fact, he descended on me with both hands outstretched, his huge brown eyes fixed on my face as if there were no one else in the room — no small feat, given that the flat was absolutely crammed. The guests parted like the Red Sea as he approached.

The nearer he got, the more handsome he seemed. The intensity of his gaze beneath his long dark lashes was unsettling, but, I had to admit, also very attractive. I guessed this was how a rabbit felt shortly before being swallowed whole by a boa constrictor – scared but oddly flattered at the same time.

'Hey,' he said in a rich, slightly accented voice like dark chocolate. He managed to wring a whole sentence-worth of meaning out of that one syllable.

My mouth dropped open but nothing emerged.

Ted nudged me hard in the back and the breath whistled out of me.

'Hello!' I managed.

'Good evening, gorgeous lady,' he said, grabbing my hands, and raised one to his lips to kiss it. 'Do *you* need to get aboard the Rolf Express to Partyville? Because it's heading into the station and I want *you* riding on it.'

I had no idea what to say to that. I wasn't even sure what it meant. But I had to say *something*. Fast. Before Ted nudged me again or, worse, intervened himself.

'Yes?' I hazarded.

Rolf — I assumed that was his name — threw back his mane of hair and laughed, and the girls behind him re-assembled themselves. One snaked her fingers through his belt loop, and another rested her head on his shoulder, closing her eyes in the sort of pose that made her look like a model. If I'd posed like that, someone would have offered me a bucket and a sit down.

'I'm Rolf. What's *your* name?' he went on, releasing my hand, but not my gaze. 'Or can I just call you gorgeous?' He frowned. 'No. In the morning. Can I just call you . . . in the morning? That's the one.' He cocked an imaginary pistol and fired it at me.

'I'm Amy.' My throat had gone dry and several really stupid comments were fighting to escape from my mouth. Rolf's extreme confidence had raised the stakes about a thousand times higher than they were at the best of times, plus everyone was looking at us.

Where was Jo? I *needed* her here.

'Amy! Sweet. And how do you know the lovely Josephine?'

'I live here?'

Clearly I was doing so badly Ted felt the need to step in. 'Can I get you a drink?' he asked. His solid presence behind me was reassuring, even if he did smell of mothballs. I assumed that was the suit, rather than a new aftershave.

'Good call. What have you got?' Rolf temporarily turned his charm beam off my face, and I was surprised not to fall to the floor.

'Beer, wine, some blue cocktail Jo's made. But' — Ted had done the health and safety course for our business — 'I have to warn you that it's been unsupervised for the last half hour and I can't guarantee what she put in it to begin with.'

'Sounds promising.' Rolf's full lips pouted in thought; then he turned his head, and addressed the nearest blonde. 'Mirabelle, go down to the car and get the chiller, will you? Cheers, bambina.'

He turned back to me while Mirabelle was still processing the instructions; as she swayed off on her heels, he slung an arm around my shoulders and steered me toward the long window where there was a tiny bit of space.

I sensed Ted's jaw drop, but something about Rolf seemed to be overriding my brain. It was like being on a hypnotist's show. I hoped he wouldn't ask me to quack like a duck or anything.

'While we're waiting for Mirabelle to make with the Moët,' he drawled in my ear, 'I want to hear all about you and why it is that you've come dressed for bed already.'

Well, Jo had been right about that. Fancy dress did get people talking with no effort!

'It's fancy dress, and I'm not dressed for bed, I'm dressed for a lie-in,' I said. In the reflection of the window I could see girls lining up behind me to talk to Rolf, hovering impatiently. I felt an unexpected frisson of triumph that he was talking to *me*.

Rolf raised a well-groomed eyebrow. 'Uh-huh. A lie-in. I like lie-ins too. Especially after a late night.'

'I've got bed socks on. Look, cashmere.' I shoved out a foot and nearly trod on a bowl of olives. My gormlessness didn't seem to put him off though; he leaned back and gave me an appraising look.

'I like to keep my socks on too,' said Rolf. 'Saves time getting dressed after. If you know what I mean. I think you and I could have a lot in common, Amy.'

He winked — but it was a wink too far, and without meaning to, I made a *bleurgh!* noise of horror, which I had to wrangle back into a *hmm?* face.

Suddenly Rolf placed his hands on my shoulders and gripped, fixing me with another smoldering gaze. He wasn't that tall. We were roughly the same height. 'You stay *right* there, gorgeous,' he said in the voice of a much taller man. 'I need to use your bathroom. Where is it?'

I nodded across the hall, and he swaggered off, apparently unaware that he had a pair of oyster satin knickers dangling from his back pocket.

The music and flirting started up again, and I tried to gather myself together. *This is okay,* I thought, as the last hastily gulped glass of Jo's punch started to take effect on my balance. *I'm hosting, I've been chatted up, the gatecrashers seem to know Jo, no one has been sick or called the police. I just need . . . more food to soak up this booze.*

I swayed off to the kitchen and grabbed two sausage rolls from the giant pile, and since I was there I poured myself another glass of punch. It tasted different from the first three cups I'd had, but after my short ride on the Rolf Express I was feeling reckless. When I tried to leave the packed kitchen, the three Britneys had gone into a tearful group hug, and as I tried to crowbar my way past, the music went off and mass yelling broke out.

This time it sounded serious.

My short-lived triumph shriveled. I dropped to my knees and crawled between the Britneys to the sitting room, just in time to see Rolf in the middle of the floor, waving an iPod in one hand and (oh my God) a green bra in the other, while Ted and a tall blond bloke attempted to grab them off him.

'If you don't let me put Abba on the stereo, I'm going to chuck this out of the window!' roared Rolf.

'You're not chucking anything anywhere! Not on my watch!' Ted roared back, putting his head down to rugby-tackle him, but Rolf nipped out of his grasp, shimmied over to the long window, and somehow managed to open it.

Visions of the Christmas balcony drama danced before my eyes. That balcony wasn't very big. Rolf was moving very fast. Where *was* Jo?

'Don't let him get out there!' I yelled. 'It's not as deep as you'd think! It's unsafe!'

The blond man in the white shirt turned to look at me, and my mind went blank, but not for the usual reasons. I couldn't do anything but look back at him. He had the bluest eyes I'd ever seen — proper deep blue, like cornflowers, with dark lashes — and when our eyes met, I felt like everything had stopped in the room. Just like in a film.

He stared back at me, and his brow furrowed; then he started smiling in a 'hey, it's you!' way, even though we'd never met. Butterflies fluttered up in my stomach. I hadn't got a clue who he was, but something about him felt instantly familiar, as if I'd known him for years. *Did* I know him?

But in the split second we were staring at each other, Rolf vanished from view; then a very unmanly squeal indicated that the Rolf Express was heading off the tracks very fast.

Ted leaped forward with more energy than I'd seen him expend at work all year, and grabbed Rolf's legs just in time.

There was a scraping crash, followed by the sound of falling pots. And then, far away, the yowl of a surprised cat.

I'm not ashamed to say that my first thought wasn't *Oh no, we've lost a guest,* or even, *Oh no, I hope Elvis wasn't having a tomcat's night out tonight,* but *Oh,* bollocks, *that'll be Grace Wright's effing Dream Seeds.*

# CHAPTER THREE

Everyone surged forward, and Ted and Rolf reappeared from the scrum of shocked onlookers, as my teeth began to chatter with shock. It was a long way down from that balcony.

Rolf, however, was doing a very good impression of someone who nearly falls out of windows at every party. He brushed dead leaves off his shiny shirt as if nothing had happened and made a 'drinky drinky?' gesture to a nearby girl, but his blond mate grabbed him by the arm and whispered furiously into his ear. He seemed less than impressed — whether with Rolf for making a show of himself, or with us for having a potentially lethal balcony, I couldn't make out.

Meanwhile, a couple of girls rushed over to Ted and patted him like a big hero. He looked startled, then disengaged himself to sort out the iPod, and to my relief, Beyoncé was blaring out of the stereo again before you could say '*awkward.*'

Rolf beckoned me over, back on the charm offensive. I went, praying Jo was on her way back up to deliver the telling-off I wasn't sure I'd be able to summon up. Even though he totally deserved it.

Or maybe we did. Who was supposed to have locked the doors? Jo . . . or me?

'This is all your fault.' Rolf shook his head flirtily. 'If you'd been here—'

'If I'd been here, I'd have told you not to go on the balcony,' I said. 'In fact, I was. Couldn't you hear me yelling?'

'Have you never seen *Romeo and Juliet*?' He pouted.

'That doesn't work on me,' I said.

'It will. Give it time. Listen, the Rolex has spoken. I need to move on. Where's the lovely Josephine?'

'I don't know.'

Rolf's pout intensified. 'Playing hard to get. At her own party. *Quel* style.' He snapped his fingers, pointing to the door. 'Anyhoo, with deep regret, the Rolf Express is departing this station. Are you on board?'

'This is my party!' I protested. 'Of course I'm not on board!'

'Too bad.' He grabbed my hand, kissed it, then made a clicking noise; two broad-shouldered men I hadn't seen before materialized and ushered him to the door, making a wall of navy-blue blazer between him and anyone trying to follow. The trio of blondes trailed behind, one of them staggering under the weight of a cooler. Rolf made one last salute at the door, which only about four people caught, then he was off.

I still had no idea who he was, but I felt as if half the oxygen had just left the room.

'Don't think the Rolf Express is taking passengers from this station,' said Ted.

'The Rolf Express should be *canceled*,' said Jo, appearing from nowhere with a dark look on her face, despite the glitter. 'I've a good mind to put a cow on the line. Rolf is such a . . . a . . .'

'Perfect example of someone you'd meet in hell?' suggested

Ted. 'Maybe even the bloke who'd be in charge of the entertainments?'

'Where did you spring from?' I demanded. 'Did you *see* all that?'

'I caught the last bit.' Jo squirmed.

'Then why didn't you stop him?' I started to ask, but she'd gone over to the stereo and was starting to whip everyone into joining her doing the 'Single Ladies' dance. We'd spent many happy hours dissecting that routine, although only Jo could do it in high heels.

From the way she was geeing everyone along, I assumed Marigold *hadn't* left the gas on downstairs.

'What's up with her?' I asked Ted, as Jo did the flippy hand action with surprising attitude for a history of art graduate. 'Did she invite him? Does she know him?'

'Rolf? Oh yeah. I think there's some history there,' he yelled.

My eyes popped. 'Rolf? And Jo?'

I couldn't hear what else Ted said, but his face was really saying it all. He was trying to make his face nonchalant, but failing as only a man allergic to emotional conversations can.

I would have hung around and been more sympathetic, but unfortunately for Ted, at that point I realized that Rolf's very handsome blond mate hadn't left the party but was trying to catch my eye over his shoulder.

It took all my concentration to walk over to him without treading on any guests or bowls of olives. By the time I finally made it to where he was standing by the door, my mind was completely blank apart from the word *gorgeous*. Because he was. Absolutely gorgeous.

*Just say hi. Hi is fine. Hello, even.*

Then he smiled at me, a quirky twitch of the lips, accompanied by an apologetic frown, and I lost even *gorgeous* in a sea of white noise.

He looked like most of the men Jo invited to her parties — white shirt open at the neck, dark blue jeans, thick blond hair cut in a tously style — but there was an extra sharpness about him, as if he were just a bit more in focus than everyone else. And he was still smiling as though we already knew each other.

'I didn't want to go without apologizing,' he shouted in my ear over the sound of wine and crisps being ground rhythmically into our carpet. His breath was warm against my neck, and I felt all the tiny hairs spring to attention. 'Don't worry, Rolf is in a car speeding far, far from your flat.'

I leaned into his ear and yelled, 'Not in the driver's seat, I hope.'

*Not bad. Where did that come from?*

He laughed, showing square white teeth, and leaned toward my ear again. 'I wanted to check that he hadn't damaged anything on your balcony. If he did, obviously he's going to want to replace it.'

I arched my eyebrow. 'He is? Or you are?'

'I am,' he said. 'And he's going to pay me back.'

I felt the same fluttery excitement that I'd had the first time I'd driven to college on my own after passing my test: as if everything were rushing toward me and I was reacting second by second, not knowing where my reactions were coming from.

We'd moved closer together as two guests (under)dressed as Botticelli cherubs tried to leave, and now we were nearly nose to nose. He had a straight nose with a few freckles scattered across the bridge, and I had to fight the impulse to tell him how glad I was to meet a fellow freckler. Either Jo's blue cocktail was kicking in or there really was something in all that claptrap about certain people just being easy to talk to.

'Shall we have a look?' he suggested.

'At what?' I squeaked.

'The damage to the balcony?'

I nodded dumbly and turned to the window.

He followed me across the room, and we had to swerve to avoid being whacked in the head by Jo and her line of would-be backup dancers.

'How do you girls learn that?' he asked, touching my arm to direct my attention to where Jo was strutting in perfect unison with four other girls.

'It's just that one dance,' I admitted, aware of how close he was to me. 'Jo does it as part of her Edinburgh stand-up act, with different words — she calls it "Single Laddies." I can do it too.' I demonstrated one quick hand move and smacked a nearby Simon Cowell in the face by mistake. 'Oh my God, sorry, sorry . . .'

Gorgeous Blond Man grinned and made a space for me to get through to the window. As I opened it, I groaned aloud: the heavy window box of geraniums was still there, but the plants I'd wedged behind it had been shoved through the railings and off the balcony. Grace's precious pots and my precious seedlings would be toast — as would her dreams, and our plans for the rental property contract.

Not that I believed all that hippie mumbo jumbo.

Still, I sobered up instantly in the chilly night air. I didn't normally get so sentimental about plants — some sprouted, some failed, Nature was mean like that — but for some reason this felt symbolic.

'What?' The man leaned to see what I was looking at.

'There were seven pots of seedlings and some herbs,' I said. 'I don't even want to *think* about what they hit on the way down.'

'Really? Oh no.' His own expression turned serious when he saw my face. 'Were they expensive plants? Or valuable pots? Can we replace them?'

'No. They're . . .'

He looked at me as if he really wanted to know, and the words tumbled out of my mouth before I had time to think about what I was saying.

'They're seeds I was growing for a client — hers haven't sprouted, so I was growing these as backup. I was going to swap these with the ones she's managed to wipe out before she gets back this week. I'm a gardener,' I added, in case he thought I did this sort of thing for fun. 'And they're not dodgy.'

'Can't you just swap them for some different seedlings?'

I shook my head, already wondering what I could tell Grace. 'She got them while she was on some retreat in Thailand. There are photos of the flowers in her meditation pack — she'd know if they suddenly came up as tomatoes.'

He frowned, then his face cleared into a smile. 'Oh, I know

the course you mean. Were they Dream Seeds? Lots of nude yoga and talking about your soul's greenhouse? Each seed represents a wish, et cetera, et cetera?'

'You know them?' I squinted at him. He didn't look the sort to go on Grace's courses. I mean, he looked wealthy, but nowhere near flaky enough. (Also, nude yoga?)

'Let's say I know *of* them,' he replied. 'And I know how important the seeds are to the fruitloops who . . . Oh, God, sorry, the, um . . .' His eyes were doing the frantic darting thing mine did when I was trying and failing to find the tactful word.

'You had me at fruitloops,' I said. 'In the nicest possible way.'

We shared a quick, apologetic smile of conspiracy.

He touched my arm. 'In that case, let's go down and see if they've survived the fall. I can't have someone's karmic journey on Rolf's conscience as well as him ruining your party.'

'Does it look ruined?' I asked. The Beyoncé dancing was reaching a new level of ferocity, and if Mrs Mainwaring hadn't been doing some kind of mashed-potato move in the middle of the floor, she'd have been banging on the ceiling with her broom. That didn't mean her cat was inside. If anything had happened to Elvis, I wanted to find out before she did.

He glanced over and when he turned back a white-hot shiver rippled through me.

'No,' he said, keeping his eyes on mine. 'Quite the opposite, I'd say.'

'Okay,' I said, before I said anything more stupid. 'Let's go and have a look for these plants.'

*

It was much quieter in the hall, and I suddenly felt conscious of not actually having introduced myself. The fact that he seemed so relaxed with me only made me worry that we *had* been introduced and I'd forgotten. That had happened before now. Although it wasn't my fault so many of Jo's friends had nose jobs without telling anyone.

'Do I know you from somewhere?' I asked, following him down the stairs.

It came out less flirty and more accusatory. I scrabbled to salvage it before I made it worse.

'I mean, I don't mean that to sound like you're forgettable, because obviously you're not, ha-ha, um . . .'

He paused by the communal post table and extended a hand, inclining his head in an old-fashioned courtly manner. I hoped he hadn't noticed the thermal underwear catalogue with my name on it, and I leaned against it, just in case.

'Leo,' he said. 'I was just thinking the same thing. But I'm sure I'd have remembered your name if we'd met.'

Leo had a good handshake. A tingly sensation spread through me as he gripped my hand and held it just long enough for me to register his smooth skin and the warmth of his grasp.

'Amy,' I said, and my voice didn't wobble. 'Amy Wilde. I'm from Yorkshire.'

'Ah. That's where your accent's from. Sorry, I'm very bad with accents. It's unusual. Melodic.'

I could feel myself blushing. 'You're the first person who's ever said that. Most people ask me where I've parked my tractor.'

Leo laughed, and if I hesitated for a micromillisecond, just enjoying the feel of his hand in mine, he did too. Just long enough for me to notice. Then he smiled and released it to open the front door.

'Very pleased to meet you, Amy,' he said, and held the door open for me. 'Now, whereabouts do you think these pots fell?'

'Round here.' I pointed down the narrow passage that led round the back of the house. From the front, No. 17 was elegant white stucco; at the back it was a rat-run of fire escapes, television aerials, and scabby window boxes. The second-floor flat, belonging to the Harrises, who were rarely there, had a bigger balcony than ours, jutting out onto a sort of extension, which they used as a storage space for junk. Currently one sandbox (no idea why, they had no kids) and a very dead Christmas tree.

It wasn't a very charming scene, and I made a mental note to offer to replant everyone's window boxes ASAP. I scanned the yard for smashed pots and a flat cat; then the security lights went on, and I caught sight of something red sticking up out of the sand.

'Up there!' Relief rushed through me. 'Look, in the sandbox!' Then the relief rushed back out. 'But they're away until the middle of next month. That's one of the reasons we had the party. I won't be able to get in for ages.'

'No probs.' Leo stepped back and grabbed hold of the fire escape, testing the brackets for strength. Then he shrugged off his jacket. 'Hold this.'

'What? No, you don't have to—' I started, but he shushed me good-naturedly and started to climb up the fire escape toward the Harrises' balcony. He made it look very easy.

His jacket was light and lined with a beautiful purple satin that gleamed in the streetlight. There was a label in it that I didn't recognize and it smelled of some expensive cologne that was far more subtle than Rolf's pungent aftershave, which I could still smell on my own clothes. I glanced up and saw that Leo was concentrating on judging the jump to the balcony from the fire escape, and while his back was turned I took a surreptitious sniff.

It was one of those colognes that bypasses your brain and goes straight to your hormones. I wasn't an expert like Jo, who could categorize all men in London by their bathroom shelves, but I could pick out geranium, rose, and something else. Real smells. Flowers and plants and grasses and air and skin . . .

'Is this it?'

I looked up so fast my neck nearly cracked, and saw Leo holding a pot aloft like a trophy. It was one of my seedlings.

'There's only one that's not broken, I'm afraid,' he went on. 'Unless you also want some — *ew*. You don't want *that*.' He gave something a discreet kick, and it fell off the balcony out of sight.

I gave him a goofy double thumbs-up, then wished I hadn't. 'Be careful coming down.'

'I know. That's the hard part.'

He stuffed the pot into his trouser pocket, and I watched him climb down in a series of confident moves. He had obviously climbed before — I could tell by the effortless way he transferred his weight from hand to foot down the scaffolding, keeping himself balanced until he reached the fire escape.

At the bottom, he jumped down from the fire escape and handed me the plant pot with a flourish.

'Thank you,' I said. It sounded inadequate, but it was all I had.

'Happy to be of service.' Leo smiled, the moonlight shading the chiseled contours of his face, and again I had that weird feeling that we'd met before. I felt like I *knew* him.

Jo was always telling me how readable my face was. I hoped it was now saying something meaningful and intelligent, but I had the sinking feeling I just looked like the pantomime horse I hadn't come as. Big-eyed and moony.

'By the way, I like your costume.' Leo took a step back to admire the bits of silk pajama visible beneath the quilted parka I'd pulled on to come outside. 'Don't tell me — your idea of heaven is . . . staying in bed all day?'

'Yes!' I felt stupidly pleased that he'd got it. 'Well, no, to be honest, my idea of heaven is a really long bath, so I suggested covering myself in bubble wrap, you know, for bubbles? And then when I ran out of conversation, I could just invite people to pop me. Jo wouldn't let me.'

'You might attract the wrong sort of poppers,' he said, his eyes serious, although the corner of his mouth twitched.

'That's what she said. But everyone likes popping bubble wrap. Saves having to make chitchat about villa holidays.'

'You're not a fan?'

'I've never been on one.'

'They're overrated.' Leo nodded. 'No one ever washes up, and there's always an "incident" with the pool. Give me bubble wrap any day.'

I grinned, savoring the intimacy of his tone, and also the outline of his shoulder muscles through the white shirt.

'For the record,' he added, 'both the long bath and the long lie-in are my idea of heaven too. But to be honest, fancy dress parties are hell. Well, any party where you have to explain your outfit is hell, but fancy dress parties more so.'

'I couldn't agree more.'

The night air was sharp, tinted with distant Saturday-night shouting and the faint waft of steak and smoke and the gray London smell I could never pin down. We stood in the yellowy streetlight, me clutching the one surviving Dream Seedling, and when Leo shivered under his open-necked shirt I remembered I was still holding his jacket.

'Sorry, you must be freezing,' I said, embarrassed. 'Here you go.'

The jacket started vibrating as I passed it over. He pulled his phone from the pocket and checked it as he slipped the jacket back on, then pulled an expression of what seemed like real regret.

'Sorry, I've got to make a move. Rolf's crashed another party.'

'So long as that's all he's crashed,' I said. 'Wasn't he in your car?'

'Don't remind me.' He nodded at the plant. 'Anyway, good luck nursing that back to health after its adventure. Sorry there was only one.'

'No, thank *you*. I'm the plant doctor. I'll just have to get someone to fly more seeds out in the next twenty-four hours.'

Leo grinned, and there was a pause where I wasn't sure if I was supposed to make more witty conversation (unlikely) or kiss him goodbye (but how many times? which cheek first?), or shake his hand, or what.

The moment was stretching out and I was going into one of my silence-filling panics when he touched my arm lightly, leaned forward, and pressed his warm lips against my cheekbone.

No man that handsome, that charming, or that fragrant had ever been so close to me, and if I could have freeze-framed it, I would have.

'Will you thank Jo for . . . well, she didn't actually invite us. Maybe apologize instead. Apologize for our intrusion.'

'I'll thank her for having you,' I said brightly.

As soon as it came out of my mouth, I thought, *That sounded wrong.*

Leo grinned. 'That sounds a bit wrong.'

'It does.' I nodded, grinning and still tingling from where he'd kissed my cheek. I still wasn't used to all the casual kissing in London. It was something all Jo's friends did, even if we'd just been introduced, but where I came from you had to know someone for at least ten years or be directly related to them (and maybe not even then) before you went further than a gruff 'see ya.' Touching was for family members, and even then only at moments of high emotional tide, like funerals or Rugby World Cup finals.

Leo gestured toward our flat. 'I'd say come with me, but I can't guarantee it'd be more fun than the party you've already got going on in there.'

'To be totally honest,' I confessed, because something about Leo was making me say things I normally wouldn't unless I was far drunker than this, 'if you offered me a sofa and a film now, I'd bite your hand off.'

A flicker of amusement lit up his incredible eyes. 'What, a whole season of something on DVD? And some nice takeout?'

'I was thinking maybe a film,' I agreed. 'But with the best pizza. And ice cream. And all the controls within reach so you don't have to get up. Maybe even a Slanket.'

'A Slanket? I don't know what that is, but I want one.' Leo looked wistful, and for a split second I thought he was going to suggest we go back in there and kick everyone out so we could watch *The Shining* and ring Pizza Hut.

The unspoken invitation hung in the night air between us, and it abruptly occurred to me that good hostesses weren't supposed to plan secret escapes from their own parties.

'I mean, I *like* parties . . .' I started.

'But there's a lot to be said for a relaxing night in.' Leo held my gaze, and I melted inside. 'With the right sort of company. And you're already dressed for it.'

In an ideal world, I would have come out with a killer line at this point, but I just stared at him and nodded. Which was, I figured, better than saying something I might regret.

Leo let out a rueful half laugh. 'If only I didn't have to save the next hostess from Rolf, eh? Another time.'

He bent and kissed my cheek briefly again (again!). And he was gone.

I sank onto the rusty picnic table left over from the summer, not wanting to go back into the flat just yet. The stars were out over London, and the moon was fat and clear in the blue-black sky. Something about the evening didn't feel quite real, but in a delicious new way, and I wanted to savor it while it was actually happening. I knew in the morning little details would have already started to flake away in my memory, lost forever, and I closed my eyes to imprint everything as much as I could.

His smell. The warmth of his breath on my neck. The cool tingle of the night air.

Then something brushed against my bare ankle and I nearly dropped the plant pot in shock.

Mrs Mainwaring's cat, Elvis, flicked his tail at me. He was covered in gold body glitter and soil, and he didn't look too pleased about it.

# CHAPTER FOUR

The one party rule we had — or rather, the rule we had that Jo enforced with steely determination — was that all guests had to leave at two o'clock, even if it meant pretending that we'd called the police. Morning-after lingerers were absolutely forbidden in our sitting room. Jo said it ruined the magic for everyone, and besides, the last thing one wanted to smell through one's hangover was unwashed guests.

She also insisted on a ritual downing of one pint of water, a vitamin C tablet, and an aspirin directly after we'd locked the door on our last guest (this time, Dickon, minus his velvet jacket but with a smear of coral lipstick on his left ear and seven phone numbers written on his shirt), and as a result I woke up on Sunday feeling almost human.

A giddy Christmas-morning feeling was flitting around the edges of my mind, as if I'd had a gorgeous dream I hadn't wanted to wake up from, and it took me a moment to work out what it was.

Then my eye fell on my bedside table, empty apart from one terracotta pot, and I remembered. Last night I'd met a blue-eyed man who'd scaled rusty scaffolding to rescue a plant. For me.

I sat up cautiously, hoping that maybe a piece of paper with

Leo's phone number might have materialized in the soil or something, but it hadn't. He hadn't scrawled his number on the pot either. I don't know why I hoped he had; I knew he hadn't, and I'd been too shy and inept to ask him for it.

Disappointment tinged the giddy feeling as I thought of all the things I *should* have said. How could I get in touch with him to say thank you now? It would be only polite to say thank you.

Although, the realistic voice in my head started, if Leo knew people who went on Dream Seed courses, he was about four leagues out of my reach. And he was friends with that appalling Rolf, so I probably wasn't really his type either.

I swung my legs out of bed to stop *that* depressing line of argument and went through to the kitchen to start my part in the morning-after routine: the miracle cooked-breakfast hangover cure.

The sitting room certainly looked a little less heavenly this morning than it had last night, even without guests slumped over the soft furnishings. I pushed open the curtains to let some light in and started to tidy on autopilot, but really my brain was only thinking about one thing. Each time I replayed the brief moments when our eyes met, or Leo's hand had touched mine, a sharp thrill went through me, and I shied away from it as if I might wear out the memory from replaying it too often.

But then I'd move a bunch of glasses or an empty bowl of olive stones and allow myself a sneaky memory of Leo kissing my cheek, or him leaning in to my neck to make himself heard over the party, and I'd shiver all over again.

In the end, I had to turn the radio on to distract myself,

and with the dishwasher humming and the windows wide open to get rid of various smells, I fried eggs, and grilled sausage and bacon, and made toast, and piled the whole lot onto one big serving dish, then took it through to Jo's room with a pot of tea so we could begin the party postmortem.

Jo was lying surrounded by all her pillows, with a silk sleep mask over her eyes. Her hair was still in last night's curls, but her skin was clean and pink. She always took her makeup off before she went to bed, no matter what state she was in, even the time we were both so worse for wear that she'd tried to use toothpaste for cleanser.

'I've made you breakfast in bed, milady,' I said, doing a pretend *Downton Abbey* bob.

She gave a languid waft of her hand, which was supposed to convey the impression that she never *ever* ate fried foods — we had to go through this each time — and I added my usual line, as of our first night out, 'Five generations of my family swear by this fry-up, and they were —'

'—proper drinkers,' Jo joined in for the last bit. 'Oh, go on. Persuade me. Maybe start with tea.'

I poured two cups of strong tea, the color of bricks, and stirred in two sugars. 'Come on. You're not *that* hungover. You've had eight hours' sleep!'

Jo struggled into a sitting position and held out her hand for the mug, sleep mask still in place. I put it carefully into her hand and went to open her curtains.

'It's a lovely day outside.' I shoved open the sash windows, and clean bright air rushed in, along with the sounds of a dog barking a few streets away and distant church bells. 'Even the pigeons look clean.'

'Are you still drunk?' Jo pushed the mask up onto her head and gave me a bleary-eyed look. 'How come you're so chipper? You did your usual vanishing act, I noticed. You missed the orange game — again!'

Jo's parties frequently ended with the orange game: you had to pass an orange from one guest to another without using your hands. Inevitably, since by this stage guests were seeing double at least and had little balance left, the orange would get stuck in someone's cleavage, and so much upper-class hooting would ensue that you'd think a flock of Canada geese had landed. It was a good way of checking who was safe to drive, and I found you could win quite easily by hiding your own orange somewhere about your person — no one ever checked.

'I, er, had to pop out . . .'

'You always *do*.' Jo winked and patted the duvet next to her. 'Come and fill me in about what happened while I was running around after Marigold. Who had the best outfit? Did you see Julian's?'

'Julian?'

'Julian Martin. He was dressed as Gordon Ramsay.'

'With the bloody jacket?' I said, trying to remember which one that was. 'Or am I thinking of the evil dentist guy? They're so easy to mix up, evil dentists and evil chefs.'

'Which means he made no impression on you at all.' Jo sighed. 'Fine. What about Max? I spotted you chatting to him by the kitchen.'

Things hadn't gone well with Max, who'd arrived shortly after I'd floated back in after my moment with Leo. He seemed intent on describing the entire plot of a film he'd just seen, and I was hardly able to concentrate as it was, and in the party crush, Max thought I'd said I was from Grenada instead of that I was a gardener, so I'd spent fifteen confusing minutes desperately trying to answer questions about some beach holiday he'd been on, and then he'd given up and left.

I took a long time spreading Marmite on my toast while I worked out which bits of this I could convey to Jo without being rude about one of her friends. I didn't like being rude. My family was of the straight-talking variety, which was probably where my tongue paralysis under pressure originated; I'd rather the stunned silence came from me than the horrified second party.

'You can be honest, Amy,' Jo pressed, her eyes alight with encouragement. 'I know Max isn't the sharpest tool in the shed, but he's a lot of fun once you get past the red trousers. He likes dogs! And he won't make you go skiing because he's a *terrible* skier . . .'

'Jo. It's never going to happen with Max.' I speared a sausage and decided to be truthful. 'I just can't talk to him. He makes my mind go blank. I can't think of a thing to say to him.'

'Max? But he's easy to talk to!' She seemed surprised.

'He's easy for you to talk to, yes. You've known these people for years. I have zero conversation to make about horses, or tennis.'

'You're being chippy.' She wagged her toast at me. 'Don't be chippy.'

'I'm not, I'm being honest.' A faint, warm wave of last night's magic rippled through me. 'I just think when you meet the right person, conversation isn't an issue. It just . . . happens.'

'Fine,' said Jo. I could tell she hadn't given up, though. She was just planning a different approach. 'What about Dominic? Did you meet Dominic? The rower?' She mimed someone rowing, adding a broad smile to indicate his perfect dentistry, or possibly a history of emotional instability.

I cut my sausage in two and bit into it. 'Jo, seriously. It's like I said yesterday, you don't have to keep trying to set me up. What if I dated someone and we fell out? I don't want it to spoil our friendship. And I'm not going to meet Mr Right if I'm on a blind date with Mr Wrong.'

'You never go on any dates! And you totally deserve one. Look at this amazing breakfast! I know men who'd marry you for this alone. Plus, it would make your life so much easier.'

'What do you mean, easier?'

Easier? Didn't she mean *more romantic*? Or *exciting*? Or even . . . *less soil-focused*?

'Well.' Jo pulled the face she always pulled when she was about to say something not very politically correct. A half-apologizing, half-really-*not* sort of face. 'Wouldn't it be easier if you didn't have to worry about other people's lawns day and night to make ends meet?'

I put down my fork, sausage still attached. 'Are you suggesting that I need a boyfriend to *pay my way*?'

'No! Well . . .'

'There's a word for that back home,' I said hotly. 'It's not a very nice word either.'

'Oh, don't get your knickers in a twist, I don't mean like that.' Jo buttered another slice of toast, unperturbed. 'Obviously he'd have to be a lovely guy who'd adore you, and you'd have to adore him, but there's nothing wrong with letting someone else take care of you a bit.'

'If I'd wanted to be taken care of, I'd have stayed at home.'

'Think yourself lucky. If I'd stayed at home, I'd have been doing all the taking care. And I'd have needed someone to take care of *me*,' Jo retorted. 'A full-time therapist, for a kickoff. My parents are *enraging*, not like yours. Can we swap?'

I ate the other bit of my sausage and chewed it for a long time so I wouldn't have to say anything.

Without meaning to, Jo had touched on — no, not touched on, punched — a real sore spot. My independence was something I was proud of, and I'd have eaten porridge for a week rather than be late with any of the bills in the flat. (Actually, I had done that once or twice in the early days, though obviously I'd never told her.) It was a point of honor for me that Mum and Dad hadn't had to lend me a penny since I left home, and I'd paid back my college fees through gardening jobs in the holidays.

I didn't hold it against Jo, but it was easy for her to accept the odd bit of help from her mum and dad — they had the money, for a start, and her family went from being very rich to very poor every hundred years, so they were used to it. My family, though, had been through a nightmare few years while I was still at school, and it had left me fiercely protective about my finances. That part of our life wasn't something my parents and I ever talked about, and the one good thing about busy, anonymous London was that no one here knew about it — unlike back home, where you could wear a hat one day and be known as 'the girl with the hat' for the rest of your life.

I knew not opening up about stuff like this made me look like a chippy northerner sometimes, but I'd rather that than tell Jo the whole story. I liked the new Amy she knew; I was quite happy to leave the old Amy back home in Rothery.

'Am I barking up the wrong tree?' Jo went on, taking advantage of my full mouth. 'I mean, if you're on the other bus, tell me. I know loads of gay people. In fact, I could introduce you to—'

I swallowed my sausage as fast as I could. 'I do want a boyfriend. Eventually. I just want a normal one. Someone with an actual job. Someone who eats at Pret a Manger at lunchtime, and has a travelcard and a mutt like Badger, not a spaniel with a family tree. I'm not saying your friends aren't nice — I just don't have much to say to very posh boys. Not unless they like gardening too. By which I mean, actual gardening, not directing their groundsmen.'

'You don't ask for much, do you?' observed Jo.

'I just want someone normal,' I said stoutly. 'I'm just a normal girl, and I want a normal bloke.'

She smiled. 'None of us are normal. We're all special in our own way.'

'Have you been reading Grace Wright's self-help books again?'

We eyed each other over the breakfast tray, and I hoped Jo knew I didn't mean any offense.

'Anyway, you can talk,' I pointed out, trying to lighten the mood. 'Who on earth was that Rolf bloke last night? I mean, was he real? Or was it some kind of reality TV thing?'

'He's real enough.' She groaned, reaching for her tea. 'Although strictly speaking, Rolf exists in his own version of reality that the rest of us aren't invited to. Just like he wasn't actually invited last night.'

'Where did you meet him?'

'Amanda Hastings's first wedding.' Jo prodded the tray with a finger to indicate something outrageous was coming. 'When the vicar asked if anyone had any just cause or impediment, Rolf stood up and coughed, and then sat down again. Then he laughed. The best man punched him on the nose at the reception, he bled over a bridesmaid's Vera Wang, and Amanda sat him next to *me* at dinner because she said I could talk to anyone.'

'Well, you can.'

Jo looked wounded. 'That's not something you should *punish* your friends for.'

'But he seemed really keen to see you.'

Jo took a big gulp of tea. 'Well, he can carry on looking. I'm not at home to Rolf Wolfsburg.'

'Why?' I was really interested now. 'Have you two got history?'

'I wouldn't call it that.'

'Ted would.' I added a raised eyebrow for good measure.

'Well, there's no need for that. Not that Ted . . . I mean, he doesn't . . .' Jo fiddled with her eye mask, then pulled it off crossly. 'Listen, even if Rolf wasn't a party-crashing egomaniac who thinks he's constantly appearing in his own James Bond title sequence, I wouldn't touch him with someone else's barge pole. My dad only gave me one piece of advice when it came to relationships.'

I'd listened to enough of Jo's stories about her parents' various marriages to be surprised her dad's advice could be boiled down to just one thing.

'Do tell,' I said. 'I'm agog.'

She put her mug down on the bedside table and pressed her lips together. 'He said, "Jojo, you can marry into any family in the world — except a royal one. They're all crazy." Well, until I met Rolf, I thought he was just being pretentious, but now I know how right he was.'

'What, Rolf's royal?' My eyes widened. Jo's social circles were glittery, but I hadn't realized they were *that* glittery. 'What? As in . . . a prince?'

Jo nodded, then shook her head, then did a sort of squinty-eyed halfway head-wobble. 'Well, *ish*. His family's from Nirona. He's one of the Nironan Wolfsburgs.'

I hadn't heard of Nirona. But then, I'd thought the Kardashians were an area of Russia until quite recently. My family weren't big readers of *Hello!* magazine.

Jo clocked my blank expression. 'It's one of those island tax-haven principalities off the coast of Italy, all yachts and casinos and gold shoes. Jake Astley had his stag weekend there last November. He said you couldn't move for hedge funders having shady meetings with their accountants.'

'Oh, *there*,' I said. 'I'm always popping over to Nirono.'

'Nirona. You might have heard of Rolf's mum, though — she's an American model? Liza Bachmann?' She made a pouty fish face, and it was a sign of how long I'd been living with Jo and her glossy fashion mags that I knew immediately whom she meant. 'With the signature cheekbones?' she mumbled, pulling her skin on her face back to demonstrate.

'Yes!' I pointed at her. 'I know who you mean. She wrote that awful vegan cupcake cookbook Grace Wright gave me for Christmas. The one with the website that tells you how to make your own yogurt out of—'

'Don't remind me! That's her!'

'And she produced Rolf? She's so . . . dignified.'

'I know,' said Jo. 'Genes are a funny business, aren't they?'

Despite myself, I was quite awestruck. Who knew we'd had a royal person in our flat? Even if he had kicked my seedlings off the balcony, trodden a load of olives into the carpet, and goosed Mrs Mainwaring.

I blanched, thinking of all the inappropriate things I'd probably said to him. Should I have curtsied? It wasn't as if he'd *behaved* like a prince. 'So he's . . . Prince Rolf? That sounds more like something you'd call a dog than a prince.'

'His full title is His Serene Highness Prince Rudolfo-Harolde de Nirona and Svetland.' Jo rolled her eyes. 'I only know that because he has the whole thing printed on his platinum credit card and insisted on showing us how they'd had to go to two lines to fit it all on.

'Don't be impressed,' she went on, reaching for another slice of toast. 'It just means he should know better. And it doesn't get him automatic entry to *my* parties. Rolf's on my outdoor-events-only guest list, for very good reasons.'

'Which are?'

'Small fires,' she said darkly. 'And puddles. Don't ask.'

'So we got off pretty lightly with a near-death balcony plunge.'

'We did indeed. Anyway, that's more than enough about Rolf.' Jo buttered her fourth piece of toast with such a ferocious swipe of the knife that I didn't dare press her any further about their exact history. 'We still haven't got to the bottom of *your* night. What was your highlight? Best three moments, then we'll do the worst three.'

I opened my mouth to tell her about the amazing man I'd met, but then something stopped me. Was it rude to say I didn't want to meet any of her friends because I was so busy, then confess that I *had* met someone? Leo was very posh. Exactly the sort of posh boy I'd just told Jo I couldn't bear. And knowing Jo, she'd insist on having a dinner party to set us up again — but that would mean inviting Rolf too, and clearly that wasn't a goer . . .

Jo was shoveling in fried egg with a fierce expression that I suspected was repressed Rolf Rage. I decided to keep it to myself. It wasn't as if I was going to see him again anyway.

My chest contracted suddenly.

'Ted. Ted was a highlight,' I said, to distract myself as much as Jo. 'Doesn't he brush up well in evening dress?'

'He brushes up fine.' Jo gestured with her fork. 'It's just when he gets talking that he makes a girl want to run screaming for some wet paint to watch.'

'That's because you rub each other the wrong way. If you didn't talk to him like he's your annoying little brother—'

'Listen, I've got a whole bunch of various kinds of brothers, and none of them is as rude to me as Ted is. I've tried to help him over the one hundred years I've known him, but he resists all attempts at improvement.'

*It's because he fancies you*, I wanted to say, but didn't. It seemed too obvious.

'He reminds me of my dad,' I said instead. 'He's reliable, he calls a spade a spade—'

'Well, he has to do that, darling. How can you trust a gardener who calls it something else?'

Jo had a habit of deflecting personal comments with a *darling* and a witty comment, exactly as she was doing now. I eyeballed her.

'It's all very well you trying to set me up, but when was the last time *you* were out on a date with someone who—'

Jo held up a hand, the gold nail varnish unchipped from last night. 'Did I tell you the latest from Marigold?'

That stopped me in my tracks, as she knew it would. I *loved* Tales from de Vere Towers. Jo's family was like an Agatha Christie novel without the body count.

'Is that what last night was about? Not the gas at all?'

She nodded. 'It was a ruse to get her emergency files out of the flat. Kit won't sign the divorce papers — he wants joint custody of all the dogs, and Marigold's holding a horse as ransom. She wants to know if she can change its name by deed poll. I mean, *God*. You'd think by now she would know the score. How many times do you have to get divorced before you learn the cheat codes?'

Jo's mother was going through her fourth divorce, this time from a very famous (apparently) horse trainer called Kit Pike who could tame any mad stallion but had terrible trouble controlling Marigold de Vere. Meanwhile, Jo's dad, Philip, Marigold's first husband, lived in *his* family's rambling pile in Worcestershire with his second wife, Laura, and their three children, Oliver, Edwin, and Betty. Marigold and Kit had no extra children, but they did have several Clumber spaniels, named after various characters from *Fawlty Towers*, plus Kit's horses, all of whom had names too. It was sometimes hard to tell whether Marigold was screeching about human family members or doggy ones. (Jo was very good about drawing people diagrams on napkins and so on while she dished the gossip.)

'It's maddening,' said Jo. 'I've told her — I've got quite enough legal drama in my life spending all day with builders, without getting dragged into her court cases.'

'But that's exactly why you need Ted,' I persisted. 'He'd bring calmness to your life. Calmness and kindness and a lawn with amazing stripes.'

'I get that from having you as a flatmate.' Jo reached for her tea again and gave me a friendly nudge. 'And you smell a lot nicer than Ted.'

'Even if I do leave mud on your nail brush?'

'I can deal with the mud in return for this fried egg,' said Jo, and she smiled at me as she chewed.

I smiled back at her and thought, not for the first time, *Who knew the best friend I've ever had would be someone who thinks fried egg is a delicacy?*

# CHAPTER FIVE

There were lots of things I loved about my job — I could literally see the fruits of my labor springing up around me (hee), and the satisfaction of watching a neglected space turn into a fragrant cloud of flowers never got old. I set my own hours, and I didn't have to worry about office politics or have an opinion about the latest reality TV show, and thanks to my digging, I could also beat most men in arm-wrestling matches. However, even I had to admit that being a garden designer was a lot more fun between March and October. The reality on a cold January morning was thermal leggings under my jeans and a moisturizing regimen that stopped just short of a light coating of duck fat, like a Channel swimmer.

January, for me and Ted, meant a series of backbreaking tidy-up jobs inspired by other people's New Year's resolutions. We'd spent two days clearing a mountain of deadwood in Battersea, which the husband of the household had chopped out of his apple trees during a trying Christmas with the in-laws, and another day discreetly fixing his frenzied handiwork. By Wednesday we were on our fifth trip to the tip with a full vanload of cuttings to be composted, and my arms felt as if they were about to fall off.

Saturday night's party seemed like a very long time ago,

although the memory of it floated in and out of my mind constantly. I couldn't stop thinking about Leo scaling the scaffolding. And also Ted refused to stop going on about Grace's ruined plants and what he'd like to do to Rolf Wolfsburg with his shovel.

'You realize that if Richard can't make Grace's dreams come true, we're going to have to think up a whole other source of revenue for — oi! Can you put your phone away?' Ted turned in the passenger seat and glared at me.

I pocketed my phone. I'd just been checking it was still working. Not that I was expecting it to ring — Leo hadn't taken my number, and anyway, what would I say if . . .

Anyway, it hadn't rung. He hadn't rung. No one had rung. Or texted.

'I was just seeing if Grace had left a message,' I improvised, because I was, sort of. 'She's back on Friday.'

Ted slapped his forehead. 'Friday! What are you going to say happened to her plants? A very specific balcony burglary? If you'd just left her plants there, instead of taking them home to swap the pots over . . .'

That *had* occurred to me. Many times.

'I could just tell her the truth.' I still had one plant, after all. One plant might be enough.

'Which part of the truth? That she managed to blight the seeds she planted? Or that you didn't trust her to do it properly, so you stole the rest to do yourself? Or, "Oh dear, Grace, only one of your wishes is going to come true"? We need to get her onside.'

'Stop it!' I bit my lip and glanced down to the footwell, where

Badger was curled up on my spare sweater. 'I could tell her that Badger was running around and they got knocked off? Because both those things happened . . . just not necessarily at the same time.'

Badger cocked his ears, as if to say, *That's right, blame me,* and I felt bad. Gran hadn't entrusted her beloved dog to me so I could use him as an excuse for out-of-control minor royalty.

'Well, *my* suggestion is that you just find some more plants and substitute them,' said Ted, as if I hadn't heard the first twenty times he'd told me that. 'And if she notices, which I doubt, then call me and I'll talk her round.'

I glanced across at him incredulously.

'Okay,' he amended, seeing my expression. 'If she notices, we'll call Jo, and she can talk Grace round. She'll probably end up booking her to refurbish her kitchen at the same time, knowing Jo.'

I gripped the steering wheel and checked my mirrors like a fighter pilot before pulling out into the quiet residential road, lined with big 4x4s and old trees. Ted frequently teased me about my methodical approach to driving, but I had to center myself before tackling the mad London traffic. I'd learned to drive in the quiet country roads near our house in Rothery, and it had taken me a few months to get past the Fear of Hyde Park Corner, but now, in my van, I was like Boadicea. No bus or cab cut into my lane. Oh no.

'Did you enjoy the party?' I asked as we headed toward the recycling center.

'It was all right,' Ted grunted, which I took as high praise. 'At least there's enough to eat now you're on board. Used to be just Pringles and those weird olives at Jo's. Now at least you get something to soak up the booze.'

I beamed. 'Thanks! Do you want any more sausage rolls, by the way? We've still got a few left over.'

Ted had taken two dozen mini sausage rolls off our hands as he left on Saturday night. There were still another seven dozen in the freezer. I'd started to give Badger two a day on the quiet, rather than chuck them out, and they were making the footwell smell somewhat fruity.

'If they're going spare.' There was a pause, which I thought was down to Ted reflecting on the succulence of my sausage rolls, but then he blurted out, 'Do girls really like guys like that total idiot?'

'Which total idiot?'

'That . . . idiot Rolf.' He looked pained. 'I can't believe Jo likes him.'

'Him? No!' I said. 'Absolutely not. She *refuses* to take his calls.'

I thought I was being tactful, but Ted's crestfallen face told me I'd actually put my foot in it.

'He's been calling her?'

I bit my lip to stop myself blurting out something worse. Rolf had been *bombarding* her with calls. There were nine unlistened-to messages on our answering machine, and so many on her mobile that she'd turned it off for a while. I'd never known Jo to turn off her mobile. She even kept it on during weddings and funerals. (Silent vibrate, obviously.)

I hurried to fill the awkward gap. 'Just to apologize, I think. She certainly doesn't want to talk to him. Jo's as upset about the plants as I am, I mean, as we are. She reckons it's the height of rudeness, someone kicking someone else's dreams off a balcony.'

Ted snorted, then ran a hand through his curly hair, which, to be honest, could have done with a wash. But then, neither of us was in fragrant condition after a morning's hard labor.

'Do you want to talk about . . . anything?' I started. I was a good listener; Jo often said I'd have made a great talk show host, or policewoman: I didn't say a lot, but I had one of those faces that made people admit the most personal things without meaning to.

'No,' said Ted unhappily, 'I don't.'

That in itself told me everything.

We drove on in silence for a few minutes. Then he said, in an entirely different voice, 'We need to think of how else we're going to do this honey project, if Grace decides we're too incompetent to recommend to Richard. Maybe we should just buy some space? Rent some gardens? I could probably get some cash off my mum. How about you? Can you get your folks to invest?'

I felt myself snap shut like a Venus flytrap, as every defensive muscle in my body twitched.

Maybe I should explain a bit about our Great Plan. And my parents. The two are sort of linked.

Okay, the Great Plan. Ted and I were going to make local honey in each of the postcodes we worked in, by planting as many large-scale wildflower borders and containers as we could, then either setting up our own hives or doing a deal with local beekeepers. The more local the honey was, the more effective it would be for hay fever sufferers in that area — I knew it worked because Mum had always dished out honey sandwiches to ward off the red eyes and sneezing Kelly and I both suffered from as kids.

Dad had kept hives in the rambling gardens of our old house in Hadley Green, before we had to move to Rothery where there was just a small yard. The beautiful flower gardens there were balanced with a big wildflower meadow, and you could taste the lavender and cornflowers and daisies in the honey. My clearest childhood memories were of watching the bees flit around the hives in the summer sun, me with an ice cream, Dad with a beer — I was never scared of them, just a bit spooked by their extraterrestrial communication abilities.

So I knew Dad could hook me up with some beekeeping equipment, and Jo knew the right sorts of deli owners who'd pay a fortune for our local honey. But ideally, we needed a big development like Palace View to plant proper swaths of wild-flowers on the roof as well as hives.

And that was the second thing: start-up money. I had very little left after my monthly outgo, and though I knew Dad would help me with the bee element, he and Mum had no spare money either, and I didn't want him to think I needed it.

'I'd rather we got it going ourselves.' I could hear my voice had gone tight and northern, like Mum's when she was in one of her moods, and I wished it wouldn't. 'Leave Grace to me. I know she'll help us out if she can.'

Ted mumbled something, but we'd worked together long enough to know — just about — when to leave a grumble before it flared up into a row. So we said nothing while we hauled all the wood cuttings into the council composter, and nothing while we drove home, and he said nothing when I asked him to drop me off at the park so I could give Badger a lunchtime run before I went over to my afternoon job in Pimlico.

We were both *thinking* plenty, though. I could almost hear the gears in Ted's brain grinding with the effort of not saying it aloud.

Badger and I had a power walk round the park, and by the time I decided to head home to make a sandwich (in the interest of my new economy drive), we were pleasantly breathless and spattered with mud.

I was thinking about the different bedding plants I could try this spring in the rather gloomy Pimlico garden, but when we turned down the street, my concentration was jolted — there was something on our front step.

That in itself wasn't unusual — Jo regularly got flowers from grateful clients — but this didn't look like the usual florist's bunch. I sped up, as did Badger, eager to sniff out what had appeared on his territory.

There was no one around, so I jogged awkwardly toward the front step, shoving wispy curls out of my eyes. To my surprise, it was a row of terracotta pots, each with a little plant sticking out. There was no note attached to any of them, or stuck under them, or left in the letter box.

*Who could have left these?* I wondered, only to rock backward in shock when Badger started barking as if the house was on fire. At the same instant, I caught movement from the steps down to Marigold's basement flat — what had been the servants' entrance in ye olden days — and stumbled as I got to my feet. Someone was making his way up, presumably having failed to get any answer from Marigold's doorbell.

I froze. Was this Kit Pike, come for the horse's birth certificate? What was I supposed to say?

Badger carried on with his guard dog routine, barking like a much bigger dog, and pulled so hard I dropped the lead. He made a dash for the top of the steps, yapping furiously; then, when the man didn't stop coming up, Badger started snapping at his trouser legs, to my mortification.

'Badger!' I yelled. 'Knock it *off*!'

'Hey! Enough of that!' the man said, much more mildly than Badger deserved — I was already saying a lot worse, in my head — and I recognized the voice at once.

A searing blush started around my forehead and spread rapidly across my whole body.

It wasn't Kit Pike. It was Leo.

As he emerged from the steps, he looked a bit different in a work suit than in the jeans and shirt I'd seen him in on Saturday night, but everything else was very much the same. The teddy-bear blond hair, the shy smile, the arresting blue eyes.

Actually, he looked better in a suit. He looked like a suit model, but capable of doing whatever job he needed to wear the suit for.

Predictably, my brain went into standby mode, just when I needed it.

'He won't bite,' I babbled, 'he's just very barky and — Badger! Stop it! He has a thing about deliverymen — I think one must have kicked him when he was at my gran's — not that I'm saying you look like a deliveryman, obviously, or that you kicked him — Badger!'

I finally stamped on Badger's lead just as he launched forward again, but not before Leo stumbled back to avoid him, and fell into the railings running alongside.

He spun, then sat down with a thump on the stone front steps, and I grabbed the growling Badger and scooped him under my arm. I wished there were some kind of rewind button I could press to do this the way I'd been imagining it in my head for *the past four days*. Most of those scenarios had ended with Leo laughing at my ready wit, then taking me out for dinner. None of them had involved this much apologizing before we'd even begun.

'I'm *really* sorry. Are you okay? He didn't rip anything, did he?' I went to help him up, then thought better of it, in case Badger went for his tie. It looked like a really expensive tie; I had an awful mental image of Badger swinging from it by his teeth. 'This is Badger. My dog. He's a bit protective of me and Jo. Thinks he's the man of the house!'

'Well, I guess he's cuter than a burglar alarm.' Leo nodded at him warily, and got up, brushing dust from his trousers. 'Unless you're a burglar. Does he do that to everyone?'

'Just, er, deliverymen.' I shook my head, and put Badger down, clamping him between my legs for safety. 'And men with hats. And men who look like the dodgy handyman who lived next door to Gran. That's why he wasn't invited to the party — he operates a really strict door policy.'

'You mean, he wouldn't have let Rolf in?'

'Not if he was wearing a hat, or carrying a parcel, no.' I grinned nervously. 'Santa gets a hard time of it. That's why he uses the chimney.'

Badger was sniffing the air between him and Leo, and I could feel his wiry body trembling through my jeans; but then Leo made some kind of clicking noise and, to my astonishment, Badger sat down and looked balefully up at him through his sparse white lashes.

'Wow,' I said, amazed. 'How did you do that?'

Leo raised an eyebrow. 'Deliveryman trade secret.'

I took a deep breath and noticed, out of the corner of my brain, that the air was tangy with the scent of next door's winter honeysuckle, which bloomed early every year. I could smell spring in the air, even though it was still winter. Being near Leo seemed to heighten all my senses, as if every tiny detail was sharp around him.

'You're very honored,' I blurted out. 'It took ages for Badger to get on with Ted. I had to make him carry frankfurters all the time — he was like the Pied Piper of Fulham, what with the dogs following us around. But without the jazzy tights, obviously.'

Leo bent down to pet Badger's ears, and glanced up, apparently not put off by my nervous waffling. 'Ted's the tall guy who stopped Rolf from falling off the balcony? Very strong? Bit cross?'

'That's Ted, yes.'

'Does Rolf owe him some plants too? Or a rare tree or something?'

'No.' I kept a watchful eye on Badger, but he was upside down now, offering Leo his muddy tummy to tickle. The tart.

'Ted's agricultural interest is strictly nine-to-five. He really only got into it so he could do some covert metal-detecting. He's convinced that there's a Roman hoard out there with his name on it.'

'And has he found much?' Leo got up, and Badger sniffed his trousers, which I was relieved to see weren't shredded.

'Three bags of assorted coins and more clay pipes than a civil war reenactment,' I said. 'But he lives in hope. At least we haven't found any dead bodies. And it leaves me free to get on with the actual gardening side of things. I do the planning. And the planting. And the design.'

Now that we were actually looking at each other and talking, I felt the same strange mixture of nerves and relaxation I'd felt on Saturday night. I was panicking about what to say, but somehow it was coming out all right — and more than that, Leo seemed interested.

'Did you leave these?' I gestured toward the pots.

'Yup. Five pots of Dream Seeds, to replace those lost in action.' Leo grinned, giving his professional City appearance an unexpectedly boyish twist. 'I don't know if they're at the exact same stage as the ones you had on your balcony, but I don't think your client's going to know the difference, is she?'

I blinked in amazement. 'But where did you find them? I've been on the Internet all week trying to track some down! I can't even find out what they're called. They're so secretive about where the course is and how much it costs — all I could dig up was that it's one of those ones celebs go on when they don't actually want to be photographed.'

'It's on a private island. And it costs a fortune. Between you and me, my contact's been on it so often she's virtually got a whole hedge of these things,' said Leo, dropping his voice conspiratorially.

'She must have a lot of dreams come true.'

He looked wry. 'Funnily enough, no. Which is odd, given that she's already got pretty much everything most women would wish for. I sometimes think she goes on it to get ideas for things *to* wish for.'

I nodded. I wasn't sure what he meant, but I liked the confiding way he said it. I wondered, awkwardly, if the 'contact' was his girlfriend. Oh . . . nuts.

He was staring at me with a smile flickering on his lips, as if *I'd* done something amazing — even though he was the one who'd just magicked these plants out of nowhere. I felt my face tingle.

'I don't know how to thank you enough,' I babbled. 'Did she mind giving them up? I mean, how did you get them? Did you pop round to hers and say you needed some dreams coming true, so could you take some cuttings?' I widened my eyes. 'Does she think you're having some kind of midlife crisis now?'

Leo had a nice, relaxed sort of laugh. 'There were a few phone calls back and forth. I think it would have been easier to fly there myself and get them — I mean, these guys more or less got their own seat in business. The pots aren't quite the same, but I guess you could say you replanted them as a Christmas present?'

'Oh, no, they're nearly ident —' I stopped, and stared. *He flew them in?* He was so normal to talk to that I'd forgotten that Leo was the sort of guy who hung out with princes like Rolf. Rolf had probably flown those girls in on Saturday. On a private jet or something.

'Anyway,' he went on, leaning against the railing, 'I was hoping you'd be here — I wanted to talk to you about something else, and I wasn't sure how to get hold of you.'

My heart bumped in my chest. 'Oh?'

'I've got this garden. It's a bit of a project, and I've been told to get some professional advice on it.' His blue eyes crinkled. 'And as you're the only gardener I've met recently, I wondered if you had time to advise me. I can't guarantee there's much worth metal-detecting, but there's quite a bit of planting.'

My heart stopped thumping so hard. A garden. Of course.

Well, maybe that one plant he'd saved had been mine. I *had* wished for a new client. Maybe wishing for Palace View had been overambitious.

'Of course I've got time, I'm always on the lookout for new clients. I mean, new challenges.' I fished my phone out of my pocket, and hoped I hadn't made it sound as though all Ted and I did was play amateur archaeology. 'When's a good time for you? Morning, afternoon?'

I paused. Leo's suit was quite a traditional one, with none of the flashy details some of Jo's friends adopted, so he probably worked in the City, without time to take off for garden consultations. This had to be his lunch break. How long had he been here? 'Or is evening better?' I added, in case he thought I was staring.

*Did that sound like I was fishing for a date?*

My mind gave up and went blank.

'Evenings are better. Let me look at my diary and get back

to you,' said Leo. 'I've got quite a complicated couple of weeks coming up, and I'd hate to arrange something and then have to cancel. I just wanted to check that you had time to see me.'

'There are easier ways of getting hold of a gardener than hanging outside her house with plants.' I couldn't help feeling a little flat that it was my green fingers he wanted, not . . . any other bit of me. I tried to cover it with a jokey tone. 'You could have asked Rolf for our landline. He must have it — he's been calling Jo enough.'

An expression I couldn't quite identify flashed across Leo's face and then vanished almost at once. If I hadn't been staring at him like a love-struck teenager, I'd have missed it.

'Has he? I haven't seen him since the weekend, to be honest. And I didn't want to ask him for your number because . . .' His mouth twisted up. 'Well, you've met Rolf.'

I started to agree, then realized I didn't know exactly what he meant by that. What? He was embarrassed to be seen calling me?

Leo saw my confusion and hastily added, 'I mean, I . . . I didn't phrase that well. Sorry. I meant, I don't do everything with Rolf. I like to keep some areas of my life straightforward.'

'Fair enough,' I said, only partially mollified.

'So?' Leo's thumb was poised over his phone, and I rattled off my work mobile number, and e-mail, and then our home landline too.

'You could let Rolf know that Jo's not listening to the messages, by the way,' I said while he was saving them. 'The first two were okay, but they got a bit . . . stalky after that? Maybe a nice bunch of flowers would be a better gesture.'

'Good suggestion. I'll let him know,' said Leo, then checked his watch and grimaced. 'I wish we could have that chat about the garden now over lunch, but I've really got to dash. I'm supposed to be in a meeting in Canary Wharf in ten minutes.'

'That's okay, I'm supposed to be in a garden in Buckingham Palace Road in fifteen.'

'Buckingham Palace Road?' He looked impressed. 'You win. Are you fitting corgi doors?'

'Oh, it's just weeding,' I said automatically, then remembered I should have told him I was doing something more upmarket, as befitting his garden plans. Doh.

'Anyway,' I hastened on, 'I should be thanking you. I can't believe you went to so much trouble with these plants. My client's back on Friday — she'll be nearly as thrilled as I am to see those.'

'My pleasure.' A warm smile spread across Leo's handsome face, and I could only just make myself keep meeting his gaze. 'I'll be in touch. About the garden.'

There was a second's awkwardness — should I offer my hand to shake? — and then he leaned forward and kissed my cheek. A tingle spread through me, under my thermals, across my skin, and then Leo bent down, ruffled Badger's ears, and, with a backward wave, dashed to catch a passing black cab.

I put the pots carefully to one side on the step, where they wouldn't be kicked over, then hurried to the front door, where I fumbled with my keys because my hands were shaking so much. I knew I was smiling like a madwoman from the ache in my cheeks, but I froze when I saw my reflection in the big mirror over the hall post table.

My hair was somehow greasy *and* flyaway, my face was flushed, and my clothes — oh God my clothes looked in a worse state than Badger did, and he'd been rolling in everything the park had to offer.

I stared at myself. Why hadn't Leo *said* anything? How polite *was* he that he hadn't mentioned the fact that I looked like I'd been sleeping rough in someone's shed for three weeks? My glowy mood shriveled with embarrassment, and then my phone buzzed.

Just checking I've got your number right, and to give you mine. Great to see you just now — glad we're forgiven! Look forward to talking soon re the garden. L

My heart raced. He must have texted from the taxi — he hadn't even waited the two days Jo said most London men waited before they got in touch, just to mess with your head.

But then, Leo was completely unlike any man I'd met in London before. He was very posh, but he was easy to talk to. He wore a suit, but he didn't mind scaling scuzzy fire escapes for broken plants. He was gorgeous, but — actually, there was no *but* there. He was just gorgeous.

The only trouble was, he was best friends with the one man my best friend absolutely, definitely didn't want to talk about.

I looked at my smeary face in the hall mirror and decided that from now on, I might start wearing a bit more makeup for work, just in case.

# CHAPTER SIX

Leo must have spoken to Rolf about the phone calls, because they stopped that night.

The presents, on the other hand, started the next day.

'You have to admit, Rolf's persistent,' I said, looking at the enormous box on the kitchen table, spilling pink and black tissue and ribbons over the jaunty plastic tablecloth.

It was a very big box for what was inside. The silky underwear we'd eventually unearthed from the multiple layers of tissue would have fitted into a medium-size Jiffy bag and still left room for a gift card and a pair of tights.

'Persistent, yes,' said Jo, picking up the fragment of lingerie with a finger. 'In the sense that the *common cold* is quite persistent. And I don't count this as an apology. I'm not sure if it's actually making things worse.'

'Is this really a pair of knickers?' I asked, curious. 'Technically speaking?'

Rolf's apology undies were a world away from my own Marks & Spencer reliables. They were more elastic than material, and I wasn't even sure how you'd put them on, since it was all holes.

The box of knickers had arrived after Jo had left for work that morning, and then sometime in the afternoon, Mrs Mainwaring had taken delivery of a Jo Malone scented candle the size of a bucket, with a solid silver lid. While we were having supper, Dickon had knocked on the door to pass on one of those ludicrous sledge-size padded boxes of Swiss chocolates that I thought only existed in Doris Day films, delivered by courier. All with cards that Jo wouldn't even let me see 'for the sake of your innocence.'

She made a snorting noise, balled up the thong, and squashed the ribbons and tissue paper back over the lot. 'The fact that Rolf thinks I'd be won over by this sort of lingerie tells you everything about both him and the sorts of girls he normally goes for. I am not a girl who can be impressed with stripper thongs. Even if they did cost a couple of hundred quid.'

'A couple of—?' My mouth dropped open. 'Are they made from gold thread or something?'

'And the rest,' said Jo. 'Anyway, Rolf's got to learn to take no for an answer. I'm not interested in a man who talks about himself in the third person. Why would I change my mind just because he thinks he can guess my bra size?'

'Did he?'

Jo looked momentarily discombobulated. 'Yes. And I don't know how, because he never got as far as . . . Anyway, no! No, no, no! It's extremely bad behavior and only makes me more determined to ignore him.'

'He must really like you, though, to go to all that bother,' I said, thinking of the thoughtful way Leo had not only found the plants but delivered them himself. They were now installed on Grace's balcony, where I'd spent several happy hours simultaneously tidying up and rehearsing the conversation I'd have with Leo when he called to talk about his garden. Which he hadn't. Yet.

'Amy!' Jo's eyebrows vanished into her fringe with disbelief. 'Men like Rolf have La Perla on speed dial. It's not that impressive. And he doesn't *really like* me either — he just can't stand the thought of being turned down. He's not used to it. It took me nearly a month to end it with him in the first place. I kept telling him we had nothing in common, and he kept saying, "Oh, tiger, you're playing hard to get! Grrr!" and sending me enormous teddy bears with diamond earrings on.'

I boggled my eyes. 'Your problem with that being?'

'The problem being that I didn't *want* them.' Her ferocious expression softened. 'Princes, even very low-level ones, don't understand normal women. They don't understand that you can't *buy* your way into someone's heart. That's why we should leave them to date loopy supermodels with entitlement complexes and princesses who are just as mad as they are.'

I said nothing. The most I usually had to worry about with the men Jo tried to set me up with was, were they going to make me pay for supper, and could I ever fancy a man who called it 'sups' in the first place?

Jo's face suddenly brightened. 'Ooh! I meant to say, I saw my friend Poppy outside Callie Hamilton's. She's having a party at the Chelsea Arts Club this Saturday — she's put us both on the guest list.' She nudged me. 'Come on, I'll lend you my red dress.'

I liked the Chelsea Arts Club. It had one of those unexpected city gardens that felt like stepping off the street into Narnia, all quiet corners and tea lights and undergrowth that rustled with artists. But what if Leo called, and asked me to come over on his day off?

*He isn't going to ask you to check out his garden in the dark,* I reminded myself.

Jo was peering at me. 'What's up? Are you worried we'll run into Dickon? Not all painters demand that you strip, you know. Poppy usually asks her sitters to put more clothes *on*. Dog costumes, usually.'

I hesitated, and wondered if I should tell Jo about Leo. Then my eye fell on the controversial thong, and I decided against it.

'I'd love to. Sounds great. What are you going to do with those?' I nodded at the box.

'Do you want them?'

I nearly laughed. They'd barely go over my arm, let alone anywhere else. 'As a novelty headband? Maybe. Not so much as knickers. Every time I bent over, I'd think of Rolf.'

'*Eeeuuugh!*' said Jo. 'That's exactly what he wants!'

We stared at the box, as if Rolf's handsome face might suddenly appear in the tissue like in a crystal ball.

'Let's leave them on Mrs Mainwaring's doorknob,' she decided. 'That'll give them all something to talk about.'

Grace flew back from Aspen first thing on Friday, and when I went round there, I found her standing over her Dream Seedlings with a glass of white wine and a pile of crumpled tissues, sniffing back tears and chanting some sort of gibberish mantra to herself.

She looked so happy, though, that I nearly cried too. With relief.

'Oh, Amy! Amy!' she said, throwing her arms around my neck. 'There's been a miracle. Look!'

I said a million silent thank yous to Leo while Grace touched the leaf of each plant with a tenderness that made me wonder whether that was her first glass of wine. And she was meant to be on a detox too.

'I can't believe I made them grow so fast,' she hiccuped. 'Me! After I killed that lovely strawberry plant and the roses. And that bay tree. Look how strong they are. They must be . . .' She covered her mouth and blinked hard. 'Maybe it means my wishes are already coming true?'

'Looks like it!' I said.

I was crossing my fingers that Grace wouldn't do some basic math and question how nonmagic seeds could go from seed to fairly sturdy plant in under three weeks, even with my green fingers waggling over them.

Grace gripped my arm and I let out an involuntary squeak, convinced she'd rumbled me.

'Amy, can I tell you a secret?' She bit her lip like an excited teenager. 'Promise you won't tell anyone?'

I'd been doing Grace's gardening for nearly two years, and in that time she'd told me a fair number of secrets, most of them about her dad, who owned the flat, and Richard. And her therapist. And how she'd cheated in her A levels, and had Botox in her hands, and all sorts of other stuff.

'Promise,' I said.

'Richard's bought the Palace View development!' she

whispered. 'He sealed the deal in Aspen. On the ski slopes. He crashed off a red run answering his phone, but it was okay in the end because there was a medi-chopper on standby anyway and the clinic had Wi-Fi so he could do it all by Skype.'

I clamped my lips together to stop myself from saying anything.

'And the sweetest thing was that while we were in the clinic, he arranged for me to have this amazing new chemical peel thing you can't even get here!' She looked thrilled and touched her nose self-consciously. It was a bit raw-looking. 'So that was fabulous too.'

'That's great news, Grace,' I said. 'I'm really pleased for him. And you.'

She sighed happily and pointed at one flowerpot. 'So that's one come true already.'

I knew at this point I should say something smooth like, 'So, Richard'll be needing a gardening service, I suppose?' but I couldn't. I just couldn't.

'Bodes well for the other wishes then!' I said instead.

Grace paused, then took one flowerpot — the one with the puniest plant in it — and handed it to me. 'There you go,' she said. 'You helped with the seeds, it should work for you too.'

'But you had a whole string of wishes!'

She made an uncharacteristically rude *prrthp* noise. 'Face it, world peace isn't going to happen with one puny seed. It'd need a whole tree. What are you going to wish for?'

I opened my mouth, as the various Amys in my brain argued among themselves.

*Wish for a nice new boyfriend.*

*No, the gardening contract for Palace View.*

*Boyfriend.*

*Gardening contract. If you're thinking of Leo, he's a bit out of your league, love. He's a crush. Not a potential date.*

*But he did such a nice thing, finding those plants . . .*

*He felt guilty about Rolf kicking them off. And what about the New Year expansion plans? What about taking the business to a new level? Priorities . . .*

'Amy? Are you all right?' Grace peered at me. 'You've gone all . . . cross-eyed.'

'I'm fine.' I took a deep breath. 'To be honest, Grace, I'd wish that Ted and I could do the gardening for Palace View. Do you think I could send a proposal to Richard? I've got some great ideas for landscaping . . .'

Grace stared at me, then beamed. 'Yes! What a great idea. That's like . . . karma in action! I grew this plant, and now you can grow more plants for Richard!'

'Um, yeah . . .'

'Wow, that's your wish sorted out!' She clapped her hands to her newly peeled face in delight, then flinched. 'So, actually, you won't be needing this. Maybe I can recycle it.'

And with a dazzling white smile, she took the plant pot back and placed it neatly back with its mates.

Grace wasn't always as stupid as she looked.

I spent the early afternoon digging over a garden in Fulham while rehearsing the off-the-cuff phone call I was going to make just before teatime, to update Leo about Grace's plants. Technically, I didn't need to, but I argued to myself that he'd want to know it had all been worth it.

Badger had long since got used to me chatting away to thin air, but he'd developed a long-suffering sigh that bordered on the sarcastic when I went over the same conversation too often.

'Hey, Leo, it's Amy,' I started to the leafless cherry tree.

Was *hello* better?

'Hello, Leo, it's Amy. Amy Wilde.'

No. Was that a bit too formal?

Remembering Jo's drama school advice about smiling on the phone, I pulled a wide grin, and my voice came out shiny and bright. 'Hi! It's Amy!'

That sounded better. Mad, but miles better.

Underneath the wheelbarrow, Badger let out a low groan and curled up tighter on my fleece.

'Grace loved the plants.' I coughed and aimed my voice slightly lower. 'Grace was so thrilled about the Dream Seeds . . .' Better, more specific, in case he'd forgotten. 'Can I take you out for a drink to say thanks?'

No. He could say, *No, it's okay*. Or *No, I don't drink*.

I was overthinking. Again. I shoved my spade into the soil, despairing. It was so easy to come across the wrong way. What would Jo do? She'd just ask. She'd have asked on Wednesday morning, straight off: 'When are we going out?'

'You know what, Leo?' I drawled, leaning on my spade in a Jo impression — she was always using her surroundings as props to drape herself on, like someone in a Noël Coward play. 'Can we go out for a drink? I would *love* to hear about some of the scrapes you've had to dig Rolf out of. And, besides that, you're gorgeous and you don't talk exclusively about your car or have an off-putting nose.'

My mobile rang in my back pocket and I nearly slipped off the spade handle in surprise. I fumbled it out with my gloved hands, and when I saw who was calling, the cool Amy vanished completely: it was Leo.

Oh God. Oh God. Should I be Amy? Or Jo?

I took a couple of deep breaths, counted to five (I didn't want him to go to voicemail), and managed to gasp out, 'Amy Wilde speaking?'

'Hello, Amy, it's Leo. Is this a good time to talk?'

My face went red, as if Leo could somehow see me in my grubby jeans. His voice was very close in my ear.

'Yes,' I said, brushing soil off myself. I frowned at myself and stopped. 'It's fine.'

'Excellent. Two things, really. First, did your client notice the replacement plants? It was today, right?'

He'd remembered. He'd actually remembered what day I said Grace was coming back. A happy feeling rushed me.

'She didn't suspect a thing,' I said. 'She's over the moon — I've never seen her so happy.'

'Wonderful!'

'In fact,' a voice that sounded a bit like mine added, 'she was so happy she promised to put in a good word for me about another big contract, so thanks for that too!'

'Then I'm doubly pleased. In fact, that makes my second question even more urgent. I was wondering how you were fixed for Thursday next week?' he went on. 'If you're not doing anything, I'd love to have that chat about my garden. If you can still fit me in. I know Thursday is the new Friday.'

I hesitated. Grace, in a fit of confidence about her early days with Richard, had explained there were rules about this sort of thing. How many days' notice you were supposed to give. How busy you were supposed to look. She made negotiating dates sound like haggling over a knockoff Prada handbag in a Turkish street market, but not as much fun.

What would Jo do? She'd say . . .

'Thursday? That's Zumba.'

I closed my eyes in horror. Where had that come from?

'Zumba? Is that some kind of religious . . . event?' Leo asked politely. 'Forgive my ignorance.'

I considered lying for a split second, but decided there was no point. I'd only make it worse. 'No, no, Zumba's a class that Jo makes me go to with her at our gym,' I confessed. 'You're meant to look like Shakira while you're doing it, but I've seen us in the mirror, and we look like two pensioners with hip problems trying to take off a pair of trousers without undoing the fly.'

Leo laughed. 'Well, I don't want you to miss that.'

*Why did I just give Leo a mental image of a dancing pensioner? Even if his laugh was making my chest feel ticklish?*

'Wednesday's fine, though,' I said quickly. 'If you're free? Wednesday's the new Thursday in our house.'

'I can definitely be free on Wednesday,' said Leo. 'It's a date.'

Date. He'd said *date*.

'What sort of garden do you have?' I didn't know why I'd dragged the conversation back to business — maybe because I was desperately trying to displace the dancing pensioner with a knowledgeable horticultural-expert woman. 'So I can sketch out some plans?'

'Oh, it's just a small one,' said Leo, and I thought I detected a tiny note of embarrassment. 'You know, city garden.'

'I do know — I'm really good at making the most of small spaces.' I could already see it in my mind's eye, the pretty mini-garden in the sky. Maybe some figs in containers, or tumbling climbers pinned to brick walls. He had no need to feel embarrassed — any garden in London was a luxury. 'I've done a few rooftop vegetable patches recently — they can be low-maintenance, and some people find it therapeutic, watching things grow. If you make a sketch of your garden and bring it, we can talk about light and shade and soil.'

'Sounds great. So, is half seven good for you? We can have a drink and grab some dinner, if you have time.'

'That would be lovely.'

'I'll look forward to it.' Leo paused, then added, as if he wanted to prolong the conversation, 'How did the apology gift go? I suggested that actions might speak louder than words.'

'Um, not great.' I wasn't sure how much I could say without being rude about Rolf. 'The action being suggested was a bit . . . adult-oriented. Flowers might be nicer? I can recommend a book on the language of flowers, if it'd help.'

'I like that. What's the international flower language for "I'm sorry for being a loudmouthed idiot"?'

'A Venus flytrap.'

Leo let out a loud, slightly guilty snort. There was some office-type noise at his end, and I heard someone speaking. 'Okay, listen, I have to dash, but we'll firm up details closer to the time. Have a great weekend!'

'And you!'

And that was it. Simple. Date arranged, nice chat, no embarrassing moments apart from the Zumba thing, but he'd laughed at that.

Heat was spreading through my chest, in direct contrast to the numbness in my nose and ears.

Badger stared at me, and I realized I was grinning like a loon at a dead wisteria.

# CHAPTER SEVEN

Obviously, I spent the next four days agonizing about what to wear, with only brief pauses to agonize over what to say — all made about a million times harder because I was too embarrassed to tell Jo I was off on a date with the friend of the idiot who was now filling our flat with orchids. I didn't want to give Rolf the faintest chance of making it a double date, for one thing.

My social life didn't usually require much effort on the wardrobe front. Thanks to the fact that Jo and I were both skint most of the time, dinners out in London were limited to the pizza place round the corner; our local pub, the Nightingale Arms; and all-you-can-eat Indian buffets in Tooting with Ted, who fancied himself as something of a curry connoisseur. I got the feeling Leo wasn't going to book a table at any of those locations, so I wasn't feeling very confident about my usual jeans and a top.

Plus, it was still a business meeting. I'd prepared some color sketches of garden ideas — a white garden, a cottage garden, a neat little raised-bed complex — and was actually quite excited about creating something new. What did top gardening experts — who wanted to appear subtly sexy — wear?

In the end, since I couldn't consult Jo herself for fear of

opening a whole can of worms, I fell back on the What Would Jo Do? reasoning, and went for my black dress. I rarely spent money on clothes, but Jo had virtually pried my debit card from my hands at a Harvey Nichols sale. She'd been right to make me buy it. My Reliable Black Dress scooped me in at the right places and skimmed over the wrong ones. It was one of those secret weapon dresses that you could literally go anywhere in, depending on whether you pulled on boots or killer heels.

I put my one pair of killer heels in my bag, just in case, and set off in my flats.

I arrived in Berkeley Square at seven thirty, as Leo had texted me earlier, and immediately saw him waiting exactly where he'd said he would be, on the park bench opposite the Bentley car showroom.

He looked smart. Really smart. Before he could see me, I ducked behind a postbox and pulled on the heels.

I straightened up, butterflies swarming in my stomach, and banked this moment in my mental scrapbook for later. On the bench a very, *very* attractive man was waiting for me, dressed in a proper navy coat, his tawny-blond hair shining in the streetlight. I thought he was checking his phone, but on closer inspection I realized he was reading a Kindle.

That just put the cherry on the cake. A man who read, when no one was even looking at him.

Unaware of the reaction he was creating just by sitting on a bench reading, Leo shot back his coat sleeve to check the time, and glanced hopefully in the direction of Green Park Tube station. I didn't want someone else snapping him up, so

I hurried across the square as quickly as I could in my unfamiliar heels, hoping he wouldn't look up too soon and witness the giveaway wobbling.

Nerves hit me when I was nearly there. So far, the two times we'd met had been very much on my turf. Now we were on his, and I wasn't even sure my shoes were totally on my side. But when he realized the irregular clacking noise heading his way was me, Leo's face lit up with a smile that crinkled the corners of his blue eyes, and something warm pushed aside the nerves.

'Hello!' he said, putting one hand on my arm as he got up to kiss me on the cheek.

I nearly swooned at the sudden closeness of his skin, and his subtle cologne, and the roughness of his coat collar, all at the same time. Every single one of my senses felt as if it had been turned up to eleven, and then had a neon-lit brass band marched through.

'Yes, hello!' I started, but he'd gone for the other cheek in a Euro double kiss, and I mumbled awkwardly into his beautiful sharp cheekbone, 'Oh, sorry, um, yes, hello!'

'Sorry, sorry!' he said, and for a moment we sort of held each other at arm's length, bobbing heads.

'No, I'm sorry,' I said to fill the unsettling silence, 'I never know how many kisses to do. One, or two — or none! We don't do kisses back home. Our family doesn't really do kisses, we're more the hearty-slap-on-the-back type. Um, I don't mean we don't *kiss* each other *ever*,' I corrected myself, in case he thought I didn't want to be kissed at all. 'Just not all that, you know—'

'Just that you don't go in for all that *mwah-mwah* stuff,' Leo suggested. 'Quite right, too, it's awful. Hate it. I've got friends who do four.'

'Four? *Really*? Are they English?'

'Ha! No, they're not. Rolf'll do up to six, if he can get away with it. More, if the girl isn't resisting. He just carries on until she shoves him off.'

I snorted, which wasn't very ladylike, but Leo didn't seem to mind.

'So, um, where are we headed?' I asked.

He gestured toward the towering Georgian townhouses that surrounded the tree-lined park. If you could ignore the two lanes of traffic circling it, Berkeley Square was quite a romantic spot, not too far from Green Park in the art-galleries-and-designer-boutiques part of London. Lights were twinkling in the windows, and the sky was unusually clear behind the lines of old plane trees that crisscrossed the square.

'I thought we could eat round here, if that's okay with you?'

'It's fine with me,' I said as we started walking. I was nearer his shoulder in these heels than I had been in my trainers the last time we'd met. 'I like Berkeley Square.'

'Really? What about it, in particular?' Leo sounded interested. 'Are you into art galleries?'

'No, it's the trees. Don't laugh,' I added, because my thoughts on London trees tended to make even Ted snigger. 'I love the squares in London where the trees are as old as the buildings — or even older, like the buildings have had to fit around *them*. I like imagining where the roots go, how far under the ground they stretch.'

'Uh-huh.'

Leo hadn't sniggered, so I carried on. 'I imagine them touching the Underground tunnels, and winding round wine cellars. I know they don't, obviously, they're not that deep, but I always loved those cross sections of London we had in history lessons. Roman roads, and medieval pottery shards, and plague pits, and tree roots joining them all up.'

'That's a very poetic way of looking at it.' We were at the pedestrian crossing now, and Leo put out a hand to stop the taxi that was trying to cut across us. It stopped at once, and I felt more special than usual as he waved me across first.

'It's a known fact that trees cut down on crime too,' I went on, in case I was sounding too flaky. 'And they're natural air filters too. Beautiful *and* useful!'

'Like the city's lungs,' said Leo. He glanced across at me. 'I sometimes think that when I look out of my office window – how green London is between the buildings. How green it must once have been when it was all villages.'

I stopped. *I* often thought that. 'Do you? Honestly?'

''Fraid so. I like to imagine the villages around the church spires. Before the streets joined them all up into one big sprawl.' Leo nodded, then pretended to wince at the geekiness of it, and I laughed, and felt something tingle between us.

'Did you know,' I said, eager to get my fact in while we were still in the square, 'that that plane tree there is worth seven hundred and fifty thousand pounds?' I pointed to a thick tree in the corner, gnarled and leafless but still dignified, like an old soldier watching the houses. I mean, I was second to no woman in my love of trees, but that was an *incredible* amount of money.

'How do they work that out?'

'It's down to age, and size, and how many people benefit from it being there. That plane's been there since the storming of the Bastille. Since George Washington became president.' I could never quite get my head round that. 'It's a living thing, isn't it? Imagine what it's seen!'

'Well, quite. I mean, all *sorts* goes on round here ...'

Leo had stopped walking to look back at the tree, then turned to me. His mouth was curled into a half smile at one corner, and he seemed genuinely intrigued. 'That is the most interesting fact I've heard today, by quite a long stretch.'

I started to say, 'Oh dear, was it a bad day?' but I stopped myself in time. That was a compliment. *Take the compliment, Amy*.

We smiled, goofily, at each other for a second; then he waved his hand toward a door with a canopy over it. 'Shall we go in?' he asked. 'Unless you've got any more good tree facts for me?'

I was confused for a moment — it looked like someone's house, not somewhere we'd go to eat.

Leo couldn't live in Berkeley Square, surely? No one *lived* here, it was all embassies and offices! My panic crept back. Was this some royal residence of Rolf's? Was I wearing the right outfit?

'Are you all right to eat here?' he asked.

I blushed. I had absolutely no idea where we were. 'Um, I don't really know the restaurants in this part of town.'

'It's actually a members' club,' said Leo. 'I thought it would be quieter, and to be honest ...' He looked momentarily ruffled. 'My secretary booked somewhere a bit . . . loud. I share her with a much more, uh, flamboyant fund manager, and I don't think she's worked out that I'm not really into restaurants where they set fire to your drinks *and* your dinner.'

'Me neither,' I said, as if I went to those sorts of places all the time and hated them. I hadn't been to a members' club either. Wasn't that something to do with lap dancing? Surely not . . .

I made an effort to channel Jo, and smiled broadly. 'This sounds great!'

'Good,' said Leo, and waved me down the stairs.

The staircase led into a narrow lobby, lined with framed paintings like a country-house hotel. It was discreetly lit and thickly carpeted, and the door was swung open by an invisible hand. As we stepped in — Leo letting me go first, butterflies now ricocheting round my chest in lead boots — a coat-check girl shimmered forward to greet Leo with a smile.

'Hello!' she said, as if they were old friends.

'Hello, Frida,' replied Leo with a courteous nod. He helped me off with my coat and handed it to her, pocketing the ticket himself.

'Good evening, sir!' The maître d' seemed to know him well, as did the waiter who showed us to a corner table, and I sat down, holding in my stomach and clenching my thigh muscles at the same time, but bathing a little in the warmth of Leo's welcome.

Dad would make a lot of that, I thought. He was always going on about how you could tell a man by how he treated waiters. Sadly, none of my meager selection of boyfriends back home had taken me to dining establishments where there *were* waiters.

I frowned. Actually, maybe that was the point Dad was trying to make.

'You look wonderful, by the way,' said Leo, as he slid into the chair opposite. 'What a great dress.'

'This? Thanks!' I could feel my face heating up. *Don't say you got it in a sale.* 'I got it in a sale.'

*Shut up, Amy. Shut up, Amy.*

'But thank you,' I added, encouraged by the admiring look he was giving it. 'It's my favorite.'

'I can see why. Very chic.'

I glanced around, trying not to look too obviously at the other diners. Some of them seemed quite familiar, but again I steeled myself not to say anything. The trouble about living in London, I'd found quite early on, was that it was all too easy to accost, say, a regular cast member of a national soap opera in Tesco and insist on saying hi, thinking it was a familiar face from your Zumba class.

My buttocks clenched of their own accord at that particular memory. I did *not* want to make that mistake in front of Leo.

'So . . .' I said, desperately trying to think of something witty and charming to say, but Leo helped me out.

'Tell me more about your gardening business,' he said. 'Have you got a favorite part of London you work in?'

I found it easy to talk about gardening, and Leo asked questions as if he was really interested in the answers. I told him about how I loved bringing pockets of the countryside into concrete balconies, and how bees kept the whole natural world turning with their pollen removal business, even in town. He told me how his late grandmother had been a keen gardener, and how he didn't have much time, since he worked long hours, but always tried to take his grandfather to the Chelsea Flower Show. After a few minutes, I forgot to be nervous, and even eased off my pinching heels under the table.

We talked and talked, and while we were talking Leo ordered a bottle of wine without bothering to check the wine list, and I barely noticed the waiter pouring it. We were still talking when the waiter appeared at Leo's shoulder and coughed, right in the middle of my story about Ted's attempt to clip a box hedge into an acorn, which had ended up as something very different and us being fired.

'Excuse me, sir.' The waiter's face was tight with awkwardness.

Leo reached quickly across the table and touched my arm. 'One second,' he said, and I didn't say anything because a bright flicker of electricity had just sparkled across my skin where his fingers had touched it.

The waiter bent down to mutter in Leo's ear, but I could hear every word. 'There's a gentleman at the door who is claiming to be you. I realize, of course, that he's attempting to gain entry by deception, but what would you like me to do?'

Leo frowned quickly, then understanding seemed to dawn.

'A dark-haired man?'

The waiter nodded. 'And he has a small party with him.' He coughed discreetly. 'Of two young ladies. We do have limits regarding guests, as you know . . .'

Leo glanced at me and his blue eyes were heavy with apology. 'I'm sorry,' he said. 'It'll be Rolf.'

'What?' My skin crawled. Not just because I couldn't cope with Rolf's personality crashing into our lovely easy conversation, but because if he saw me, he'd tell Jo. And Jo would demand to know what I was doing out with someone I hadn't told her about. And Rolf might demand to know what Jo had done with his fancy underwear, and I'd probably blurt out what we'd done with it, and how Mrs Mainwaring and Dickon had had an almighty row about . . .

It didn't bear thinking about.

'Rolf isn't a member here, but he knows I am,' Leo murmured, leaning forward so only I could hear. I tried not to look at the couple at the table opposite, who had stopped trying to talk to each other and were openly staring to see why the waiter had come over. I ended up nearly bumping noses with Leo. He pretended not to notice, but my breath suddenly became shallow as I breathed in his cologne.

'I don't come very often,' Leo went on, 'so sometimes Rolf says he's me and tries to blag his way in. Which is stupid, because the guys on the door here know everyone in London.'

'But wouldn't they just let him in, I mean, what with him being a prince and —' I realized too late how gauche that sounded, and clapped a hand over my mouth. Which was a habit I thought I'd broken up till then.

Leo didn't react. 'Listen, if you could bear it, I think it'd be easier to have a quick drink with him and then make some alternative plans,' he murmured, as the sound of someone making a fuss at the door drifted through the room. A few people tutted and turned their heads to see what on earth was kicking off by the coat check.

As they did, it dawned on me why the couple at the next table looked familiar. He was our local MP, the very posh one who'd turned up to a protest Jo and I had been on to save some local theater from closure. And the woman he was with had been in a film we'd just had out on DVD. A straight-to-DVD one, but *a film* nonetheless.

When I looked back, Leo was talking to the waiter in that discreet under-the-breath tone. Since his attention was fixed elsewhere, I snuck a good long look at the firm line of his jaw, and the soft slope of skin just under his ear. Jo and I often mused how rare it was to find a man with a perfect mouth, but Leo's mouth was just right — a pillowy lower lip and a top lip that had just the right amount of fullness.

A mouth that would be very good at kissing. I went red.

'The man at the door is a guest of mine — we're expecting him to join us, he's obviously running late,' he was murmuring to the waiter. 'And can I ask a favor of the kitchen, please?' He muttered something else I couldn't catch, and the waiter nodded and scurried off.

Leo turned back to me and reached out to touch my hand, and again the stream of sparks tingled up my arm as his fingers lingered a little longer than they needed to. 'I'm really sorry. I've got a backup plan, don't worry.'

'It's not a problem,' I said, trying to look cool but probably failing. He wanted to spend the evening with me, rather than with his best mate? 'I'm having a great time already. I've never been somewhere like this.' I waved my free hand at the plush walls of the club, covered in gilt-framed pictures and swagging.

Leo smiled. His hand was still on mine, but he removed it, just to take a large, preparatory gulp of wine. I followed suit.

There was a swish of coats and cold air, and the maître d' appeared, apologetically herding in Rolf and his 'small party' of two skinny, shivering model types with bare legs, blue underneath the fake tan. They weren't the same girls from our party, as far as I could tell.

'Leo! And who's your lovely young friend?'

Rolf started bellowing three tables away, causing a ticker-tape tutting reception as he drew nearer. He was wearing a green velvet dinner jacket over a purple striped shirt. Despite the chilly weather, three buttons were undone to reveal a lot of tanned chest and a flash of well-tended chest hair, and he didn't seem to be wearing any socks with his deck shoes.

'Rolf. Are you too hot?' Leo inquired, rising from his seat politely.

'Me? Too hot? Ask Paloma here!' Rolf hooted and slapped the bottom of the nearest girl, and she giggled.

'It's just that you might want to do up a button or two,' said Leo. 'Before someone asks you to.'

Rolf started to argue, but something in Leo's eyes stopped him, and he did up one button as if he were being asked to don a burka.

Since Rolf's manners didn't extend to introductions, Leo introduced himself, shook each girl's hand, and indicated our table. 'Would you girls like to sit down?'

A chair appeared for Rolf, and I scooched round the velvet couch to make room for Paloma and her friend, painfully aware of the comparison that would now be going on. From where Leo was sitting, it probably looked as if Badger had gatecrashed the Afghan hound final of Crufts. I reminded myself that at least all my features were my own, and I wasn't here with Rolf.

'Do I know you from somewhere?' Rolf squinted at me. 'I don't forget a pair of—'

'Rolf,' said Leo in a warning tone.

'— green eyes like that.' Rolf grinned, and I heard the girl next to me (Sienna, I think) giggle, although her face didn't move.

'We met at my party,' I said, rather crushed. I didn't look *that* different out of pajamas. How drunk had he been? 'I'm Amy.'

'Your party?' Rolf's shaggy brown eyebrows met in the middle. He was clearly having to think hard. 'I go to lots of parties. Need more than that. Location? Theme?'

I stared at him. Was he trying to be funny? Was he trying to make *me* look stupid? Did he have any idea how much of this conversation I'd be relaying to the object of his orchid bombardment?

'In Victoria! The theme was heaven or hell! You weren't wearing a costume.'

*Unless you'd come as a complete cliché of a playboy prince,* I managed to stop myself saying.

'You kicked a lot of plants off my balcony,' I went on, annoyed by the amused grin on Rolf's face. And the way he was cutting into my date with Leo with every minute I had to spend telling him who I was. 'You punched my friend Ted?

You nearly fell thirty feet off my balcony and broke your neck? You were at the helm of the Rolf Express? You won't accept my friend's very reasonable request to leave her alone?'

'Jo's party! That was you?' He looked amazed. 'You look so different in clothes.'

'You what?' The other girl spoke this time, and she would have looked furious if her brow had been up to it.

Leo coughed. 'I think our car is here.'

'Really? You have to go?' Rolf was looking at me very differently now he knew I was Jo's flatmate. The arse. I glared back at him, and when Rolf looked over my head to Leo, I could see by his reaction that Leo was glaring too.

Leo stood up and gestured for the waiter to bring them another bottle of wine. 'You'll excuse us, won't you, ladies? We have a reservation.'

'Have you indeed? Hotel or restaurant?' Rolf winked, and the two-hundred-quid undies floated before my eyes. I felt a bit hot.

'Dinner,' said Leo firmly, and put his hand on the small of my back to steer me away from Rolf's leering face. Possibly to stop me from smacking it.

A couple of beads of sweat had formed on Rolf's upper lip as his brain caught up with itself.

'Lovely to meet you all,' said Leo. 'The wine's on me. Please leave quietly and without upsetting anyone. *Rolf*.'

And with a smile, a nod to the maître d', and a discreet tip to the coat-check girl, we were swanning back up the stairs to the outside world.

My heart, though, didn't know whether to burst or sink — was that the end of our date, or just the beginning?

# CHAPTER EIGHT

The moon was unusually full over Berkeley Square, like a waxy pearl in the navy sky. The air felt chill after the warmth of the bar, and I shivered. Something else had changed too: I'd been quite relaxed until now, but I was off-balance again. I wasn't quite sure what happened next. Usually, it was a shouted conversation in a late-opening bar, then the last Tube home, but with Leo, none of the usual usuals applied.

'Cold?' said Leo at once. 'Want my coat? My car's just here.'

He pointed to the other side of the square, where a Range Rover with blacked-out windows was parked next to a yellow streetlight.

His car? Not a taxi? He couldn't drive, surely. We'd knocked back a bottle of wine between us and had just started the one that Rolf was now guzzling inside.

And did 'my car's just here' mean . . . he was going home? Was it over?

*Was that an invitation? Should I say yes — or no?*

My heart plunged in my chest.

'I'm fine,' I said, hugging my jacket nearer me. My feet were aching, but I wanted to hang on to the glamour of my heels a bit longer. 'But should you be driving? We can share a cab if you want.'

'Oh, *I'm* not going to drive, don't worry. I've got a driver. It's cheaper than keeping a car in London,' he added, seeing my surprise. 'I always forget where the congestion charge zone is. Costs me a fortune in late fines. But . . . a cab? Are you heading home already?'

'No, I . . .' I stammered. 'I wasn't sure if . . .'

'Not hungry?' Leo tilted his head hopefully. 'Can't I tempt you to dinner? 'Cause I'm quite peckish. And we haven't even talked about my garden yet.'

'Well, if you put it like that . . .'

He grinned, and the mood slid back nearer to where it had been before. Somewhere between easy and charged.

'Where are we going?' I asked.

'Ah. Surprise.'

As we approached the car, a driver in a long gray coat jumped out and opened the nearside door, and Leo paused to wave me into the backseat.

I was about to get in, then saw the driver's black gloves and had a bit of a *Crimewatch* flashback. The Dad voice in my head would have plenty to say about this. Getting into a car with a man I'd just met? That was on the list of things Dad had warned me never to do, along with lend a boyfriend money, believe everything he told me, and get on a motorbike. (There were more. A lot more. But those were the main ones.)

I struggled with my inner voices, the one telling me that Dad had a point, and the one telling me that Dad had gone semi-bananas after Kelly's antics and that the world was not filled with men like Christopher Dalton. Leo clearly wasn't like Christopher — he had no facial hair, for a start, and I'd seen him pay for something.

But I didn't know that much about him, even if every instinct was telling me that he was far more of a prince than Rolf would ever be.

'It's just that . . .' How could you say it without sounding rude?

'What?'

'It's just that I don't really know you,' I blurted out. 'You don't seem like the abducting type, but then who does? I mean, I don't know where we're going, no one knows where I am . . .'

*Brilliant, Amy. That's exactly what you should say to a potential abductor: 'No one knows where I am.'*

To his credit, Leo didn't laugh or look outraged. 'That's fair enough. Do you want to get a cab instead? That's fine with me too. Do you want to call Jo? You can give her the registration if you want.' He kept a straight face.

'You could have false plates.'

'That's true.' He pressed his lips together. 'What if I give you my wallet?' He took it out of his inner pocket and offered it to me.

I actually considered that, but then reasoned that if he was an abductor, he'd probably have fake ID too. 'No, it's okay. But be warned, I have a really sharp shin-kick move.'

'I'll bear that in mind,' he said gravely, and got into the back of the Range Rover. After a second's pause, I did too.

We headed away from Berkeley Square through the illuminated carriage drive of Hyde Park, and out toward the lights of Kensington; then the car stopped in a square of white townhouses surrounding a gated garden with tall bare-branched trees arching over the perfectly flat-topped hedge that hid the gardens from public view.

Leo leaped out and went to talk to the driver, then opened my door for me.

'What are we doing here?' I asked. 'Is this where you live?'

'Ah, nearby.'

*Blimey,* I thought. Even the flats round here ran into the millions, let alone the houses. Ted and I didn't have many clients in this area; if you could afford a house, you could afford a full-time gardener, as well as a nanny, a cook, a driver, and an assistant.

Leo walked up to the padlocked gate and rummaged in his pocket. He held up an old-fashioned key on a ring, undid the padlock, and swung the gate wide for me to go through.

Any lingering paranoia was swept away by rampant curiosity; I'd always longed to nose around a private garden. They were rarely open to passersby, even on those Show Off Your Garden open days in London; and I didn't know what the groundskeepers did to their hedging shrubs, but they were so dense there was no way you could see through. Even if you practically shoved your head in there (cough).

These gardens were about as exclusive a chunk of London air as you could get — even owning one of the astronomically expensive houses around it didn't guarantee you entry. There were committees to go past, and key-holder agreements, and annual fees. Jo had a friend of a friend who lived near one with a tennis court in the middle that was about as easy to get a game on as Centre Court at Wimbledon.

I stepped into Leo's private garden, my eyes darting everywhere as I tried to take it all in at once. It was a medium-size gem, and although it was meticulously tended, it had park benches and croquet hoops — signs that the resident actually enjoyed spending time in it. The garden was laid out formally, in squares like a Battenburg cake, with sections of mown lawn next to knot gardens, all separated by low box borders that sent a dark green scent into the night air. Converted Victorian gas lamps threw warm yellow pools of light over raked flowerbeds, while scatterings of delicate snowdrops stippled the clean borders — not in the ramshackle clumps I planted but in elegant sprays like paper doilies.

'Wow,' I breathed, completely enchanted.

'I thought we'd eat in the summerhouse,' said Leo, indicating a wooden gazebo in the middle, with white-painted shutters and a beautiful scalloped roof. 'If that's fine with you? I know it's not exactly summery, but there are heaters. And blankets.'

'It's fine with me,' I said, virtually running toward the summerhouse to see what was inside.

Leo followed me and flicked on a couple of electric lights, which spoiled the *Secret Garden* effect, but he flicked them back off and started opening cupboards instead, using the moonlight to see by.

'There should be some candles . . . Would you mind inspecting the garden for a minute, please?' he said, flapping his hands to make me leave.

It wasn't easy to walk on the gravel in my heels, but I didn't want to take them off; fortunately the third glass of wine was taking the sting out of my blisters. I followed one of the paths round to a stone fountain and pretended to inspect a statue of a leaping salmon, but I couldn't concentrate. I was buzzing with delight. The only thing that felt real about this entire evening was the tiny stone now wedged in my shoe.

I reached for my phone to text Jo, to prove to myself that this was actually happening, but stopped. Bad idea. She'd ask me where I was, I'd be bound to blurt something out about seeing Rolf, then she'd want to know where I was and with whom.

I knew I *should* tell her, or someone, where I was — but every minute I spent with Leo made me feel more and more as if I'd known him forever. In fact, the worst thing that could happen would be to text Jo or, worse, Ted.

'Amy?'

I saw Leo on the steps of the summerhouse, waving me over, and my feet started to move without me even having to think.

Inside, it smelled dark and green, but in a nice way. The wooden table was spread with a white cloth, and in the middle were three big candles, casting shadows around the already shadowy room. On either side was a china plate with proper silver cutlery and a snowy napkin, and between them were three small domed dishes.

'Where did they come from?' I asked.

'I asked the chef at the club if he could rustle up a takeaway, and Billy brought it in from the car. The cutlery and stuff is here all the time, for picnics.' Leo looked pleased. 'My idea, actually. It's a great garden for picnics in the summer — quick game of croquet after, convenient for cabs . . .'

The sensation of being inside a fabulous dream went up another notch. This was Leo's idea of a takeaway? Silver dishes and porcelain? What was going to be under the domes? Swan fricassee? The Mad Hatter?

'Dinner is served!' He flicked out his napkin with a flourish, then peered under one of the domes. 'But don't get your hopes up too high. If I'd had a bit more time to warn the kitchen, they might have been able to do something a little more, um . . .'

Leo whisked off the dome to reveal a pair of club sandwiches. The second dome revealed three packets of crisps.

'Perfect picnic food. And they're good crisps,' I pointed out. 'Organic. Handmade.'

'Only the best.' Leo decanted half a packet onto my plate as if he were sharing out caviar. Then he opened the wine — pre-chilled in a silver sleeve — and poured us each a glass.

'Cheers,' I said, and raised it. 'To picnics and gardens.'

He smiled, dimpling in the candlelight. 'Picnics and gardens.'

I inched off my heels under the table and heard the lump of gravel fall out.

'So.' I took a sip of wine. It was probably the nicest wine I'd ever tasted, all honeyed and crisp. 'Tell me how you come to have a key to this amazing garden.'

'I'm a volunteer on the gardening committee.' Leo picked a gherkin out of his club sandwich. 'And I can tell you that, because you won't think it's sad. Most people do.'

'By most people, do you mean Rolf?' We'd already had a few jokes about Rolf in the car on the way over. I'd confessed all about the fate of the thong and how we'd been using the latest box of chocolates as a tea tray; Leo had told me how much worse some of his earlier ideas had been. I didn't think Jo would have thanked him for a Vietnamese house pig. Neither would Badger.

'Rolf's idea of a good garden is anything with a sun lounger in it,' said Leo. 'I once won a hundred quid off him, betting that oranges grew on trees and not in a big orange pod. I'm sure you could make a fortune off him.'

'I'm sure I could,' I said, then, before I could stop myself, I added, 'if he can't even remember who I am, there's no way he'd remember I'm a gardener.'

I wished I hadn't said it, because at once Leo looked mortified.

'Not that he has any reason to remember me.' I scrambled to fix it but it was too late; Leo was fiddling with the stem of his wineglass as if he was just waiting for me to stop talking so he could launch into something himself. 'I'm sure he meets a lot of people . . . being a prince and . . . going to four parties a night. But, you know, I *am* taking deliveries for him most days, and I'm not *that*—'

'The fact that he's a prince means he should know better than to hurt someone's feelings so carelessly,' Leo interrupted, with a Mr Darcy-ish impatience that turned my insides to pure water. 'He should be grateful for the gracious way you handled his ridiculous behavior earlier. Is it too much to ask you to ignore it? Rolf's honestly not that bad when he doesn't have an audience. His reputation goes ahead of him and he always chooses the wrong people to try to impress. And . . .' He paused, obviously weighing whether or not to share a confidence.

'Go on,' I said. 'Whatever you're going to tell me about Rolf can't be worse than him thinking a girl would take the gift of a piglet in a good way.'

Leo smiled. 'Not that. I was going to say that the reason he didn't recognize you tonight was that one of his lenses fell out on the way to Jo's — please don't ask me how — and he was too vain to wear his glasses. He's blind as a bat without his lenses, but he's too scared to get laser treatment. I think that might be why he almost fell off the balcony.'

'He managed to find the loo all right,' I pointed out. 'And the drinks.'

'Rolf's developed a bat-sense for loos and drinks. Years of practice in darkened environments.'

'It's fine,' I said. I didn't want to look as if I was *bothered* that I hadn't registered on the Rolf Scale. If anything, I was a teeny bit more bothered that Leo hadn't told Rolf who he was seeing for dinner. 'I don't have a very memorable face.'

'No,' said Leo. 'No, I don't think you could *be* more wrong about that.' He looked at me intensely from under his lashes. 'There's no way I'd have forgotten it, lenses or no lenses.'

My heart expanded in my chest like a peony opening in speeded-up motion. This was an actual date, wasn't it? This wasn't about his garden at all. He couldn't mean this garden; it clearly had gardeners already. We hadn't even talked about his own place. Unless . . .

I knew I should say something, but my mind went blank; and then a clock somewhere outside struck the hour, and Leo looked at his watch in surprise.

'Midnight? How did that happen?'

'Do you turn into a pumpkin now? Or do I?' I inquired. My voice sounded a bit too high. I really didn't want this evening to end.

'Neither. I'm afraid I turn into someone with a squash lesson tomorrow morning at seven. And I'm useless enough on a full night's sleep.' He wrinkled his nose apologetically. 'Sorry to be so boring, but I have to call it a night.'

'I never thought I'd meet someone who actually played squash at seven in the morning,' I said, impressed. 'I thought that was just in films.'

'If only. I bet you get up early, though.' Leo offered me the last profiterole (under the third dome) and then finished it himself when I declined. It was nice to see a man who enjoyed a pudding, I thought; Mum would *love* that.

'Well, yes. But that's only because if I get a couple of hours' work in early on, I can have a bacon sandwich at ten and not feel guilty.'

'I have a similar arrangement with a danish pastry. I've found an amazing bakery round the corner from my office — I should send you some croissants.'

'I'd take a decent croissant over a Vietnamese house pig in diamond earrings any day,' I said. 'I'm a very cheap date.'

Leo held my gaze, and I held my breath, wondering if he was going to lean over the table and kiss me.

He didn't, but his eyes darkened and sent electricity tingling right through me, as his beautiful mouth curved in a smile. 'That's not cheap. That's discerning.'

We tidied away the crockery in the sputtering candlelight — him washing, me drying — and when everything was packed up, he locked the summerhouse, and together we walked to where the car was parked. It still felt quite dreamlike, even though I had my flats on now. Leo didn't comment on the sudden drop in my height. So gallant.

The Range Rover was waiting where we'd left it, and as we approached, I saw the driver hastily put away a newspaper and leap out to take the picnic basket from Leo. I felt sorry for him, sitting there doing the crossword while we ate dinner.

I felt Leo's breath on my ear. 'Don't worry, I got Billy a sandwich too,' he murmured. 'I'm not a complete slave driver.'

'Glad to hear it,' I replied. Not because it was very witty but because I wanted an excuse to put my lips as close to Leo's ear as his had been to mine.

When he'd handed over the basket, Leo turned to me. 'Amy, can I drop you home first?'

'Thank you. That would be nice.' It came out more stiffly than I'd meant. Now that I was facing the social obstacle course of ending the evening, I was nearly palpitating with fear of doing the wrong thing and ruining everything.

I gave Billy my address, and he drove there far more efficiently than most London cabbies would manage, using all sorts of cut-throughs I'd never known about.

Leo chatted but didn't try to kiss me or put his arm round me; by the time we pulled up outside Leominster Place, the outside of Leo's knee was only just resting against mine — damn those luxuriously wide backseats — but even so my heart rate had reached practically Olympic levels.

'Well, here we are,' I said.

*Oh God. How to leave? Handshake? No. Kiss? Bit forward. And which side first?*

'Thanks for a lovely evening. And we never even got to talk about your garden!' I squeaked nervously.

Leo looked at me as if I were joking, then realized I wasn't. 'Amy, that *was* my garden. That's where I live.'

'I mean your balcony garden. For your flat. The fig tree. The vegetable patch.'

'I don't have a flat,' he said patiently. 'I've got a house in the square. I want you to do something in *that* garden.'

I made a faint noise. That put a very different perspective on things.

Leo touched my hand. 'Sorry we didn't get round to talking about it. I suppose I'm going to need to see you again for that. Is that okay?'

'Yes. Yes, it is.'

He leaned forward, and for a dizzy second I thought he was going to kiss me; instead, he brushed his lips against my cheek, and I nearly fainted anyway, from the scent of him and his warmth.

'Goodnight. I'll call you.'

I managed to splutter a goodnight back, and then let myself out of the car. It was a long way down and I nearly fell out, but managed to recover myself, say thank you to the driver, and stumble up the stairs.

I probably looked drunk, but I'd never felt more sober in my life. It was all the stars exploding around my head and in my blood that made me so deliciously uncoordinated as I tiptoed up the sweeping staircase to our darkened flat. And as I trailed my hand along the worn oak handrail, trying to not wake anyone up, I felt like winking at the naughty spirits of Leominster Place who'd once danced home with stars in their eyes and pearls around their throats. I felt like we finally had something in common.

# CHAPTER NINE

I didn't sleep that night, thanks to the endless replay going on in my head, but I didn't even feel tired when I got up the following morning and headed off to prune Mrs Troughton's wisteria in Chelsea.

Ted's flat singing (he liked to dig to the sound of hymn tunes, not always with the right words) did not bother me.

Badger rolling around in a pile of fox poo at the bottom of Mrs Troughton's big garden did not bother me. (It did bother her, to be fair.)

Even getting home and discovering, (a) a four-foot teddy bear from Rolf lolling suggestively against our door, and (b) our postwoman storming down the stairs from Dickon's flat, clutching her regulation jacket firmly to her chest, and (c) another overdue gas bill on the post table did not bother me.

Nothing bothered me because I was happier than I could remember being in London. Or, in fact, anywhere. The last time I'd been this happy was the summer I did my GCSEs, before Kelly screwed everything up and we moved and . . . all that.

Badger ran into the flat ahead of me, looking for Jo and/or food. I left the gas bill on the kitchen table and the bear sprawling on the sofa, and after I'd fed Badger, I waltzed into the bathroom for a long soak, with my phone propped up against the window for best reception in case Leo called.

While I was submerged in the warm water, I replayed various key moments from the previous night, lingering over the bits where Leo's eyes had locked with mine or our hands had brushed, in the car, in the club. I didn't have to edit out any cringe-worthy faux pas or fast-forward over awkward pauses. I wasn't struck too late by much wittier things I should have said. I'd *never* had a date like that.

I guessed it was a bit like what my dad used to say about playing cricket with the one decent pro cricketer Hadley Green CC ever had — Dev Bhattacharya was so talented with the bat that he made everyone else play better too. It was the same with Leo. He was so charming and natural he made it easy for me to be natural too. Even quite charming.

As I twiddled the big brass hot tap with my foot to top up the cooling water, the front door opened; I sank back into the bath and waited for Jo's screech of horror at the enormous teddy to echo round the flat. I knew her routine: come in, drop bag, wail skyward about the ineptitude of builders, check answering machine for invites (many) or calls from her agent (fewer), ask if there was any wine needed finishing up for economy reasons, and so on. But tonight Jo walked straight in and hammered on the bathroom door.

'Amy? Amy, are you in there?'

'Yes. I'm *relaxing*.'

'So you should be — what time did you get in last night?'

I sat up in the bath, surprised by the urgency in her voice. 'Not late. About half twelve? What do you mean by that?'

'I mean, I was worried. I didn't know where you were. *Badger* didn't know where you were.'

'Neither did my mum, and she isn't ringing me up to give me the third degree.'

I knew that was my guilty conscience talking. *You should have phoned,* I reprimanded myself. *I told you you should have phoned.*

'Hello?' I could *hear* Jo's incredulous expression through the bathroom door. 'You're normally in bed with your electric blanket on by ten! I was a whisker away from ringing round the hospitals! And you were up and out before my alarm even went off this morning. I only knew you'd come back in because there was no milk left in the fridge.'

Oops.

There was a pause.

'Can I smell your good bath oil?' Jo demanded. 'Are you really all right? You're not . . . trying to wash away a bad experience? Because you can tell me. Amy? Amy!'

Jo had a very vivid imagination. If I left her to guess, it would escalate fast, and she'd have Dickon breaking the door down before we knew it.

Although that might take some time.

'I'm fine,' I said. 'Honestly. I've been pruning all day, my back's killing me.'

'And the bath oil? You usually use that hideous muscle relaxing one when you're knackered. Not that expensive one Grace gave you for Christmas that you've been eking out like truffle oil for two years.'

Reluctantly — the water had reached the perfect temperature — I hauled myself out and pulled on the fluffy dressing gown Jo had pinched from the last boutique hotel she'd stayed in. It had STOP: THIEF embroidered on the back.

'Oh no, don't get out of the bath on my behalf,' came the wounded response through the door. 'I'm only your *flatmate.*'

I opened the door and saw Jo standing there in her leopard-skin coat, with her arms folded and a hurt expression barely covering her blatant curiosity.

'So?'

'If you must know,' I said, unable to stop myself smiling, 'I was on a date.'

Jo's jaw actually dropped. She'd done a course in mime at her drama school and reverted to it at times when words were not enough.

'Don't look like that,' I said. 'It was more a work consultation that sort of turned into a date.'

'No, no. Stick with date. It sounds good. Where? And who? Do I know him? How do you know him? It is a him, right?' She was steering me into the kitchen, and toward the table. We chewed over most of our problems at the kitchen table. It was handy for the fridge. 'Sit. Is there any wine needs finishing up?'

'You know there isn't. Just open a bottle. You might as well, because I haven't replaced the milk, sorry.'

'Don't worry about the milk. You've been on a date! I should be popping champagne! Ooh! Shall I open one of the ridiculous bottles Rolf sent?'

Jo's tone had changed completely: she was genuinely excited for me, like a father in a Russian play whose eldest daughter has just found a gnarled suitor who also owns all the orchards in town.

She opened the fridge door to reveal the magnums of champagne Rolf had been sending. They nestled next to normal bottles of wine like giant babies. There wasn't much room for anything else in there.

'Normal wine is fine,' I said.

Jo had two glasses in front of us in seconds, and was leaning across the table before I'd had time to blink. 'So? Spill the beans! Who is he?'

'Well, his name's Leo,' I started shyly.

'Leo Hendricks?'

'No, Leo —' I stopped, and suddenly realized that I didn't know Leo's surname.

He must have mentioned it at some point, but I'd been too embarrassed to ask him again, in case it sounded like I wanted to Google him. I thought I'd heard the waiter say something like Mr Prinz or Preece, but hadn't liked to check.

'What?' Jo scrutinized my confused face. 'You don't know his name? What sort of business consultation was this?'

'I . . .' Oh my God. I'd got into a car with a man whose surname I didn't even know. Dad would pass out.

*Note to self: Never tell Dad.*

It didn't seem to faze Jo. 'Okay, we can work this out. Where did you meet him?'

'I met him at the party, here. Last weekend.' There was nothing for it, I was going to have to come clean about my 180 degree turn on the posh boy thing. 'He's a friend of Rolf's. Blond. Quite tall. Works in the City.'

She stared at me. 'Leo Wolfsburg?'

'I don't think so. He doesn't sound German.'

'He isn't German. He's half-Nironan.'

It vaguely rang a bell. 'Is that a description? Like Sagittarian?'

Jo seemed to be vibrating with excitement. 'Was he quite serious? Amazing blue eyes? Incredibly wealthy? Hotter than a nuclear fondue set?'

'Er . . . yes to the eyes. We went to a members' club for drinks, so . . . I guess quite wealthy? We didn't really talk about that. We mostly talked about trees, and gardens. And London.' I turned red. It was hard to remember exactly what we'd talked about, but I knew there hadn't been a second's pause in the conversation all night.

'Don't say it,' I warned her. 'I know he's quite posh. But he's also normal. He agrees with me about the ludicrous social kissing situation.'

Jo threw her head back and laughed. She hit the table a couple of times for emphasis — again, the mime classes.

When she'd got it out of her system, she straightened up and grabbed her wine. 'You are the funniest person I know. Amy "I don't like rich guys, I have nothing to say to them" Wilde. Ha!'

'Meaning?'

'Meaning, you had dinner with a prince and you didn't even notice.'

'Leo's not a prince, he's a fund manager.' I grinned at the rare chance to correct Jo on a point of social standing. '*Rolf's* the prince. Duh.'

'Well, duh yourself. Leo's Rolf's *older brother*.'

'He's what?' I was so shocked, it didn't even register as shock. More disbelief. 'No. They don't look anything alike.'

'Neither do Prince Andrew and Prince Edward, but you try telling them they're not brothers.'

My brain furiously tried to process clues that Leo might have dropped, but I couldn't remember a single one. I wasn't *stupid*. I'd have picked up on it.

Wouldn't I?

More pressingly, distinct memories of some of the things I'd said about *his own brother* swilled back like flotsam. 'Oh my God.' I put my hands over my mouth. 'I was so rude about Rolf.'

'Forget about it. Everyone is. Leo's the rudest of all. So, where did he take you? The Ritz? Nobu?'

'We had a picnic. In a private garden.'

Oh, that had been a clue right there. You'd have to be a member of a royal family to afford a house like that. I must have looked like such a yokel. What else had I said? I moved my hands up from my mouth to cover my whole face. It was hot to the touch.

'You're so sweet,' said Jo. 'You really had no idea? Who did you think he was?'

'I thought he was just Rolf's mate,' I wailed from beneath my fingers. 'I thought he was the sensible friend idiots like that usually have in tow to stop them driving Rolls-Royces into swimming pools, you know, like a butler or something . . .'

I trailed off. Leo was clearly *not* a butler.

'Rolf could do with a butler.' Jo topped up her wine. 'Suggest it to Leo. See if you could get him a Jeeves. Or even a Nanny McPhee.'

I sat up and gave her a straight look. 'Jo, are you having me on?' I demanded. 'Just because I don't know anything about this sort of thing . . .'

'Royals don't walk round with crowns on all the time, you know.'

'So why aren't you giving me the big lecture about not touching royalty with a ceremonial barge pole? How come Rolf's awful and Leo's not?'

'Because, off the record, Leo Wolfsburg is the one royal personage I'd make an exception for. He's nearly a normal.' Jo narrowed her eyes so I'd know she was making a big concession. 'Nearly. But he has a cocktail named after him at the Casino Del Rois, and he's something like the twelfth most eligible prince in the world, so not normal in the usual run of things. Haven't you Googled him?'

'Of *course* I haven't.'

Jo pulled a 'what are you waiting for?' face and flipped open her laptop. She pushed it over to me with a wicked grin. 'Go on, type his name in and see what comes up.'

I hesitated. I didn't like Google. I was the only person I knew who'd never Googled herself, because after the whole thing with Kelly, even though it was years ago, I didn't want to see what came up about me or my family. I'd never even told Mum about Google; she'd have been straight back on her anxiety meds. Ted said Google was like walking into a room where everyone was bitching about you, but they didn't stop bitching when you opened the door, and that was enough for me.

'Fine. I'll do it,' said Jo, and started to take the laptop back, but I hung on to it.

'No.'

I took a deep breath, struggling with the idea that if Leo had wanted me to know any of this, he'd have told me himself.

But then he hadn't, pointed out the chippy voice. He *let* you make a complete arse of yourself.

'I feel like a stalker,' I complained, typing Leo's full name into the search engine. 'What if I find something I don't want to know?'

'Leo's family pays good money to make sure that can never happen.' Jo scooted her chair round to get a better look.

'Even for Rolf? Have they got someone working round the clock with a big Internet red pen?'

'Liza Bachmann has a full-time press agent,' said Jo darkly. 'There's an incident with two racehorses and some pink paint in Dubai that I don't think ever made the papers. Anyway, no need to be squeamish — it's perfectly sensible to check your dates out online first. I do. It's when they *don't* have any history that you want to start worrying.'

'Isn't that a trust issue?' There was plenty Jo didn't know about me, for a start. 'That maybe you should wait till they tell you?'

She didn't respond because the screen had loaded with page after page after page, all about Leo. Some had photos, and his shiny blond hair caught my eye. I was transfixed despite myself. Was this why he felt familiar? Had I seen him before in the papers?

'Oooh, look,' said Jo. 'Is that the Little Black Book eligible men list? Open that.'

I clicked on the fourth link down. It was some society gossip site called YoungHot&Royal.com, featuring a list of the World's Most Eligible Young Royals. Leo was at number nine; there was a photo of him smiling broadly and shaking someone's hand with an explosion of flashbulbs around him. He was with an older man who looked like a film star and one of those glamorous, sharp-clavicled Hollywood women whose faces set at forty-four and don't change until they die. She was wearing an impressive diamond tiara in her tawny hair, and she too was working the adoring crowd like a pro.

Rolf was lurking in the background, also in black tie, but with his hair slicked back in a style that even I knew was really only acceptable on superyachts.

'His parents,' said Jo helpfully, although there was a caption. 'Prince Boris of Nirona and his lovely wife, Liza Bachmann, who is so famous she tends to be known as that rather than Princess Eliza.'

I wasn't listening. Now I knew, Leo really did look royal. That was the man who'd shared a bag of crisps with me last night, in a glorified garden shed. And then washed up. And I'd more or less accused him of being a date abductor.

My insides clenched with embarrassment.

'He's up to number nine!' said Jo. 'Good for him. What was he last year?'

I peered. 'Twenty-one.'

'Ah. That would be while he was dating Flora Hardy-Torrence, you know, the jeans model?' said Jo, as if I'd say, '*Oh, yeah,*

*Flo-Har-Tor, of course!* 'Everyone thought those two were halfway down the aisle.'

'And she's fine to date him, being a supermodel?'

'Oh, she's mad on her own account — her dad's an earl. Is Rolf on the list?'

'Rolf?' I started to scoff, 'If Leo's only number nine, Rolf isn't going to —' But I choked when I saw that Rolf was ranked even higher than Leo. His deeply tanned face shone out of a photo that seemed to have been taken at a zoo. Or a private party with a lot of free-range monkeys. 'No! He's number seven! Down from number five last year! How is that even *possible*?'

'Because Rolf is everything these prince-hunting types want.' Jo counted on her fingers. 'He's rich, he's good-looking, he's got absolutely no responsibilities whatsoever. All the glamour of dating a prince with none of the irksome tours of duty in Afghanistan.'

'I don't get that,' I said.

'Don't worry,' said Jo, 'plenty do.'

I was trying to keep my voice casual while my eyes widened at the details scrolling up the screen: Leo's net worth (considerable, from his banking job alone), his previous girlfriends (the aforementioned Flora plus one Swedish princess and two 'philanthropists'), his bronze medal for skiing . . .

It was like reading about someone totally different. Some of it fitted with the friendly, unassuming, yet focused man I'd met, but most of it felt almost surreal. I never met people like that. People who dated Swedish princesses.

But, thinking about it, *had* I met Leo? I felt as if we'd clicked, but he hadn't told me about any of this. It was almost as if he didn't want me to know. Maybe it hadn't been a date. Maybe it *had* just been a very informal meeting about his garden.

*With a very gentle kiss on the cheek at the end of the night.*

They all did that, I reminded myself, crossly. Kiss kiss kiss kiss. What else was he going to do? Shake my hand?

But the fact that he *hadn't* tried to take advantage and go in for a big snog suddenly seemed more romantic than not. It was gentlemanly. I couldn't decide if I was flattered or disappointed or what. It was all incredibly confusing.

'Your eyes have glazed,' Jo observed. 'You're thinking, aren't you? What are you thinking?'

'I'm not sure I want to see any more,' I said slowly.

'Why not?' She clicked on photos of Leo skiing. I'd never skied. The closest I'd come to skiing was sledging down Weatherburn Hill on a tea tray.

There he was at a ball in Vienna with a stunning girl-woman in a tiny slither of a silver dress and not a hint of side-boob. Flora Hardy-Torrence. Of course. And again, with her in Verbier. She was barely wider than the skis she was carrying, and her teeth were whiter than the snow.

'Because . . .' I couldn't finish. I knew Jo was going to wheel out the whole chippy thing again, and it wasn't that.

She stopped scrolling and turned to look at me. 'Because what?'

Because I didn't want to get excited. Because I didn't want to get carried away. Because this funny sparkly feeling inside me, like champagne bubbles, wasn't going anywhere — I was starting to feel flat already.

'Because I've clearly got the wrong end of the stick,' I said. 'Stop it.'

Jo seemed on the verge of disagreeing with me, and then changed her mind. She pushed my wine glass nearer to me and I took a big swig, but my marshmallowy happy mood had gone. I felt cold inside my bathrobe.

The wine wasn't as nice as last night's either. I'd probably been knocking back Châteauneuf-du-Pape and not even realized.

'I can't believe he didn't tell me,' I said unhappily. 'Why did he let me make a fool of myself? Going on about Rolf . . .'

'There are all kinds of reasons why he wouldn't want to tell you.' Jo's voice was gentle and reasonable. 'I mean, maybe he assumed you knew? Most people he meets know exactly who he is. Maybe he didn't want to embarrass you when it was obvious you didn't.'

That made me feel even more of a clueless bumpkin. I squared my shoulders and tried to find something positive to cling to. 'It doesn't matter anyway. He wants me to plan a garden for him.'

'That's *great*!' Jo's enthusiasm made it sound not that great. 'Maybe it's *better* that you've found a new client. Weren't you looking for someone with a really big garden to use for this bee thing? Imagine how much garden space Leo's family's got!'

I forced a smile; that was exactly what I'd hoped she wouldn't say. It was such a runner-up prize.

'Don't take this the wrong way,' Jo went on. 'I don't really know Leo, but from what I've heard about him, he seems like a nice guy. I just think you're a *nicer* girl. I wouldn't want you to get sucked into the madness.'

'I'm not that nice,' I said. People were always telling me

how nice I was. You'd think it would be a compliment, but it was amazing how sometimes it just felt like a kinder way of saying 'blah.' 'I just keep my horrible side well hidden.'

'Shut up. You're a peach. I mean, the Wolfsburgs are weird,' said Jo. 'And coming from me with my family, I think you can tell how weird that means they are.'

'In what way?'

'Well, Rolf's pretty much your typical Wolfsburg.' Jo sat back in her chair and swirled her wine. 'Wolfsburg men do crazy, pointless things like land speed record breaking or extreme hot-air ballooning, and they usually marry singers or models or actresses who are madder than cats. Marigold had her second honeymoon on Nirona — even she was shocked at what used to go on in the marina. I mean, there were so many shenanigans there in the eighties that the whole monarchy nearly got kicked out. It was only thanks to some serious financial wheeler-dealing that they didn't.'

'But surely Rolf has to be sensible if his dad's going to inherit?'

Jo leaned forward again. 'That's the whole point, he won't. Boris is the younger son — by about ten minutes. His brother Pavlos is the heir, and he's spent the last however many years keeping his head down and making sure he's photographed filling out his tax return and wearing a seat belt in his Prius. Like his dad, Rolf has all the money, none of the responsibility.'

Jo was talking about these people as if she knew them. It sounded like the setup of an eighties miniseries starring Joan Collins. 'But what I don't understand is, if Leo's a prince, why's he working in Canary Wharf for a bank?'

She shrugged. 'It's not a bank like the one you stick your salary in. He's probably managing the family's charity portfolio, or something. I suppose it's the rebellious thing to do in his family, having a job. Maybe he wants to make sure no one confuses him with Rolf.'

As Jo spoke, Badger's ears flattened, and he got up from where he'd been lying on my feet. I ignored the sounds of his claws clattering like castanets on the hall parquet and stared at the table, trying to get my thoughts in order.

Sensing my crestfallen mood, Jo didn't launch into some excited story of exactly what her mother had seen in the marina, although I could tell it was an effort for her not to.

There was a cross bark from the bathroom: Badger's 'I can't reach this!' bark, the one he used to try to bark squirrels down from trees or Bonios down from countertops.

'I'll go.' I pushed my chair back. 'Put some toast on. I need bread. It's in the washing machine today, by the way.'

Jo was 'off carbs' for January, which wasn't helping the sausage-roll mountain go down. I'd had to hide the bread in a different place each day to stop her raiding it.

'Oh, you read my mind.' She sighed. 'January is just too insufferable without toast. I nearly cried in front of Callie's plasterers today. I can't get stroppy on miso soup alone. And she's pestering me about what happened at the party — who was there, what we wore. I'm starting to think it might just be easier to invite the lonely old bat to the next one.'

In the bathroom, Badger was standing by the loo, his stumpy tail wagging back and forth. His beady brown eyes were fixed on my phone, propped against the candy-colored glass of the privacy window.

I had a message.

Thanks for a lovely evening — and for putting up with al fresco supper! How about Monday lunchtime to review garden situation? Will send car at twelve. L

An hour ago, that message would have filled me with rocketing joy. Now it made me feel uncomfortable. And I couldn't put my finger on why.

Was that a date? Or a meeting? Was I embarrassing myself just by thinking that? And how was I going to retract what I'd said about Rolf without looking like I didn't mind his appalling rudeness?

'Do you want to take your newly washed hair out to a party tonight?' Jo shouted from the kitchen. 'There's a choice of two — one eighties-themed in Chelsea, one dinner-in-the-dark in Islington, which frankly sounds like an excuse for Freddie Henderson to molest people at will. Or do you fancy a pizza and a rom-com marathon at home?'

I bit my lip and stared at the message. I needed to get this into perspective. I already had more than an entire forest of Dream Seeds could provide. Incredible flat, job I loved, brilliant flatmate who didn't always understand but always tried to. How could any reasonable person be disappointed because the ninth most eligible royal in the world hadn't decided to unburden himself to a total stranger?

*Who do you think you are,* demanded a flat Yorkshire voice in my head, *Kate chuffing Middleton?*

'I'm leaning toward pizza myself,' yelled Jo. 'If we're going to have carbs, we might as well make a night of it. Oh no! I'm ordering dough balls! Stop me! Oh, garlic bread! Help!'

Badger looked up at me and wagged his tail. We were a long way from Hadley Green, him and me.

Hadn't I told Leo what my ideal night in was? Pizza and a film? Well, here it was. It was as if someone somewhere was telling me something.

'I'll have a Quattro Formaggio,' I yelled through. 'And get extra garlic bread!'

It wasn't as if I'd be snogging anyone tonight.

# CHAPTER TEN

Having dropped the Prince Leo bombshell, Jo spent the weekend trying to distract me from examining the fallout. She banned any further conversation about Leo, Nirona, casinos, or Rolf, and propelled me into a weekend of nonstop London-market-browsing activity. Portobello antiques, Columbia Road flowers, some random organic farmers' market in Victoria; she marched me round every single one, as if to prove that you didn't need a tiara and/or millions of dollars to have fun.

I mean, having-fun-for-no-money was what I did most weekends; although, this being Jo, it did involve a certain amount of spending. But I got a scary glimpse into what it must be like for her clients. I don't know if she went so far as to confiscate *their* mobile phones to 'encourage' them to keep their minds on the tiling/plastering/wiring and off the texts that were not arriving.

She did allow me one text, the one replying to Monday's date/nondate. When I told her about Leo's text, her reaction was, I thought, a teeny bit of a projection.

'He'll send a car, eh? Without even checking you're free? Rolf tried to send a car for me to go to Tramp last week, and I told him where he could send it. Honestly. Tell Leo you'll make time to see him but you'll get there yourself. *Send a car.* Honestly.'

'He works in Canary Wharf,' I pointed out. 'I have literally no idea how you're meant to get there. Do you have to go on the river?'

Jo narrowed her eyes. Columbia Road was about as far east as this Chelsea girl went in London without an armed escort and a map. Not even the Olympics had tempted her farther into the wilds of East London. 'Fine. Let him send the car, but make sure you leave on the dot of two. If he wants to sweep you off your feet, he needs to send a helicopter, at least.'

Once I'd sent the text, Jo shoved my phone in her own enormous tartan shopping trolley and I wasn't allowed to see it again until Sunday teatime. She also yanked the Wi-Fi router out of the wall to stop me Googling, but that was a bit of a mistake, as we couldn't work out how to install it again, and Dickon had to come downstairs and do it for us.

I did some cursory container-tidying at Grace's on Monday morning, and the car arrived outside 17 Leominster Place on the dot of twelve, as Leo had said it would. But seeing it sweep up, all huge and silent and expensive, only reminded me that the first time I'd seen it, waiting in Berkeley Square, Leo had let me think he was just a businessman with a company driver, and I felt stupid all over again.

It would have been very easy to drop a hint then. Or maybe he had and I'd just not noticed. I started to feel embarrassed, but then remembered what Jo had trumpeted — 'It's simply the height of bad manners to make someone feel stupid! He should know better. It's the kind of thing Rolf would do!'

(I don't think Jo realized it, but she did turn into the Judge

Judy of etiquette after a few glasses of wine. She started banging a virtual gavel all over the place.)

I wasn't even sure now that I was wearing the right clothes. For either work, or a business meeting, or a lunch appointment with the ninth-most-eligible prince in the world. And anyway, I'd got mud on my best jeans, so . . . great.

Leo's driver, Billy, started to get out to open the passenger door for me, but I lunged forward to stop him.

'No, honestly, there's no need!' I grabbed the handle myself. 'I can open the door. I'm a gardener!'

Billy's friendly face creased in confusion. I couldn't blame him.

'I mean, I'm just a normal person,' I added. 'Nothing special.'

'As my old mum used to say, we're all special in our own way, miss,' he said with a dry smile. I smiled back and started to get in, whereupon I was poleaxed with *another* flash of panic.

Did he think I thought it was a date with a prince, when *he* knew it was a business meeting about Leo's garden? Or did *he* think it was a date, and that he was secretly spiriting me off for how's-your-father in the gazebo? That was more likely. How many other women had Leo sent a car for? They were probably all supermodels, or socialites. Well, one of them would have been Flora Hardy-Torrence, for starters.

*She'd let chauffeurs open doors for her*, I thought, tetchily. There were probably clauses in Flora's modeling contract about not operating heavy machinery like Range Rover doors. My imagination obliged by conjuring up the long-lens image of those willowy arms wrapped around Leo's neck on a yacht in the

Bahamas, then added another of him and her at a black-tie gala for good measure. I really wished I hadn't seen those photos. My arms had never felt so beefy.

*That's why this is a business meeting to talk about his garden,* said the voice in my head. The voice that sounded quite a lot like my sister Kelly's.

*But what about the plants?!* wailed a more hopeful voice. *And the romantic midnight picnic?*

*And that website?* The bolshy voice was merciless. *Do you know any of the people on it? Do any of them look like they might get secret pleasure from popping bubble wrap?*

'Miss?' Billy was looking at me. To be fair, for someone who couldn't hear the epic row going on among the various voices in my head, it did look as if I was struggling to decide how to get into a car.

'What? Oh, sorry.'

I made a quick decision. From now on I'd treat it as a business consultation only. Ted and I needed the work, and I needed to demonstrate that Leo being a prince didn't make any difference to my ability to handle his garden. If he wasn't going to mention it, neither was I.

I told all the voices to shut up, and slid onto the leather backseat.

I sat with my knees clamped together, tormenting myself with the faux pas I'd made, until Billy asked me politely whether I had any useful tips about wisteria.

Apparently, his wisteria had now blocked out two windows, and since pruning was one of my specialties, we were soon chatting about the best time to cut it back — right up to the moment when he stopped the car by the iron gates to Leo's garden.

My stomach had been fine till then, but now it leaped back into my throat. The railings looked more imposing in daylight. More exclusive.

'. . . cut back all the side shoots to about finger-length . . .' My voice trailed off as my mouth went dry.

Billy turned round with a friendly grin. 'Thanks for that, most helpful.' He undid his seat belt and went to get out — to open my door.

'No, really,' I insisted, embarrassed, but now I wondered if maybe Leo was watching, and if Billy would get into trouble if he didn't go through the whole 'there, milady' routine.

I couldn't remember a car journey that had required quite so much active thought. It was giving me a massive stress headache, and I hadn't even seen Leo yet.

Billy opened the door just as I was struggling with the handle, and I half-fell out and had to swerve to miss a taxi.

While I fiddled with my clipboard and panicked about whether you were supposed to tip private drivers, Billy got back into the front seat and picked up a copy of the *Racing Post*.

'I'll be waiting right here when you're finished,' he said easily. 'I'll have to take his lordship back to work anyway.'

'Back to work?'

'This is his lunch break.' Billy dropped his voice, and regarded me over the paper. 'Told them he had a business meeting.'

'He has!' I said hotly. 'I'm helping him with his garden layout! I'm a gardener!'

Leo had appeared behind the gate — on his phone — and unlatched it from the inside while he carried on talking, so I had no time to dwell on whether I'd just made myself look like I was protesting a bit too much.

I tugged my parka tightly around myself to give my hands something to do. If the garden looked more impressive in daylight, Leo looked even more handsome than I remembered. But, like the car, somehow different. I didn't want to think that — I wanted it to feel just the same — but it *was* different. I'd felt as if I'd known him for ages, but now I knew that I didn't know him at all. I'd imagined something that wasn't there, and in doing it, I'd been incredibly rude.

Looking at him still sent a silvery shiver through me, even as I was telling myself it shouldn't.

Leo's blue eyes twinkled as he tried to mime *hello* while winding up the call, and because I couldn't quite bring myself to look at his handsome face, I stared at his wrists instead, just visible beneath the cuffs. I had a thing about a man's hands — a strong hand with long fingers and clean nails made my knees go weak, and Leo had beautiful hands, slightly tanned with broad nails and . . .

I tore my eyes away. I didn't want Leo to think I was gawping at his posh watch. Or the signet ring I'd now noticed on his little finger.

'Amy! Sorry about that. Thanks so much for coming.' He slipped the phone into his inside pocket and smiled at me.

I started to smile back until it struck me that princes were probably trained to do that, in order to cope with all the random people they had to meet every day. Wasn't that what everyone said afterward in the paper — 'Prince Charles talked to me for *ages*. I had no idea he was so interested in antique snuffboxes/go-kart-racing/Barrow-in-Furness!'?

Leo held his hands out in an ambiguous way that could have turned into a social kiss, but some indignant instinct got hold of me, and I shook his hand briskly instead.

'My pleasure.' It came out more northern than I'd meant. 'So, we got a bit sidetracked on the garden front last time. Which part were you wanting to redesign?'

*What?*

Leo looked wrong-footed by my greeting, and I wanted to stop and say, 'No, let's start again' — like I did when I'd rehearsed this whole conversation earlier and it went wrong — but we were walking down the path and there was no turning back. Literally, and metaphorically.

He gestured toward some circular beds in a far corner, empty apart from some bedraggled shrubbery. 'This is the main area I'd like you to look at, to begin with. There's a lot to do, but I thought we could break it down into projects, so you can fit it in around your existing commitments.'

'Maybe I should give Ted a ring and see if he can get over here too?' I couldn't stop the stiffness. It was spreading up me. Soon my lip would be jutting. Why hadn't he started by saying, Listen, there's something we need to clear up? 'This is potentially quite a big project.'

'No, I want a *creative* opinion on the garden. A design opinion.' Leo paused, then added, 'If I'd wanted Ted to be here,

I'd have asked him along. It was you I wanted to see. I thought . . .'

He was clearly trying to work me out, but two could play at being pointlessly mysterious, I thought crossly. I'd been so relaxed with him on Wednesday that I'd told him things I hadn't told anyone in London, not even Jo. Things like imagining all the Tube stations as people (Victoria: elegant Sloane Ranger in pearls; Pimlico: little old lady in hat; Tooting Bec: lady trumpeter, etc.).

Clearly, he'd been smiling because he didn't even *use* the Underground.

'You thought . . . ?' I prompted.

'I thought you might be interested in creating a modern rose garden for me,' he said, persisting with the friendly tone. 'There was originally a large rose garden in the center, but it was dug up by some previous committee. I thought it would be a nice project to restore it to the old design. Maybe track down some of the original roses, and find some new ones?'

It was true. It was a real project. He did just want me to garden.

At the same time that I saw the lifeline being thrown to my pride — Leo respected my skills enough to offer me the job — disappointment began to pool in my stomach. It was irrational. I know. But it was still there, curdling now with the embarrassment about Rolf.

'I've got the original sketches, if that would help,' he went on. 'They're rather lovely. Watercolors.'

'Really?' I couldn't help a flash of curiosity breaking through my reserve. Historical garden plans were like maps of undiscovered lands for me, full of symbols and colors you could bring to life, and forgotten plants you sometimes had to track down like lost relatives.

But at what point was he going to tell me that he *lived* here? And that he was doing this in his *time off from being royal*? I was really struggling with myself now; the more he kept talking about the stupid garden, the more I wanted to yell, '*Why didn't you tell me who you are?*'

But that would make me look like I thought it was a big deal; and if Jo had drilled one thing into me, it was that the posher someone was, the less you were supposed to refer to it, 'even if they turn up to dinner in a crown and start knighting people over pudding.'

I bit my lips while Leo carried on talking about the designer, and how his great-grandmother had used him for her own gardens 'at home.' It was as if the elephant in the room were following us round with its hands behind its back like the Duke of Edinburgh, making discreet coughing noises every so often.

We were at the edge of the central flowerbed, the area that had apparently once billowed with English tea roses and now held a few lone rosemary bushes. I forced myself not to get distracted by imagining which roses I'd plant back into it, and instead looked at Leo.

He stopped talking, and he knew I knew.

The silence between us grew, but he didn't say anything at first. If anything, he looked a bit anxious. And that threw a match into the combustible mixture of embarrassment and humiliation inside me.

I heard my voice blurting out into the silence, 'Why didn't you tell me you were Rolf's brother?'

'I—'

'Did you and Rolf think it was funny that I didn't know already? Because I feel *so* stupid now!'

My hands were on my hips. I made a conscious effort to remove them.

Leo's expression froze. 'I don't think you're stupid at all. That's the last thing I think.'

'Well, I feel stupid.' I kicked a stray stone back into the flowerbed. 'I mean, it was *rude. I* was rude. There's no way I'd have said some of the things I said about Rolf if I'd known you were related to him.'

'You haven't said a thing I don't agree with.' He wiped a hand across his face. 'I just assumed you knew who we were. Most people do. Sorry, I hate the way that sounds. Surely Jo told you about Rolf when you were planning the guest list?'

'Well, if Rolf had *been* on the guest list, maybe she would have done.'

'Of course.' Leo looked embarrassed now. 'But what about when I saw you for dinner? Didn't she say something then? Didn't anyone at the party mention it?'

There was something about his assumption that everyone at my own party knew who he was *except me* that made me feel even more of an outsider.

I lifted my chin. 'I'm friends with Jo, but I don't exactly move in the same social circles as she does. But she told me everything the other night. We Googled you.'

More images of Leo and Flora slid sideways into my head, and I struggled to push them out.

'You Googled me.' He groaned, almost like a normal person. 'Oh, tell me you didn't. What did you find?'

'That you're a ski-champion prince with a personal fortune and an ex-girlfriend who is the spokes-bum of Lady F jeans.'

Leo gave me a level look. 'I'm a fund manager.'

Oh, that was a bit much. I couldn't stop myself. 'Just a fund manager?'

'Just a fund manager?' He pretended to look outraged. 'It's a full-time job, I'll have you know. I'm there from eight till eight most days. Don't believe everything you hear about bankers. Some of us work pretty hard for the money.'

For some reason, that annoyed me more than the car and being sent for.

'No, you're not a banker! You're a prince! Why didn't you just *tell* me that I'd just had a drink with the ninth most eligible prince in Europe?'

He winced. 'Up to ninth, eh?'

'Rolf's seventh. I don't know what they grade it on.'

It came out a bit too sharp and I hated myself for messing it all up so badly. This wasn't how it had gone when I'd rehearsed it in my head all last night, but again there was no way of going back and trying it with more diplomatic phrasing. Jo had suggested some easy ways of getting this conversation over and done with, but they all needed to be delivered with her breezy confidence. And deep down, I knew I was over-reacting. This wasn't about Leo being a prince — it was about someone not being who they'd led me to believe they were. I had a real loathing of that, for good reason.

Even if we did get the gardening contract now, I thought

unhappily, it would just remind me, every day, of how I'd cocked up this whole situation.

'Not that it matters,' I said, too quickly. 'Ted and I have no objections to taking on royal clients. We just like to know for . . . security reasons.'

'But that's not what you're . . .' Leo gave me a clear look then pressed his lips together. 'Shall we take a walk?' Before I could answer, he'd started to crunch down the gravel path that ran around the flowerbeds.

I considered not following him, but I had the sickening feeling I'd been melodramatic enough already. And I found it easier to talk while walking, or gardening, or doing something else entirely, so maybe it was for the best, to get the air cleared.

We walked in silence for a few paces; then Leo dug his hands into the pockets of his overcoat, and shot me a guarded look from under his lashes.

'I'm sorry if I made you feel stupid,' he said. 'Really, I am. Most people make a huge deal about my family background, and to be honest, I find it embarrassing. When I realized you didn't know, it was so refreshing to be starting off without any of the usual assumptions that I didn't want to . . .' He paused, searching for the diplomatic word.

I ploughed into the silence. 'I'm sure you'd have given it away eventually. Some mention of the palace. A spare scepter in the back of the Range Rover. A supermodel in the summer-house.'

Leo stopped. The unexpected vulnerability in his eyes sent a shiver through me. 'I meet a lot of girls who know *exactly* who I am. Not what I'm like, or what I do, just who I am. They know everything about me before they meet me, but they're not the kind of girls I'm interested in meeting. They want to meet a prince. Not necessarily me.'

'Rolf doesn't seem to have a problem with it.'

Leo rolled his eyes. 'No. But I don't want to meet the kind of girls Rolf likes to hang out with. Jo being the honorable exception, of course.'

'She's not that keen on hanging out with him.'

'That's why I like her. Because she doesn't care about the title, just the man. And . . .' He hesitated, then the words spilled out. 'I'm not like Rolf. I mean, Rolf's not as bad as Jo thinks he is, and as I said the other night, a lot of it's an act, and I do love the guy, but just because we're related doesn't mean I am *anything* like him . . .'

Leo didn't finish, but I understood the conflict in his face so well that something leaped out of me.

I touched his arm and said, 'I understand that just because you share the same genes as someone doesn't mean you have to be alike. You and Rolf couldn't be more different. There are people in my family that I can't even believe . . .'

*This is not the moment to bring up Kelly.*

I stopped myself, just in time, but he was turning to me with a relieved expression in his eyes and that familiar connection I'd felt before crackled between us.

'Leo, I wish you had told me,' I said seriously. 'I already worry enough that I'm putting my foot in it somehow. I mean, Jo seems to know everyone, and how they met and where they went to school, and—'

'Look,' said Leo, 'would you have treated me any differently if you'd known?'

I shook my head. Then nodded, confused. Then shook it again. 'No, but—'

'You would. You'd have been uptight. You wouldn't have told me about the Tube stations, for a start. See?' he half-laughed, as I reddened. 'Amy, I don't know what websites you've been reading, but my life really isn't all fancy balls and flybys. I bet on a day-to-day basis it's not so different from yours.'

'Oh, *come on*!' I protested. 'You've got a driver!'

'Well, there's a reason for that.' He started walking again, casually tucking my arm into his as he did so. There were at least four layers of clothing between us, but the contact still made me feel warm inside. 'Driving in London's a nightmare when you don't know it very well. And parking — have you tried parking round here? Of course you have. You park your van every day.'

'I do. I've got a resident's permit for Westminster. It's one of the reasons Ted lets me do the driving — where there's parking permits, there's power.'

'But you drive round town all day. That would scare the pants off me.'

I allowed myself a glimmer of pride, but tried not to let it show. 'You don't get a special prince permit?'

'That is a very sore subject. We had a diplomatic permit up till last year, but Rolf ran up over five grand in various fines, congestion and otherwise, and it's suspended till the bill's settled. Dad won't pay it, Rolf refuses. Mom would pay it, but

Rolf's too scared to tell her. Meanwhile, I have to have a driver.' He looked at me pointedly. 'Which I pay for myself, to save the arguments. Now, does that sound like the glamorous life of a royal family to you? Or just a normal bloke who doesn't want to drive in London?'

My irritation was ebbing away with every glance Leo gave me. His eyes kept flicking my way, as if he was genuinely anxious about my reaction. I was bad at maintaining a huff.

'It wouldn't have made a difference to me,' I said. 'My mum's met Princess Anne, you know. We're like this with the Windsors.' I held up two crossed fingers. 'Great Yorkshire Show, 2001. She said Mum's Eccles cake was "perfectly fruited."'

When Leo realized I wasn't trying to wind him up, he smiled, and an echo of Wednesday night's romance sang back at me. He had a way of locking my gaze that made everything else go out of focus in the background.

'Can you forgive me?' He tipped his head. 'I'm so sorry for not being up-front. From now on, I'll tell you everything you ask me.'

'As long as there's nothing else you're holding out about. Like, you actually own this square?' I knew I should shut up and let the moment breathe, but I couldn't. 'Like, you're actually a vampire? Or married?'

Oops. Too far.

'I'm not married, or a vampire. But in the interests of full disclosure, yes, my family does own this square. But no, wait, I should also say we've owned it since it was built on a particularly unfashionable bit of marshland. My great-great-great-whatever owed the developer a favor, so put up the cash. It was a lucky break. We're a notoriously lucky bunch, the

Wolfsburgs. We got most of the family fortune gambling, one way or another.'

I shot him a sideways glance. 'Luck is banned in our family. My dad says the harder you work, the luckier you get.'

'Well, I believe in fate,' said Leo. 'If Mom hadn't given me orders to keep Rolf under control that weekend, then I wouldn't have followed him to your party, and he wouldn't have wrecked your balcony, and I wouldn't have met you.'

He paused, and I stopped walking. I felt as if Leo were looking all the way through to the secret me inside, with the arguing voices and practiced conversations, and he didn't seem to mind. He smiled, and shivers ran up and down inside my many layers, tingling up to my scalp.

Very gently, he put his hands on my arms and leaned forward, until I could feel his warmth against my half-frozen cheek.

*Shut up, Amy,* warned the voice, even though for once I had no intention of saying a thing.

He paused like that for a moment, as if he wanted to give me every opportunity to say *Oi, no.* But I didn't say no. I didn't say *anything*.

And then he leaned forward and pressed his lips against mine, and kissed me very gently on the mouth.

I closed my eyes, leaned forward, and kissed him back, as if I were in some sort of dream, and tried to impress every single breath and touch and smell onto my brain for later. He smelled of that herby cologne, and tasted of coffee, and his lips were really soft, like the underside of a perfect nectarine, and I could smell hyacinths and the pale-gray tang of wintry city air around us.

After a few delicious seconds of exploration, Leo pulled away and I was left, my eyes still closed. I didn't want to open them. I didn't want this moment to end.

He cupped my jaw with his hand, and stroked the smooth skin under my ear with his thumb.

'Your eyelids are moving,' he observed. 'Are you thinking?'

Not another one who claimed to be able to see my brain working. What was it about my face?

I squinted, and saw him studying me with an amused expression. 'If you treat all your gardeners like this, I'm not surprised you're in charge of the gardening committee.'

'And I was thinking you were stunned by the romance of the moment.'

'I thought you were summoning me to a business meeting about your herbaceous borders.' I paused and opened my eyes properly. 'What, um . . .' Awkward. But necessary, I reminded myself. 'What, um . . .'

'Yes, I need your advice about my garden. But mainly I wanted to see you again.' There was something touchingly hesitant in his tone, as if he wasn't quite sure what my reaction would be.

'The two aren't mutually exclusive, you know.'

Leo pulled me close, kissed my forehead, and then slipped his arm around my waist. 'How about we separate them out? Do you want to come over and see the garden plans, and give me a quote on the work as my garden consultant — and then let me take you out for dinner as a date?'

'That would be great,' I said. 'I mean, on both counts.'

'Excellent,' he said, and I was quite glad of the gravel chip of reality that had once again worked its way into my boot, because even in the watery light of day, Leo's garden felt more like a waking dream than like real life.

# CHAPTER ELEVEN

Jo took the news of my lunch-date/business-meeting/prince-kissing better than I'd expected, given that we were both still suffering the aftershock of Rolf's latest attempt to win her attention: a crystal-studded iPod loaded, as it turned out when we plugged it into the speakers, with Barry White's greatest hits and a playlist called, chillingly, 'One Night with Rolf.'

'I'm so glad you've finally let some romance into your life!' she cheered, bouncing us both up and down as we tried to wipe away the mental image of Rolf sprawled over satin sheets miming along to 'I'm Gonna Love You Just a Little More, Baby.' 'What are you going to tell your mum and dad?' She mimed me on the phone and did her useless Yorkshire accent. 'Hi-ya, Moom. I kissed a prince and I liked it!'

'I'm not,' I said at once. 'I'm not going to tell them anything. They get very . . .'

I hunted for the right word. Mum and Dad weren't the sort of puritanical parents who refused to believe I was no longer six, but they were naturally protective. Plus, I was now living in London, home to serial killers and handsome caped men with twiddly mustaches and evil intentions. The first few times I'd been out on dates with Jo's friends, my mum had made me phone home to reassure her (by which she meant, *my dad*) that I was safely at home and not tied to a train track with my bag stolen, or similar.

Jo arched her eyebrow. 'Very what? Very excited? Very involved?'

'They get very protective,' I finished.

'Ah, but you'll *have* to give them plenty of notice if you're going to hook your own royal boyfriend.' Jo waggled her fingers. 'They'll need a while to set up their own multimillion-pound Internet business, for a start! And you need to get your mum booked in for her skinny jeans fitting if she's going to compete with Carole Middleton!'

I stiffened. The protectiveness went in both directions in my family. If Jo had actually met my mum, in addition to the long phone chats they'd had, she'd have known that there was about as much chance of Mum getting into Carole Middleton-esque skinny jeans as there was of me getting into the Vatican's fast-track seminary. It was something else we never talked about, and another reason why my parents had gone from being pillars of the community in Hadley Green to very private people in Rothery.

Jo sensed my sudden awkwardness and released me with a playful swat.

'Oh, I'm just teasing. I'm pleased you've found the one gent in London who wouldn't try to have his wicked way in a locked garden. He honestly didn't try to grope you under the pergola? Wow.'

'Let's not get carried away,' I said, more to myself than her. 'It's dinner. And a garden with possible beehive opportunities for Ted.'

'The romance. Divine.' She looked wistful for a moment; then the familiar Jo came back. 'Do one thing for me, though, darling?'

'What?'

She picked up the sparkly iPod between her perfectly manicured fingers as if it were one of Badger's poo bags. 'Ask Prince Charming to tell Prince Rogers Nelson to knock it on the head before I send *my* stepbrothers round there to scrub out his tiny mind with soap and water.'

I didn't normally share the ups and downs of my private life with Ted, but I had to explain where the sudden flurry of work had come from. Our new contract with Trinity Square Residents' Association — several hours a week, plus planning — made a great start to our business expansion plans. I could expand my design portfolio, and, Ted was particularly pleased to hear that Leo was amenable to letting us put some hives and flowerbeds up on the roof of his four-storey townhouse.

We climbed up to Leo's roof one morning the following week — Leo was at work, but he'd left the key with his housekeeper (Aggie, Scottish, very stern, 'probably ex-secret service,' according to Ted, who suddenly seemed to know a lot about royal bodyguards) — and while Ted busied himself with his new laser tape measure and muttering about hive access, I sneaked a moment to take in the perfection of the scene. The flat roof space with its thick redbrick chimney stacks was ideal for hives, but also offered a stunning aerial view of the city. I could have stayed there leaning against the fire escape for hours, gazing out at the curling terraces and thumbprint parks and the church spires poking through the bare-branched trees, but Ted was more alive with interest than I'd seen him in ages. It was almost certainly the prospect of introducing more gadgetry into his working day.

'Four hives here ... Maybe some wildflower beds here around the chimney stack ...' He looked up and caught me gazing dreamily at a water butt. I was daydreaming about dancing on the rooftop with Leo and watching the sun come up over the private garden, but obviously Ted didn't know that. His voice was providing a soothing sound track of *blah-blahblah* to my choreography.

'Hello,' he said sarkily. 'Are you listening to anything I'm saying?'

'Er, yes?' I said.

Ted carried on clicking his measuring whatsit. 'You know what would really help? If your dad could come down and set this up for us. I know roughly what I'm doing, but he's the bee expert.'

I chewed my lip. 'Um, I don't think that's going to happen.'

'Why not? He could invoice us for the train fare, if that's an issue.'

'It's not that,' I said quickly. 'My parents aren't ... big on London. Anyway, I'm going home for Dad's birthday in a few weeks' time. I'll talk to him then. I'll get a whole list of stuff we need.'

Ted's face lit up at the mention of 'stuff.' Sometimes I thought he'd only gone in for gardening because it required more heavy equipment than teaching.

'Anyway,' I said, 'don't you want to know about the rose garden? It's fascinating — so many old varieties, from all over the place. I've been making a list of the original roses, and not all of them are going to be easy to get hold of.'

Ted beamed his laser tape measure over to the massive chimney stack and scribbled down a figure.

'Are you listening to *me*?'

'Yeah, course. Roses. Lots of them.'

'It was planted so cleverly, for color *and* fragrance, in so many layers,' I went on, because I was almost as dazzled by the meticulously sketched plans as I was by Leo. The thought of bringing it back to life, with some updating, was making me giddy with excitement. 'The varieties were arranged so the place must have been a cloud of gorgeous scent from April through — what are you doing?'

'Working out how much this roof space is worth per square foot. Do you have *any* idea how much this house would be on the market for?'

This was possibly the first time Ted had ever used the quantity surveying portion of his course, and it made me feel awkward. I'd never wondered how much the houses we worked at were worth. I knew they cost millions, and that the rooms I glimpsed through the sash windows were stunningly designed; but I also noticed that the staff lurking in the background often seemed bored, and the residents never seemed to have much time to enjoy the shady green oases I created for them in the precious pockets of outside space. The white Kensington mansions like this one of Leo's had always felt like a different world from the one I lived in, one I wasn't actually envious of because it wasn't a life that I wanted. Or had had anything to do with, until now.

'No.' I pushed myself off the railings. 'And I don't need to know either, thanks. Let's measure for the wildflower beds.'

The gardens in the center of Leo's square were worthy of Kew, but I was secretly thrilled that he'd allowed me to create a hidden corner of wildness up on his roof, where no one would ever guess there were poppies and buttercups and long grasses.

When I met Leo for dinner a few nights later, he was surprisingly interested in my notes about the rare roses I'd tracked down — or at least, if he was pretending to be interested, I was keen to believe he meant it.

'You don't have to ask questions,' I said with a blush when I realized I'd been rhapsodizing about the delicate perfumes of old English tea rose varieties for so long that the waiter had had to be waved away twice.

'But I *am* interested,' he insisted with an eager smile. 'The roses are my favorite part of the gardens at home.'

'At home . . . in the palace?' I was going to have to practice saying that until it sounded a bit more casual.

Leo nodded easily, and poured me some more wine. 'There are formal gardens all round the palace and they're all themed. You'd like them. My great-grandmother was very keen on gardening — she was one of those pioneer women who had to be doing something. There's an English country garden for the English side of the family, and an Australian garden because she was from Australia, and an alpine rockery part for the German side.' He grinned. 'Good job we're a mongrelly sort of family — gave her plenty to do.'

'Were they gardens you could go in? Not just for show?' I asked, trying to imagine what it must have been like, growing up in a stately home.

'Oh, definitely. We spent hours there as kids because we weren't allowed to run around inside. The head gardener used to lay on treasure hunts for us — it's still disappointing for me that chocolate eggs apparently don't grow under rose-bushes.'

'It can be arranged,' I said, pretending to make a note on my pad.

'Can it?' His eyes twinkled. 'It might make me do more gardening.'

'It all sounds very fairy-tale. Well, it would be, with the castle.'

I'd seen pictures of the Wolfsburgs' Nironan castle on the Internet. I wasn't going to let him pass *that* off as a holiday home.

Leo shrugged. 'We didn't think of it as a castle; it was just where my grandparents lived. Our apartment there is quite modern, not like the state rooms that tourists can go round. I liked the gardens best, though. Some of my happiest child-hood memories are of lying on the grass with my cousins, watching clouds and drinking this mint tea that my grand-mother used to make. Just the smell of hot mint takes me right back. Very embarrassing when I get misty-eyed in Turkish restaurants.'

I couldn't stop myself smiling at the romance of it all. The fact that Leo loved the gardens more than the palace made me like him even more. We'd reached that stage of falling upon shared interests as if we were the only people in the world *ever* to hate blackcurrant Jelly Babies, and childhoods in gardens was Amazing Coincidence number eighty-one, after proper cotton hankies (love of), recorder (as first instrument), etc.

'I'm like that with lavender! Dad used to grow it for the bees, and every time the dogs ran through the bushes you'd get a gorgeous gust of lavender on the breeze. I plant it everywhere I live, in pots, so I feel at home.' It was lovely sharing things with Leo. I couldn't think of the last person I'd talked to like this. 'That's why I like planting herbs in people's window boxes — I think smells are such a big part of memories, even in London. Cut grass, and rosemary, and sweet peas. I like the idea of tying them into people's lives so that whenever they smell hyacinths or something, they get that nice *aaah* memory.'

Leo smiled soppily at me as if I'd said something profound, and I felt self-conscious. 'What?'

'I love the way you talk about your job,' he said. 'It's so much more than getting the perfect lawn for you, isn't it?'

'Ted does lawns. I want to create somewhere peaceful for clients. Somewhere they can go to get away from everything. Somewhere they can see that no matter how crap their day was at work, this little plant will keep growing, and even though that tree looks dead now, in three months' time there'll be green shoots, and in five months' time there'll be apples again. It's good to be reminded of the seasons in London. Smelling the roses now and again is good too. You can't stop and smell the roses unless you've got some to smell.'

That was definitely a family thing. Dad had said it a lot,

during the grim times after the move, his face set with defiant dignity — 'The tree might look dead, Amy, but the roots are still there. It'll be flowering again before you know it, love.' He hadn't needed to add, 'And so will we.' I heard it anyway.

I pushed down the fierce pang of homesickness for Dad, and our old garden, and those familiar things. Leo was talking, his hands moving animatedly, long fingers playing with the silver salt cellar.

'We've got some amazing photo albums of my great-grandmother directing operations in her gardens,' he said. 'Someone's written "Rolling up the royal sleeves!" underneath one photo, although to be accurate, she's in a crinoline and an enormous veiled hat, with about forty sweating workmen behind her, trying not to fall over her various Pekinese dogs.'

I blushed. 'I'd really love to see that.'

'I'd love to show you the gardens — you're the only person I know who'd appreciate some of the rare plants they've still got. I mean, I'd love to show you the whole island.'

Leo looked up at me with the sweet sideways glance that sent the blood shooting faster through my veins. He did everything else with the easiest confidence I'd ever seen — ordering food, directing Billy, tipping — but sometimes, like now, a self-consciousness peeked through, as if he wasn't quite sure how I'd react.

'Are you inviting me back to your place?' I said cheerfully, without quite thinking it through.

'I suppose I am. No, I'm inviting you back to my *palace*.'

We grinned, and it hung in the air between us. I shivered:

I'd been chatted up before, but never on such a glamorous scale. I'd wished for something new, but this was more than *new*.

'Just the gardens, mind,' he said seriously. 'You have to pay extra to get into the castle.'

I thought for one awful, crushing second that he meant it, and then a mischievous smile twinkled into his blue eyes, and I swatted him, the same way that Jo swatted me.

Leo kept finding excuses to call me, and I kept finding excuses to discuss plans for his garden, and pretty soon we were seeing each other nearly every day, even if it was just for a lunchtime coffee in the frosty square while Billy read the *Racing Post* in the Range Rover.

Each time Leo revealed a little more about his family. Within a few lunches I'd learned that his mother, Liza Bachmann, spent half her time in New York directing her fitness DVD and control lingerie empire, which currently made her the seventh richest model in the world; that his dad, Prince Boris, the fourth in line to the throne of Nirona, was currently in London to raise funds for his feral-cat charity; that Leo had just flown home for the night to celebrate the twenty-ninth birthday of his sister, Sofia, who worked for a big international law firm and specialized in family inheritance dispute resolution.

'Sofia doesn't like being mistaken for a royal freeloader like Rolf either,' he explained. 'But it helps that she also enjoys a good legal wrangle.'

In return, I told him carefully selected details about my own family: how my dad was a retired bank manager who'd won every prize going in the local vegetable show (not for nothing was he the Marrow King of Hadley Green, which Leo pointed out made me the Marrow Princess); how my mum had run the kitchens at the local school and invented several new puddings that were now on the national menu. I told him about my town councilor gran, who'd left me Badger, and mentioned my older sister Kelly again, who'd left home while I was at school.

And, of course, we always had Rolf to talk about. Rolf and/ or Jo. I tried to pass on Jo's message about the iPod with as much tact as I could, but Leo scratched his chin thoughtfully.

'The thing is, I've never known Rolf to make so much effort for a girl before. Normally he's bored by now. You say he's sent an iPod? With songs on it? He can't even work his own. Is she really not interested?'

'I don't think so.' I wasn't sure what the tactful way to convey Jo's reaction was. She did seem to be enjoying the outrage quite a lot, given that she could quite easily make it all stop with a simple restraining order. Maybe she saw something in Rolf I couldn't. Maybe her outrage was an advanced version of the insulting banter she and Ted enjoyed. I was much happier to make excuses for her double standards, since it was Leo's brother causing them. 'If it's just the challenge Rolf's looking for, can't he take up a new language? Or learn to knit?'

'Or maybe he really likes her.'

We both looked shocked at that.

'She could be the making of him. He needs someone with a bit of common sense,' Leo added. 'Jo doesn't take any of his nonsense seriously.'

'Well, if that's the case, I think what would impress Jo more,' I said very carefully, 'would be if he stopped *trying* to impress her. If he could make it less about himself and more about her? A lot less about himself, actually.'

Leo nodded solemnly. 'I'll pass it on.'

What I really wanted to say was that Rolf should start being a bit more like Leo. Although he answered my predictable questions about heating in castles and whether it was weird seeing your family on humorous postcards, Leo seemed determined to make our dates as normal as possible. We ate out at simple French restaurants near his house, and he wouldn't let me pay for anything, even though I tried. And at the end of the evening, even when I was literally trembling with the sort of desire I'd only ever read about in Kelly's Judith Krantz novels, rather than whisk me back to his luxury townhouse for a princely ravishing, he kissed me — slowly, until my knees turned weak and the blood raced round my veins — and sent me home with Billy.

'I don't want to rush things,' he said, in the long phone calls in the dark that followed. 'This is special.'

I agreed. The time Leo and I spent together *was* special, but in a way that had nothing to do with him being fifth in line to the throne of Europe's most exclusive island tax haven, after Pavlos, Pavlos's sons, Serge and Guillermo, and Boris.

# CHAPTER TWELVE

I got my first glimpse into just how different Leo's life was from mine at the start of February when he rang me at work one morning, to ask if he could take me to a charity gala event at the Royal Opera House in Covent Garden.

He was using the same sort of voice Jo used when she begged me to go to one of her actor friends' plays — the 'I don't really want to go to this on my own, and I'm not saying it's going to be any good, but I said I would, and it's only for a couple of hours, and you never know, there might be chips' sort of voice.

'It's one of Dad's charities,' he explained. 'Sofia's bailed out because of some hearing she's got at the European Court of Human Rights, and Dad doesn't want to have to talk to Rolf all night on his own, so I'm getting a fair bit of pressure to turn up and support the old man. Will you come and support *me*, please?'

'Of course!' I said, without even thinking. Leo made it sound very run-of-the-mill. In fact, he sounded more worried that I'd be put out by going. 'What's the charity?'

'The Boris Wolfsburg Foundation for Feral Cats.' Leo coughed. 'I know. Dad's got about five foundations, and all of them are a bit . . . out there, but there weren't many left.

Granddad's got all the serious ones, and Uncle Pavlos bagged any interesting ones that were left, since he's the official heir. At least Dad's got some of Mom's friends on board for his. I think Elle Macpherson might be coming. And Lulu.'

'Really?' I was impressed. I'd heard of them. 'And will she be there herself?'

''Fraid not. She's in New York this week, launching her Valentine's control lingerie range. Don't ask about that either.'

I didn't. I'd Googled it, though, with Jo. Though my slightly wobbly tum could have done with Liza's help, I hadn't invested in a Take Control Girdle. As Jo put it, even if your date was so impressed with your board-flat stomach that he took you home, that'd be about as far as it'd go, unless either of you had a pair of scissors handy.

'So when is it, this do?'

'Friday.' Leo sounded apologetic. 'I know it's short notice, but my assistant put it in my work diary, not my personal one, so I missed it. Will you have time to get something to wear?'

'Of course!' I said. There were four shopping days to Friday. That was loads of time.

'Great! I'll have the invitation couriered round to you right now.'

I put the phone down in a state of fluttery excitement. A gala! With film stars!

Although, I thought, glancing down at the lingering after-effects of my mother's Christmas baking extravaganza, still making my jeans billow a bit, maybe it mightn't be a bad idea to see if Liza did any girdles with easier access.

*

'You can't wear that,' said Jo in a no-arguments tone.

'Why not? What's wrong with it?'

We looked at my reflection in Jo's mahogany cheval mirror. Neither of us looked very happy, to be brutally honest.

'Darling, you're going to the opera, not a piano lesson.' Jo tweaked my gray velvet knee-length dress, my second-best event outfit. I'd already worn my black dress in several different accessory permutations so I'd had to fall back on this, zhushed up with a pair of red shoes that I could walk exactly one hundred meters in before I started to limp. It was what I called a go-anywhere dress, and what Jo called my nun frock.

'But it's a charity night,' I protested. 'I don't want to look overdressed.'

'It's not *that* sort of charity,' said Jo briskly. 'There won't be a raffle for a fruit basket, it'll be Katherine Jenkins singing selections from Puccini and everyone jangling their diamonds in time to the music. And his family will be there!'

'I don't want Leo to think I'm making a bigger effort for his family than I do for him,' I said stubbornly. 'I don't want him to think I think it's a big deal for me. Him being a prince. He's already said how refreshing it is that I'm not some prince-hunter type.'

I paused, as the Other Voice in my head started to point out the stupidity of what I'd just said. Of course it was a big deal. Me deliberately not making it a big deal only underlined its big-dealness — and, if I was being honest, made me look a bit chippy.

I prodded the messy emotional reasoning churning away inside me, stirred up even more now by Jo's reaction. It wasn't as if Leo's family was just any old family. In fact, wasn't it rude *not* to make an effort? For anyone's family? God, it was so complicated.

'Or have I got that all wrong?' I asked in a small voice. Any normal rules about dating had gone out of the window ages ago. I was literally clueless.

By way of an answer, Jo swung open her wardrobe door and started to rifle critically through the hangers.

I stared at my reflection in the mirror and tried to decide if I felt more excited or scared. On balance, I *thought* I was excited.

Leo sent a car to collect me at seven, but it wasn't Billy in the Range Rover, and when I got in — quickly, because the huge blacked-out limo was holding up two taxis in the road outside our house — he wasn't in the backseat.

Rolf was. In evening dress, with his bow tie undone and his hair messy. He was texting, and barely bothered to look up when I slid in. A strong smell of expensive aftershave hung in the air, and I had an unwelcome mental blast of the 'One Night with Rolf' playlist. Thankfully, it was in my head, not on the car stereo.

'Evening,' he said, squinting at his phone. 'Be with you in a second.'

The backseat was so wide I wasn't expecting him to lean across, but a wave would have been nice. Something to acknowledge the efforts I'd made to wriggle into Jo's best full-length silvery silk evening dress, now carefully double-taped to my front and back to avert any embarrassing slippages.

'Hello, Rolf,' I said pointedly, to avoid an embarrassing repeat of the incident in the club. The driver closed the door behind me with a discreet clunk.

Rolf's head turned and he did a double take, so hard his floppy fringe fell into his eyes.

'Well, hello.' He gave me the slow, sexy smile that worked on the stupid half of my brain. 'Look at you! Don't you look gorgeous?'

I blushed and tried to pretend that I hadn't made that much effort. Admittedly, Jo had spent about two hours painstakingly tonging my hair into bigger curls than normal, and then doing my makeup to a depth of approximately one inch, but I didn't think I looked *that* different.

Rolf stared at me for a moment, then gave me a wolfish wink, glanced across at our flat as if Jo might be at the front door, and went back to his phone.

' 'Scuse me,' he said, 'but I've got an awkward sitch with tonight's guest list. Too many girls, not enough Rolf, if you know what I mean.'

I thought there was probably more than enough Rolf to go round, but I didn't say anything. It was much easier to warm to Rolf when Leo was talking about his childhood terror of penguins, caused by an unfortunate incident at the Royal Zoo, rather than faced with the real thing in all its manicured glory.

'Where's Leo?' I asked instead. 'He is still coming?'

'Yup. He's been delayed at the office. Says he'll meet you there.'

My heart sank. I'd got my invitation in my bag, but no

actual ticket, and I had no idea what I was meant to do on arrival. Leo hadn't put any instructions in with the thick white envelope. 'Must be something important.'

'I'm sure it is. It always is with Leo. I don't know if he's told you, but he's the only person in London with a job.' He paused, glanced across at the house once more, then as the car purred away, said, 'Text Tatiana.'

'I'm sorry?'

'Text Tatiana. I'm talking to my phone.'

'Oh, right. Sorry.'

'Hey, baby. Total nightmare.'

It took me a second to realize he wasn't actually talking to me. 'Mine doesn't do that,' I said, feeling I ought to explain.

'What?'

'Mine isn't voice-activated. Although I do shout at it quite a lot!'

Rolf frowned. 'Delete. Delete. No, not that. Text Tatiana.'

'Sorry, did I mess that up?' I gripped my — Jo's — evening bag and tried to focus my thoughts before I blurted out something else that might crash Rolf's phone by accident. I wasn't sure how this texting of Tatiana fitted in with Rolf's determined wooing of Jo. I resisted the temptation to shout 'Delete Tatiana.'

'Double booking,' said Rolf, with an ambiguous wink.

'On the Rolf Express?'

'Exactly.' He fiddled with his phone. 'If someone hadn't been washing her hair tonight, there might have been room for two . . .'

Jo was *not* washing her hair; she was having dinner with

Marigold at J Sheekey. I could have told him that for nothing, but I bit my lip and smiled enigmatically.

While Rolf fiddled with his phone, I turned my head away and watched the nighttime streets of central London flash past. I never got tired of seeing the postcard sights, all lit up for the evening as if they were onstage: the round face of Big Ben above the spiky Houses of Parliament, orange taxi signs like eyes in the darkness, and the pearly strings of lights along the Embankment.

After a while I noticed that people were looking at me. Well, at the car. As we swished past, their heads turned automatically to see who was in such a massive look-at-me limo.

The first time a tourist pointed, I shrank back in my seat, as if they could see me as clearly as I could see their curious faces. But as we went on and I realized I was safe behind the tinted privacy glass, I started to enjoy it. If Rolf hadn't been there, I might even have indulged myself in a royal wave, just to see what it felt like.

It wasn't a long drive to the Royal Opera House from Jo's flat, but the traffic was gridlocked, and by the time we pulled up outside, we were nearly twenty minutes late. My heart was racing with tension.

Well, *my* heart was racing. Rolf was still smarming at his phone: 'I'll totes make it up to you. Big love. Delete big love. Text, kisses. Yeah. Rolf. Ex ex. Ex. Send. What are you doing?' he added, seeing me struggling with the car door.

'Trying to get out. We're so late!' I checked my nails. I'd been to a salon down the road that afternoon, and already one was chipped. I wasn't used to varnish.

'It's deadlocked, babe,' he said, as if it were very obvious. 'And the doors are armor-plated.'

I turned to look at him, to check if he was joking or not. 'Why do you have an armor-plated car?'

'Because some nutter tried to have a go at Granddad once. Anyway, everyone's got them. The Saudis. The Grimaldis. The Ecclestones.'

The Ecclestones were my parents' neighbors in Yorkshire. I didn't think they were the same ones, though.

'And don't try to open the door!' he added, as I was digesting this startling information. 'That's what Mark's for.'

'But I'm perfectly capable of—'

'That's not the point,' said Rolf. 'It's about the show. The entrance. The *magic*.'

As he spoke, the door swung open and the driver offered me a hand out, as if I were some elderly granny. This driver actually wore a peaked cap, as well as driving gloves. I didn't know drivers had formal wear too.

I stuck one foot out, but before I could remember what I'd seen in the films about exiting cars like a lady, there was another hand on my back, giving me a none-too-gentle push. I was already distracted by the banks of people with cameras waiting outside the door of the Opera House — some of them now pointing at me — and the unexpected shove nearly made me fall out onto the pavement.

'Hurry up, and don't show your knickers,' said Rolf with a wink that said exactly the opposite. 'I hope you're wearing some?'

Somewhere in the seconds between finishing his text and

copping a feel of my bare back, he'd done up his bow tie, smoothed down his hair, and somehow transformed his sleazy appearance into a more presentable version. Like Wonder Woman but in a limo rather than a phone box.

I swallowed. Dare I say it, a more princely version.

'Of course I am wearing knickers,' I said haughtily, and got out.

Immediately the cameras started flashing, and I had to fight my instinct to jump straight back in the car. I really didn't enjoy having my photo taken — my best side was the back of my head — and the flashes were giving me black spots in front of my eyes. I hoped they would stop once they realized I wasn't anyone famous, but they seemed to get more intense.

*Stand up straight. Smile. Not like that. Don't show your wonky tooth.* I turned my head so my beauty mark wasn't facing the cameras, and the flashes went mad.

Then, of course, I realized Rolf was playing up to them behind me. He'd slipped on a pair of sunglasses, which he was now taking off again, while grinning and turning very slowly to give everyone his best side. While the cameras were still whirring, he yelled, 'Okay, that's enough!' He held up a hand and shepherded me into the foyer of the Opera House.

I really mean shepherded. I was so stunned he practically had to push me in, and this time he seemed to be checking whether I was wearing a bra.

Once inside, I pretended to be looking around while I recovered my composure. I'd never been to the Royal Opera House, and the first thing I noticed wasn't a thing, but a smell

— the drowsy scent of tiger lilies arranged in stripy starbursts all round the room. They were the most strongly scented lilies I'd ever come across and I wondered where they'd been flown in from.

Long gold banners with the Prince Boris Foundation logo hung from the ceiling, and waiters in dazzling white shirts and black cats' ears circulated with trays of champagne flutes. They slid through the crowd of chattering guests, keeping their trays straight, all the streaming bubbles in the flutes aligning perfectly, despite jeweled hands reaching out of nowhere to grab them.

I turned to ask Rolf if he knew how long Leo would be, but he'd vanished, and my nerves reappeared in one panicky *whoosh*. I didn't exactly feel comfortable with Rolf, but he was the only person I knew here — plus, he was the only one I could easily ask about what to do. Should I have shown my invitation to someone?

I looked around and sent a silent thank you to Jo for refusing to let me wear my nun dress. Everyone was *seriously* dressed up. There was more fur in here than at Battersea Dogs and Cats Home, and every other face was familiar in that 'Are you from Zumba? Oh no, you're the foreign secretary' way.

'Champagne?' A waiter materialized silently in front of me. He didn't look too chuffed about the cat's ears.

I probably shouldn't have, but the prospect of some Dutch courage was too tempting. I took the glass from the tray with a nervous smile, accepted a tiny canapé on a napkin from the waiter behind, and got out my phone to pretend to be checking some urgent e-mails. Everyone around me was doing the same.

The only difference was that other people were talking to their phones at the same time. And I didn't have e-mail on my ancient phone, so I had to content myself with checking my own contacts list, frowning at it every so often.

No missed calls from Leo. I typed Where are you? How long will you be? then deleted it and texted I'm here! in what I hoped was a cheery manner.

I gazed around at the milling crowds as if I were looking for a friend — one of Jo's top party tips — but when several other guests looked at me and started muttering to each other, I put the phone to my ear and pretended to be taking a call instead.

That's when I heard the voices behind the lilies.

'. . . with Rolf?'

'I don't think so. Isn't he seeing Tatiana Solzenhoff?'

'Yuh, she told me. But he arrived with some other girl, did you see how she . . .'

I gripped my glass. They were talking about *me*. Me!

Frustratingly, the voice dipped — with, argh, a low chuckle — and I missed whatever I'd done that had been so amusing.

I wanted to part the lilies and lean through to say, 'No, I'm not with Rolf, not in a bazillion years. I'm with his much more attractive brother,' but I was temporarily stunned at the thought that two people I'd never met were discussing me, just because I'd arrived with Rolf. They'd noticed me, because I'd arrived with him. How did that make me feel?

The two women started talking again, but as I leaned forward to peer through the lilies, I brushed against a pollen-loaded stamen, and my attention swerved.

What sort of florist hadn't taken the stamens off the lilies? Lily pollen stained everything in sight, and there were a lot of white dresses around, mine included. Jo had already warned me that this dress was so vintage it required specialist dry cleaning, and that I wasn't to let Rolf anywhere near it with a red drink. Any drink, for that matter.

Without thinking, I started to nip off the heavy orange stamens, dropping them into the cocktail napkin that I hadn't been able to off-load onto a waiter. I was focusing on doing that as cleanly as I could when a warm hand touched the bare skin on the small of my back, and I squeaked with shock.

I spun round, ready to apologize for defacing the arrangement (or slap Rolf's face), and saw a much more welcome sight: Leo, effortlessly stylish in black tie, his blond hair brushed back, and two glasses of champagne in his hands.

The relief. I can't even tell you. Also, the *burn* of excitement at seeing him in a dinner jacket. Hot. Hot hot hot.

'Hello!' He smiled his familiar eye-crinkling smile, and already the situation seemed less alien. 'Don't tell me — you've got some notes for the florists?'

'Oh, they stain, and this dress . . .' I waved the napkin pollen-bomb stupidly.

'Here, let me,' he said, juggling the glasses to take the napkin off me. He handed it to a waiter who'd materialized out of nowhere, as had three women in plunging dresses that seemed to be held up by sheer willpower. Leo smiled at them, then led me away to a quieter corner.

'Can I get my apologies in first?' he asked, before I could speak. 'I'm so sorry about leaving you with Rolf. I was on a conference call with New York that overran, and I couldn't get away without jeopardizing the deal. And second, sorry we couldn't schedule dinner beforehand, but I thought at least this way you only have to talk to Dad and Rolf before and after the performance. Start you off gently.'

'It's fine,' I said. I could feel curious eyes drilling into the back of my head. People were staring at us. Well, at Leo. 'Thank you for sending the car.'

'You're welcome. I just wish I could have been in it. You look incredible,' he added. 'I spotted you straightaway from the foyer.'

'Why?' Panic flickered in me as people glanced over, then pointedly looked away. 'Am I not wearing the right thing?'

'No! Because your hair is about a foot higher than normal.' Leo touched one of the curls Jo had pinned up in a high bun, then touched my ear as if he couldn't stop himself. 'It really suits you. Shows off your lovely neck.'

I stashed the compliment away for later and blushed. 'Jo did it for me.'

'And the dress is adorable, very on-trend with the vintage detailing.' He pretended to grimace. 'I am allowed to say that. My mother's in fashion.'

I smiled, mainly at the conspiratorial wink he was giving me, the one no one else could see. 'It's all held up with sellotape, you know. I'm a bit worried it might peel off if it gets too hot.'

'In that case, there's no way I'm letting you sit near Rolf.' Leo's face was straight, but his eyes were roguish above his champagne glass.

I leaned forward anxiously, and he leaned forward too.

'What?' he stage-whispered. 'Was there an incident in the limo?'

'No! Leo, are you sure I'm wearing the right thing?' I whispered. 'Everyone's wearing diamonds and — and tiaras! People keep staring at me. I mean, I don't have a tiara, but — should I have got one? I didn't know the dress code was *heirlooms*.'

Leo straightened up and spoke in a normal voice. 'They're staring at you because you look adorable, you *nut*. It's a charity gala, you're wearing exactly the right thing. I always think there's something in bad taste about coming to a fundraiser in a million pounds worth of jewelry and only donating ten quid to the actual cause.'

He touched my arm lightly as he spoke, and a calm sensation spread through me. I had donation money in my handbag. Mum would have killed me if I'd forgotten that.

'Now,' Leo went on, 'if I can tear him away from his adoring public, let me introduce you to my father.'

He nodded toward a gaggle of guests standing in what I assumed was the VIP area. As Leo approached, they parted, and in the middle of them was a tall man wearing the most impeccable black tie I'd ever seen, but with a bright pink bow tie. And pink Converse All Star trainers.

'Ignore the shoes,' muttered Leo, seeing me freeze like a rabbit in the headlights. 'It's his thing. He thinks they make him look like a film star.'

Leo's dad *did* look like a film star. Or rather, Boris looked like one of those eighties film stars who'd moved from leading-man roles into characterful father parts, with a sideline in high-profile humanitarian charity work. He had the same striking blue eyes as Leo, and his hair was sandy blond, swept back off his forehead in a thick swoop. His tan glowed against the sparkling white collar of his evening shirt, and when he reached forward to greet me, his cuffs gave off a sudden flash of bright light so sharp my head spun round to see where the photographer was.

I later found out this was because he had diamond cuff links the size of pebbles.

'Leo! And who is this beautiful woman?' he said, taking my hands and fixing me with his warm gaze.

I had no idea what he was going to do with them, but I had to fight back the stupid grin forming on my face. It was like being bathed in the most flattering sunlight in the world. Keeping his unsettlingly blue eyes fixed on mine, Prince Boris raised my right hand to his lips and kissed the backs of my fingers while still holding the left.

Obviously, I melted like an ice cream. I tried not to simper too hard, but I heard a weird kitteny noise seep out nonetheless.

'Oh, for heaven's sake,' said Rolf, who clearly didn't like anyone muscling in on his charming slimeball act, least of all his dad. 'Amy, that's his standard greeting. If you were a guy, he'd ask who your tailor was so he could get himself a set of shoulders like that too.'

'So I could send my son to him for a proper suit, you mean,' said Boris without taking his eyes off mine.

'My suits are far more fashionable than—' Rolf started, but Leo coughed and took charge of the situation.

'Papa, this is Amy Wilde,' he said. 'Amy, my father, Prince Boris of Nirona and Svetland.'

Boris inclined his head, and my smile stuck as my brain finally caught up.

Should I curtsy? *Could* I curtsy in this tight dress? Was it better to curtsy and rip it? I did a jerky sort of bob, which made me look like I'd got a cramp; as I did, the two glasses of champagne I'd knocked back finally reached my head and collided with my jittering nerves, and I slipped forward.

Leo put his arm out and stopped me lunging into his dad's chest. He managed to make it seem as if he was just putting a protective arm around me, but I turned red all the same.

*Oh, great start.*

'Save that for later, maybe,' said Rolf from somewhere behind me.

'Let's not stand on ceremony,' said Boris with a gracious smile and a trace of an accent. 'You can call me Your Serenity, or Prince Boris, or just Boris, it's up to you.'

'Thank you,' I said.

'Are you a fan of opera, Amy?' he inquired.

'Or feral cats?' inquired Rolf in the same cordial tones.

'Mmm! Both!' I smiled and nodded. From that point onward, I decided, polite smiling was going to be my default response to everything. Hopefully Leo would guide me through some more specific conversation later.

An official appeared and murmured to the man in dark glasses standing two feet to the left of Prince Boris; the man then put his finger to his left ear, murmured something into his cuff link, and said, 'If you'd like to take your seat, sir, everyone's ready for you.'

Boris nodded. 'When we're ready,' he said. 'I haven't seen what the interval refreshments are going to be. You did make sure about the ice cream?'

The man nodded. 'Neapolitan. Soya.'

'With wafers? Organic? The fan ones, not the tube ones? My grandmother was an opera singer,' he added to me, as if this explained everything.

Leo was glancing at his watch. 'We should go through, everyone's waiting.' He nodded at the security guard. 'Amy? Are you set?'

The room had emptied in the space of a minute, apart from the ushers glaring at us, and I felt the familiar missing-the-train panic I got every time I went home. We were holding everyone up. They'd all be tutting and checking their watches. Like the ushers were.

'Leo, you're so . . . nine-to-five,' drawled Rolf, but Leo ignored him and directed me toward the corridor that led to the private boxes, offering me a program as we went.

Rolf and Boris followed a majestic three full minutes later, and then the house lights went down and the royal gala performance began.

# CHAPTER THIRTEEN

I have to be honest with you. I spent more time boggling at the glittering surroundings of the Royal Opera House than I did listening to what was going on below. People came on, they sang beautifully (selections from *Cats*, I think, and *The Lion King*), everyone clapped. But there was just too much going on around me to look at the stage.

For a start, we were in what I assume was a, if not *the*, royal box. Deep raspberry velvet seats, gold leaf and crystal in every direction, champagne in ice-beaded silver buckets by our sides. Rolf was getting through a bottle all on his own, although it didn't affect his ability to text. His fingers never stopped. After the first performance, a willowy Chinese girl in a leather dress slipped into the box and took the seat next to him; although Leo acknowledged her arrival with a polite smile, no one said a word, which I thought was a bit odd, but frankly unless Rolf got drunk and fell off *this* balcony I intended to keep quiet.

The man in dark glasses stood behind us, but after five minutes, he slipped out and returned with a crystal dish of Neapolitan ice cream, which Boris ate with a miniature silver spoon. Every so often Boris would guffaw and clap uproariously, and Rolf would accuse him of showing off for the cameras, and Boris would deny there were any, although I did spot the occasional flash that seemed to coincide with the guffawing/clapping.

I was trying to take it all in to tell Jo later, but I couldn't quite get beyond how delicious it was to be sitting next to Leo in the dark like this. He was the only one in the box paying proper attention to the performances on the stage, but he still kept sneaking the odd sideways glance in my direction to see if I was enjoying it. Once or twice he caught me staring at his handsome profile, and I wondered if the same shiver ran through him that did me.

I think, once or twice, he looked at me when I wasn't looking too, and that was even nicer. I just hoped my face wasn't giving me away, so I kept it set to 'entranced.' That was not hard.

The curtain fell after forty minutes, and Rolf got up before the applause finished. 'I'm just nipping out to —' he started, then his phone rang. He looked at it, and said, 'Oh, jeez.'

The beautiful Chinese girl had risen too, and was smiling uncertainly at me, as if not sure whether to introduce herself. Rolf saw me opening my mouth to save him the trouble and said, 'Oh, this is Ida. Ida, this is Amy.'

'His personal trainer,' said Ida with a smile, and Rolf looked slightly put out as he glanced at his phone again and flinched.

'Hello,' I said, and shook her hand.

At least he'd got my name right this time, I thought, then noticed Rolf was shifting from foot to foot.

'What's the problem?' asked Boris through a mouthful of ice cream.

'It's that nut-job Tatiana.' Rolf thrust the phone at me. 'Answer this and say you're my therapist and I can't take calls in session.'

'What?' His phone had a big *R* on it in crystals. Or diamonds. It matched the iPod he'd sent Jo, and the ring tone was some kind of hunting horn. I gave him a dark look, emboldened by another glass of champagne. 'Are you sure *I'm* the person you want to deal with your excess of girlfriends?'

'For God's sake, turn it off!' said Leo. He grabbed the phone, turned it off, and dropped it in the slushy ice bucket. 'That's been driving me insane all night.'

'Like father, like son,' said Boris indulgently. 'Too many women, too little time.'

My jaw dropped. I could *not* imagine my dad saying that. I couldn't imagine casually dropping a phone worth hundreds of pounds into an ice bucket either.

'Too little *brain*, you mean.' Leo ignored Rolf's attempts to dry off his phone and turned to me. 'Amy, can we get you anything?'

'No, no! It's all perfect. I'm just going to . . . freshen up,' I said, levering myself out of the velvet seat with a wobble.

Actually, what I needed was air. And a large glass of cold water. The canapés weren't soaking up as much alcohol as my own sausage rolls usually did. The usher assigned to the box steered me discreetly toward the ladies' room, and when I pushed open the door, the marble-tiled loos were thankfully empty.

I swung over to the mirrors with a swagger in my step now no one was watching, and was surprised to see, in my reflection, a sparkle around my eyes that had nothing to do with Jo's smoky Mac eye palette.

I looked glamorous. That was quite a surprise for me, and now that I was a little bit, um, relaxed, I didn't feel like such a traitor to my normal 'take me as I am' state to admit that I liked it.

Apart from a stray curl here and there, my makeup and hair were holding up pretty well. In fact, I thought, adding another layer of rose lip gloss with a shaky hand — the only part of the makeup process Jo had entrusted me to top up unsupervised — it was *all* holding up well. Hair, dress, conversation. Boris and Rolf were rather intimidating, and I was going to tell Jo *all* the gory details of Rolf's girlfriend shuffling later, but Leo seemed happy with the way things were going. Maybe we'd go on somewhere else afterward, just us.

Maybe tonight, with me in my beautiful dress and him in his black tie, might be the night he decided that we'd done enough taking things slowly and could get on with the princely ravishing.

I shivered and saw myself in the mirror, grinning like a loon.

But first, I had another hour of light opera and chitchat to get through. As I was thinking of some intelligent questions to ask about feral cats, the door swished open and a magnificent blonde stalked in, her eyes flashing almost as much as the huge gold necklace around her throat.

I smiled at her since she was staring at me through the mirror, but instead of turning left into the cubicles, she made straight for where I was standing.

'Are you the girl who came here vith Rolf?' She had a faint accent and very, very toned biceps. They were pulsing, along with her jaw. She looked much more like a personal trainer than Ida did.

'Well, technically, I suppose I am. Are you looking for him?' I said. 'He's still in the box, I think.'

'Really?' she said, her eyes narrowing.

Or was this the sister? Sofia? Not very friendly if she was.

I opened my mouth to ask her, but before I could speak, she grabbed the vase of oversize Dutch tulips by the basket of towels.

'You can tell him from me,' she roared, 'that he is dumped, and you are a cheating slut.'

'Now, hang on, I'm not *here* with Rolf—' I started, holding up my arms to defend myself, but she didn't throw the vase at me — she yanked the waxy flowers out of it and deliberately poured the water over my head, soaking my dress and flattening my hair.

I gasped as the cold — and stinky — water coursed down my back and into my shoes. Everything was sticking to me, and my eyes stung where my so-called waterproof mascara was running.

I was too stunned to speak. All I could think of was poor Jo's beautiful vintage dress. And my own brand-new shoes. And the fact that no one had changed that water for *days*.

'Don't *lie* to me!' The woman jabbed her finger at me, her nostrils flaring. 'And you don't vant to know vhat I'm about to do to that scumbag! Tell him Verbier is *off*! And so vill his balls be if I catch you vith him again!'

And then she turned and stormed out, just as two older ladies in crushed-velvet floor-length gowns were opening the door to come in. They took one look at me and backed out, their eyebrows nearly in their wigs.

I wanted to cry, but I was in shock. Every time I moved, something squelched, and the air conditioning was freezing. I squinched my eyes half-shut and risked a peep in the mirror: my hair was plastered to my head in the most unflattering way imaginable, making my ears seem enormous, and as if that weren't bad enough, the water had turned the dress completely see-through. I wasn't wearing Liza Bachmann Muffin Top Wranglers either.

Somewhere in the main hall, a bell rang and an announcer requested that the audience retake their seats for the beginning of the second half.

I gripped the edge of the basins with one hand and slapped my face with the other, hoping it would make my brain start working again. Quickly. What was I going to do? Even if I *wanted* to go and punch Rolf for this — which I was already doing in my imagination — there was absolutely no way I could go back into the *royal box* looking like I'd wet myself, *then* fallen in a lake.

I couldn't tear my gaze away from the hideous outline of my thong in the mirror. You could see *everything*. Much as I longed to punish Rolf, I really, really, really, *really* didn't want Leo to see me looking like this. It would ruin everything. And as for his dad . . . His *royal* dad.

My coat was downstairs in the cloakroom. Could I grab it, then sit in that until my dress dried? The wild-eyed stranger in the mirror cringed.

No. No, I couldn't. This wasn't a student party. This was a black-tie gala, with actual celebrities, and photographers . . .

*Oh my God, the photographers outside!*

I would have died inside all over again, but I didn't have the luxury of time.

I knew what Jo would do. She would storm back in there and show Rolf up, teaching him a lesson and turning the whole thing into a brilliant anecdote. But she was confident and didn't mind people staring at her, whereas people staring was, as everyone now knew, my absolute worst nightmare.

I didn't want to do it — it was the one thing my dad had impressed on me, that decent people didn't run away — but in my panicked state I couldn't see what choice I had left. I was going to have to make a swift exit. Quickly, before Leo saw me. Thank God I had my bag — I could text him once I was safely out of the building, and pretend there'd been some emergency at home.

Which there would be, once I got back. I would officially be having a meltdown.

The cloakroom lady wouldn't give me my coat at first; she practically accused me of stealing someone else's ticket, and it was only when I told her exactly what was in the pockets (Oyster card, lip balm, dog treats — embarrassing, but they were in every coat I owned) that she handed it over. Her beady eyes, and the eyes of all the security guards, followed me through the front door until I was safely out of the Royal Opera House. My one stroke of luck was that the first wave of celebs going on somewhere else had left during the interval and now the photographers were busy wiring their pictures. They didn't notice Prince Rolf's 'date' slinking out in the shadows.

At least when I was freshly soaked, there was an obvious reason for my disheveled state; but as I dried off, my hair just looked greasy and I smelled worse than Badger after a roll in the bushes. Even when I'd buttoned my coat up to my neck, I felt as if every single tourist in London was staring at me as I stumbled toward Trafalgar Square, my new heels scuffing and squelching on the pavement. Grace Wright would have said it was karma that I'd decided to give the feral cats a generous donation — which was still in my bag — so I was able to afford a cab home, although the first two refused to take me, on the grounds that I looked like I'd been dragged out of the fountains by Nelson's Column.

Jo's dinner with Marigold must have finished early, because I could hear her bellowing the opening number from *Chicago* as soon as I opened the front door; she tried to keep her rehearsals for her one-woman show to times when I was out, since I now couldn't hear 'All That Jazz' without twitching. As I reached the first landing, Jo let out a showstopping shriek, and Mrs Mainwaring's door popped open and Dickon's head appeared over the top banister.

When they saw me, though, they both stared, said nothing, and vanished while I carried on trudging up the stairs.

Jo stopped singing the instant I staggered in, her jazz hands frozen in place.

'What happened to you?' She had one foot up on a kitchen chair and was wearing a silver trilby. 'Don't tell me Rolf pushed you in a fountain?'

'Half right.'

'Which half?'

I collapsed in a stinky heap on the sofa and told her. Even Badger's usual affectionate greeting had been cut short after some tentative sniffing — warm flower water was a stench too far for him.

'That is the final straw! I'm going to phone that *pig* right now and tell him what I think of him and his harem of insane fembots,' said Jo, reaching for her phone with a black look. 'If he thinks—'

'No! No,' I said. 'Run me a bath instead. I can't think while I smell like this.'

Jo hauled me up by the armpits and steered me into the bathroom, where she started to run a hot bath. Without a word, she poured a generous amount of her best bath oil into it. That bath oil only came out for contract terminations and dumpings. She was grinding her teeth in fury, and she hadn't even mentioned the state of her dress.

'Get into that,' she said. 'What did Leo say when you told him what happened?'

I paused, one shoe off, and pulled a face. 'He doesn't know. I texted him and said Badger had had an accident and I'd had to leave.'

'Why didn't you tell him?' Jo demanded. 'It's not like it was your fault!'

'What, and let him see me like this? I didn't want a big scene, I just wanted to get out of there.' With Jo looking at me like that, it did seem a bit ... wet to have slid away like that. But at the time ...

'There's a difference between making a scene and — and *bringing someone to their senses.*' Jo narrowed her eyes. 'You don't look as bad as you think. If that'd been me, no one would have noticed my appearance for the sight of Rolf weeping on the floor. Royal, schmoyal.'

I should point out that at that exact moment, Jo was wearing a silver trilby, gold hot pants, and Ugg boots. That was the trouble with really confident people. Their embarrassment scale was calibrated entirely differently.

'Well, I disagree,' I said weakly. 'There were photographers.'

'So what did Leo say, about this mysterious emergency?'

'Dunno. I turned my phone off. I couldn't bring myself to look.' I hiccuped; delayed shock. 'Oh, Jo. He's going to think I'm incredibly rude, isn't he? It just seemed like the only thing to do at the time.'

'Rude? You? After someone assaults you in a powder room?' Jo looked as if she was about to explode with fury.

I suddenly felt exhausted, as if all my energy had been used up in getting home. 'I know you don't understand, but I already felt like everyone was staring at me for not wearing a couture evening gown. I didn't want to be the sideshow on the way back down too. If I could do wisecracks like you, then maybe. But look!' I pinged my thong. 'I don't want the first glimpse of my knickers that Leo gets to be *these* ones.'

She acknowledged that, at least.

'And I'm so sorry about your dress.' I gulped. It was such a delicate thing. There was no way I could afford to replace it. 'I don't know if you can save it, but I'll pay for any—'

'The dress doesn't matter.' Jo flapped her hands. 'So what?

It died in a love triangle outside the royal box of the Royal Opera House. It's what it would have wanted. I'm more worried about *you* and what—'

The doorbell rang, and we both flinched.

'What if it's Leo?' I panicked.

'What do you mean, *what if*? It's bound to be him. Talk to him. Tell him what happened!'

My mind went blank. It wasn't just a case of telling him about Tatiana now; I also had to apologize for leaving without saying goodbye, lying to him, leaving him to explain to his *prince father* where I'd gone . . . I needed to think about that conversation. I needed time to prepare it. Hadn't this evening only proved what happened when I went off-piste?

The doorbell rang again.

'I'll get it.' Jo pulled off the trilby. 'If it's Rolf, I can't promise I won't lamp him.'

She stormed off downstairs, but I didn't get into the bath. Instead, I pulled on Jo's bathrobe and crept out onto the landing to listen, out of sight.

If I angled myself right at the very edge of the banisters, I could just see Jo opening the door, and — I cricked my neck — there was a dark evening suit and just a hint of white shirt.

'Good evening, Jo. I've come to check that Amy's all right.'

My heart dropped like a stone. It was Leo.

Oh God. Was Jo going to lay into him? Was she going to invite him up to see the damage? I felt sick, and very sober.

'She's fine, thank you.' Jo sounded posher than I'd ever heard her, all clipped and shiny like piano keys.

'And Badger? I got a garbled message from her about him

being taken ill.' He paused. 'Quite ironic, at a fundraiser for cats. Is he all right? I've put our London veterinarian on standby, just in case.'

I leaned my forehead against the cold wall as the full extent of the mess gradually revealed itself, in all its horrific glory.

Downstairs, I could tell Jo was struggling not to tell Leo, because she was sticking to a grim sort of truth instead of inventing spiraling lies about canine defibrillators and vet medicopters as she would normally have done. 'Amy wouldn't have left unless it had been a real emergency,' she said crisply. 'She was very upset.'

'I've been trying to call her,' Leo went on, 'but I suppose the vets don't allow cell phones?'

Jo made a strangled noise, which I knew was the truth trying to escape from her.

I couldn't bear it. I struggled to my feet and stumbled down the stairs, slipping on the worn carpet.

'Leo!' I said, arriving at the bottom with a lurch. I tried to ignore his manful struggle not to grimace at my lank hair and smeary face.

It occurred to me — too late — that the bathrobe might make it look less like I'd been camping out at Badger's basket side and more like I'd been relaxing in an early bath — after escaping a boring night out at the first opportunity.

Oh. Maybe this wasn't such a great idea.

'Is everything all right?' Leo sounded more confused than ever. 'We were worried, especially when your phone was off.'

'Well, the thing was . . .' I drew a deep breath. I could save this. Leo's expression was eager and attentive. Jo was silently urging me on.

'The thing was . . .' I said again but a depressingly familiar hum of white noise had started to spread through my mind. Words slithered through my brain like sand as I struggled to put the evening's surreal events in an order that wouldn't make me look like even more of a flaky liar than I already was. 'I, um, bumped into someone in the loos and . . .'

At that precise moment, I heard a clatter, followed by a familiar pattering noise and realized that Badger had let himself out of the dog flap and was making his way downstairs to see what the noise was about.

I watched in mounting horror as he bounced across the entrance hall, careered into Jo's legs, and came to a halt just in front of Leo, his favorite lunchtime treat dispenser. Whereupon he started wagging his stumpy tail furiously. The very picture of health.

There was a long pause, then Leo bent down to scratch Badger's ears. Jo glanced at me, a pleading expression in her eyes, but my mouth had gone dry.

'It's not what it looks like,' I gabbled, which, as everybody in the entire world knew, meant, *it's exactly what it looks like.* I might as well have written LIAR across my forehead.

Leo straightened up, and looked me in the eye, but his own expression had turned unreadable. 'Seems absolutely fine now,' he said. 'So that's good.'

'I'm so sorry, I . . .'

'Don't apologize. You were right to bail. Your disappearing act helped us all through quite a dull second half. As Rolf pointed out, even he's never been stood up in the *middle* of a date before.' Leo's tone was dry but there was a grown-up anger beneath it, and I knew that I'd just dropped him into an entire evening of alpha-male teasing.

'So,' he said. 'Now that I know you got home safely, I should be, ah, getting back to the drinks reception. I'll be in touch.' And he turned and opened the door to leave.

I stood there in Jo's bathrobe, dumb with remorse and self-loathing. I didn't dare open my mouth in case I said something even more stupid.

Jo couldn't hold it in any longer. 'Leo, that's not what—'

But the heavy door was closing, and as she spoke we both heard a car start in the street outside.

The evening was over. I shut my eyes, and my runny mascara stung. It was too late. The front door opened again as Jo darted outside, but I didn't have the energy to stop her.

I don't know how long I stood there, but when I opened my eyes, Jo was shaking me, her face right in mine, contorted with the effort of not busting out the Jo de Vere Shiny Boots of Justice.

'Amy, what the hell is wrong with you? Phone him! He'll be *furious* when he knows what Rolf did! And as for that mad Tatiana — you should press charges!'

My lip wobbled. I hated confrontation. And I wasn't cut out for this sort of high-drama nightlife. Photographers. Mad exes. Evening dress you had to stick on with tape. 'You're the one who said royals were too mad to get mixed up with. Don't you think this proves your point?'

'Let me—'

'Please, Jo.' I drew a shuddering breath. 'Let me sleep on it. I don't think I'm going to do anything right tonight.'

One of the doorknobs turned, and we both knew at least one of the other residents was earwigging.

Jo dragged me back into our flat, kicked the door shut behind us, and gripped me by the arms. 'Listen to me,' she said fiercely. 'None of this was your fault. You're better than this sort of carry-on. Mr Right is out there for you, and I am going to help you find him.' She hugged me. 'And I will not let you kiss any more frogs, okay? No more royal frogs. Just lovely normal ones.'

'Okay,' I said weakly. Only Jo could imagine that kissing any royal frog was anything other than a once-in-a-lifetime experience. My heart broke another inch, as I realized that I'd thoroughly screwed up my one chance.

# CHAPTER FOURTEEN

Leo didn't call on Saturday, despite me staring at the phone alternately willing it to ring and then not to ring because the recurrent flashbacks were making me want to die all over again. On Sunday, Jo confiscated my mobile because she was sick of me staring at it, and then she hid it to let the battery go flat in case I cracked and left some garbled message.

I made her promise not to phone Rolf and go nuclear on him, but in return I had to swear on her signed photo of Daniel Craig that I would tell Leo the truth, so I could move on.

'Ring him on Monday and explain,' she urged. 'But for God's sake, think about what you're going to say so *you* don't end up apologizing.'

When I charged the phone on Monday for work, the only messages were from Ted, telling me he'd found 'part of a Roman helmet, or possibly a tin plate' on Wimbledon Common, and from my mum, wanting to know when my train got in for Dad's birthday party the following weekend. Nothing from Leo or Rolf. Or even Tatiana.

I promised *myself* that I would phone Leo at midday on Monday, not least because I was supposed to be planting some roses that afternoon — I wasn't sure if I'd flounced myself out of a contract. My morning job was at Grace Wright's, and she was out at her Pilates class, which allowed me to rehearse some opening gambits in private. None of my imaginary conversations were very satisfying. Already the whole evening was starting to seem like one of those weird Christmas-afternoon nightmares you get after too much Stilton and sherry trifle and *Upstairs Downstairs*.

Grace arrived home at the point I was self-righteously taking Rolf to task for treating all women like extras in his own crap videos. When she saw me, her face lit up with glee.

I hoped her glee was to do with Richard's apartment block; if Leo was going to change his mind about employing runaway gardeners, I'd need Richard's balconies more than ever.

'Oooh, Amy!' she cooed, her eyes all wide. 'Was that you I saw in the paper?'

'What? No,' I said automatically.

'I rather think it was! Stay there!' Grace rushed into the flat and came back with a copy of the *Daily Mail*. I was about to tell her she'd made a mistake when she flicked through and then thrust a party page at me.

Blimey. It *was* me. Me and Rolf arriving at the Royal Opera House, albeit in a much smaller photo under the one of Prince Boris and a gallery owner I didn't know. Rolf's show-off body language obscured most of my face, but those were unmistakably my hips in Jo's beautiful — and now ruined — dress.

'You scrub up *very* well,' said Grace approvingly. 'Where did you get your hair done?'

'Oh, um, my flatmate did it.' Why was everyone so obsessed with my hair? I wasn't sure what to make of the swirling mess of emotions churning away inside as I peered at the tiny photo.

Did I look like that? I looked fierce — not in the fashion/ Beyoncé way Jo meant, but literally fierce. Like I was about to deck someone. My hair did look rather good actually, very glossy and curly, but you could see my bra strap through the dress! And was my bosom really that pneumatic? And my hips that . . . wide?

'If I didn't know it was you,' said Grace, 'I would *totally* think Rolf was going out with a model. Well, maybe not a model. Maybe an Olympic dressage rider. Or one of those tall blond Amazons you see doing the America's Cup!'

'Thank you,' I said. 'I think?'

Grace nodded emphatically. 'Mm-hm. Very glowing. Healthy!'

But there I was in the paper . . . with a prince. A prince who was known by one name by people like Grace. A horrified excitement crept into me. I wondered if Mum's next-door neighbor and the bane of her life, Di Overend, had seen it. Di got the *Daily Mail* and was a bit obsessive about the royal family, on account of once having seen Princess Michael of Kent on holiday in France.

'Well, fancy that,' Grace said, pleased. 'My gardener, dating royalty! Are you going to tell me now that you're really a countess's daughter? Like Lady Di slumming it at the kinder-garten?'

'Definitely not,' I said. 'And I'm not . . . dating royalty.'

As I said it, it finally sank in properly. That had been my one and only official date with Leo; he wasn't going to risk that happening again. I didn't care about the royalty thing, but the thought of it being the end of the road with Leo . . . He was the only man I'd met in London whom I'd woken up each morning hoping to see. The breath stuck in my throat.

'You can tell me,' said Grace, nudging me with her skinny hip. 'I'm very discreet. I know all sorts about some of Richard's tenants. Is Ted your police protection officer? I've always thought he looked rather *special forces,* if you know what I mean!'

My phone rang in my rucksack, and Grace squeaked with excitement.

'That'll probably be my *mum,*' I said. 'Calling to see if I've remembered to book a train ticket for my dad's birthday.'

I went over to the far corner of the balcony to answer, but it wasn't Mum; it was a withheld number. My heartbeat quickened as I picked up the call.

'Amy, it's Leo. Wolfsburg,' he said, before I could speak.

I removed myself to the very edge of the balcony so Grace couldn't see my stricken face. Leo sounded so adult, and cool. The chatty intimacy I'd got used to in his phone calls had gone. And he'd used his surname. As if I'd mistake him for anyone else.

I reminded myself to count to five before saying anything. No elaborate excuses. No rushing into new sentences before finishing the last. Just let him lead the conversation. Remember, you were about to call *him.*

'Hello, Leo,' I said calmly — *one, two, three* — but the apology burst through. 'Leo, I need to talk to you about Friday night. Something happened that I should have been up-front about—'

'You don't have to apologize,' said Leo stiffly. 'I should have briefed you properly about what the evening would entail. I don't like these sorts of things much myself. I didn't realize there would be quite so much Andrew Lloyd Webber, for a start . . .'

'No!' I said. 'No! That was fine. I liked that bit. I recognized some songs. It wasn't that, it was—'

But Leo seemed determined to get through his list of apologies. Even though his formality was killing me, hearing his voice was giving me shivers. 'It was absolutely out of line for Rolf to ask you to lie to his girlfriend, given your friendship with Jo, but I understand from him that it was some sort of cretinous attempt to make Jo aware of his stream of female company, if you can believe that.' Leo's voice dripped with disdain. 'Apparently it got somewhat out of hand. I told him he owed you an apology as well as her, so if you start getting deliveries of knickers—'

'No! Stop!'

I was churning inside. Clearly Rolf hadn't told him the whole story of what had happened. Maybe Tatiana hadn't even made it to the box. Maybe security had bundled her out.

At the other end of the balcony, Grace gave me a *yoo-hoo* wave.

I turned away and closed my eyes. *Now. Do it now. Tell him. So what if he's a prince? He's also a decent bloke who just happens to have a complete idiot for a brother, and he'll understand that when her thong is out on show, a self-respecting girl doesn't have a choice but to do a runner.*

I dropped my voice. 'Leo, I need to talk to you. In person. And you'd better tell Rolf to get his apology engine started.'

I met him in the small public garden outside Markham Place, just off the King's Road. Grace very kindly allowed me to freshen up as best I could in one of her three bathrooms, but I still looked like someone who'd done a morning's gardening.

If Leo noticed the difference between my gala hair and my normal corkscrews, he didn't make any comment. His expression was guarded, and he kissed my cheek so politely it was like a reverse show of affection. I noticed he was unusually scratchy around the jaw, as if he hadn't shaved.

'You got here quickly,' I said politely as we sat down. 'How fast did Billy drive you from Canary Wharf?'

Leo drew a deep breath and rubbed his face ruefully. 'If you must know, I've been working from home today.'

'Oh.'

An awkward silence developed, so I leaped straight in, before the niggling voices had time to put me off.

'Leo, I shouldn't have made up that story about Badger, but I didn't bail out of the gala because I was bored,' I said, all in a rush. 'I left because some psycho girlfriend of Rolf's mistook me for his new girlfriend and emptied a vase of flowers over me. I didn't know what to do, my whole outfit was wrecked, and I mean, no one's ever even thrown a *drink* over me before. I didn't want you to see me looking like that, and I didn't want to make a scene with Rolf in front of everyone, and I knew the place was swarming with paparazzi and I thought I'd show you all up if—'

Leo had been staring fixedly at his hands, but now he turned to me, his brow furrowing as the words spilled out. 'Wait, what? Tatiana?'

'Was that who it was? The girl he was texting on the way over? I guess it wasn't technically Rolf's fault either, but I realize I shouldn't have left without explaining. I'm so sorry if I offended your father, I know it was rude, but . . .'

'That is *not* the story I got.' Leo put his head in his hands, and when he looked up, he shook his head as if he couldn't quite believe it. 'I don't know where to start.'

'Well, you could start by getting Rolf to replace Jo's dress.' I suggested. 'Whatever they put in the flower food has destroyed the silk.'

'Of course. Of *course*. But what about you? How did you get home? Why didn't you *call* me? Why didn't you just come back to the box?'

'I wasn't sure what the royal protocol was about re-entering the presence of royalty in a see-through dress.'

'Forget that!' Leo actually looked annoyed. 'What's protocol got to do with anything? This is about someone assaulting you, and your evening being ruined — and *my* evening — because of —' He scrabbled in his jacket for his phone. 'I'm going to have it out with Rolf. He's lucky you're not suing him.'

'It's fine,' I started to say, but Leo wouldn't let me shrug it off.

'It's not fine. Really, it's *not* fine. I only agreed to go because I wanted to take you, and I thought you'd enjoy it, and, by the way, you'd still have looked beautiful even if you were drenched in pond water.' Leo paused, so I'd look up, and when I did, his intense gaze was fixed on my face. 'When I saw you from the door, the only person there taking the time to smell those amazing flowers instead of networking, I kicked myself for not canceling my meeting and getting an extra hour in the limo over with you.'

I melted inside at the way his eyes flashed when he said that. I'd never met a man who made compliments sound as sincere as Leo.

He rubbed his chin again, but this time he looked grim, as if he were already having the conversation with Rolf. Then he turned to me and took my hands in his; they were a lot warmer than mine.

'Is there any way you'd agree to see me again, to let me make this up to you?' he asked. 'Anywhere. You name it.'

'Jo did warn me this sort of thing tended to happen a lot with royalty,' I said, only half-joking. 'I'm not sure I'm up to fighting off furious would-be princesses every time we go out. I don't photograph well either.'

'It won't happen again,' he urged. 'Let me prove it. You choose. New York? Paris?'

'What?' I wasn't sure I'd heard him right. 'New York? For dinner?'

'Too far? Okay, then. Bowling? Cocktails? What was that dance class you said you and Jo do? Zumba? Can guys come along?'

'God, no!' I clapped my hands to my mouth. 'No one sees me Zumba and lives to tell the tale.'

Although now he mentioned Jo, something did occur to me. I shot him a sidelong look. 'Honestly anywhere?'

'Anywhere.'

'Well, Jo's doing a one-woman production of *Chicago* next week. It's off-off-off-West End.'

Leo frowned, trying to place where that might be. 'Islington?'

'No, it's in a room above a pub in Battersea. Not even the main room. If you come with me, you might just double the audience. But it would be doing me a favor, and it would make Jo very happy. She's given me a script with CLAP NOW and SHRIEK NOW marked on it.'

'I'm an excellent clapper,' said Leo. 'We had a clapping trainer when we were little, to make sure everyone could hear us applauding at public events.'

'Seriously?'

''Fraid so. Also a walking coach and a small-talk coach, so we'd always have something to say to people. Mom's idea. Not that useful at home, but it's come in handy at English house parties. Once you've done the weather and how bad the soccer team is, you're really fighting for air with some people.'

'Well, I've seen the script for this thing. There's a reason she's told me when to clap.'

Leo shrugged. 'You're obviously not familiar with the Royal Nironan Theater Company. They're obliged to perform one play a year in Esperanto. We're obliged to attend.'

'There'll be jazz hands,' I warned him.

'I can take jazz hands.' He gave me a quick demonstration of his own jazz hands, which were surprisingly jazzy for a man in a Savile Row suit.

'If you're really sure . . .'

'I am. It's a date.'

A date.

A DATE. WITH A PRINCE.

I opened my mouth to make a lame joke, but when I looked

up into Leo's handsome face, framed by the perfectly arranged gray scarf wrapped round his neck, my mind went blank. His face wasn't familiar because I'd seen it in magazines; it felt familiar because we just clicked together. Something in the way he was gazing at me, as if he was feeling the same giddy homecoming that I was, made the rest of the King's Road vanish around us, and I let the awkwardness of Friday night slide away as he pulled me closer to him.

*Chicago-a-go-go* might have been a one-woman play, but it had a full-time understudy, viz me.

Thanks to Jo's constant bellowing of 'When You're Good To Mama' and other highlights in the bath, bus, and bedroom, I could have performed the whole thing myself, plus most of the hoofing. Sometimes I did, miming along in the bathroom mirror when she had her tap on full in the sitting room. Callie Hamilton's builders could probably have acted as Jo's backing dancers, if she'd been practicing on the job as much as she had at home.

The pub theater didn't have a dressing room as such — Jo had commandeered the biggest loo cubicle to change in, and stuck a gold star on the door — so once she'd gone in to start plastering on her makeup, I hung around by the picnic tables outside the pub, waiting for Leo.

As usual, when I saw him appear round the corner, his coat collar turned up against the night air and his hair gleaming under the streetlights, I had to give myself a quick pinch.

'Hello.' Leo's smile lit up his face as he leaned forward to drop a kiss on my lips, resting his hand gently on my shoulder.

'Have you been out here long? You've got lovely pink cheeks.'

'What? Oh no, am I—?' I started, touching my face; that photo in the *Mail* had made me very mindful of my flushed cheeks, but Leo stopped me.

'No, pink like you've just been skiing. It's pretty.' He pretended to frown. 'Do I have to send you to my compliment-accepting coach?'

'You had one of those too?'

'Yes,' he said. 'My mother.' He cupped my face with his hand and rubbed his thumb against the hollow under my ear. 'First lesson for free: if I say you look gorgeous, just smile and say thank you, okay? Like you hear it a million times a day but still appreciate the effort. That's straight from the horse's mouth.'

I couldn't really argue with that. I didn't even tell him I couldn't ski. Which was a step forward.

Leo held the frosted glass door open for me, and I walked into the pub acutely conscious of the prince at my side, but no one seemed to notice I was with one. Leo blended in with the crowd of City workers in their suits and heels, except his coat was a tiny bit better cut, and his scarf was a tiny bit softer. And — to me, anyway — he had a polish you could see a mile off.

'What can I get you?' I asked, searching in my bag for my purse. I waved away his protests. 'No, please. This is my night. And don't even try to pay for the ticket — we're on the guest list. They're tickets money can't buy.'

'I'm flattered to be invited to the premiere.' Leo squinted at the wine list. 'I'll have a . . .'

I crossed my fingers and prayed he wouldn't order champagne or a fancy cocktail served in a whole melon or something that might blow my spare cash for the rest of the month.

*Or,* my dad's voice added, *a half-pint of shandy or some other girl's drink.*

'. . . a bottle of Beck's, please.'

I released my breath. Normal, straightforward, and quite cheap.

I ordered two Beck's, and when I'd paid we wandered upstairs to the theater area and waited. On our own.

'So,' said Leo, who didn't seem at all fazed by the empty seats around us, 'has Jo been acting for a long time? Is this her first solo performance?'

'She goes up to the Edinburgh Festival every year, usually with a stand-up routine about builders,' I said. 'It's very funny, but she had to change a few things for legal reasons. This is her first musical.'

As we chatted, a few people wandered in and sat down. I started to feel a little less tense about Jo's ticket sales. She'd put the thumbscrews of guilt on her entire Facebook friend list (roughly equivalent to the population of Southampton), but it was a Thursday night, and as she said herself, Thursday was the new Friday.

Leo didn't mention Rolf, and I thought it best to avoid the topic of the truckload of orchids clogging up our entrance hall. For me this time, not Jo. At five past eight, the lights dimmed. Well, the lights went off at the switch, and Leo extended an arm along the back of the seat. I leaned into it happily and held my breath.

Jo strode onto the stage in her silver trilby and fishnet tights, put one foot on a chair at a semi-gynecological angle, and opened her bright red mouth to start singing, but as she did there was a clatter and a blast of light from the landing as some latecomers shuffled into the empty seats.

I turned round to see who had come in, but the room was too dark to make anything out beyond the general shapes.

Jo didn't seem unduly fazed. 'The opening's the best bit, darlings, as the actress said to the bishop, so let's do that again.' She rammed her trilby back on, disappeared off the stage, and went through the booming intro and spotlight routine once more.

'Is that in the script?' Leo whispered, his breath tickling my ear.

'No. She practices her put-downs on plasterers,' I whispered back. My lips were close to the smooth, tanned skin on his neck and, as my senses sharpened in the darkness, my heart did a cartoon thump in my chest. I was surprised not to see an outline of it appear through my top.

Maybe Leo noticed, because he turned his head and our eyes locked. I didn't say anything, and he didn't either, but suddenly the distance between us felt very small and filled with a crackling tension. He'd been devastating in a dinner jacket in the Royal Opera House; but somehow here, in a Battersea pub, in his work suit, I wanted him even more.

And then Jo marched back on and started hoofing like her life depended on it, and we had to concentrate on not getting a size-seven silver tap shoe in the face.

*

Wisely, Jo had decided to condense her show into one hour rather than risk losing anyone to the interval bar, so *Chicago-a-go-go* whipped past at breakneck speed, much like Jo's black and blond wigs, which went on and off more times than a Piccadilly Circus traffic light.

When she exited the stage, high-kicking like a demon, there was a stunned silence, followed by the sound of loud clapping — coming from next to me. Leo hadn't been lying when he said he was a professional applauder. It sounded like a thunderstorm.

I started clapping too, albeit at a much more amateur volume; then I registered a sort of stereo loud clapping effect coming from somewhere behind us. That clapping was then augmented by a furious whistling, then whooping, then a sound that I didn't think humans could make.

I spun round and saw Rolf sitting in the back row surrounded by the usual gaggle of women with hair like Afghan hounds.

I spun back to Leo, who was now calling, 'Encore! Encore!' but not quite loud enough for Jo to hear.

'Why's Rolf here?' I hissed.

'He's here to support Jo.' Leo beamed a job-well-done beam. 'I told him he had some serious making up to do, to you and her, and that it had to be thoughtful. He said he'd bring along a theater producer friend and a reviewer — he knows lots of people in the entertainment industry whom Jo might find useful for the show.'

'Oh!' That *was* thoughtful. And the little room seemed to be packed too.

'Rolf's very sorry about what happened,' Leo went on. 'He wants to apologize in person, to both of you. Properly.'

I made a vague noise of appreciation, but my brain was throwing out car-crash scenes of Jo ramming her trilby over Rolf's head until he was wearing it like a necklace. Despite Rolf's orchids and apologies, Jo was still livid on my behalf and had already got anyone who knew Tatiana to defriend her on Facebook. Tatiana was now persona non grata all over West London and was apparently finding it very difficult to get into any of the clubs in Soho.

'Maybe not here, though?' I said, already hearing Jo's mighty roar in my head. 'Maybe . . . over a quiet drink somewhere else?'

A couple of hands clapped down on my shoulders from behind. 'It's Runaway Amy!' oozed a voice in my ear. 'And Jilted John!'

'For God's sake,' said Leo.

I spun round and tried to scramble back to the happy place I'd been a few moments ago.

'Amy,' said Rolf, taking my hands and fixing me with what I now realized was the trademark Wolfsburg family melting look. It was a bit less impressive now I'd seen his dad's version. 'Amy, Amy, Amy. I don't know what to say.'

'You keep saying sorry.'

'I'm more than sorry. I'm contrite. I'm repentant. I'm prostate at your feet with—'

'Prostrate,' I said. 'I don't want to know about your prostate, thanks.'

'Saucy,' replied Rolf, after a second's thought. 'I have told that bad Tatiana that she will never board the Rolf Express again, and she is so grateful that you're not pressing charges that she has—'

I saw the curtain twitch out of the corner of my eye. I really didn't want Jo to kick off at Rolf if there were useful theater contacts here. She could kick off at him later, when no one was reporting.

'Well, it's all water under the bridge now,' I babbled. 'Thanks for coming! How many parties have you got to fit in tonight? Don't want to keep you. I'll tell Jo you were here if you want to dash off.'

'Oh, there's nothing until about midnight-ish,' said Rolf, to my dismay. 'Thought we'd have a bite to eat here, then mosey up to Knightsbridge.'

'But this is just a pub!' I exclaimed. 'Pub food! It's all chips and peas and — and I don't even know if it's organic.'

The curtain parted and Jo's face peeked round. When she clocked Rolf, her eyes darkened and she yanked the curtain right back and marched across the stage, wearing her fishnets and tap pants with an old Downe House hockey shirt over the top. Since the stage was only about three meters long, she was right up behind him before I had time to say, 'Brace yourself.'

'You've got a nerve!' she started, but Rolf was right on it.

'You. Were. Magnificent!' he yelled, then turned to the blondes. 'Sukey! Saffy! Over here! And where's Sadie?'

Sadie. Sukey. Saffy. I tried to tell them apart, and failed.

'Sukey's from the *Evening Standard*,' Rolf explained, as one blonde got a phone out of her bag and another blonde started taking photos of Jo. 'Saffy's her snapper. She's going to splash you in the diary feature, aren't you? She's going to say I was here, and Leo was, and you'll be sold out.'

'And Sadie?' I asked with a raised eyebrow.

'A dear friend from school,' Rolf replied, hurt.

'How can you dare to — hang on, let me take my hockey shirt off!' Jo glanced back and forth from me and Leo, to Rolf, to the blond *Evening Standard* pair.

'And these are for you!' Rolf went on, thrusting a gigantic bunch of flowers into Jo's arms. I had no idea where they'd come from; they were big enough to have needed their own ticket.

Leo shot me a look. It started hopeful, but when he saw me unable to control my amazement, it turned to amusement too.

'Amy and I are going downstairs to the bar,' said Leo. 'Join us when you're done so we can buy you a drink!'

And while Jo was busy being photographed with her flowers, he swept me out and down to the bar, where it turned out there was a bottle of champagne on ice for us.

The rest of the evening was a bit blurry. In a good way.

Jo, Sukey the writer, Saffy the snapper, and Sadie the random reality TV star (and dear old school friend) got on like a house on fire. Once they'd dispensed with the small matter of Sukey's column and the burger Sadie had to eat under the table in case anyone saw her, all four bundled into a taxi to some nightclub, with Rolf in the middle like a playboy Buddha, leaving me to my bar supper with Leo.

I rubbed a clear spot on the steamed-up pub window with my napkin; as the taxi pulled away, it was suddenly lit up by a barrage of flashes, photographers running alongside it. A shiver ran across my arms.

Leo didn't even break off from the steak and ale pie that the waiter had just put in front of him. 'I thought I saw some photographers earlier,' he said, more to himself than me.

'For who?'

'Rolf. And Sadie, probably, if her press people are on the ball.'

'Does that happen everywhere you and Rolf go?' I asked, thinking of the barricaded photographers outside the Royal Opera House. I'd thought they were just there because it was a big event.

'Pretty much.'

'Will they still be there when we leave?'

'Maybe. Depends whether they got enough good pics of Rolf falling into the cab.' He looked up, and saw my anxious face. 'Joke. Look, it's because of Mom — she's in the news in the US at the moment because she's spearheading this campaign to get teenage girls to respect their inner princesses or something, so it'll be freelancers trying to get photos of Rolf to sell to the US gossip rags. And we have a big bicentenary coming up too. No one's really interested in Uncle Pavlos because he and his family never do much, so they go after Rolf.'

I couldn't help thinking about the YoungHot&Royal website that Jo and I had found. We were both pretending not to look at it, but it was like having an open box of chocolates in the house. I wasn't supposed to know, for instance, that Rolf had slipped down a place in the eligible list since he'd been spotted going to a trichological clinic in Harley Street. But I did.

'Don't think about it,' he said, tucking into his steak and ale pie. 'I don't.'

Even so, when we did leave — after I'd paid the bill; I insisted — I noticed Leo glance round quickly before we pushed our way out of the pub, and pull up his scarf.

There was someone who looked a bit like a photographer hanging around outside on the benches. He was on his phone, and took no notice of us as we walked down the deserted residential road. I breathed out, quietly, so Leo wouldn't notice, but my heart was hammering — and not just because, at that moment, Leo slipped his arm around my waist and pulled me nearer.

Ten thirty was always the awkward bit of a London evening. A bit too soon to go home, but not really enough time to go on somewhere else.

Our footsteps echoed in the quiet, and I fidgeted at the silence. With every step, we were nearer the main road, and taxis, and going our separate ways. Or not going our separate ways, if you know what I mean.

'This is going to sound a bit Rolf,' said Leo, pausing as if he could read my mind. 'But I don't really want to go home yet.'

'Me neither. But I don't want to go to Tramp, thanks,' I added quickly, in case he thought I was angling to follow Jo and the others.

'Wild horses would not drag me to Tramp,' said Leo solemnly. 'Not even with you.'

I shivered, but not because I was cold. 'It's such a gorgeous evening,' I said. 'Look at those stars. So clear. It's almost like we're not in London.'

'I wish we weren't in London.' Leo gazed up into the sky, then looked back down at me. 'I know I should say goodnight and put you into a cab,' he said. 'But I don't really want to.'

'I know. They're ridiculously expensive at this time of night,' I started to gabble, then made myself stop. I had to learn how to be a bit more cool and calm. Now would be a good time to start.

We stood there for a very long, quiet second; then he murmured, 'Can I kiss you?'

I nodded twice, and very slowly Leo leaned forward, tilted his head to one side and closed his eyes.

I closed mine and held my breath, and suddenly his lips were on mine, just touching at first, then kissing, harder. Sparks flew all round my body as his hands slid under my coat and around my waist, stroking and pulling me closer.

And my hands, I have to confess here, were inside his coat too, but he didn't flinch at my chilly fingers against his warm body.

'Amy.' Leo's voice sounded thick in his throat. 'Can I take you home?'

I didn't say anything, but I didn't need to. I think my kisses were saying everything I needed to say, and quite a bit more than that.

# CHAPTER FIFTEEN

My dad's birthday was one of the non-negotiable home visits of my year, along with Mum's birthday, my birthday, Hadley Green Agricultural Show, and Christmas.

This year, I'd bought my train tickets up to Yorkshire weeks in advance to get the cheapest fare. Mum and Dad lived in a small town in the middle of nowhere, and the combination of trains and buses required to get there made it only slightly less of a trek than walking. But not going, as I tried to explain to Jo when she found me at the laptop at 5:30 a.m. grabbing the discounted tickets, wasn't an option.

For one thing, birthdays allowed my mum to bake for a reason other than to off-load her nervous tension. My parents dealt with stress in different ways: Dad dug for hours on his allotment, and Mum turned into a one-woman all-night bakery. She'd always been a keen home cook, testing out recipes for the canteen on us in scaled-down portions; but since she'd given up her job at the school, she baked so much that our house now smelled permanently of fairy cakes.

I mean, it was lovely — much better than the house smelling of cats, like Di Overend's did — but all the cake had to go somewhere, and most of it was going into Mum and Dad. Mum was now at least two or three times the size she'd been when I lived at home, and I'd had to persuade her to set up a cake stall at the hospital, just to give Dad's pancreas a break.

But the main reason I had to go home, the reason we all knew but never actually said, was that Dad's birthday was two days before Kelly's, and me being there for his party meant that Mum and Dad could celebrate Kelly's birthday too, but without any of us mentioning her at all.

It was amazing what complicated emotional knots my family could tie themselves into without talking about anything. We were the emotional equivalent of Jo's mime classes.

Typically, this year Dad's birthday party landed on a weekend filled with all sorts of London delights. Jo was on the VIP list at three different clubs, Mrs Mainwaring had invited us both to a sherry party in her flat for the first time ever, Dickon had an opening (although we were privately a bit dubious about that one), and Leo had tickets to a completely sold-out gig at the Royal Albert Hall that was so popular the tickets were allocated by lottery.

He'd revealed this surprise to me over hot soup and take-away coffee in his garden, where I'd spent the morning planting Souvenir du Président Lincoln rosebushes, delivered straight from the French rose specialist I'd tracked down online.

'I've got a surprise for you,' he said when we were huddled up on the bench together with our minestrone. 'Call it a late Valentine's present.'

'But you've already given me a Valentine's present,' I protested. 'I'm not one of those girls who has to be constantly plied with gifts, you know. Though obviously they're much appreciated.'

I'd got back to Leominster Place after the most eye-opening night of my entire life in Leo's antique sleigh bed to find he'd had the flat filled with flowers — not forced scentless blooms, but proper garden-grown roses, with delicious fragrance that was almost edible, lilac Blue Moons and blushing White Mischief interlaced with china-blue hyacinths and flag irises and tangles of greenery.

'They were just flowers. Coals to Newcastle, I know. Here. And don't tell me you don't like the bands playing — I checked out your iPod.' He reached into his jacket pocket and pulled out the tickets: front-row stalls.

I boggled. 'Seriously? Leo, I know for a fact that this is sold out because Jo failed to get tickets when they went on sale *last year*. How did you get these?'

He grinned, and pulled a piece off his bread roll. 'Magic. Don't ask.'

'I won't.' I grinned back. Maybe dating a prince had unexpected advantages. But then I looked at the tickets again, and my heart sank. 'Oh . . . these are for Saturday night.'

'Are you seeing someone else?'

'No. Well, yes. My dad. It's his birthday.' I felt awful. 'I'm going to Yorkshire for the weekend. I don't think I'll be able to get back in time.'

Leo's face fell. 'You can't leave a little early?'

'It's not quite as easy as that — it takes two trains and a bus to get there. And I can't leave until all the sandwiches have been eaten and everyone's checked me over to make sure

I haven't started talking like a southerner and eating crème fraîche. You know what family dos are like. Well,' I added, 'maybe you don't.'

'What if I came with you?' Leo beamed as if he'd just had a great idea. 'Hey, let's do that! I'll drive you there and back — we can do it in a day. I've never been to Yorkshire. It'll be a nice day out.'

I choked on my soup.

'What?' Leo frowned. 'Don't you want me to come?'

'No, it's just . . .' I was going to say, '*I can't even imagine you in my parents' house*' but changed it to, '. . . this soup is very hot. And it's a long way.'

I know. Not great. But it was the first thing that came into my head. The thought of Leo and his gorgeous princely glow in my parents' cramped front room made me feel panicky. They'd need at least six months' notice — (a) for my dad to rebuild the whole house, and (b) for my mum to have enough therapy to deal with the stress of hosting someone who wasn't an immediate member of our family.

I regretted it as soon as I'd said it, because Leo looked crest-fallen. Admittedly, sitting on a park bench in his winter coat, with a gray cashmere beanie over his expensively tousled hair — and, okay, his nose red with the cold — he looked rather more normal than he did in black tie, but even so. My last boyfriend had been an apprentice scaffolder.

'I don't see what the problem is,' he said, hurt. 'Don't you want them to meet me? Unless . . . you haven't told them you've got a boyfriend? Is that it?'

Ironically, that *was* it. 'Not in so many words.'

Leo's mouth dropped open. 'What? You haven't—'

I hurried to explain. 'It's just that my parents tend to give anyone I bring home the third degree. Especially my dad. They're quite protective of me. They worry.' I was editing a lot here. 'It's nothing to do with you, they're just a bit mad. Sometimes you've just got to . . . you know, humor your folks.'

'Listen, they can't be more mad than my family.' Leo stretched out his long legs, crossing them at the ankle to reveal a flash of discreet black sock. 'You know I said Mom was involved in this campaign to' — he employed heavy air quotes — 'make every American girl an everyday princess? Well, Mom made me and Sofia fly back to Nirona for the afternoon on Monday, just so we could be in a photo shoot for *Vanity Fair*, talking about how important a down-to-earth upbringing was and how we'd always eaten our greens, et cetera, et cetera. Sofia was *not* happy. She kept following the journalist around, telling her that actually she wasn't "normal" at all, she'd been a member of MENSA since she was twelve.'

'No Rolf?'

'Definitely no Rolf.' He twisted his lips in wry amusement. 'And of course Mom couldn't let rip at Sofia while the journalist was there, but she more than made up for it when the woman left. I thought something was going to get broken. The windows, maybe. That's not in the American Princess Plan, let me tell you.'

I smiled and blew on my soup. Then stopped myself. That wasn't good etiquette. Or was it? I'd have to check.

Leo sighed and dipped his bread in the soup. 'So you're telling me I'm going to have to take Rolf?'

'Well, that'd be perfect for your mother's big campaign! What could be more mannerly than taking your own brother to a rock concert! There's bound to be a photographer there,' I added.

'I'm not going anywhere with Rolf if it has a backstage area,' said Leo. 'No way, José.'

'Take Jo, then. Take Jo *and* Rolf, and you can teach him how to show a lady a good time.' That wasn't what I meant. I spluttered on my soup. 'I don't mean, like that! I mean—'

'I know what you mean.' Leo shook his head. 'But I don't really want to go without you.'

I thought for a moment that he was trying to get me to cancel on my parents, but I shook my head. I wasn't going to do that. And I couldn't bend the laws of time and physics to do both.

'Another time,' I said. 'I promise.'

It was only a few weeks since I'd been home to Yorkshire for the annual unofficial mince-pie eating record attempt, but as usual my parents acted as if I'd been on some round-the-world voyage, not digging a few gardens at the other end of the East Coast rail line.

'You're skin and bones!' wailed my mum, before I'd even heaved my rucksack over the threshold. Badger lurked behind me, letting Mum's attention wash over me first before it could turn to him and his 'hygiene issues.' 'Aren't you eating? Are you too busy to eat?'

'You're looking worn out, Amy,' added my dad. 'Have you got one of those colds going round? They say they spread round the Underground network like wildfire. Germ cocktails. Mutating all the time.'

'Oh, Stan, be quiet. Amy's not *ill*,' Mum corrected him, stroking my arm. 'When she's ill, she looks more *gray*. She looks *peaky*, not ill. Underfed, if you ask me.'

Dad made a snorting noise, because only remote tribes in Tonga where women weigh more than horses would consider me underfed.

'Happy birthday, Dad,' I said, before he could start arguing with my mum about my body fat. 'I've got you a present.'

'You shouldn't have,' he said automatically, but I could tell he was pleased. 'Is it seeds? Or bulbs?' He eyed my rucksack hopefully, then spotted Badger behind me. 'Oh. I see you've brought the demon dog with you.'

'Yes,' I replied. 'He's the reason I had a table seat to myself on the train. Wouldn't travel without him.'

'I've just hoovered,' said Mum. 'I hope there won't be a repeat of last time.'

'Oh, come on, Mum, it's not Buckingham Palace!' I said, and immediately wished I hadn't.

My mum and dad's end-of-terrace house was nice enough by Rothery standards — Victorian, with bay windows, a narrow kitchen, and a faint air of gloom that wasn't helped by the noise of the railway line running behind the street. But if you went through the house into the back garden, it was like stepping into a different world. Dad had crammed every inch of available soil with an ever-changing patchwork of plants and shrubs, the pride of which was a vine that he'd actually coaxed grapes from during the very hot summer of 2010. Thankfully, not enough to make any wine.

We'd moved to Rothery ten years ago, after Kelly's Shame had forced my parents to downsize from our lovely thatched cottage in the much nicer village of Hadley Green, with a huge garden that was the star turn on the Neighborhood in Bloom poke 'n' preen. Kelly and I'd had swings on the apple tree and rabbits in the garden, and Dad had presided over a huge vegetable patch that was so impressive they eventually made him a judge at the local show because they ran out of categories for him to win.

Now Dad had an allotment on the other side of town and blagged exotic seeds off me from a contact I had at the agricultural college. Badger hadn't exactly covered himself in glory last time Dad took him up there at New Year's, although he *had* covered himself in soil and pigeon droppings from the pigeon loft next door.

'Don't be mean to Badger,' I said. 'He's been looking forward to seeing you.'

'I'm only going on his past record,' said Mum darkly.

'You're okay, aren't you, lad?' Dad gave him a roughhousing stroke, and Badger barked, rolled onto his back, and, I think, made a terrible smell.

'Go through,' said Mum, waving us down the hall toward the sitting room. I waved too, to dissipate Badger's indiscretion. 'I've put a few things out in case you were hungry on the train, just to carry you on till teatime . . .'

I edged past her — no small feat, given the narrowness of the hall and the width of my mother — and went into the conservatory. Pale Yorkshire sunlight filtered bravely through the net curtains, falling on the groaning table of plates and glass cake stands waiting for me.

Chocolate birthday cake. Thick slices of fruitcake. Cookies, various. Brownies in a tumbling nutty pile. Five types of sandwiches cut into tiny quarters with the crusts trimmed off. I blinked. Had I got it wrong? Was this a surprise birthday party for our whole family?

I glanced at Dad.

'Your sister's card arrived yesterday,' he whispered. 'It set her off. Thought she might be coming.'

A familiar weight draped itself on my shoulders like a moody cat. Kelly sent cards every birthday and Christmas, but never said where she was or when she'd be back. It didn't stop Mum pulling out all the stops, just in case. 'And is she? Did she put a letter in this time? Was there a postmark?'

Dad shook his head sadly. 'No. Nothing we could make out. Just "Happy birthday, lots of love from Kelly. Kiss kiss." That's one more kiss than last year.'

On the table between all the cakes were five cards — mine from the Kew Gardens collection, one 'to my dear husband,' one 'to my dear brother,' one 'to a special neighbor' (well done, Di Overend), and a big sparkly card that dwarfed the others.

A white-hot ribbon of anger ran through me. If Kelly could spend ten minutes writing a simple note in these cards, instead of just picking the most expensive one in the shop, then Mum might not be in such a state. It was almost worse than not sending one at all. It just got their hopes up three times a year — as usual, it was more about Kelly salving her conscience than helping them with the chaos she'd left behind.

Over the past few years I'd tried to track her down myself via Facebook and friends, but Kelly had covered her tracks pretty well for someone with that big a mouth. She obviously didn't want to be found. I was only sixteen when it all happened, and I hadn't properly understood the full extent of Kelly's stupidity then; but now, looking at Mum comfort-eating herself into XL smocks and Dad lost in enforced early retirement from a job he'd loved really made me realize that it wasn't Kelly who'd been punished for what she'd done — it had been us.

She, on the other hand, had the luxury of starting over.

'How hard is it for her to pick up the phone?' I hissed. 'I mean, it's what? Nine years now, nearly? Can't she get over herself and *ring*?'

Dad suddenly looked older than sixty-five. His mustache, once the badge of his bank-managerial respectability, drooped. 'It's hard, love. I suppose she'll come back in her own time. We all said things we regretted—'

'For very good reasons!' I snapped. 'I didn't get to say enough at the time!'

'Amy! It's not like you to be sharp.' He seemed genuinely shocked.

'Sorry, Dad, but I just get so—'

'Now, then. What can I get you?' Mum bustled in, piling another small wall of millionaire's shortbread onto the cake stand, and Dad and I straightened up like guilty schoolkids.

'This cake is amazing, Mum,' I said, reaching for the nearest plate. 'So light!'

A shy smile spread across her round face, making her blue eyes shine. Mum was still a good-looking woman despite her extra weight, and that seemed to make her even more self-conscious about her billowing curves. She'd been a local beauty for years and years; but now she felt everyone was looking at her with even more reproach when she went out. Looking and whispering. Mum rarely left the house because of her paranoia; the hospital cake-stall lady had to come and collect her bootful of light-as-a-feather sponge cakes.

'You'll have to take some back for Ted,' she replied. 'And Jo.'

'And that new boyfriend of yours,' added Dad through a mouthful of parkin.

'What?'

I was very glad Leo wasn't around to see the crumbs spraying as he said it, or the murderous expression on Mum's face.

'Stan!'

I looked between my gleeful dad and my mortified-but-at-the-same-time-agog mum and realized that not even the British tabloid press could match the Rothery grapevine when it came to the spreading of hot and potentially scandalous news.

My plan to break the news of my new boyfriend to my parents in a sensitive fashion we could all look back on with affection in years to come had been comprehensively scuppered, it seemed, by the intervention of the friendly neighborhood gossipmonger, Di Overend (who else?) — in this case, via her henpecked Other Half, Barry.

Dad had been the unlikely bearer of the tidings to my mother only that morning.

'I had Di Overend's Barry on at me today up at the allotment,' he explained, while I tried to reshuffle my prepared speech about Leo into something that might fit whatever they'd heard. 'Asking why on earth you'd pay good money to go to a boxing match when the lads round here put on a good show for free most weekends.'

'She saw you in the hairdresser's,' Mum explained. 'In *Hello!* magazine.'

'With a lad who called himself a prince.'

'At a boxing match!' Mum added. 'You don't even *like* boxing. I didn't think it could be you until Di said she recognized your friend Jo from that washing-up liquid advert.'

My head flicked back and forth between the two. This was not how I'd wanted to lead into it. For a start, I'd have to explain why I'd been at a charity boxing match in the first place.

Dad gave me a beady look. 'Well, come on. What nonsense is all this?'

Fine. The potted version was this. Whatever Rolf had done or said to Jo while he and the Three Blondes were sinking fancy cocktails in Tramp after *Chicago-a-go-go*, it seemed to have succeeded where boxes of cutaway knickers and several jeroboams of champagne had failed, because she'd agreed to go with me and Leo to watch him in a charity boxing match, fighting a very pretty former boy-band singer in aid of abandoned potbellied pigs.

Hostilities hadn't been totally called off – Jo still referred to Rolf as the Frog Prince, and claimed that she'd only agreed to go so that there'd be some more glamorous paparazzi shots of her on file than the blurry ones of her leaving the pub – but I could tell from the odd thing she'd said that Rolf had managed to reveal a more thoughtful side. I hoped so, anyway. He didn't seem the type to be that good at hypnotism.

Anyway, to cut a long story short, Jo had insisted that she call in all sorts of favors from various salon-owning clients, and we spent an entire day being waxed, tanned, styled, buffed, tanned again, professionally made-up, literally sewn into plunging dresses, and then deposited at a London hotel where about three thousand paparazzi went berserk thinking we were two of the famous guests.

Much to our amazement, Rolf won his bout (possibly because his unusually waxed body hair distracted his opponent); he then donated his gold medallion to the charity, Jo kissed him (I'm condensing here, you understand), and in the car on the way home, Leo gave me a bracelet made up of tiny white and yellow diamonds set like a daisy chain — 'so next time I take you to a gala, you'll have your own heirlooms for the dress code.'

If I made that sound like a normal night out, it wasn't. It really wasn't. But even if it felt like a hysterical dream, I woke up the next morning with a bad headache, a diamond bracelet on my wrist, and a snoring prince, so it must have been real.

'So?' Dad repeated. 'Have you got a boyfriend who calls himself a prince or not?'

They were both staring at me. Mum had the teapot poised, as if my next answer would release the flow of tea. Instead of looking thrilled and excited, they both looked worried.

'Um, yes,' I said. 'I have. His name is Leo. I was going to tell you today, actually.'

'And he's a prince?'

Well. This was blowing Kelly's nonappearance off the agenda.

'Yes,' I said. 'He is a prince.'

Mum's bosom heaved up and down anxiously. 'Are you sure, love?'

'What do you mean, *am I sure*?'

'We've seen it on television,' Dad informed me. 'These con men who claim to be Arab princes and take advantage of much cleverer folk than you. It's nothing to be ashamed of, Amy. Did he say where he was a prince of? Di Overend couldn't remember.'

My face went hot. 'It's a principality called Nirona. It's an island off the coast of Italy. Very famous for lemons and celebrity honeymoons.'

Mum seemed more impressed by that. 'Ooh, now, didn't Betty and Ike Thwaites stop off there on their anniversary cruise?'

'Probably,' I said. 'There's a marina. It's very exclusive. People who can't get a berth on Nirona have to go to Monaco instead.'

Dad put down his cake and spoke his mind. 'He hasn't asked you for any money, has he?'

'Dad!'

'Stan!'

'Well, we all know how easy it is to be led astray by folk who seem to have lots of cash.'

Mum, Dad, and I flinched at exactly the same instant.

I thought about showing them my diamond daisy chain,

but decided that Dad would have it off me and down to the local jeweler for carbon testing before I could say Cartier. And I didn't have to defend Leo to them.

'He's not like that,' I said hotly. 'He's got a job in the City, he earns his own salary even though he doesn't have to. He didn't even tell me he was a prince for ages, because he didn't want me to judge him!'

'Didn't tell you for ages,' said Dad, all but tapping his chin with a finger. 'Hmm.'

'I'm sure Amy wouldn't have got that wrong,' said Mum. She helped herself to another fairy cake, delicately peeling off the starry paper wrapper. 'Would you?' The cake vanished into her pink mouth in one bite.

'Of course I haven't got it wrong.'

'And how long have you been seeing him?'

'Since just after New Year's.'

'But it's only the end of February now!' Mum looked shocked. 'That's no time!'

'It's long enough for me to know that . . .'

I had to raise my voice because the lunchtime train was going past the back window. We had to wait until it stopped. I wondered how they put up with it; our old cottage had been so quiet you could hear birdsong during the day, if Kelly wasn't singing or having an argument with someone on the downstairs phone.

'Long enough for me to know he's a nice guy,' I finished, and took a slice of cake. I put it all in my mouth so I wouldn't have to answer any questions for a few seconds.

Mum and Dad exchanged glances.

'Di said she barely recognized you in the photos,' said Mum. 'She said you looked like a right glamour puss.'

That cheered me up a bit. 'Good. I was picking false eye-lashes off for days,' I said crumbily.

I was explaining the outlandish concept of false eyelashes to my dad when Badger's ears pricked up and he scuttled toward the front door. Ten seconds later, there was a knock. Three loud knocks.

My heart broke at the hopeful expression that transformed Mum's face. She hoped it was Kelly. It was so obvious.

It would also be typical of Kelly to crash my special moment too, I thought waspishly.

Dad leaped to his feet. 'I'll go,' he said.

'It's probably Di Overend,' I said to Mum as her eyes followed him down the hall, 'come to show us that copy of *Hello!* Was it really a nice photo of me?'

'Apparently so. But you take a lovely photo, Amy. You always have done.' Mum smiled and offered me the scones. 'Go on, have another. It's your dad's jam!'

Our ears were straining to catch the conversation in the hall, but it didn't sound like Di. I heard Dad say, 'Come on through' in an overly polite tone that gave me a horrible flash-back to when the police had first come round looking for Kelly, and then, all at once it was my worst nightmare.

I don't know who looked more shocked, me, Mum, or Dad. I could see the three of us in the mirror over the fireplace, slack-jawed. It wasn't a good look for any of us.

Leo, though, looked perfectly relaxed in his jeans and cash-mere hoodie under a peacoat. He looked more like a Hollywood actor than a prince. Although that didn't make him look any less incongruous in my parents' conservatory.

'I hope you don't mind me dropping in,' he said with his most charming smile. 'I tried to call Amy, but her phone was off. Oh, is that Battenberg cake? That's my absolute favorite.'

I think that was the point where Mum fell in love with him.

Once I'd got over my initial shock at Leo's unannounced arrival (and that took a couple of cups of tea), I had time to marvel at how thoughtfully he won over both my parents.

He chatted to Dad about the rose garden, and laughed at his jokes — most of which were about me (thanks, Dad). He ate Mum's cake. Not just the Battenberg, but a bit of everything. And then he asked for some to take home. Actually, maybe that was the moment Mum tipped over from love into outright adoration.

The tin lid was put on everything when Di Overend *did* knock on the front door to ask if we knew what was going on with the helicopter parked on the cricket pitch at the other end of our road.

'I thought Pam might have been taken badly.' She was craning her neck to see if we had guests. 'Or maybe you were on one of those reality shows where they reunite you with a long-lost relative,' she added darkly.

'None of the above, Mrs Overend,' I said, closing the door. 'We don't know anything about the helicopter.'

'I saw you in *Hello!*' she shouted through the letter box. 'It's amazing what they can do with Photoshop these days, isn't it?'

But while I was really happy that Leo and my parents were forming their own mutual appreciation society in the conservatory, I was struggling with some shabby feelings I wasn't proud of.

I was suddenly conscious of how small the house was, crammed with all our things from the old cottage. The horse brasses that had looked so right on the half-timbers of the cottage looked tacky here, and you could barely walk down the hall without knocking Mum's china ornaments off the shelves.

As Leo relaxed on the creaky wicker chair from the old music room where the piano had been, I wanted to explain *why* my gentle dad and lovely mum were living in these crowded, ugly rooms, *why* they'd quietly sacrificed all the things they loved and moved to this place where they didn't know anyone.

But I didn't want to think about that, and I definitely didn't want to tell him about Kelly, so it curdled into a churlish irritation that he'd sprung this on me — a romantic millionaire's gesture that made me feel defensive, not swept off my feet.

I spent longer than I needed to washing up the teacups. I was so long that Leo came to find me, giving me a sudden panic that he'd want to use the loo, which was full of old copies of *Private Eye*; I'd had no idea till I moved to London that reading matter in the loo was only just worse than keeping a pig in the backyard.

'There you are,' he said, slipping his arms round my waist. 'Come through and talk — your mum's telling a hilarious story about how you won your first vegetable competition with a squash nearly as big as you.'

'Not the marrow story,' I groaned.

'I've just been promised the story about you and the swing.' He jiggled his eyebrows. 'But apparently you have to be there for that.'

I moved away and grabbed a tea towel.

'What's up? Don't you think I'm ready to hear the swing story?'

I turned round and dropped my voice so my parents wouldn't hear. 'How did you get my address?' I hissed.

'Jo gave it to me.' Leo seemed surprised at my wild eyes. 'Why? Is it a state secret? Are you in a witness protection program?'

'No, I just think my parents would have liked some time to . . . prepare.' I rolled my eyes at the stacks of seed trays on the stairs and the piles of newspaper ready to go to the allotment.

'Why? I don't need a red carpet,' said Leo.

'*They* might like to roll one out, though,' I snapped back. 'Round here you're not supposed to drop in on folk without written warning.'

I wished I hadn't said that. I sounded like a right pious snob. I'd only let it slip because I was cross with myself.

Leo shoved his hands into his blond hair. 'I thought it'd be a nice surprise, me coming to pick you up for this concert — it wasn't meant to be a big "meet the parents" production, just—'

'Leo, it's a big deal for my parents.' I twisted the tea towel between my fingers. 'It would be a big deal even if you weren't who you are.'

'You told them about the whole . . . prince thing?'

I boggled at him. 'Flying visits in Rothery don't generally involve an actual helicopter.'

'Well, they seem fine about it to me.' Leo fixed me with one of his piercing looks. Sometimes he let me get away with a bit of self-deprecation, but this wasn't one of those times. 'It's only you who's in a state of nervous tension. I hope this isn't some kind of weird inverse snobbery at work?'

'Absolutely not,' I said hotly. Although the kitchen did suddenly feel quite small with both me and Leo in it. And Badger's paw prints all over the lino. And Dad's wellies by the door.

'Listen.' Leo pulled me closer so our noses were touching, and whispered in my ear, 'I don't like people judging *me* on the basis of where I live, so I don't judge anyone on theirs. And since you obviously can't see it, this place is fascinating. Your dad's been showing me his old posters for the village sports.'

'It's not as nice as our old house,' I started to say.

'Then that must have been even more fascinating. Look. We've got three more plates of cake to eat, and two more really embarrassing stories to hear, and then I'm taking you back to London in my helicopter, if that's all right? Or would you rather get the train?'

'Ooh, I heard that!' Mum was at the kitchen door, beaming all over her round face as if she were at the best party ever. 'Room for a small one?'

That was the first joke I'd heard her crack in months and months, and for that I was more grateful to Leo than he knew.

# CHAPTER SIXTEEN

Leo invited me to stay with him in his palace in the same relaxed way that he brought up most things that, even after several weeks of official dating, I still couldn't say aloud without pulling a satirical face. Things like 'an informal ball' or 'your mother, the supermodel.'

March had breathed some welcome spring warmth into the London air, and as my work diary ticked over into April I could smell the summer coming on the fresh leaves. Leo and I were sitting in the rose garden eating lunch — homemade egg and cress sandwiches and coffee, as it was my turn and funds were low. Now that all the roses were planted, uncurling their roots into the soft earth and preparing for the summer's exertions, Leo was musing aloud about what might be missing from the display.

'It needs something else,' he said. 'Something . . . central.'

'What? Are my meticulously sourced and historically accurate rosebushes not enough?' I half-turned to him on the bench, and he leaned back and slipped an arm round my shoulders, kissing me on the temple as he pretended to inspect the view with a critical eye.

I loved these picnics with Leo. I didn't know how long it took him to get from the City to Kensington at lunchtime, or what he told his PA he was doing in his long lunch break, but at least twice a week he met me in the garden with a takeout bag from Pret or M&S, and we just sat and talked. And talked and talked. He explained how his job worked, as a fund manager for a large charitable-investment portfolio, and I rambled on about wildflowers and how even the commonest meadow-mix daisies and poppies kept the bees going and the ecosystem ticking over.

The food was ordinary, but the setting wasn't: it was like having a table for two in the most beautiful garden restaurant in London, especially now that the yellow daffodils and crimson tulips that had sent pops of color in every direction were giving way to frothy blossom in the cherry trees, like clouds of delicately scented champagne over our heads.

'I think it needs a birdbath,' he said, regarding the central bed thoughtfully. 'Or a fountain. Something tall, in the middle.'

'There's nothing about that on the plans!' I reached into my bag for the copy of the original plans, but Leo put a hand on my arm.

'I know.' He smiled mysteriously. 'I just wanted to put our own mark on it. Something old and new. I thought you could come and choose something from the gardens at home.'

'From the . . .' I had to brace myself to say it. 'Palace gardens?'

'Yup. They won't miss a small one. I asked Granddad, and he said I could ship anything that wasn't cemented in.'

That would be Leo's grandfather, the Sovereign Prince Wilhelm. Another thing I found quite hard to say with a casual expression.

'Did I tell you he used to live here, in the fifties?' Leo went on, jerking his head backward to his own house. 'Keeps trying to tell me about all the various hijinks he got up to in my house.' He held up his hands, as if trying to keep back some particularly hair-curling specters from the past. 'Some of it makes Rolf look like he isn't even trying.'

I bit into my sandwich with a smile. 'I think it's fine to have scandalous grandparents. What sort of thing did he get up to?'

'Oh, the usual — wine, women, song. Racehorses. Film stars. Escapades with various naughty duchesses.'

That was not the usual in my family. They were more wine, women, and whippets.

'What sorts of escapades?' I asked, letting my imagination wander. 'Are we talking undone bow ties and white gloves discarded over the grand piano?'

'Ha! Exactly. According to Granddad, there are a couple of very famous movie party scenes that were directly based on parties he threw in the palace. Ask him about them — he'd love to tell you.'

'I will,' I said, boggling inwardly at the thought. If Boris was Rolf to the power ten, what would his father be like?

'It was really because of Granddad that Nirona was so fashionable in the fifties,' Leo went on, as if he were discussing the founding of the local Neighborhood Watch. 'Granny had a few Hollywood actress friends, and he let them film on the island for very advantageous rates, then quickly built some ritzy hotels for them all to stay in and hustled them down to the casino to blow their fees. No one really knew where the island was, so the press couldn't interfere with the merry-making, and before you know it, Bob Hope's your uncle. And Bob Mitchum. And Bob Redford.'

'Wow.'

'Well, sort of wow. It all got a bit hot in the eighties when helicopters and telephoto lenses came in — that's why Uncle Pavlos has been building his reputation as a very, very responsible and reliable pair of hands. Poor sod. He likes being photographed about as much as you do.'

'Well, I think that's totally understandable.'

Jo and I had already had our paparazzi photos posted on YoungHot&Royal.com, and neither of us came out of it well (although I had found out that Jo was actually the *Honorable* Josephine Frenais de Vere, something she'd kept very quiet until now).

Leo finished his sandwich and looked at the lunch box. 'These sandwiches are very moreish,' he said. 'Can I have another?'

'Yes,' I said absently, still processing all the glamour dismissed in a few sentences. 'It's Mum's secret recipe. A touch of English mustard.'

'Oh, your mother. Did she tell you she'd sent me my own box of Battenberg? She should have her own cooking show.' He bit into the sandwich with relish. 'So, how about it? Are you doing anything this weekend?'

'You want to go back to Rothery for more cake?'

'No, I mean back to mine. Unless you've got plans?'

I swiveled on the bench and gazed at Leo, the prince in a suit and overcoat, eating an egg sandwich with his eyebrows raised in question as if I seriously might have something better to do than be flown to a castle to choose a priceless piece of antiquity to go in a garden.

Since the visit to my parents, he'd been even more careful to ask before he sprang surprises on me. It had niggled me since, I have to be honest; I didn't know that it wasn't a case of throwing money at a problem but forgetting there were people involved, but I'd pushed it aside, because I was fairly sure being annoyed at someone whisking you away in a helicopter to go to a sellout gig fell under the heading of 'inverse snobbery.'

'No,' I said. 'I'm not doing anything this weekend.'

'Great,' said Leo with a cheerful grin. 'I'll book the plane.'

You know the usual minibreak panic you get the first time your new boyfriend takes you to Paris or New York or somewhere for the weekend:

*What do I take?*

*How can I prevent him from seeing my passport photo?*

*Should I take sexy pajamas?*

*Is there such a thing as sexy pajamas?*

*How can I engineer that moment you always get in films where the girl slips on his oversize white shirt and slinks around the bed looking kittenish?*

*Etc.*

Now multiply it by a factor of Meeting the Parents, then by another factor of Staying in a Castle, and then multiply all that by a factor of ROYALTY, and you have a rough idea of the nervous hysteria I was suffering by the time I was in the car on the way to the airport on Saturday morning.

I was traveling light, but that was only because Jo had gone through my wardrobe *and hers* and even then deemed only four items of clothing appropriate. Two of those were cashmere cardigans.

'Royalty appreciates thrift,' she insisted when I was wailing in panic at my limited selection. 'They wear the same clothes for years and years. Look at Princess Anne. She has blouses older than her children.'

'I don't think Liza Bachmann and Princess Anne are the same sort of princess,' I protested. 'Remember that blog that tracks Princess Eliza's outfits to make sure she never repeats them?'

'Oh, but she's a *supermodel*!' Jo clapped me about the arms. 'Anyway, Leo's been out with a model and he dumped her. He likes the normal-girl thing better. He won't *expect* you to turn up looking glam.'

I think she meant that to sound reassuring; but the more I saw myself on YoungHot&Royal.com, the more I secretly wondered if my carefree 'no-makeup makeup' look was actually looking *careless* rather than *carefree*. And I hated myself a bit for even thinking that.

'Here, take these.' Jo dumped her collection of vintage scarves into my bag. 'Ring the changes with accessories.'

'Just because you read that in a magazine doesn't mean they won't notice that I've worn the same thing with four different scarves.'

'Darling,' said Jo. 'If there's one thing I've learned about models, it's that they'll be so busy with their own outfits they won't notice what you're wearing at all. And anyone royal will be far too polite to mention it.'

That was consoling. Sort of.

When Leo said he'd book the plane, I'd naively thought he meant to flex his BA frequent flyer card; but Billy drove us to a private airfield south of London, where a charter jet was waiting on the tarmac, just for us.

I was beginning to realize that the more exclusive and private something was, the more unassuming it would seem to be — until you clocked the people around you. The loos in the private terminal didn't have gold taps, but I won't tell you who I saw using the hand dryer when I nipped in to check my makeup. It would be very indiscreet. But suffice it to say . . . *American Idol*.

From the second I stepped onto the private jet, I was taking mental notes to pass on to Mum (and, from a technological point of view, Ted). It felt more like being in a very big luxury car than a plane, with big leather seats and clunky belts, but there were three cabin attendants waiting on us for the two-hour flight with handmade chocolates and champagne on ice.

I had a couple of chocolates, but I couldn't risk the champagne, not in the tight pencil skirt Jo had zipped me into. She said I looked very sports luxe. I wasn't so sure I knew what that meant. Leo, of course, was perfectly relaxed and even joked with the crew when turbulence started to bounce us across the English Channel a bit quicker than planned.

'Sorry there's no film on these things,' he said, gently peeling my white-knuckled fingers off the armrest. 'Or duty-free. Although I can tell you all about Mom's Be an Everyday Princess campaign, if you can bear it?'

I nodded. Jo and I had spent the past week extracting every single scrap of information about Liza's campaign and Nirona in general from the Internet, and then condensing them into a series of 'intelligent dinner-party questions' I could ask. It was like the Max Barclay party chat, but about a million times more upmarket.

Leo's voice was so soothing that even Liza's waffle about personal dignity and community spirit sounded profound and even relevant to someone like me. I stared out of the window and tried not to be sick. The choppy water of the Channel turned into patchwork fields over northern France, and then snowcapped mountains spiking up from the clouds, and suddenly we were coming in to land at Naples.

I glanced across at Leo. The nervous butterflies had returned, but now they were joined by a different kind, the glamorous, tropical 'I'm going on holiday' fun butterflies.

'It'll be fine,' he said before I even said anything, and squeezed my hand.

A helicopter flew us over to the island, and landed in a paddock behind a sprawling cream stone villa with stocky turrets at each end, the walls wrapped in green vines and the roof tiled in warm terracotta. It was built into the side of a hill, and I could already see the different gardens laid out around the grounds, as if the castle were a grand lady with her skirts spread around her, each panel neatly embroidered in its own bright colors and patterns.

'Wow,' I murmured, lost for words as I tried to drink in every detail at once. 'It's . . .'

How did you compliment someone on his castle?

'Breathtaking, isn't it?' said Leo. 'I get the same reaction every time I come home.'

'I just want to run around all those gardens,' I said, touched that he seemed as in awe of it as I was. 'And climb up the turrets and smell all the flowers.'

A footman was stacking our bags onto a golf cart, and Leo put his arm around my shoulders. He seemed amused but pleased with my reaction. 'That can be arranged,' he whispered in my ear.

The golf cart took us around to the family entrance at the back of the castle; Leo explained that there was a tour on today, so the main entrance hall was occupied by four busloads of German tourists. Underneath a stone arch topped with a blue and yellow flag, Leo's father, Boris, and an elegant woman were waiting for us. I thought they were having a row, from the waving arms and open mouths; but when we got nearer, I realized that the woman's mane of tawny hair — seriously, I finally understood what fashion magazines meant by a mane — hid a phone, into which she was speaking with some force.

Boris was just talking away to himself, I think.

Leo jumped off the cart and went to greet them with air kisses and a hearty handshake, respectively.

I slid off the seat with my knees together and tried to minimize the embarrassing wrinkles in my pencil skirt, which now looked a lot less Grace Kelly than when I'd wriggled into it that morning. I felt Leo's hand on the small of my back before I had time to pull it down properly, and suddenly I was being shoved into the presence of Princess Eliza.

'Mom, this is Amy Wilde. Amy, Liza Bachmann, my mother.'

'Hello,' I squeaked, and stuck out my hand, which she took, gracefully, in both of hers.

Liza Bachmann was properly, premiere-league beautiful. Everything about her face was perfectly even and symmetrical, from her almond-shaped eyes to her wide cheekbones to her generous mouth. When she smiled, it felt as if a very large light were being shone in my face. I blinked, amazed at the star quality she exuded, then twigged that she'd positioned herself with the sun behind her. What a pro.

'Amy,' she said in a melodious low voice, as if I were a top new perfume by Estée Lauder. 'How wonderful to meet you.'

The Internet said Princess Eliza was a princess but not *the* Sovereign Princess and so I didn't have to curtsy, but I found myself bending my knee a little anyway, and Liza seemed pleased.

'Ah-ha, it's the runaway date!' Boris was pointing at me, then did a weird boxing gesture at me which I guessed was meant to be a greeting. 'Got your passport ready this time? You're going to have a hard time getting away from us on this island unless you're a good swimmer!'

I turned red. Red-hot red.

'I beg your pardon?' Liza inclined her head and a mass of mane tumbled to one side, revealing her small ear and her huge diamond earring. 'Is this something I should know about?'

Boris winked at me. 'Gotta keep an eye on this one, Liza. She might decide to go home if we're not being entertaining enough.'

'No, no, that wasn't what happened!' I protested, mortified. 'It was—'

'It was one hundred percent Rolf's fault,' said Leo. 'He's lucky Amy is incredibly forgiving, as well as everything else. Are we in time for lunch? Because I want to show Amy the gardens while the weather's good.'

'Sure.' Liza seemed to be filing the runaway thing for later. 'Come this way, honey.'

My luggage had already vanished as we made our way into the castle, and I had to make a conscious effort not to let my wide eyes dart around me too obviously. Everywhere I looked there was something old and interesting; I guessed the massive swords and spears that usually hung on the walls of places like this had been kept for the main tourist areas, because these airy apartments were much more like a stylish art gallery. If the art gallery had stone-flagged floors and walls filled with medieval frescoes of various battlefields.

'I thought we'd just have a light lunch,' said Liza as we swept down the corridors at some speed. Large oil paintings of blue-eyed blondes in hats slithered past in my peripheral vision. 'I've got some appointments this afternoon.'

'As have I,' Boris added.

Liza shot him a look that said, 'Yes, dear,' more acidly than words could have done.

A liveried staff member ushered us into a bright dining room with a huge bay window looking down into the tiered beds and trimmed hedges of an English country garden. I wondered if there were any English-speaking gardeners who could tell me how they'd managed it, given that we were three worlds away from the soggy English climate here.

'Is Sofia joining us?' Leo asked. 'I heard she was around this weekend.'

There was a microscopic pause before Liza smiled and nodded. 'She said she'd try. She has some meetings herself today.'

It was Saturday. Did everyone have meetings on the weekend?

'Not work meetings,' Leo said, sensing the question threatening to burst out of me. 'Sofia's writing an article for *Time* magazine about our family. For the bicentennial. She's doing some research this weekend with Uncle Pavlos and Granddad.'

Boris let out a short bark of amusement, which Liza closed down fast.

'But she's very much looking forward to meeting you, Amy,' she added, with another gracious smile.

The large table in the center of the room was set for six, and Leo held the elegant mahogany chair out for me, beating the two footmen to it by seconds. I was relieved to see just eight pieces of cutlery in front of me to negotiate. Jo had thoughtfully hidden a guide to social etiquette in my bag, in case they sprang any royal galas on me over the weekend.

'Is Granddad joining us?' Leo asked, nodding at the sixth space.

'We don't know. He might just arrive. He's so busy at the moment. Anyway, Amy, Leo tells me you're a garden designer?'

Liza began as a starter of scallops materialized in front of us, and with some discreet boosts from Leo, I managed to tell Liza and Boris about the wildflower mini-meadows now taking shape on Leo's roof and my plans for (or, through the Leo-filter, my 'fantastic transformation of') the Trinity Square rose beds. I was halfway through a sentence about how the original designer had cleverly managed to create a subtly shifting cloud of fragrance all summer long, when the sound of high-speed marching ricocheted down the tiled corridor, and a woman dressed in several shades of beige swept into the room.

Her narrowed eyes took in the scene at the table and settled on me. I had a very real sense of how Goldilocks must have felt when the three bears popped home unexpectedly, and found her mid-snore.

'Ah, Sofia,' said Boris jovially. 'Are we early or are you late? Actually, no, don't answer that,' he added, as the smile faded from his face under the thundercloud of her gaze.

# CHAPTER SEVENTEEN

'Oh, please start,' said Sofia sarcastically, even before Leo and Boris could rise to their feet. 'No, really. I'll just jump in when the main course arrives, shall I?'

Liza made an imperceptible motion to a footman, who produced another porcelain plate of scallops from nowhere.

'Sofia, honey, do sit down, we'd barely started.'

Sofia rolled her eyes but moved so the footman could pull out her chair, then sank into it with a dramatic sigh. Even without being introduced, I'd have known who she was. She was the image of Liza, but not quite as polished; her eyebrows were quite bushy, for a start, and she wore a pair of stern glasses that reminded me of Jo's 'don't mess with me' prop glasses she put on to bully architects. I wasn't 100 percent sure Sofia's had prescription lenses in either.

'Don't bother, Mom, Oprah's *gone home,*' she huffed. 'Yeah, yeah, hi.' She waved a hand in my direction. 'Carry on.'

Everyone's eyes turned back to me, but I'd totally lost my place. 'Um, I . . .'

The ormolu clock ticked loudly on the magnificent sideboard behind me.

Silence. Silence in my head. Horrible silence in front of me. *Say something. Anything.*

For one awful second I was back on the balcony with Jo, listening to her Max Barclay chat tutorial and fighting my mental shutdown.

'So, Sofia, are you named after Sophia Loren? Or is there a special connection with the city?'

Oh, God. That was my voice saying that. I wanted to sink my head into the scallops.

'Are you asking if my parents conceived me in Bulgaria?' asked Sofia with a deadpan expression. 'I don't know. You'd better ask them. Mom? Can you remember where you conceived me?'

Boris roared with laughter. 'Ha-ha-ha-ha-ha-ha! What a question! If it was down to that, we should have called you HMS—'

'Boris!' snapped Liza at the same time that Sofia yelled, 'Have you people never heard of a rhetorical question?'

'Sofia is named for our great-great-grandmother, Anna-Sofia Diedrich, the opera singer,' said Leo over the chaos. 'She was a famous diva.'

'Oh, go on, say it,' snapped Sofia. '*Too*. She was a famous diva *too*.'

'I had no intention of saying that. Would you like me to?'

'Kids! Kids!' Liza raised her hands and laughed a lovely caramelly laugh with just a hint of steel underneath. 'Honestly! I know it's healthy to be able to tease each other with love, but come on! You're going to make Amy think we need family therapy!'

'Not at all,' I mumbled.

'Pavlos's kids don't argue like this,' Liza carried on, making a cute pointy gesture with her fork.

Jo's book said you weren't supposed to gesticulate with your cutlery, but I supposed royalty got a pass on that one. As Sofia had so correctly observed, Oprah had gone home.

'That's because they're not allowed to talk unless it's all been cleared by Pavlos's Speech Police,' replied Sofia. She polished off all her tiny scallops as if they were scampi in a basket. The second she stabbed the last one, our plates were removed and replaced with the main course of perfectly cooked white fish and tiny vegetables carved out of the original-size ones. 'Oh my God, I was talking to him for an hour this morning and I can't remember a single thing he said. I hope the people of Nirona are looking forward to their robot leader and his tiny robot army.'

'Sofie!'

'Well, it's ridiculous. I know you're twins, but did you get all the charisma as well as all the hair, Dad? Did you suck it all out through the umbilical cord?' She wriggled her fingers at him.

Boris shrugged modestly. 'He got the crown, I got the personality. That's how it goes in most royal families, my darling. Only fair to share things out between the siblings.'

Leo glanced at me, and I quickly closed my mouth, which had dropped open in surprise.

'Well, Rolf certainly got all the personality in our family,' he said with the amiable charm that seemed to defuse tension at a stroke. Well, usually. 'What did I get?'

'A penis,' snapped Sofia. 'And because of that, everything else.'

Liza's eyes widened so far I thought her cheekbones would crack.

But Boris seemed to be considering. 'Hmm, I'd have said Leo got the empathy, and you got the smarts, Sofie.' He nodded. 'But yes, a penis. Who could ask for anything more?' he added tunelessly.

My eyes darted from Sofia to Boris to Leo and back again to Liza. I wanted to imprint it all on my brain to text Jo later, but they kept talking so fast. What was it like when there were more than four of them here? At least the relentless back-and-forth meant I didn't have to say anything. I'd never be able to keep up with this.

'Sofia's spent the morning chatting about the rights of succession with her Uncle Pavlos's advisors,' Liza explained across the table. 'For her wonderful *Time* magazine feature, which is coming out around the time that my television series premieres. You're going to stress how important support and unity are in a modern royal family like ours. Right, honey?'

Sofia turned her attention toward me, and I leaned back involuntarily in my chair as she addressed me directly. 'Don't you think it's ridiculous, in this day and age, that women are passed over in the line of succession?'

I swallowed. This wasn't the sort of lunchtime conversation I was used to, even when those lunchtimes were spent sitting with my feet on a prince's knee.

'Um, yes?'

She turned to Liza, flicking her hand in dismissal. 'See? Even the gardener thinks it's ridiculous.'

There was an uncomfortable pause, in which I wondered if I'd heard her right. I heard Leo take a sharp breath, but I didn't want to make things any more awkward, so I spluttered, 'Is that not the case here?' in as intelligent a tone as I could muster.

'No, it is not.' Sofia looked about to launch into a long speech but Leo coughed before she could get going.

'And even if *the gardener* is ethically correct, it makes no difference, because *the lawyer* would have to knock off not just her Uncle Pavlos but Serge, Will, and her own father before she got anywhere near the throne. And that's quite a food-poisoning incident to engineer,' said Leo. He patted his lips with the crisp linen napkin and pushed his chair back, even though he'd eaten only half his fish.

'Would you mind if Amy and I took our coffee into the garden?' he said, turning to his mother. 'I'd really like to catch the groundskeepers while they're there, so they can answer any questions Amy might have.'

I hurriedly put my knife and fork together.

'Have you finished, Amy?' asked Liza. 'Don't let Leo rush you out!'

'Oh, I, er, don't eat pudding,' I lied, even though my inner pudding scoffer was wailing for whatever delicate confection was doubtless being plated behind the scenes. I knew that would be the one thing Mum would ask about — what had the royal pastry chefs created for pudding?

'Just as well. Don't forget, dinner with Pavlos tonight,' said Boris.

'And his tiny robot army.'

'Sofia!'

I wondered if she was like this in court. I wouldn't know

whether to be relieved or very concerned that she was on my side.

Leo took my hand and led me back down the corridor toward the main area of the palace, past a crocodile of tourists in shorts who stared at us as we ducked under the red velvet rope separating the private apartments from the public tour.

I could hear the guide talking as we carried on through the state reception hall.

'. . . site of a Greek myth in which a peasant girl was turned into a rosebush by Zeus, in order to escape ravishing. The rosebush, which flowers all year round, can be found in the gardens to the front of the grounds. The castle, now the elegant villa you see around you, has been inhabited continuously since 1092 AD . . .'

'All nonsense,' whispered Leo. 'I made up the bit about the Greek myth when I was fifteen, slipped it into the guide's spiel. No one noticed.'

'You're joking!' I whispered back.

'No, I had a bet with Sofia — she tried to get them to say that the peasant girl foretold that when a princess named Sofia was born, the rosebush would flower yellow, the succession would change, and a wise woman would inherit.' He paused. 'Kind of gave herself away by telling them the future female ruler's name would begin with S.'

'Good on her for trying, though,' I said. 'At least she didn't have some sea monster carrying you all off.'

Leo raised his eyebrows. 'Don't think she wouldn't try.'

We were in the main hall now, an impressive open space

with marble pillars, filled with oil paintings and huge vases — and tourists taking photographs of everything.

'It's rush hour,' he explained. 'We only let visitors in for three hours a day and during certain months, so it gets busy. Let's take a shortcut.' He guided me down a black-and-white-tiled passage, past a sign in seven languages for the Princess Eliza Costume Collection one way, and the gardens in the other.

The palace smelled calm, of figs and sun-warmed stone, but the air changed the second I stepped into the gardens. At once the saltiness of ozone from the shimmering sea hit me, fizzing over a tumultuous rainbow of floral fragrances — old-fashioned roses sweetening the greenish notes of broad tropical leaves I'd never even seen before. I spotted copper markers in the soil picking out each plant, and if Leo hadn't been by my side I'd have been nosing around each one, making notes and taking pictures for Dad.

Leo turned to me with a proud glint in his eye. 'What does the English gardener think of the Italian gardens?'

'She loves them.' I couldn't stop grinning. I really did. So many unusual flowers, tropical plants — it was how I imagined Jo felt when the new clothes arrived in Harvey Nichols. My fingers tingled, longing to touch everything.

'I want to show you the English garden.' Leo guided me down a set of steps, and I blinked at the spectacular view of the harbor below us, white yachts bobbing gently in the aquamarine water next to multicolored umbrellas. 'I've asked the head groundsman to contact you about some of the roses you planted in London. I'd like to have the same ones shipped here.'

'Isn't someone else in charge of decisions like that?' I asked, taking in the croquet-lawn smoothness of the pocket-size English garden. I had no idea how they'd managed to make cottage garden hollyhocks and lupines grow in one corner, with tea roses in another and scented wisteria climbing up an old brick wall; it was like something from *Alice in Wonderland*. 'Don't you have to go through your grandfather?'

'He's a busy man. And he likes it when someone takes an interest in the gardens — the rest of the family tend to be more focused on the crown jewels and who's got the apartments with the best views.' Leo put his arms round me and pulled me close. There was no one else around, but I cast an anxious glance toward the palace; I didn't want to be spotted doing anything untoward.

And to be honest, I was twitchy about photographers. There'd been a particularly mortifying shot on YoungHot&Royal.com of me and Leo leaving the neighborhood bistro near his house; from the angle it was taken, it looked as if I was doing something very rude to his trousers. Which I wasn't, seriously.

'Don't worry about tonight,' Leo murmured into my hair. 'Sofia will be on much better behavior when the rest of the family are around for dinner.'

'Is it a big dinner?' Nerves gripped my stomach as a mental image of a table full of tiaras and sashes flashed before me. The lunchtime banter squared with formal wear. 'I mean, when you say the rest of the family —'

'That's all it is, a family meal. Nothing official. Pavlos is here with his wife, Mathilde, and my cousins. They're a bit younger than us. And Granddad will be here — just remember to be nice to his greyhounds, if he brings them.'

By now, the greyhounds were the only family members I felt at all comfortable about meeting.

'And if Mom tries to get you to —' He stopped. His phone was ringing inside his linen jacket. 'Sorry, hang on.'

Leo's expression changed as he picked up the call, and to my surprise he rattled off a stream of fluent Italian. I'd never heard him speak Italian before. It was *very* sexy. I decided I wanted to learn Italian ASAP.

Whatever the call was about, it made him tap his brow testily, and then hang up.

'Would you excuse me for a minute?' He touched my arm. 'The office is trying to get hold of me, I need to send a quick e-mail. Can I get a drink sent down to you? Some lemonade? Iced coffee? What would you like?'

'It's fine! I'm more than happy to potter round here.' I gestured toward the glorious flowerbeds. 'You could leave me here all day.'

'Oh, but I won't.' Leo grinned, then bounded up the stone steps and vanished behind the tall palm trees.

The Mediterranean sun was warm, and fat bees were buzzing around the lilac spikes of the lavender bushes. The honey from this garden must be the sweetest ever, I thought, full of sunshine and colors. I closed my eyes and smelled the pink roses nearest me, inhaling the powdery fragrance, then opened them to check the slate labels next to each one. I was so fascinated by the lengths to which someone had gone to bring the Cotswolds to the Mediterranean that I didn't even notice there was someone else in the garden until a cultured voice said, 'Are you a gardener?'

I looked up with a start. An elderly gentleman in a white linen suit was standing over me, his face shaded by an ancient gardening hat. Judging from the deep tan and the lines on his face, he'd spent a fair bit of time outside, as had the hat. I could make out a pair of sharp blue eyes underneath the floppy brim. The sharp eyes were taking me in, but not in an unkindly way.

'I'm admiring these slate labels,' I said. 'I'm too disorganized to label my own borders, but I always mean to. Then I forget what I've planted.'

'Ah, one must always label. It's like photographs. One never thinks one will forget names and places, but one always does.' He had a slight accent that I couldn't quite place beneath the genial plumminess of an old-fashioned public school, and there was something devastatingly charming about his manner.

'That depends on how special the plants are.' I rose to my feet, hoping I hadn't been looking too nosy. 'Or how big your garden is, of course.'

'Indeed. And I have had a good few gardens in my time,' he said with a wistful smile. 'I hope I haven't disturbed you, my dear. It's nice to see someone taking a moment to enjoy the roses, rather than snapping away with a camera.' He produced a small Tina pruning knife from his baggy jacket and cut an apricot-yellow tea rose from the thick climber.

'My own favorite,' he said, presenting it to me with a courtly inclination of his head. 'Lady Hillingdon. A dependable old climber, but very sweet. And the color of your rather lovely hair, if you'll permit me to say so.'

'Thank you.' I buried my nose in the velvety petals, and decided not to think too hard about the reference to the climber. 'Lady Hillingdon's one of my favorite roses too. I've planted one of these in the garden I'm working on in London. It's a historical rose garden, lots of traditional varieties like this.'

The old man tipped up the brim of his hat with a crooked finger, and raised his white eyebrow. 'How interesting. I know London well. Whereabouts?'

'Kensington. Not too far from the Royal Albert Hall.'

The blue eyes twinkled conspiratorially. 'Ah, yes. The Royal Albert Hall. Now, these are exquisite too, these deep pink blooms. Amy Robsart, do you know it? See, even the leaves have a fragrance.' He cut me another with a professional nip, and rustled the leaf between his fingers to release the smell.

I met his gaze over the top of the petals and found an equally old-fashioned shyness creeping over me in response to his chivalrous attentions. This was a man, I could tell, who'd known a rose to match the eyes, hair, and name of every film star in the marina.

I smiled. Even so, he still had the knack of making a girl feel special.

'Let me show you the red roses,' he said, offering me his arm, and we walked slowly along the thickly flowered beds, pausing to admire one variety or another. Soon I had a round posy of perfect roses, the thorns deftly removed, and a promise of cuttings to take home with me. From the man's encyclopedic knowledge of the gardens and the proud way he reeled off answers to my questions about the care of them, I guessed he was either the head groundsman or — I wasn't *daft* — Leo's grandfather. I didn't want to show myself up by asking, and in any case, it didn't matter; we were talking plants, not palaces, and I was far more confident when it came to black spot and rust than I was on tiaras.

We'd probably have got through the whole conversation without mentioning the elephant in the rose garden if he hadn't brought it up himself, but he did so with such grace that I barely had time to feel embarrassed.

We'd paused by a smallish stone fountain with a dancing woman at the center. Water was pitter-pattering off her outstretched arms in pretty arcs, and blush-pink rose petals from the climber wrapped around the nearby arch floated in the water.

'You like this statue?' he asked, with a sidelong glance.

'I do. It's very elegant. Not too big.'

'It's modeled on my mother. Adelaide. She was a wonderful dancer in her youth, although she wasn't able to continue with it after her marriage, of course.' He left a discreet pause for me to catch up. 'She also designed these gardens. These are her own roses here, named in her honor. Princess Adelaide — very delicate in appearance, but almost impossible to kill off with a bad winter. We prize our beautiful imported varieties here. They bring such strength and character to our garden.'

Oh, nuts. I wasn't sure what to do now he'd told me who he was. Would a curtsy be appropriate? Could you do a retrospective one? I didn't want to do the wrong thing. Prince Wilhelm didn't have Liza's 'curtsy now' aura, but he had a definite old-school dignity about him that I wanted him to know I'd noticed.

I started to fumble with my skirt, but he just patted my hand and gave me three flowers on a stem, each one the color of ballet slippers.

'Please, no. No ceremony. One thing I enjoy most about these gardens is that here I am Willi, and I can talk with people who love these roses as much as I do. There is enough bowing and scraping inside. Outside, it's the flowers who deserve the attention. And if I take an hour out of the day, at my age, then I will. What is the point of being a prince otherwise?'

He smiled, and I remembered what Leo had said about his grandfather's playboy heyday in London: the wine, and the women, and the song. I could see that. I could definitely see that in his smile. I could see him in Leo's rose garden, watching the dawn break over the wet grass from the summerhouse.

'Thank you, Your Highness,' I said. 'You're very kind.'

'You must call me Willi,' he said solemnly.

'I'm Amy,' I said, and he took my hand and kissed it. That was the wrong way round, etiquettely speaking, but I was beginning to realize that hand-kissing was very much par for the course round here, royalty or not.

'And what have you done with Leo?' He gestured for me to sit down on the bench. It was identical to the benches in the Trinity Square garden, except instead of 'To Dodger, a True Friend and Shooting Companion, 1985–1998' on the plaque, it read, 'Princess Adelaide of Nirona and Svetland, a Mother, an Australian, a Gardener.'

'He's dealing with his office inside.' I paused. 'Has he told you about the rose garden? Has he shown you photographs of it now?'

Willi coughed, and I realized he wasn't quite as fit as I'd thought. When I offered to go for some water, he waved away my concern.

'He has indeed. Leo has been sending me photographs, you know, of all the work you've been putting into my square. It's brought back some wonderful memories for me.'

'Really?' I felt proud. 'And do you like what we've done?'

Prince Wilhelm smiled distantly, as if an old film was running through his mind and he didn't want to interrupt it. 'I am *very* happy with what you've done,' he said. 'Do you know, I met my wife in those gardens? We used to have supper in the summerhouse when Evelyn's chaperone was otherwise engaged. I used to leave the light on, and Evelyn would pretend she was going to a dancing class in Marylebone and take a taxi, and we'd eat smoked salmon from Harrods and . . . It was all very innocent. But tea roses always remind me of those special evenings. I'm sure they will for you too. Such happy times.'

I blushed faintly at the 'happy times' I'd already enjoyed in that garden without a single rose having yet bloomed. (Not like that.) 'That's what I love about gardening. Flowers always bring back memories for people, and they come back every year — if you're reasonably careful.'

Prince Wilhelm sighed and nodded, and we sat on our bench gazing out over the English garden in companionable silence while white-winged butterflies flitted from bush to plant. A few French tourists wandered in with maps of the formal gardens, and he rose politely from the seat to answer their questions, very much the distinguished head gardener, albeit with a perfect French accent.

When an English couple wandered in, I did the same, and was able to advise them pretty thoroughly about growing similar flowers at home — what I didn't know about pre-1925 English rose varieties by now wasn't worth knowing. And halfway through my pruning advice, I caught Prince Willi gazing at me with a conspiratorial smile on his face, and without thinking, I winked.

And he, the Prince of Nirona, winked back.

# CHAPTER EIGHTEEN

I made my first solo appearance on the YoungHot&Royal website shortly after the weekend in Nirona. It was a bit of a wake-up call, to say the least. I'd had no idea that my hair had got so 'out of control,' or that anyone would ever describe me as 'mysterious.'

'But I'm the least mysterious person I know,' I protested to Jo, as we both stared at the home page in shock, transfixed by the banner headline 'After Flora: Prince Leo's Mysterious New Love Interest!' 'How can they say I'm mysterious?'

'They mean they haven't managed to find you on Facebook or in the back of *Tatler*.' Jo clicked on the comments box.

'What are you doing?'

'I'm leaving an anonymous comment to say you're a natural beauty. Your hair doesn't *need* a Brazilian blow-dry, we don't all have to look like Middleton clones.'

'What? Where does it say that? Jo, have you read this page before? You have, haven't you? You've been Googling us again! Show me.' I leaned forward, but Jo covered the screen with her hand.

'Nothing! It's nothing. Go and make us a cup of tea.' She flapped her hand. 'Go on. Tea.'

Reluctantly, I went through to the kitchen, trying not to let my imagination fill in the blanks.

Jo and I had repeated our solemn vow not to keep checking the royal gossip websites to see what they were saying about Rolf and Leo, but it was like accidentally eavesdropping on a conversation and hearing your own name mentioned, and then walking on by. As Jo said, only the virtuous or the very stupid wouldn't care.

I was neither of those things, and I was freaked out, to say the least. Not just about what fashion verdict they'd slapped on my outfit (I was already regretting our gleeful hoots of derision at some of their comments about other royal girl-friends' fashion mistakes) but what they'd managed to find out about me and, more to the point, my family.

When the photos of Jo and Rolf had been dissected on the site, they'd got a fair bit of mileage out of the Honorable Jo — between her various festival fringe shows, and her well-connected exes, and her frequently married parents, and her great-great-grandmother after whom the Prince of Wales's fourth yacht was named (who knew?), there was a lot to hoot about. But they hadn't found much to say about me with Leo until now, and we'd been dating for well over four months.

I stared blankly at the boiling kettle. Seeing this new post made something else fall into place. A photographer had been lurking around our house on and off for the past week; Jo had spotted him from the kitchen, and we'd left by the back door every day. He'd got bored by Thursday and rung the bell to ask to use the loo, but Mrs Mainwaring had told him to get lost in very robust terms. It was a good job he hadn't got

Dickon's bell, or he'd have been upstairs posing with just his long lens to cover his modesty before he could say 'nudey angel.'

I made the tea, gave the tea bags one more dunk, and dropped them in the bin. A photographer hanging around *our* house to photograph Jo and *me*. It was surreal. Like it was happening to someone else. Except the evidence was right there on the Internet, for every single person in the world to read if they wanted to. And now putting 'Amy Wilde' into Google would lead to this photo of me with three-day-old hair and a distracted (polite version) expression — possibly for the rest of my life.

Jo attempted to close the laptop as I got back with the tea, but I stopped her.

'No, I need to know what they're saying.' I took a deep breath. 'It's better to know.'

'Is it? Half of it's made up. At least half.'

'Show me.'

Jo narrowed her eyes as if she was about to argue.

'I'm being brave,' I said. 'Hurry up before it wears off.'

She sighed and lifted the screen. As she did, my stomach lurched and I had to hang on to the chair because my knees had turned to water.

It was worse than I'd thought at a quick glance. They'd put two photographs side by side: one taken at the charity boxing match, of me in my shiny ballgown with half a ton of fake tan covering my freckles and most of my cleavage, but the other was — I blanched — not quite so glam. It was a paparazzi shot of me outside Grace's flat in my dirty jeans and fleece, loading spades and compost into the back of the van, while trying to stop Badger charging down the street in pursuit of a squirrel. The photographer had managed to catch me mid-yell and Badger mid-bark so we both looked as if we were about to savage a passerby.

'It's not your best angle,' said Jo diplomatically. 'But who does look their best at ten in the morning?'

I opened my mouth, but no words came out. What if Leo saw that? What if *Mum* saw that? Well, that at least was unlikely, given her fear of the interwebs.

Jo noticed my expression, and hurriedly made the evening photograph much bigger, so it filled the screen. 'Look,' she said. 'They love your natural beauty, and your amazing triceps—'

I jostled to get back to the text. 'From all the digging I do in my *laboring job as a contract gardener.*'

She jostled me back out of the way. 'I'll get them to correct that. You're a garden designer. You're a horticultural artist. They'd know that if they'd bothered to check out the website clearly displayed on your van.' Jo sounded indignant. 'Lazy! Anyway, they think Leo's absolutely besotted with you. And he is — just look at the way he's staring at you there!'

'Well . . .' That was the only consolation — they'd chosen a shot in which Leo was standing behind me looking incredibly handsome in his dinner jacket, with his gaze angled proudly toward me as if he couldn't quite tear his attention away.

And once I'd got used to the grinding shame of seeing my own wonky grin outlined in very red lipstick, I had to admit that, actually, I didn't look that different from the other shiny-legged socialites in the background. My hair looked glossy and my dress clung in all the right places. If you didn't know, you might have thought I was called Tilly or Viola or something.

Something else stirred underneath all the internal memos to get my brows threaded and stop eating biscuits: I was the official girlfriend of Prince Leo of Nirona.

Or as the caption put it, 'Sorry, girls, but it looks like London-loving millionaire Leo is off the market again . . . for the time being.'

'Out of the way,' said Jo, reaching for her mug. 'I have a few corrections to make.'

'What? No! Are you going to tell them you're my flatmate? Isn't that the saddest thing possible?'

Jo sipped her tea. 'No, I will be e-mailing them in my pseudonymous capacity as your press agent. There are a few key details that they need to clear up.'

I started to laugh, then realized she was being absolutely serious.

I'd be lying if I said there weren't some incredible upsides to dating a man who not only had a lot of money of his own, but who seemed to have a key to doors I didn't even know existed.

Leo asked me if I'd go to another charity ball with him, this time for the Liza Bachmann Foundation for Makeup to Make Up.

'It's not as trivial as it sounds,' he said, in a tone that suggested it wasn't the first time he'd said as much. 'They donate makeup to women's refuges and work with birthmarks and stuff. Mom will be there, and I'm sure she'll insist on us being photographed, so I can't possibly ask you to come without buying you a dress. Please let me.'

'Oh, there's no need —' I started automatically, but then stopped. I did need a new dress. I'd now worn everything in my wardrobe once, borrowed everything of Jo's that would fit, and even considered wearing a bizarre number from Jo's mother Marigold's wardrobe of '70s classics.

'It'd be a favor to Mom, actually, if you went to Zoë and got something,' said Leo. 'She's best friends with Zoë Weiss, the dress designer — I don't know if you know of her?'

I nodded. I had not heard of Zoë Weiss. For all I knew, she was Edel Weiss's sister. 'Mm-hm.'

Leo didn't respond, and I looked across the bench. A half smile was twitching his lips. 'Do you know who Zoë Weiss is?'

I contemplated lying, then shook my head. I'd dropped my long-term habit of pretending to know stuff I didn't with Leo; he read me like a book. And besides, I liked the way that we could be honest with each other.

'No,' I admitted. 'So she's a fashion designer?'

'Yup. She is. Anyway, she's in London this week, so if you go to her suite at the Ritz, she'll sort you out with a dress for the ball, and Mom will be thrilled that she's got her some press coverage. Everyone's a winner.'

He took a bite of his Subway sandwich, then winked at me over it. He reminded me of his grandfather when he did that. Of the three generations of Wolfsburgs I'd met, it was hard to decide who was the most charming.

*

What Leo didn't tell me — but what Jo did, in a loud, disbelieving voice, shortly after my appointment — was that Zoë Weiss had dressed three of the nominees at the last Oscars and was in London to open her new flagship store on Sloane Street, opposite Gucci. It was probably a good job Leo hadn't filled me in on that, because I would have been too freaked out to remove so much as a shoe in front of her.

Zoë was a tiny pepper pot of a lady, with tiny feet in leopard-skin ballet pumps, and she flitted around me with a tape measure in one hand and a series of espressos in the other. She didn't seem to mind my hips or my strange gardening-inflicted muscles, but draped material over me with quick, precise movements, occasionally bestowing a compliment on my 'angel hair' or my 'great calf.' I stared at my reflection in amazement while she hummed and sketched and barked instructions at her assistant.

'Ah! Blushing! I love it!' She spun round to her assistant. 'No colors that clash with that blush.'

The assistant snapped me again on her iPhone, then held up some swatches while Zoë went, 'No, no, no, no, maybe, yes.'

I made yet another mental note to start Googling properly before every appointment involving Leo or any member of his family. No wonder all these people had assistants; they were there for *research*.

'We're done,' she said, and touched my cheek. 'I love dressing girls when they're not sample size. So much more of a creative challenge for a designer. I am going to make you look *stunning*, my darling.'

'Um, thank you,' I said.

It wasn't easy to work out what was a compliment and what wasn't these days; but thanks to my compliment coach, I was getting better at accepting them.

The ballgown that subsequently arrived by courier in a huge tissue-lined box redefined the term *evening wear* forever in our flat.

I knew what was coming — I'd had two fittings — but Jo didn't. When she zipped me into it in front of her cheval mirror and stepped back to see the result, she burst into tears.

'I'm never going to be able to shop on the high street again,' she croaked. 'It's like eating McDonald's after going to Gordon Ramsay. This is what real dresses should taste like.'

Zoë had chosen the exact shade of rich navy-blue satin that made my hair gleam like gold and my bosom (I totally had a bosom in this dress) seem soft and creamy. She'd nipped the bodice in at my waist and balanced the sleeves exactly at the sweetest part of my shoulders, so they looked as if they might fall off at any moment, while the skirt swirled around me, flattening my stomach and lengthening my legs so I looked even taller than I was. It was classic but not old-fashioned, modern but not on-trend — it was me, but through a glamorous Nirona filter.

I wore my diamond daisy-chain bracelet, and Leo had sent a box round from Chamuet with a matching necklace in it. He must have had it made specially for me, because there was a handwritten note inside: *'For a girl who could make a daisy chain look like diamonds. All my love, L.'*

Jo did my makeup, although she had to keep stopping to

blow her nose ('with emotion — don't want to get snot on your frock') and curled my hair with her tongs. By the time Billy arrived, with Leo in the back of the Range Rover, I knew I looked like a princess. But the difference was, for the first time ever, I actually felt like one.

The evening went by too fast, in a whirl of champagne flutes, delicious nibbles that I didn't eat in case I spilled them on my dress, and turns around the dance floor with Boris and Leo. They both danced so well it didn't seem to matter that I hadn't a clue what I was doing. I had to take a photo call with Liza, but she nudged me into position each time (she actually kicked the back of my knee to make me stand better at one point) and no one asked me anything directly, so I didn't have to worry about getting an attack of Party Paralysis. I just smiled, dazed, and tried to remember each moment as it flashed past.

At midnight, Leo indicated that he wanted to leave, and we sneaked out through a side door, where only one or two photographers caught us. It felt weird when they shouted my name, as well as Leo's, and I had to stop myself from glancing backward — I knew I'd look tipsy in the photos. It had started to drizzle, but Billy was waiting close by, and Leo helped me into the backseat of the Range Rover, scooping my dress up with a practiced flick and tucking me inside before I had time to get my shoes wet.

I leaned my head happily against his shoulder as we set off home. I was quite drunk on the champagne, and the warmth of the car was making me both pleasantly sleepy and somewhat amorous.

'Do you mind if we make a bit of a detour?' asked Leo. The windscreen wipers sloshed comfortingly in the background as Billy negotiated the late-night traffic. 'There's something I need to show you.'

I snuggled into Leo's jacket. I loved the smell of his dinner jacket — the hot wool mingled with his distinctive cologne. I made a mental note never to tell anyone at home that. It was right up there with 'Caviar is surprisingly versatile as a storage cupboard staple.'

'Well, that depends what it is you've got to show me,' I mumbled, thinking of how warm his house was. Particularly his enormous oak sleigh bed, shipped over from the palace. I was quite keen to get back there. 'I don't know if you've noticed, but it's pouring down.'

'I think you'll think it's worth it.'

'If it's Nelson's Column by night, I've seen it. As the actress said to the bishop.'

Leo nuzzled the top of my head. 'It's not Nelson's Column by night.'

He leaned forward and said something to Billy, then pulled me closer. I watched the yellow streetlights blur past, mingling with the orange taxi signs and red brake lights, like a messy border of wallflowers in the night sky.

Billy seemed to be driving us home. We passed the golden Albert Memorial, and the shopfronts of Kensington High Street, and — we *were* going home. This wasn't a detour at all.

The car stopped in Trinity Square and Leo jumped out. He grabbed an umbrella from the backseat, opened it, and held it up with a wide smile.

It was chilly now, as well as wet. And I only had a cobweb of a shawl with me.

Billy turned round and saw my unenthusiastic expression. 'If you'd prefer a coat, miss, I keep a spare one in the boot.'

I got out of the car rather reluctantly, I have to admit. Billy's raincoat was about twelve sizes too big for me and didn't do much for the couture evening look.

Leo reached out a hand. His eyes were bright. 'Come on. I need to show you the garden!'

'The garden? Why do I want to see the garden? I know what's in the garden.'

'Stop moaning and come with me.' Leo grabbed my hand in his and pulled me gently through the iron gate.

The leafy trees held off the worst of the rain as we crunched down the gravel path, which was illuminated with tiny spotlights — I couldn't remember whether they'd been there the first night we'd come — and there were fairy lights in the trees too.

'There,' he said proudly. 'What do you think?'

I drew a deep breath.

The Adelaide fountain from the English garden stood in the middle of my roses, shooting plumes of water into the air, and water-lily lights picked out each crystal splash. The dancing figure on the lip raised her throat to the London sky, even prettier by night-lights than she'd been in the Mediterranean sun.

She looked as if she'd been waiting to come here all her life.

'Leo,' I breathed. 'It looks ... magical.'

'You think it works?'

'It makes the garden complete.' My eyes filled with tears, and I stopped trying to remember everything and surrendered to the powerful surge of emotion sweeping through me. As with so many things that happened around Leo, I couldn't quite believe that something so romantic could be real, here, happening to me.

I felt his strong arms wrap around me from behind, very real, very solid, and I leaned into his body, letting my tired eyes close with happiness.

He pulled me close and whispered down into my hair. 'Thank you. Thank you for bringing this garden to life.'

'It was alive already,' I protested. 'I just replanted this part.'

'No.' Leo nuzzled into my neck. 'No, you've given it something else. You've given it a soul. Those roses you chose, their fragrances and names and history — that's more than just sticking plants in soil. That's creating a story that'll continue year after year. And you've done the same with me. You've planted things in my life that I can see growing every day.'

'What? That sounds terrible—'

'No, really.' Leo turned me round very slowly and held me at arm's length so he could look into my eyes. His blue eyes were serious, but something in his expression made me tingle with anticipation.

I opened my mouth to say something to fill the awkward pause, but he stopped me.

'Amy. Before I met you, I worked, I played squash, and I bailed Rolf out of situations. Those were the highlights. After

I met you . . . well, I can't even remember what it was like before. I don't ever want to live like that again.'

My heart hammered against the bones of my corset.

'I know it's all happened very fast,' he went on, 'and I don't want you to think I'm being weird, but I feel as if we were only waiting to meet each other.' Leo paused and held my gaze. 'Do you know what I mean?'

'Yes,' I said, and decided to take a leap of faith. I closed my eyes, so that if I ended up talking rubbish I wouldn't have to see the look on his face. 'I do. We're not exactly the same, but we fit together. You feel right. You *smell* right. When I'm with you, it's like I'm at home, even here in London, where I never thought I'd properly be happy. I don't know what it is, but I could talk to you forever and never run out of things to say. And I could never get tired of looking at you. Ever.'

I drew a breath and opened one eye cautiously, and saw Leo smiling at me. A slow, relieved smile that made my insides turn to water. Splashy, moonlit fountain water.

'Plus, I can't believe that someone I fancy so much can possibly feel the same way about me,' I blurted out.

Leo pulled me close. 'I have felt exactly the same from the very first moment I saw you,' he murmured, his lips a breath away from mine.

He kissed me, gently at first, then hotter and harder, and my hands were starting to explore the fine cotton of his evening shirt when he pulled away and looked me straight in the eye.

'Amy. I think . . . we should drink a toast to the fountain.'

That wasn't what I was expecting him to say.

'What?' I said, a bit ungraciously, since I felt as if my whole body was now throbbing with lust. He'd felt pretty lusty too a second ago.

'If you have a look in the water, you'll find something I left there earlier. Come with me.'

Leo took my hand and led me right up to the fountain, where he passed me the umbrella, then rolled up his sleeve and fished about in the water until he found a silver ribbon. 'Pull that.'

I pulled it, but it was attached to something heavy, which clanked against the stone basin with a familiar sound. I reached in and pulled out a chilled bottle of Krug champagne, and Leo reached up into the upper bowl of the fountain and produced two flutes. With a couple of practiced motions, he unfoiled the bottle and filled my glass.

'There. To the garden of love, and all who garden in it. From the roses in the beds to the daisies in the grass.'

I took a sip of champagne and felt the bubbles on my tongue. It was amazing how quickly I'd started to enjoy champagne. I'd drunk more in the four months I'd been dating Leo than my parents had probably consumed in a lifetime of weddings and christenings and office functions.

Leo was watching me drink, and I felt rather self-conscious.

'Am I supposed to say a few words too?' I asked. 'I'd have prepared a speech if you'd given me notice.'

He frowned. 'You probably ought to do something. Why don't you throw the first coin in the fountain, for luck?'

'Okay.' I put my glass down on the edge and started to root around in my evening bag. I was a bit cack-handed, I have to confess — this wasn't my first glass of the night.

'No, here.' Leo produced a two-pound coin from his pocket with suspicious speed. 'Make a wish and toss it in.'

He had such a strange look on his face that I couldn't take my eyes off him as I took the coin. My pulse sped up.

I fixed the fountain with my best intent gaze, then closed my eyes and wished. Unlike my wishing on Grace's Dream Seeds, this time there was no arguing between the voices in my head. I wished for everything, greedily, like a child running through a sweet shop, just in case I never got a perfect moment like this again.

*I wish that Leo and I can always be this happy together.*

*I wish that Mum and Dad could have our old house back.*

*I wish Kelly would come home and make things right again.*

*I wish that Jo would realize that Ted's the man for her.*

Was it greedy to wish for so much stuff?

As I was trying to put things in order, I felt Leo's arms go round me again, and the thought that flashed through my brain like lightning was:

*I wish Leo would ask me to marry him.*

It was so loud in my head that I was scared I'd spoken it aloud, and threw the coin at the fountain more in surprise than anything else.

The coin landed with a splash and a clink and a tiny shower of water flew up; then one of the water-lily lights went out.

'I think you hit something,' said Leo.

Oh God. That wasn't a good sign.

'Oh no! I'm sorry,' I said, and dashed over to see what I'd broken.

Another silver ribbon was dangling over the side of the fountain.

'What's this?' I asked stupidly. 'Is this electrical?'

'Why don't you pull it?' Leo suggested innocently.

'What? Is there a bowl of bar snacks at the other end to go with the champagne?'

'Try and find out.'

I pulled, but this ribbon was a lot longer. It was wound around the carving of the lower basin and I moved around slowly, untangling it, until finally something detached and floated up to the surface of the water.

A white plastic shell.

I looked up and, on the other side of the fountain, Leo nodded at me to open it.

Everything felt very quiet all of a sudden in the garden, behind the splashing of the fountain and the distant rumble of traffic. Inside one box was another, and another, until finally I found the smallest antique box. And inside that was a diamond ring sitting in a deep ruby-red bed of velvet. Three big diamonds, glimmering and glinting in the lights from the trees and the path.

I heard myself gasp and the blood pounded in my ears. I'd dreamed about how I'd want to be proposed to all through the lonely teenage years when I'd longed for a boyfriend, but I'd never dreamed of a proposal as sweet and private as this.

Silently Leo came up behind me and took the box out of my hands. He removed the ring and then dropped to one knee on the gravel in front of me, and took my cold, wet hand in his.

'Amy,' he said solemnly, 'would you do me the great honor of being my wife?'

I couldn't speak. I just stood there in my couture ballgown and Billy's jacket, and made a jerky nod and smiled through the tears and rain running down my face. *Any second now,* I thought, as my heart swelled with too much joy for one woman, *I am definitely going to wake up.*

He looked up at me from under his long lashes. 'Is that a yes?'

I didn't know whether to pull Leo up to standing or crouch down or what, but I dropped to my knees too and grabbed his face in my hands.

'Of course it's a yes,' I said, kissing his eyes, his face, his lips. 'The honor would be all mine.'

# CHAPTER NINETEEN

When Leo and I announced our happy news to my parents, they managed to look surprised for all of ninety seconds, before Mum disappeared into the kitchen and came back bearing an enormous *Congratulations on Your Engagement cake.*

It had two tiers, topped with sugar-paste figurines of a girl with wild blond hair and a man with a tiny gold crown, and it looked suspiciously like a trial run for an even more enormous wedding cake.

'How did you know?' I demanded, then saw Leo and my dad exchanging proud manly looks, the sort that often end in back-slappage.

'Leo here did the decent thing and asked my permission first.' Dad's chest was actually inflating with traditionalist joy. Then he spoiled it a bit by adding, 'And I said, "Take her, by all means! If you're daft enough!"'

'When?' I ignored the guffawing from both parents and eyeballed Leo, who shrugged modestly. 'When did you find time to do that?'

'Oh, I popped up last week while I was in Manchester for work. Wanted to do things by the book.'

'Just a flying visit, ha-ha-ha,' added Dad helpfully. 'In his helicopter.'

'It was very thoughtful.' Mum's cheeks were bright pink. 'We were so touched he asked us. As if we'd say no . . .'

This was something of a turnaround, given that Martin Ecclestone, my last boyfriend, had virtually had to hand over three years of bank statements and his passport just to be allowed round for tea. But clearly they'd fallen for Leo as much as I had. And asking my dad if he minded this millionaire prince marrying his daughter told me Leo had somehow understood my parents without me having to explain an awkward thing, and for that, I loved him a tiny bit more.

I was very slightly niggled by his cavalier use of the cricket pitch, though. 'Does the cricket club mind you using their crease as a heliport?'

'He gave them a donation,' Mum piped up. 'Di Overend was telling me. Her Barry's on the team. They're building a new tea hut – very excited. You might get asked to open it!'

Leo grimaced. 'Sorry, that was meant to be a discreet donation.'

'Nothing round here's a secret for long,' I said, and then immediately wished I hadn't because a cloud passed over Mum's face.

'Tea!' said Dad quickly. 'Where's that tea! Let's have a Yorkshire toast!'

Later, when Leo was patiently telling Mum about the various types of cakes native to Nirona, Dad cornered me over the washing-up.

'Now, just because I've given my blessing doesn't mean you have to get married, love,' he said in a discreet undertone.

'You've only known this chap, what? A few months. That's not long at all. There's no rush to get wed. You have a nice long engagement.'

'Dad, I want to marry Leo. I just . . . know he's right for me.' I glanced at the windowsill where my priceless diamond ring sat on the cat-shaped ring tree Kelly and I had given Mum for a birthday ages ago.

Leo'd told me the ring had belonged to his great-grand-mother, the Australian gold-mining heiress who'd planned the international gardens, and she'd worn it every day of her seventy-one married years, 'even when she was in the bath or gardening.' It was sometimes hard making his world and my world match up, so it was nice when there was a tiny crossover. It made it feel more real.

'How, though? Can you know someone this quickly?'

I turned and saw the anxiety on my dad's honest face. I could understand why he felt it. It was hard to explain, especially to a bank manager who'd dealt squarely in hard facts for so long. Even Jo had been a bit taken aback by our news, although she'd recovered well enough to ask if the Pippa Middleton role was up for grabs.

'I think you taught me to know a decent person when I see one,' I said.

Dad looked squarely at me, and a hundred unspoken things flew up between us like ashes.

I knew Dad wanted to believe it too, from the half-reticent, half-eager way he chatted to Leo while Leo ate everything Mum put in front of him. The fact that Leo was a prince was almost a drawback, compared with his steady job and his polite manners. But Dad had given his permission for a man to marry one of his daughters before, and it hadn't ended well for anyone. Of all the things that Dad beat himself up about, I knew that was the one that still hurt most. However, I wasn't Kelly, and Leo certainly wasn't Christopher 'You can trust me, Stan' Dalton.

I grabbed his hand awkwardly. 'I know he seems too good to be true, but honestly, Leo's like this all the time. It's not an act. He sometimes even irons his own shirts.'

Dad's eyebrows shot up in surprise. He hadn't ironed a shirt since August 18, 1972. The eyebrows then fell as another concern broke through.

'But what'd you have to do? What are you signing yourself up for? Would you have to parade around with horses, and . . .' Dad's knowledge of royal duties abruptly ran out.

'It won't have any real effect on us. Leo's fifth in line — I'll just be getting married to a City banker with an amazing holiday home. You'd love the gardens, Dad. I don't know what they've done to the soil, but they've got roses there next to succulents – it's like Kew Gardens.'

He sighed. Maybe the shirts had swung it. 'Well, I'll only say this once, love, but don't forget — you can always change your mind. It's like I said to him, "Leo, lad, you might be a rich man, but Amy's the most precious thing in the world to me, and if you don't look after my beautiful girl as she deserves to be looked after . . ." '

I never found out what Dad had threatened to do, because we were both in tears over the sink, and it took us a good few minutes to compose ourselves enough to go back and face another round of cucumber sandwiches.

Leo wanted to put our engagement announcement in every paper, from the *Times* to the *Rothery Gazette*, but he couldn't understand why I was so reluctant to phone my parents to give them the details, since etiquette decreed it had to come from them — and, of course, they had to pay for the privilege.

'The *Times*, fine,' I said, trying to work out how much that would cost per word, given Leo's complicated name, 'but not the *Rothery Gazette*.'

He seemed surprised. 'Why not? They're so proud of you! And they like me, right?'

'They love you.'

He reached across the crisp white tablecloth and laced his fingers with mine. We were in Claridge's, waiting to have a celebratory dinner with Boris and Liza; they'd flown in the previous day and were staying in a suite upstairs, but they were still half an hour late for dinner. If Boris's PA was sending updates, we weren't getting them, as Leo had courteously turned off his phone as soon as we sat down.

'So why wouldn't they want to announce it to the local community?'

I loved Leo's relative normality, but he had some weird blind spots.

I gave him a patiently sarcastic look. '"The engagement is announced between Lauren, daughter of Pat and Richard Lewthwaite, and Matt, son of Debbie and Keith Scoggins, blah-blah." Then, "The engagement is announced between Amy

Rose, daughter of Pamela and Stan Wilde, and Prince Leopold William Victor, son of Prince Boris of Nirona and Svetland and Princess Eliza Top-Supermodel of New York and Milan, blah-blah." People would think they'd gone mad.'

'I'd be happy with "Amy Wilde is now engaged to Leo Wolfsburg of London." ' He raised an eyebrow. 'That's who I am — just some guy who's met the girl he wants to spend the rest of his life with.'

'But you're not just some guy. You're a guy who lands his helicopter on the village cricket pitch and then buys them a new pavilion as a make-do heliport.' I fiddled with my napkin, trying to make it cover my stomach. I was wearing Jo's pencil skirt again, and it was cutting into my circulation. I'd also been gardening all day to make up for the appointments I'd missed on my long weekend, and I hadn't had time to straighten my hair. I hoped Liza wouldn't comment on it.

'I beg your pardon?' Leo's expression was surprised. 'That wasn't the right thing to do?'

'Well, no, it . . .' I wasn't sure I could explain it without starting a row. But it had been eating away at me. It wasn't just that Leo had money; it was his attitude to it that sometimes made me stop and wonder if we were actually living in the same world. That you could just throw money at a problem, and if you threw enough money, even people ceased to be a problem.

Like flying up that first weekend. He'd dressed it up as meeting my parents, but actually he'd wanted to take me to that concert. And he hadn't asked them first. To be honest, the only time that Leo struck a wrong note with me was when he reminded me a bit too much of Rolf.

I tried to pin my elusive misgivings into words because I really didn't want them to start driving an invisible wedge between us. 'Leo, where I come from, even marrying someone from London is regarded as freakishly exotic. The better you do for yourself up there, the less you're meant to tell people about it.'

God, the tight skirt was giving me indigestion and we hadn't even eaten yet. I could really have done with a night on the sofa, just this once.

'Anyone would think you were embarrassed to be marrying me.' Leo's voice was light, but I glimpsed a steeliness in his eyes that I hadn't seen before, and I immediately wanted to row back.

'Don't be daft!' I reached for my water glass, but he moved it to one side and made me look up.

'What's the problem?' he said. 'Tell me if there is one, and we'll fix it.'

What could I say? How could I explain the entire 'no showing off' mentality of the North of England to a man whose eighteenth-birthday photograph had been taken by Bryan Adams? (Yes, Jo and I found it online.)

'They're just . . . private people, my parents,' I said. 'They don't like being talked about. And it's such a hive of gossip up there because nothing ever happens. The helicopter's taken over from last year's power cut as the hot topic of conversation.'

Leo squeezed my hand, and turned my engagement ring round so the diamonds twinkled in the candlelight; I'd made more effort with my nails in the past week than I had done in my whole life, and he nodded toward them, noticing the fresh beige manicure. 'Liking the nails,' he said.

I was distracted by that. For a second. 'But the thing is—'

'It's just that I'm so happy,' he said. 'I want everyone to know, before . . .'

'Before?'

'Darling! Or darlings, I should say!'

Our hands sprang apart as Liza and Boris approached the table in a starry trail of charisma and personally blended perfume. Even in Claridge's, stuffed with celebrities and millionaires, conversation paused, cutlery clattered against tableware, and, although heads didn't turn, eyes definitely swiveled sideways as they passed through.

It was impossible to tell whether they were late because of a steaming row, or a wardrobe change, or a bout of passion — maybe all three. Liza looked regal in a simple dove-gray wool dress with a tangle of gold chains, and Boris was rumpled, but in a good way, in a lounge suit. He mouthed a few cheery hellos to tables as he passed, a bit like Frank Sinatra.

No one could accuse this royal family of being chilly: Liza reached us first and enfolded Leo in her arms; then she grabbed me. She put her slender hands on either side of my face and gazed into my eyes as if we were sharing a significant moment. I was suddenly grateful we'd been seated at a discreet corner table and not in the middle of the room.

'Amy,' she said in her silky-smooth coo. 'Welcome. Welcome to our family.'

Her diamond rings dug into my cheeks. They were quite cold, and made my cheeks feel fat.

'Thank you,' I said. It came out a bit Donald Duck, on account of the way she was squeezing my face.

'You make my boy happy, all right!' she said, this time in a jokey Noo Yawk accent (I think it was New York; I was less sure she was joking), and I nodded nervously until Boris elbowed her aside and delivered two smackers on each cheek, then another for luck.

(Was that the official Nironan number of kisses? I made a note to check with Leo later. From now on I needed to know this stuff; I didn't want to offend anyone by underkissing them.)

'Congrats to you both. Leo's a smart guy,' he said. 'Big girls are always good news in our family. As my own father said to Liza when I brought her home all those years ago —'

'Not that many years ago.'

'— the crowds love a tall girl — means they can see 'em better in walkabouts! What did he say to you that made you so mad? Oh, yeah! "At least we already know you can walk in a straight line and wear a tiara!" ' Boris guffawed, ignoring the daggers shooting forth from Liza's flashing eyes, and added, 'Of course, in your case, at least we know you're not allergic to bouquets either!'

Boris and Liza were both looking at me as if I should say something, so I obliged. 'And I'm very handy with a shovel if you need to bury anything in a hurry!'

Oh. That sounded better in my head.

'What Dad means is that we know you're no stranger to a day's hard work,' said Leo, pulling out my chair and gesturing for us to sit down. 'Right, Dad? It's great that you've got a passion — like Mom has her campaigns. It shows people there's more to us than just parades and hats.'

'Well, your grandfather clearly adores her,' said Liza, nodding at my engagement ring. 'Did you ask him for that? I thought he was going to give it to Sofia.'

'Granddad offered it to me himself.' Leo calmly poured some water for her. 'If you must know, he came by my room before dinner, that weekend Amy came to stay, and told me he thought I might be needing it sooner rather than later. And he was right.'

'Really?' I asked without thinking, and felt a flutter of affection for the old man. If I'd known there was a ring hanging on that conversation about climbing roses, I'd never have dared open my mouth.

'Really,' said Leo, and smiled. 'He said your views on pruning were sound, and he liked the way you chatted to the tourists and didn't give him away. Whatever that means.'

My tetchy mood evaporated. Leo had adjusted to my parents far better than I'd coped with royal life so far. We both had to learn how to handle this, and I ought to cut him the same slack that he was cutting me. He'd never even mentioned some of the daft things I'd said at that dinner.

Liza wasn't letting the ring thing go, though. 'Let me see,' she said. 'I haven't seen this one in years. Sofia and I did a book a little while ago about all the family jewels — there are some magnificent pieces, you know. A lot of Cartier, a lot of Piaget . . .'

Shyly, I showed her my left hand. 'I still can't get used to seeing it there. I'm taking great care of it, obviously.'

'I hope you are,' she said. 'Did Leo tell you how much it's worth?'

'No,' said Leo quickly. 'But it's on my insurance.'

What? I hadn't actually thought about that until now. Was I going to get mugged for wearing it? Should I be giving it back to Leo every night? I glanced at him.

He shook his head imperceptibly at me.

'Good. But Sofia's not going to be happy.' Liza sighed. 'You might have to buy her a present.'

'Why? I'm the first one to get engaged. And Granddad gave it to me.'

'But she feels she's got a right to something—'

'Mom. You need to talk to her about this succession thing,' said Leo. 'Pavlos e-mailed me this week to ask if I could do anything to calm her down. She's talking about taking the whole thing to the Court—'

'So, have you two lovebirds set a date?' Boris asked, cutting across the fierce brow-furrowing going on across the table. 'We need to give the palace souvenir people time to get their tea towels ready!'

He winked at me. Or maybe he was winking at the waiter, I didn't know — a vast chilled champagne bucket appeared, anyway. I didn't mind; I quite liked Boris's winking. It didn't have quite so much of an agenda as Liza's sympathetic head-tilting.

'Yes, what were you planning? The cathedral? That would make such a magnificent setting.' Liza's eyes lit up and she tapped her cheek with one perfect greige nail. 'And so spectacular for photography. But maybe the family chapel would be more intimate? For an additional blessing?'

My heart started to sink. Leo and I hadn't discussed the details, but we were pretty firm on the basics, and I had a feeling they weren't going to go down very well.

Leo put his hand on mine. 'Actually, Amy and I were planning on having a small informal wedding near her parents' house in Yorkshire,' he said firmly. 'Followed by a blessing back home in the chapel and a reception in the gardens.'

Liza nearly dropped her glass. 'What? But you have to get married in Nirona. People expect it, honey!'

'No, they don't. We're not heirs to the throne. They might expect it for Serge and Guillermo —'

'I don't think those two are getting married in a hurry.' Boris pulled an 'if you know what I mean' expression.

'They're *fifteen*, Boris.'

'— but I'm marrying as a private individual,' Leo went on. 'I love the cathedral, you know that, but this is Amy's wedding day. I want it to be in a place that's special to her too.'

Liza was silent for a moment, then snapped, 'How about we do a blessing in the cathedral? And the reception in the palace banqueting hall?'

'Cathedral, and gardens,' Leo shot back. 'Not budging on the gardens.'

'Done. And the date?'

'Soon,' said Leo.

'But not too soon,' I said quickly. 'I need to give my mum and dad time . . . to prepare everything.'

To be totally honest, I wanted to give Mum a chance to see a doctor about her anxiety, since there was no sign of Kelly reappearing — the one thing that might cure Mum's miserable, paranoia-driven comfort eating. She was so reluctant to leave the house in case anyone saw her that I wasn't sure how she'd get through a whole wedding service. Especially once someone — top royal correspondent Di Overend, probably — reminded her that my new mother-in-law was an international super-model and had been, just this week, hobnobbing with the First Lady about the importance of thank-you notes.

On top of that, Dad would want time to redecorate the house from top to bottom, and that wasn't a ten-minute job, as he'd put it. I hadn't discussed the ceremony with them yet — I wanted to let them get used to the idea slowly — but they were happy I'd chosen the tiny church near our old house. St. Cuthbert's was so small the guest list would *have* to be minimal.

'There's no . . . reason it needs to be soon? Not that it's a problem, but I should let the PR team know. If you know what I mean.' Liza arched an eyebrow and I blurted out, 'What? No!' a bit too loud.

'That's a mind-your-own business, Liza,' said Boris. 'In English.'

Under the table, I felt the gentle pressure of Leo's ankle against mine.

'The only reason I want to get married soon, Mom, is because I can't wait to introduce Amy to people as my wife,' he said, slipping his hand around mine again, and I thought my heart would burst with happiness.

The waiter took our order, and Liza asked me questions about Yorkshire while Boris pulled faces she couldn't see to try to put me off. The wine gave me a touch of extra confidence, and I was beginning to think that having dinner with two princes and a princess-supermodel wasn't actually that hard. I was even enjoying the curious glances we were getting from some corners of the room, as other diners recognized Liza and maybe even Leo.

As the waiter reappeared with pudding menus, I could see Leo frowning at something, and eventually he put his knife and fork down.

'Dad, is that your phone buzzing? You know you're meant to turn them off in here.'

'What?' Boris slapped his jacket pocket. 'Is it?'

'Come on, turn it off. Mine's off.'

Boris looked like he was going to argue, but Leo raised his eyebrows, and Boris reluctantly extracted the phone.

'Fifteen missed calls,' he said. 'Fifteen. You'd better hope none of them were George Clooney.'

'I thought you weren't taking his calls after the villa thing.'

'I'm not. But now I need his villa.'

'Mom!'

Liza was surreptitiously checking her phone. Well, phones. She had two.

'I've got twenty missed calls,' she said.

'George?'

'Two from him. But ten from Nina.'

I cut a sideways glance at Leo.

'Nina is Mom's assistant,' he muttered. 'She doesn't do missed calls.'

'I should call her back,' Liza announced. 'It might be about the meetings tomorrow. I'm here to speak with the prime minister's wife about my Everyday Princess campaign,' she told me. 'I'm very much hoping to get the Duchess of Cambridge on board too, if she's not too busy with her, well, I shouldn't say what.'

Heads swiveled at the nearest tables.

But before she could start shimmying between the tables, the maître d' approached. His nervous tension was visible from across the room; he had the windblown expression of someone who'd recently been yelled at.

'I'm so sorry to interrupt your meal, Your Highnesses,' he said, 'but your assistant is outside and is very anxious to speak to you.'

'Can it wait until we've had some pudding?' asked Boris. 'I spotted something on that menu that—'

'No, I think she would like to speak with you now. It was . . . very difficult to stop her coming in in person.'

'Of course we must speak with Nina.' Liza pushed her chair back and unfolded her elegant frame. There wasn't a single lump or bump in her wool dress, which was more than I could say for my skirt. 'Leo, Amy, would you excuse us for a moment?'

Leo stood politely while the maître d' escorted them around the tables, and as soon as he sat down, Leo took my hand in his.

'Listen, I want to say this while they're gone — I don't want you to think that you're not worthy of the cathedral and a big wedding.' He searched my face. 'It's just that being second-tier royal means we're allowed a little more privacy. We get to do things our own way.'

'I understand that.' Still, though, the cathedral was magnificent . . .

He pressed on, clearly anxious that I didn't get the wrong end of the stick. 'I want you to have the day you want, not feel like you're in someone else's production. I love the idea of marrying in your village church. I'm honored to be part of that tradition.'

'Well, it would mean a lot to me. It's where I always practiced getting married.'

'And don't think you have to scale down the budget, just because it's small. I can set up an account, and hire a planner to help your mom, and—'

'No,' I said. Hadn't he been listening? 'No, I want to organize it myself. Please.'

Leo took a big slug of wine, and I realized he was tenser than he was letting on. 'That's fine with me. Small is good. If Mom wants to stage-manage a big family number, she can do it when Sofia gets married. This is our day. Right?'

'Right.'

I turned the gold signet ring on his little finger round and round, then looked up.

'I sent one of the old English roses I sourced for your garden to your grandfather, for his garden,' I said. 'I got the nicest note back. He said he hoped we'd invite him round for dinner in the summerhouse one night.'

'That is so typical of him, the old fox,' Leo began, but out of the corner of my eye, I saw a gray column moving between the tables like one of those big American twisters you see on the news.

In seconds, Liza was back at the table. Her smile was fixed at an unnatural angle with the effort of remaining calm; I recognized it from Grace's strained conversations with her daddy on the phone.

'Mom, are you okay? What's happened?' Leo was so worried he didn't even drop his voice.

She slipped onto a chair and took his hand in hers. 'Leo, honey,' she said. 'Your grandfather's had a heart attack. He's been flown to the mainland and the doctors are doing all they can, but he's in a critical condition. He was in the garden and they think he was there for a while . . . on his own.'

'Oh my God.' Leo went pale.

I gripped his other hand tightly.

'Your father and I are flying back right now. He wants us there. And you. Nina says . . .' She glanced around her to make sure no one could hear. 'Nina says he's been talking about Pavlos and the succession and—'

Leo pushed his chair back, and threw his napkin on the table. 'Let's go. Right now.'

And that was when everything started to get very blurry.

# CHAPTER TWENTY

Leo, Boris, and Liza were whisked away to the airport with a police escort and blue lights and sirens and everything. Nina and their team of assistants followed behind in a minivan, making calls and lugging Louis Vuitton bags as they went.

I stood on the pavement as the Wolfsburgs left, almost hidden by the curious crowd that had slowed down to watch, and blew Leo a kiss as he raised his hand from the back of the car. He looked upset, but had still managed to call Billy to take me home, and now the dark Range Rover was waiting for me at the curb.

Billy didn't open our usual conversation about his wisteria, and we drove through the London night in silence. I couldn't stop thinking about charming Willi in his rumpled linen suit; how different he'd been from the dignified statesman I'd met over dinner that same night. Only the twinkly eyes had been the same. I'd only spent an hour or so with him, but I could feel why Leo had looked so devastated as he sped away. I felt a hollowness in my own chest too.

As I put my key in the lock of our flat, Dickon appeared on the landing with Badger, who had streaks of blue paint up his white legs. The final trace of royal glamour vanished from my evening, banished by Dickon's revolting slipper-socks and the smell of microwave curry.

'Your dog is even worse at modeling than you two,' he complained. 'I've got one crap sketch of him and four canvases covered in blue paw prints.'

I gave Dickon a weary look. I wasn't in the mood. 'To be honest, Dickon, I've seen that canvas you've been drying in the airing cupboard, and I'd rather look at blue paw prints than Mrs Mainwaring in the nip with a sponge cake covering her business.'

'There's nothing wrong with my nudes,' said Dickon huffily. 'The pictures of Irene are very Lucian Freud.'

I picked Badger up and he licked my nose, probably because I still smelled of Claridge's finest Kobe beef. 'Why's he with you anyway? Where's Jo?'

'She's out. With that loud posh guy.'

'That doesn't narrow it down.'

'The one with the Porsche. And the tight trousers.'

'Again, narrower?'

I sensed a smidgeon of jealousy from Dickon. He'd have to join the queue behind Ted if he was going to have a crush on Jo.

'The one who keeps sending stuff that *I* have to sign for because neither of you is *ever in*.'

My brow furrowed. 'Rolf? Jo's gone out with —' I stopped. Oh no. Maybe Rolf didn't know about his grandfather!

At that moment, the front door opened again, and Jo stumbled in with a furtive expression on her face. Then she looked up and saw me and Dickon glaring at her over the railing and looked positively guilty, as if she'd been caught scoffing an enormous Big Mac meal.

'It was just a drink!' she protested, running up the stairs — in her highest heels and shortest skirt, I noted. 'I was at a loose end! And the arse walked out on me anyway! I'm back now, aren't—'

'Jo, come on in, I need to talk to you. And no, we don't need any company, thanks,' I added, as Dickon tried to sidle into our flat behind her.

'Thanks so much for looking after Badger, darling.' Jo planted a sloppy kiss on Dickon's unshaven cheek, which made me think that, (a) Rolf must have been keeping the mojitos flowing, and, (b) she must have left Badger at the very last minute. And, (c) Dickon looked a bit too pleased.

I locked the door behind us, and didn't even bother when Badger trotted across to the sofa with his painty paws.

'Pleeeease don't give me a lecture,' Jo sang, throwing herself on the sofa and kicking off her heels. 'Rolf took me out for dinner to apologize for the last time, seeing as he's going to be my flatmate-in-law and we'll be going down the aisle together. You know, he's actually quite sweet. In a sort of lounge-lizardy way. He asked me if I needed any help planning your hen night.'

'Oh God,' I said faintly.

Jo gazed up at me, her face wreathed in smiles. 'You have *no idea* what a hit you were in Nirona. Rolf told *me* that Leo told *him* that his grandfather's been telling everyone who'll listen how thoroughly charming you are. Leo's English rose! Apparently everyone's started hanging around the gardens pretending to be interested in flowers because roses are the new—'

I couldn't let her go on. 'Jo. Their grandfather's had a heart attack. He's in the hospital, and Leo's flown back to Nirona with his parents to see him.'

Jo stopped rubbing her aching feet and looked up, shocked. 'No! So that was where Rolf dashed off to.' She looked mortified. 'I knew I shouldn't have sent him those stroppy texts . . .'

'Well, he should have warned you he was leaving in a rush.' I pushed myself off the sofa and went to make a cup of tea, before remembering there was no milk in the fridge because neither of us would admit we'd finished it. The chasm between Leo World and my own had never felt so sharp.

I made us two cups of out-of-date instant hot chocolate instead, and we sat and stared morosely at our phones waiting for messages, trying to resist the temptation to check online to see if the royal-watching sites had got hold of the news yet. *That* was weird.

I was about to crack and text Leo again when he rang from the hospital.

'How is he? How are you?' I asked breathlessly. Jo pretended not to listen in.

Leo sounded croaky. 'Not good. I saw him for ten minutes, but he was covered in tubes and wires, and he's had all the lawyers and advisors in there ever since. And they don't turn up unless it's serious.'

'I'm so sorry.' I gripped the phone, wishing I could be with him, even though I had no idea what I'd do. 'I remember when my grandmother died . . . it's awful when you can't do anything. But it'll mean a lot to him that you're there.'

'I don't know if he even knew I went in.'

'He will. Gran knew I'd been. I told her I'd do anything to make her better when I thought she couldn't hear me, but the last thing she did was to tell the doctor I'd offered to take Badger.' I hesitated, not sure if it was appropriate, but Leo seemed to want to talk. 'Mum was a bit put out, she thought Gran's last words should have been about God or her kids or something, but apparently they were all to do with house-keeping.'

Leo tried to laugh, and my heart broke for him. This was something all the money in the world couldn't fix.

'So he'll know you came,' I said, feeling close to tears myself. I'd really liked Willi. He'd had that knack of making someone feel really special within just a few moments, just like Leo did. There were so many stories I wished I could have heard about 'our' Trinity Square garden. And now I'd never get to know him properly.

'Amy, can you fly out in the morning?' Leo said. 'I really want you to be here.'

'Won't I be in the way? It's a family time . . .'

'You're part of the family now. And I need you. Will you? I'll ask Billy to pick you up, and Nina will arrange flights.'

'Of course,' I said without thinking, 'I'm packing right now.' My eye fell on the overflowing basket of unwashed laundry, and I remembered I was wearing my spare, spare, spare knickers; thanks to my crammed work diary and my even more crammed Leo diary, housework had gone to the wall.

Without a word, Jo put her cocoa down and started loading the machine.

When I arrived at the palace the next morning, it seemed that every single member of the immediate Wolfsburg family and all their attendant staff had flown to the hospital, so I spent three hours sitting in a high-ceilinged reception room in Boris and Liza's east-wing apartment, waiting for someone to appear to tell me what was going on. I didn't dare poke around too much in case someone caught me snooping, so I studied the oil paintings (Leo and Rolf were classic examples of blond/dark Wolfsburg manhood, give or take a breastplate or two), and drank cup after cup of Darjeeling tea from a bone china cup with the Nironan crest on it. (Two lions rampant, with gold ribbons and white roses.)

Eventually I had to stop drinking tea because I was too embarrassed to go and find someone to tell me where the loo was.

When Leo finally appeared at half two, in jeans and a fresh white shirt and hair that looked slept on but all the more sexy for it, he wasted no time in spiriting me out through a side entrance into the gardens. He marched me through the Italian garden and the Australian bush garden to the private family gardens that tourists weren't allowed in; then he grabbed me and gave me a tight hug that made the blood shoot round my body.

'I'm so glad to see you,' he said, pressing his nose into my hair. 'Thank you for coming.'

'Leo,' I said, gently wriggling free, 'is everything okay? What's happening?'

He pulled a 'not really' face, then sat me down on the nearest stone bench.

'Granddad died this morning.' I could tell he was struggling not to cry.

'Oh, I'm so sorry!' I took his hands, threading my fingers through his.

'In a way, I'm glad. He was there at the end, but he was weak and there were problems — serious ones. He was a very active man, he'd have hated being on machines. It's as if he was only hanging on long enough to . . .' He stared out over the garden and pressed his lips together.

'You don't have to hold anything back for me,' I murmured into his shoulder. 'It's okay.'

Leo turned back to me with wet eyes. 'You were saying how the last thing your grandmother did was to give you Badger?'

I nodded. 'She thought I was the only one who'd look after him properly. It was typical of her that her last thought was about tidying up.'

'Well, the last thing Granddad did was to change the succession. Dad's the new sovereign prince now. Not Pavlos.'

I blinked in surprise. 'What?'

'Granddad apparently "remembered" that Dad had been born ten minutes before Pavlos, and that he'd only said Pavlos was older because my grandmother had thought he was born first, and he didn't want to contradict her in public.'

'But isn't it on the birth certificate?'

Leo pressed his thumbs into his eyes wearily. He didn't look as if he'd slept at all. 'You're not going to believe this, but they've produced a birth certificate that says otherwise. If I were a really suspicious person, I'd wonder if he'd had two done at the time for this very reason.'

'But why would someone do that?'

'To see how your two heirs shaped up and then decide later?'

'What? Like *The Apprentice*?' I realized a nanosecond too late that that probably wasn't the most tactful way of putting it.

Leo shrugged and nodded. 'It's like I said, at the time the cabinet wanted a serious heir. Pavlos's always been serious. He's a qualified tax accountant — he does the family tax returns for fun. He represented Nirona at chess. The most controversial thing he's done in his entire life is marry a Frenchwoman.'

'That's not controversial.'

'I know. He's . . . a bit dull. But, God, I should have seen it coming — things are different now, banking isn't what it was, tourism's on the way up again, and . . .' Leo wiped his face with his hand. 'I guess Granddad felt that glamour's where the money is, and that Mom and Dad will do a better job of keeping Nirona on the map. Mom's got her media profile in the US, and Dad's very popular. Sofia's got some historical credibility, with the books she's published about the family, I've got the banking experience, and even Rolf's got connections in the entertainment industry . . .'

He trailed off as his words sank in. I made myself count the seagulls flying across the bay to connect myself to this surreal conversation. I couldn't take it in.

A leaden feeling was pooling in my stomach. I didn't have connections to the entertainment industry. Or academic credibility. Or anything else that would count in Wolfsburg PLC. And it was so easy to get rid of people who didn't fit.

I wondered how much money Boris was going to throw at the Pavlos problem. What sort of pay-off did princes need?

*One. Two. Three. Four.* There were a lot of seagulls here. *Five. Six.* Keep counting, don't speak. *Seven. Eight.*

'But what about Pavlos!' I said, unable to hold it in. 'He's devoted his whole life to being taken seriously! How does he feel, having it taken away from him? What about his kids? Haven't they been sitting in every night eating pizza instead of going wild in Boujis?'

'I know it sounds harsh, but it's not about him. It's about what's best for the country,' said Leo. 'That's always been drilled into us, even me and Rolf. Nirona's like an extra dad. You've always got to put it first. How you behave, how you spend your holidays, what job you choose. If Granddad thought that what Nirona needed was a more glamorous, proactive monarchy, then Pavlos will just have to deal with it.'

I couldn't think of anything to say. I was trying to relate the situation to something I'd felt myself, but the closest I'd got to this sort of thing was when Dad's brother Terry had wanted my cousin Steve to take over the family bakery and he'd refused because of his skin condition and there'd been words. Even though, as Di Overend put it, no one likes a scabby bun.

'I mean, Pavlos might be happy for all we know.' Leo turned his palms up with a shrug. 'He couldn't do his orienteering at any sort of competitive level while he was the heir to the throne, in case of injury.'

'Well, that's okay, then.' I knew I was taking it too personally, but there was nothing wrong with Pavlos. He was a bit dull, and a bit balding compared with Boris and Liza's luxuriant manes, but not *dispensable*. 'I'm sure Mathilde will be *relieved* she doesn't have to be the reigning princess, if Pavlos can spend more time running around the local forests with a compass and a whistle. It's every little girl's *dream* to be married to a man in an anorak.'

Leo ran a hand through his messy hair, making it stick up even more. 'Amy, that's what I wanted to talk to you about on your own. Before anyone else gets back.'

'Um, okay.' This sounded ominous.

'The situation now's very different to what it was last week. Whether we like it or not, things have changed for me.'

He swallowed, stared at the ground, then looked straight at me, his expression disconcertingly serious. His familiar face had an edge to it I suddenly didn't recognize, and I had the sickening sensation of being on the other side of a widening chasm.

'If you want to break off the engagement,' said Leo, 'I will completely understand.'

I blinked in shock. Break off the engagement? 'What?'

'If you want to break it off, then I understand,' he repeated.

'Are you saying . . .' I really did feel nauseous now; I could taste the tea rising in my throat. 'Are you saying . . . that now you're the crown prince . . . we shouldn't get married?'

As soon as the words left my mouth, I was embarrassed. How could a gardener stand next to him in a tiara and state robes? The country would be expecting someone like Liza, or Sofia. I knew I couldn't do what Liza did. Leo was trying to give me a dignified exit, making it look like my decision, while they got busy restructuring their new royal family.

Icy prickles of humiliation sliced through me, despite the warm sun.

I started to take off the diamond ring on my finger, but my hands were shaking and I couldn't get it over my knuckle.

'What are you doing?' he asked.

'Giving . . . you . . . your . . . ring back.' I finally got it off, and offered it to him. 'There. You can find someone more princessy to give it to.'

Leo's jaw dropped open. 'No! Oh my God, no, what gave you that idea?'

'You did! Just now! You asked me to break off our engagement!'

'Amy, no, it's the other way round.' He grabbed my hands, but didn't push the ring straight back on. 'It won't just be me you're marrying now. When Dad's crowned, I'll have to be here much more. I might be able to carry on my job part-time, but I'd have official duties too, especially if Mom's going to be back and forth to the US with this campaign. She wants to be a UN goodwill ambassador. It's not like the royal family runs the country, but our role has always been hands-on, lots of public appearances and charity work. As my wife, you'd have to take on some fundraising of your own . . .' He paused. 'I know you're not mad about public appearances. You don't enjoy that side of my life. That's fair enough.'

I stared at him. If I said no, was that giving them ammunition to fire me too?

'I would try,' I heard myself say. 'For you. If it's important for you . . .'

Leo suddenly looked older. More like a man, a man with responsibilities that were weighing him down. 'That would just be the start. Ultimately, you'd have to be with me when I take over from Dad. You'd be taking on the top job too. I've got no choice in the matter. But you have. I know you'd be wonderful, you're so natural with people, so good at listening, but I don't want to force you into it.'

My heart banged so hard against my chest I could hardly breathe. It was dreamlike but thrilling at the same time, that Leo honestly believed I was up to taking on a job he cared so much about himself. That he wanted me next to him.

'I mean, I'm assuming Dad isn't going to change the succession so Rolf inherits instead of me,' he added.

'I think Rolf would have to get some shoes with laces first,' I said. 'And a shave. Stubble is not a good look with a crown.'

Leo managed a quick smile, but his expression still seemed wary. 'Do you need a little time to think about this? I don't want to rush you. It's a big decision.'

'I don't need any time at all,' I said, all the whispering doubts in my heart swept away. 'I want to marry *you*. I want to be with you. If you're going to be a banker or a prince or a gardener, I'd want to be with you, helping you to do whatever you had to do. Making you happy. And I hope you'd do the same for me.'

'You know I would,' said Leo. He gazed at me, relief mingling with the sadness in his red-rimmed eyes. He traced the line of my cheekbone with his finger, touching the bump of my nose. 'And I will. I promise I will.'

He took his great-grandmother's diamond ring from my

fingers, and tried to fit it back on. But my knuckles had swollen up with friction, and it wouldn't move.

My heart sank. Oh God. It was an omen. I'd broken the spell. I'd thrown away the ring!

'Oh no. You don't get away that easily,' he said, and grabbing my hand, he plunged it into the water feature behind us, holding it down until my skin chilled. Then he slid the ring on my finger, and smiled triumphantly.

I looked at the diamonds sparkling in the sunshine and tried to make the moment stick in my head: I was Amy Wilde from Hadley Green, and I was going to be a crown princess.

And then Leo leaned forward, took my face in his hands, and kissed me, slowly and sweetly, while the fountain trickled behind us, and the bougainvillea tumbled in front of us, and it was as if he'd proposed all over again but this time in Technicolor.

# CHAPTER TWENTY-ONE

Back in London, the reality of where my life was now headed began to sink in when I had a sneaky look at the prince-hunting websites and discovered that I now had my own official page on YoungHot&Royal.

My hit-rate was second only to Rolf's; he had celebrated his promotion to second in line by buying a racehorse called Daft Mare. But whereas online posters were lining up to lust after Rolf's luscious lips and chest hair, they were mainly concerned with making personal comments about my 'manly' calves and taking bets on how long it would be before Leo got back with Flora Hardy-Torrence.

'It's not fair to use a photo of you at a funeral,' Jo complained on my behalf. (I had to pretend I didn't check it four times a day.) 'You're supposed to be looking sad and dignified. There's no need for the "miserable" caption. You're wearing a fascinator, for God's sake. Those things *pinch*.'

'They're not blackheads either,' I pointed out from the kitchen, where I was potting some seeds. 'That's the veil.'

'I'll write and correct them.'

'No! Don't.'

The photograph was of me outside Nirona's beautiful Gothic cathedral, on top of the island's highest hill. Leo's grandfather's funeral had been a magnificent state affair, and it gave me the first big culture shock of our new relationship. Until now, Boris and Liza hadn't seemed too different from some of the wealthier clients Ted and I worked for in London — thanks to recommendations from Jo's limpetlike client Callie, we'd worked in some spectacular houses. Even the glamorous nights out as Leo's black-tie date had started to feel almost normal, given that they often ended with us curled up on his squashy sofa, me eating cereal in my evening wear while he rubbed my sore feet and checked the markets one last time before bed.

But the crowds that greeted Prince Wilhelm's horse-drawn carriage made me realize that in Nirona, at least, Leo wasn't just some wealthy businessman. He was *their* prince of hearts. Thousands of people lined the streets around the cathedral, many waving flags and wearing black armbands, and banks of international cameramen jostled for pictures of Leo and Rolf walking in the procession behind a somber but tanned Boris and a haggard Pavlos. (Further Internet research suggested that haggard was his default expression, but clearly orienteering wasn't quite the compensation Leo thought for losing the top job.)

Both Leo and Rolf looked as brooding and handsome as film stars, with purple state sashes over one shoulder and jet-polished shoes you could see your face in. Some girls screamed as they went past and were roundly shushed, but even so, I got the message. If Leo was going to break the hearts of all Nironan women under the age of thirty-eight, I was going to have to prove to them I was more Cinderella than Yoko Ono.

The paparazzi aimed their lenses at me too, even though I didn't walk with the family, our engagement not yet being officially announced in the court circular. That made me feel uncomfortable; my makeup was heavier than normal, and I was terrified of smiling by accident and someone posting it on the Internet as 'Amy's Disrespect.' Leo had told me to go to Harvey Nichols and buy whatever I needed, but I'd stuck to a plain black coat and a hat that the assistant talked me into against my better judgment. I'd never worn a hat; my masses of hair had always been enough of an event on their own. Liza had had her hairdresser do an emergency restyle on me so my fascinator stayed clamped on my head, then put me in Car Five with Nina the assistant and some distant cousins.

'It's better to keep it low-key,' as Liza said. (Actually, we were all supposed to be calling her Eliza, now she was the sovereign princess.) 'We can shoot the official engagement photo when all this calms down. It'll cheer people up. Everyone loves a royal wedding.'

So that was the next big thing preying on my mind as I went back to London, to a grumpy Ted and a gardening diary full of postponed appointments: the official engagement photo. I'd never enjoyed having my photo taken, as I never looked the way I did in my head; and now, thanks to the fashion police at YoungHot&Royal.com, I knew that my natural resting expression was 'vacant.' However, I tried hard to believe Leo when he persuaded me that it would be fine, and that Liza's team of makeup artists and stylists would make sure I looked as gorgeous in the final photograph as he assured me I did in real life.

Or as Ted put it, as he reluctantly helped me with a rescheduled border-planting session in Fulham, 'There's always Photoshop.'

Three days later, I got the e-mail from Liza informing me and Leo, with Nina and her press officer, Giselle, cc'ed in, that plans for the ceremonial blessing of Prince Leo and Princess Amelia were now 'very near the top of her agenda!' and that I should be prepared to clear diary space at short notice.

From my wedding onward, I would be known as Princess Amelia. I found that out from the glossy press release that Liza's office had prepared for us to sign off on.

'Amelia? What's wrong with Amy?' said Leo when I read it aloud to him. We were having a picnic lunch in his office; he didn't have time to make it across town on his shorter hours, but I didn't mind. The panoramic view from his window over the City was something I was happy to trek across town for.

'She says she thinks Amelia sounds more royal. She told me she changed her name to Eliza from Liza. What could I say?'

He snorted. 'You'll notice that she's not calling me Prince Leopold. That's a *lot* more royal. And she chose it.'

'Look, I don't mind,' I said, although it already felt as if the press release was about someone else. Giselle had gone very heavy on 'Amelia's' expertise in organic horticulture and garden design, her commitment to preserving biodiversity in the form of honeybee protection schemes, her interest in fringe theater, and her delight in outdoor pursuits (which I assumed was the Duke of Edinburgh's Award I'd told her about).

I mean, technically it was all true — and I had just signed the Palace View landscaping contract, which was a huge deal to me, at least. In a way, it was quite flattering to see myself through their eyes — but also a bit . . . scary.

'If she thinks Amelia's better . . . Technically it is my name, I've just never been called it.'

'Is it?' Leo swung round on his office chair. He looked surprised. 'Did you tell her that? Or did she subpoena your birth certificate?'

'I think I told Giselle . . .' I couldn't remember. Giselle had a way of extracting details that made you feel you were in a centrifuge — i.e., dizzy and eager to give up information. 'I had that chat with her after the funeral.'

Leo's expression changed to one of sympathy. 'I forgot you talked to her. What else did she winkle out of you? You know the CIA had to sack Giselle for unsafe practices?'

Giselle's first words to me had been, 'So, Amy — sell yourself!' which was an immediate problem, since it had been drilled into me from an early age that talking about yourself was bad manners, not to mention boring. And to be honest, there wasn't a huge amount to tell her — there's only so many ways you can spin your mother's encounter with Princess Anne at the Great Yorkshire Show. Giselle's questions seemed geared to flushing out much more high-ranking details, like where I'd done my degree or what my most significant achievement to date had been. Mindful of Pavlos's recent sacking, I'd done my best to give her whatever she needed.

Both Liza and Giselle had demanded to know what charities I'd be representing; under pressure, I'd suggested I could found a therapy garden — since digging seemed to have stabilized my dad's depression — and 'maybe something to do with baking?'

'Home baking is a wonderfully inclusive, nourishing skill,' Liza had said. 'You know what would be great? If you could do some baking classes for underprivileged kids! Maybe your mom would like to join in! Wouldn't that be cute? Me and your mom and you?'

I'd tried to hide my horror and had agreed to about four things in a row just to stop the questions. I spotted on the press release that the Princess Amelia Green Shoots Project would be launching 'this summer.' When was I going to do that? My work diary was already running three weeks behind. And I could have come up with a better name than that. Especially if I was going to be designing it.

At his desk, Leo stabbed the send button on the e-mail he'd been rushing to finish, then joined me on the executive leather sofa. His assistant had been told not to put any calls through for half an hour, and we were down to eleven minutes now.

He pinched a California roll from my sushi box and put his feet up on the chrome table. 'I'm sorry about Giselle, but in my experience, it's always better to give the press something to run with, and then they don't come looking for more. And by the same argument, it's better to agree to this engagement photo session for Mom, and then she'll leave us to handle the wedding plans ourselves.'

He flashed me a crooked smile that gave no hint of all the wrangling about cathedrals and banquets that had gone on when I wasn't around. I knew that because Rolf had told Jo that Liza had tried to barter a honeymoon on Richard Branson's ultra-exclusive Necker Island in return for a cathedral wedding, and Leo had refused point-blank because it was still my day.

I felt bad. I didn't want to look like I was causing trouble already.

'Seriously, have you read this? *"Amelia Wilde is one of London's most in-demand outdoor experience creators, and comes from a long line of horticultural experts."* She sounds great. I must get her on board!'

'She is great.' Leo slid his arm around me, mindful of the glass walls that surrounded his minimalist office space. 'I particularly like it when she wears those jeans with the rips in the wrong place and then digs until she gets this very attractive flush all over her . . .'

My stomach knotted with excitement, and I had to resist a powerful urge to wrestle him to the ground. Leo looked extremely suave in his business suit. All chiseled and professional and . . .

A secretary walked past and stared in at us, and I sat bolt upright. Leo just helped himself to more sushi.

'Will I have to do much preparation for this photo shoot?' I tried to phrase it so I didn't sound quite so clueless.

'Ah.' He scrunched one side of his face up, as if he'd found something untoward in his fish.

'Ah, what?'

'Ah, I meant to warn you about that. Sofia's going to be in London next week, and she said she'd come round and give you a heads-up on the sort of prep you might want to do.'

'Such as?' I asked warily. Sofia was supergroomed. That totally understated New York-style supergrooming that made Jo look like Helena Bonham Carter.

Leo shrugged. 'I have no idea, I'm not a girl. But you shouldn't have to do too much. You're gorgeous as you are. I keep telling you.'

I put back my last bit of sushi and pushed the box away. I had the sinking feeling that I was already about five bazillion calories too late.

Sofia came round in person to begin the princessing process while I was in the bath deliberating about whether shaving my legs before being taken on a beauty boot camp was like tidying up for the cleaner.

I know. I could have kicked myself. But to be fair, she arrived at eight o'clock, and I honestly had no idea she'd turn up herself — I'd assumed she'd call me and send a car or her assistant like the rest of them did. Sofia either didn't have the staff or, as I soon realized, didn't trust anyone to do anything properly.

Dickon had to let her in, because I was in the bath and Jo hadn't heard the door buzzer (she was on the phone to Callie Hamilton, who was trying to persuade her to oversee the new subcellar under her cellar). By the time Sofia had stalked up two flights of stairs, she'd probably added at least two more to-do's to her list of improvements, starting with sacking the doorman.

'Good morning,' she said when I opened the door wearing only a towel and Jo's Ugg boots. 'You should get your landlord to upgrade that intercom. It's hopelessly outdated and a security risk. If you give me his number, I'll deal with it for you right now.'

Panic spread through me. How could anyone look so groomed so early? Did she have a hairdresser living in her flat?

'Um, I'll look for the number.' I didn't like to say that the landlord was currently in the kitchen yelling at a needy client.

Sofia peered at me down her long tanned nose. 'Are you ill? Did I get you out of bed?'

I clutched the graying towel closer. It was Sod's Law that this morning I hadn't used one of our many good towels. I made a massive effort not to tell her that this one was Badger's (although I should stress it was fresh out of the washing machine). 'No, I, er, just wasn't expecting you quite so—'

There was a cough behind me, and Jo moved me firmly out of the way.

'I'm so sorry about my friend,' she said, extending a gracious hand. 'She's positively incoherent until she's had her first gin of the day. Hello, I'm Jo de Vere. You must be . . .'

'Sofia Wolfsburg. How nice to meet you.'

The two of them shook hands like a pair of boxers squaring up before a title fight, and eyed each other with the sharklike politeness of the upper classes. From where I was standing, hopping from foot to foot with working-class embarrassment, it looked like quite an equal match: Sofia was pin-sharp in a navy suit that fitted her exactly, whereas Jo was wearing her 'I mean business' Vivienne Westwood skirt that I'd thought, for six months, was tucked up in her knickers. (It wasn't. It was ruched like that.)

I noted that Jo didn't fluster about whether to curtsy or call her Princess Sofia, but simply smiled and waved toward the kitchen. 'Have you had breakfast yet? I was just about to put some coffee on. Would you like some toast?'

*Yes!* I thought privately. Score one to Jo.

Sofia smiled. 'No, thank you, I had breakfast before I saw my trainer.'

Oh. Maybe one all.

'Your trainer? Heavens! What time did you get up?'

'I see my trainer at six. We work out for an hour, then I cycle in to the office and shower there,' said Sofia, as if this were entirely normal and not the schedule of a maniac. Or an insomniac.

She turned back to me. 'Would you like to get dressed? We've got quite a lot to get through.'

'I'll put on the coffee and toast,' said Jo, and sailed into the kitchen.

I had no idea now who was winning, but I knew for certain it wasn't me.

I stood in my bedroom and panicked. I had never in my entire life been quite so paralyzed about what on earth to wear, not even for my first dates with Leo. Sofia probably had scorecards in her briefcase to hold up when I walked in.

I reminded myself that Leo had told me he liked my 'natural' style, then pulled on my best jeans and a Breton top, and added my engagement ring and the diamond daisy chain to make myself feel better. I loved my sparkling daisy chain; it was a mixture of the ordinary and the precious — and, if you wanted to be all metaphorical, the precious in the ordinary — and more than that, it reminded me that Leo had actually been listening when I'd been rambling on about wildflowers and how much I loved them.

I stared at the priceless slices of diamond fringing the yellow centers, a funny sensation fluttering just out of reach in the back of my mind; then I snapped myself out of it, and went back to face the music.

In the kitchen, Jo and Sofia were having one of those chess-like conversations that involved working out how many mutual friends they had, but without revealing how well they knew them. My brain ached just listening to it.

'Have you got coffee?' I reached for the jug. 'And do you mind if I make some toast?'

'Not at all,' said Sofia. 'Could you pop that in some boiling water for me, please. Filtered.' She reached into her briefcase and pulled out a ziplock of herbal tea bags. 'We have a lot of ground to cover and I have an important meeting in the office at four.'

'Oh, really?' I dropped the tea bag into one of our better cups and seized the opportunity to show I'd been paying attention in Nirona. 'Would that be a will-related matter?'

Sofia stared at me as if I'd just asked her how much she earned a week. 'Interfamilial litigation is my main field, yes.'

'That must be fascinating,' said Jo. 'Families are the absolute worst. My mother's rewritten her will about thirty times in the last ten years — I can't even remember if I'm in the latest one or not.'

I furrowed my brow at Jo — family wills weren't the most

tactful topic right now — but Sofia reached for her transparent file without reacting.

Jo's nostrils flared in well-bred surprise. She wasn't used to being blanked.

'Amy, I've prepared a checklist of objectives that my mother and I feel it would be realistic for you to achieve by the end of October, which is when we're scheduling the coronation, as well as some shorter-term strategies that we'd like to get in place before the official engagement photo shoot and press release, and then again some longer-term goals.'

With each *goal*, *strategy*, and *objective*, she slapped stapled spreadsheets in front of me.

'I know that makes it sound rather businesslike,' she went on with an apologetic smile, which actually wasn't all that apologetic when I looked more closely, 'but I think it would help you to think of it in those terms, so it doesn't feel so . . . personal. This isn't a reflection on you, it's more an indication of what the role of Leo's wife entails. Think of it more like a job specification.'

The haggard specter of Pavlos floated before me; I blinked him away and started to make 'no, no, it's fine' noises, but then my eye snagged on the first page of targets, specifically the phrase 'Achieve BMI 18,' and I felt as if someone had grabbed my muffin top and squeezed. Squeezed and then sniggered.

Beneath that particular heading were the notes: 'AW to meet with dietician and personal trainer in London; SW to accompany. AW to supply details of dietary requirements to String Beans, daily meal plan supplier. AW to confirm best times for biweekly weight check/Harley St.'

# CHAPTER TWENTY-TWO

I was hoping Jo might have been able to come with me on Sofia's Improving Amy Roadshow round Mayfair, but she had to go and deal with Callie's latest drama. Callie, I was willing to bet, was agog at the developments. She didn't seem to get out much, thanks to the boyfriend she always seemed to be waiting in for.

'Text me your whereabouts and I'll try to bump into you,' Jo hissed, while Sofia was on the phone to her manicurist; she hadn't bothered to drop her voice when she instructed her to 'book out a double appointment. Actually, make it three.'

I tried to look on the bright side, I'd seen a lot of makeover shows in which normal girls like me were transformed into glossy beauties by a ruthless glamour puss in glasses. The more unrecognizable the end result, the more pleased everyone was.

'It's like when you made me try on skinny jeans for the first time, right?' I asked in an undertone. 'I should face my fashion fears. I mean, it might be fun? Going shopping with a princess?'

We both looked over at Sofia at the same time. She didn't look much like a princess. She looked like a corporate lawyer, albeit a very, very senior one. The stroppy madam I'd seen over the dining table in Nirona had been replaced by a woman with superflicky blond hair who was on a mission.

A woman whose brother had just been promoted over her. A woman who might take it out on her brother's fiancée using the terrifying weaponry only a hairdresser could offer.

Jo grabbed my arms. 'Try to enjoy it,' she urged. 'I know she's a bossy cow, but if it makes life easier for you to have the right clothes, do it. At the end of the day, it's just a hairdo.'

I nodded. Aside from the lemon-sucking face, Sofia did look fabulous, and I knew I needed some help in that area. Now wasn't the time to get on my 'real women don't wear mascara' soapbox.

'And if you get offered any limited-edition Chanel nail varnish, bag it and I'll give you the cash,' Jo added fiercely.

Sofia had borrowed Leo's car for the day, and I was pleased to see Billy's familiar figure standing by the Range Rover as I stumbled out of 17 Leominster Place behind Sofia. She wasn't hanging about, towering heels or not.

'Good morning, ma'am!' he said as he opened the door for me.

'Morning, Billy!' I replied. 'How's the wisteria? It should be springing back thick after that second pruning?'

'It's doing very nicely, thank you, ma'am.'

I frowned. I'd thought he'd said Amy the first time, but that was definitely two *ma'am*s. I opened my mouth to say something, but he flicked his eyes meaningfully toward Sofia, and closed the door behind me.

The dark leather interior swallowed me up, and I felt smaller. But the smell at least was reassuringly familiar.

Sofia leaned forward and said, 'Harvey Nichols, please,' then leaned back and said, 'Amy, one thing before we start — it's best for everyone if you maintain the correct distance from staff right from the outset. That goes for any job. There is no *we* in management, just *me*. I like to feel my department is a team, sure, but my office manager doesn't need to know about my weekend plans, unless they involve working late and requiring additional admin support.'

She actually spoke like that. In full sentences that went up and down with 'thoughtful' modulations, like one of Jo's voice-overs.

'Okay,' I said.

I glanced forward and saw Billy's gray eyes, guarded in the rearview mirror. He was very good at not seeing or hearing things, if you know what I mean, but he'd obviously heard every word Sofia had just said, and I felt embarrassed for him. And me.

I tried to telegraph 'it's fine, it's just for today' using only my eyebrows, but then it struck me that actually Sofia was his employer, and I wasn't. She knew the rules; Billy knew the rules; I didn't.

So I shut up and listened to Sofia reeling off all the appointments we had to fit in before three. I didn't even want to think about what Ted would be saying when he got my text message about not being able to make it to Palace View to measure the big landscape boxes because I was having my teeth fixed.

*Just go with it,* I told myself. *Stick it out. For Leo.*

*

If this were a film, there would now be a montage of me being marched around the West End in a flurry of high-end bags, nail files, and hair dryers, with maybe a jaunty shoe-trying-on sequence to the tune of, say, 'Rich Girl' by Gwen Stefani. And at the end of it, I'd emerge beaming in triumph, all polished up and looking like a million dollars. I mean, I've seen *Pretty Woman*.

It didn't really work out like that.

For a start, Sofia didn't have a rail of fabulous evening wear wheeled into the personal shopping suite of Harvey Nichols. Instead, she gave me a lecture about flattering my figure with simple basics, and how I should stick to a palette of cream, oatmeal, and caramel, which is a fancy way of saying 'no colors.'

I didn't mind the styling advice, which came from her and the personal shopper in a sort of bad cop/good cop routine. The stylist kept smiling and complimenting me on my 'fresh' skin, and Sofia kept frowning and throwing out fascinatingly random details of etiquette, like how all royals wear closed-toe shoes, and that bare legs were totally out from now on. And some of the things they made me try were amazing — I had no idea how tall and elegant I could look in the right skirt.

But as the clothes started being wrapped, as well as being piled up on the velvet couch, a disturbing thought struck me: Who was paying for all this?

Slowly, panic clamped around my innards as I realized the probable answer was: me. My bank balance was teetering on the thin line between black and red, thanks to my new social life. Leo wouldn't let me pay for much, but the more I noticed his casual chucking around of money, the more important I felt it was to pay my own way some of the time, if only to prove to myself that I was staying true to the life I'd built up. It was a point of principle: I didn't want him to think I could be bought that easily.

Sofia wasn't checking the price tags, but I was — when they weren't looking — and I'd had no idea you could even find a T-shirt that cost so much money. There was about three months' salary currently draped over the arm of one chair, and Sofia hadn't even started on closed-toe shoes yet.

My mouth dried as the Card-Declined Shuffle played out in my head. Should I go to the loo and text Jo? Or Leo?

Not Leo. I didn't want Leo getting involved in this. I needed to show him I could handle situations with his sister.

Sofia caught me looking at the door. 'Problem?'

I glanced anxiously at the assistant, who was busy calling down to the shoe department for reinforcements. I wasn't sure how to start, especially with someone who seemed to treat Harvey Nichols like Topshop.

'Um, are we taking all these clothes?' My voice sounded quite high. 'Could I maybe just take the skirt and the jacket and—' That was five hundred pounds right there. For me, that was a week's salary.

Sofia furrowed her brow. 'No, this is your capsule wardrobe. If Leo asks you to come home for the weekend, you'd need all these.'

I'd already stayed there for the weekend. How bad had my outfits been? Had they prompted some kind of fashion intervention? My armpits prickled.

'It's lovely that you've got that . . . shabby chic thing going on, nothing wrong with it at all, but you need to upgrade to investment pieces. You need at least one go-to silk shirt,' said Sofia patronizingly. 'And a versatile trouser. And a luxe cashmere knit. And a timeless shift in at least two foundation colors. You build from that. You see?'

'Right.' I swallowed, and my panicky eye fell upon a sign by the desk. I could almost hear the celestial hallelujahs. Store cards! Of course! I could open one of those accounts. I was in the personal shopping suite with a princess, wasn't I?

'Do you think I should apply for a store card?' I asked as nonchalantly as I could. 'You know, for the loyalty points? If I'm buying a lot, makes sense . . .'

'If you want.' Sofia seemed nonplussed. She was clearly a stranger to M&S gift vouchers, or paying things off over about twelve months.

'Good. Good. Right. Let me go and . . . talk to the assistant.'

I scuttled off in search of the assistant and tried to steer her into a discreet corner, just in case my application was declined. Mum had refused to have credit cards for the past ten years, just in case the credit check ran into Kelly's history and set off some big red alarm above the tills; Dad, as a bank manager, saw them as a slippery slope, and had written me a four-page guide as to why they could end up ruining my life when I went to uni.

But needs must. And in two shakes of a ballpoint pen, I was welcomed into the charging classes.

Sofia and I left Harvey Nichols with my brand-new credit card charged up to the limit with four bags of the most expensive plain clothes I'd ever clapped eyes on. While she phoned for Billy to collect us, I tried to work out how I was going to pay it off. There were a couple of extra balcony jobs I'd put on the back burner because Ted and I were already booked up till July, but if I focused my time and cut out all unnecessary activities, like sleeping and eating, I could fit them in. Just.

From Harvey Nichols we went to a Harley Street dietician, who clamped my muffin top and bingo wings with calipers and prescribed a bag full of supplements, in addition to the diet that'd be delivered to our house every day; the personal trainer swaggered in, and ran through the ex-marines boot-camp exercise schedule I was on (although my aerobic capacity amazed them all — thank you, years of digging); and finally, two doors down, was the orthodontist who fitted me for my new invisible braces. And reconstructive work. When he examined my fillings, he actually made that 'which cowboys did *this* work?' sucky noise that builders make.

I tried to chat with Sofia throughout all this, but while she was cordial enough, she didn't give me anything other than answers to my questions. I wondered if that was part of the training too — how to be so royal you never actually said anything.

We arrived at the hairdresser's on the King's Road at three, and there wasn't a single area of my body that wasn't earmarked for improvement. In a way, it was quite Zen. I seemed to remember Grace Wright had been on an extortionately expensive monthlong retreat to 'break down her ego' and had only got as far as throwing away her hand mirror. Sofia had broken me in under seven hours.

I sank into the chair while the salon manager and Sofia (and Liza on the phone) chatted about my hair as if I weren't there. It was almost soothing not to have to take responsibility for it. Sofia swanned off to get her own hair blow-dried, and I relaxed, until the junior brought my coffee and a pile of magazines, the top of which was the *Hello!* with me and Leo at the premiere of the new Keira Knightley film (Leo in black tie, looking like one of the Hollywood A-list, me looking like the Radio 1 listener who'd won a competition to go to a premiere).

I shut it quickly, looked at my be-foiled reflection, and flinched. Then closed my eyes.

When I thought back to that boxing gala Jo and I had gone to, just a few months ago, it almost made me laugh. I'd thought getting ready for that had been hard work, but it was nothing compared to this. Nothing. This was international-level maintenance carried out by trained professionals, not your flatmate wielding her hair irons, and Sofia hadn't even started on the sinister-sounding 'program of personal education' that would apparently cover things like the Wolfsburg family's position in the European hierarchy of monarchy, and their charities, and their personal responsibilities within Nirona.

Not for the first time that day, I wondered whether there was a way I could subtly ask Sofia if every day was like this, or if this was a one-off, but I didn't want to look like I couldn't handle it. I didn't want to give her another constitutional stick to beat Leo with.

When my phone buzzed in my bag, I nearly didn't answer, in case it was Liza with another beauty to-do, like 'be stretched three inches'; but when I saw Leo's name pop up, a warm feeling of relief spread through me.

Hope all going ok. Let me take your new hairdo out tonight — Delaunay at 7? L

I pulled my shredded personality together. Leo, I knew, loved my old hair, my old nails, and my old muffin top. He could only love this new improved version even more.

'Wow,' said Leo when the waiter showed me to his table, and pulled out my chair.

I held my smile, because he didn't follow it up with anything else; instead he seemed to be taking it all in — the sleek blow-dry that made my hair look so much longer, my subtly applied makeup, my understated camel cashmere T-shirt (new) over my best jeans (old) and platform shoe-boots (concealed). I had noticed heads turning when I walked through the packed restaurant, something that had never happened before, but that might have been because I was swaying dangerously in my unusually elevated state. Sofia hadn't thrown in walking lessons with the new shoes.

'Is that a good wow?' I ventured.

Leo gave me an appreciative smile that made my stomach flip over. 'Of course it is. You look amazing. I mean, you always look amazing, but this is a new sort of amazing.'

'Why, thank you.' I shook out my napkin with a careless air and immediately knocked over my water glass. 'Oh, nuts! Sorry, sorry.'

We both scrambled to stop the water coursing across the pristine white cloth, and I accidentally put out the candle in the middle. The waiter was there relighting it, and another two were replacing the cloth before I could finish apologizing.

When they were gone, he let the smile drift from his eyes down to his lips, and leaned across the table. 'The thing I like best about the new you,' he murmured, just loud enough for me to hear, 'is that I can still see the old you underneath it.'

'If you mean the klutz who knocks glasses over' — I pulled a regretful face — 'I'm afraid she's never going to go away.'

'I absolutely insist that she doesn't.' Leo held my gaze for a charged moment, then shook out his own napkin. 'So, how was your day with Sofia? I see she's dressed you as herself. Do you feel ready to march into the European Court of Human Rights and start reducing seasoned lawyers to jelly?'

'I don't think I could march very far in these heels, to be honest with you.'

'In those heels, you'd just need to turn up to have them eating out of your hand.'

I decided that maybe grooming wasn't such a bad thing; it certainly seemed to be turning our dinner into a live-action episode of *Mad Men*. I'd never felt so grown-up, sitting here in the Delaunay in my diamonds and my blow-dry with my devilishly handsome fiancé. For the first time, my normal boring world and Leo's glamorous world seemed to be merging into one. And I was actively enjoying it. I wasn't even worried about mistaking a fellow diner for a waiter.

'How was she?' he went on. 'Apparently it's all kicking off back home — they're not happy about Rolf driving across the desert in a clapped-out Fiat in some rally.'

'Because it's too dangerous?'

'Well, Mom thinks it is. Sofia probably doesn't think it's dangerous enough. And, of course, Giselle can't be with him twenty-four seven to make sure he doesn't do something outrageous, and it's very hard for her to spin Rolf to begin with.'

The thought that had been gnawing away at me all day finally slipped out. 'Leo, be honest with me. Is Sofia really fine about the change of succession?'

He looked up from the menu at once. 'Why do you ask? Has she said something?'

'No. It's just . . . a feeling I get. That she's not exactly thrilled.'

He looked momentarily flustered, as if he hadn't really thought about it.

How could he not have thought about it? I wondered, amazed. She was his own sister! It was like Pavlos all over again.

'I think she's fine about it, far as I know. She seemed to be involved in some of the legal execution of the handover, so . . . Better to be the daughter of the guy in charge than his niece.'

'But if Sofia's always had a bee in her bonnet about the succession and how it can't possibly be changed to accommodate women, it must be pretty galling to see it changed just like that for someone else?'

Our appetizers arrived, and Leo waited until the waiter had gone before answering me. He seemed to be considering it properly.

'I love that you're so empathetic, Amy. God knows we need

some of that in the family. But it's like I said, normal rules don't apply. We all know that's the way the cookie crumbles. I hope she hasn't said anything unpleasant to you about it?'

'No! No, I just . . . can't believe that you . . .'

Oh dear. This wasn't coming out the way I'd wanted.

'Forget it,' I said lightly. 'It's probably just me, misunderstanding her sense of humor. Sofia's quite hard to read.'

'I've known her for twenty-seven years and I still can't tell when she's joking.' He paused. 'I'm not sure she often is, to be honest. Anyway, there's plenty of time for you two to get to know each other.' Leo beamed at me, and his eyes crinkled at the edges. 'I was talking to Mom today about the Coronation Ball she's hosting the weekend before the coronation — the palace staff are starting to plan that now, and she wanted to know which jewels you'll want to wear.'

'Which jewels?'

He nodded, as if we were talking about shoes. 'One of the traditions of the Coronation Ball is for the ladies of the family to get the state jewelry out of the vaults and wear it, for everyone to enjoy. Most of the pieces have got stories attached, how they wound up in our sticky hands.'

'Such as?' I was agog already. Not just jewels, but jewels with stories!

'Well, there's the Rudolfo suite — emeralds and diamonds, tiara, choker, earrings, et cetera, et cetera. They're traditionally worn by the Princess of Nirona, Mom, now. Rolf's named for this guy, Rudolfo — he was a Wolfsburg younger son who made a fortune playing cards all over Europe, mostly from other younger-son princes. Granddad used to tell this great story about a scandalous divorce caused by just one night of black-jack in the room in the palace when Rudolfo won the Empress Josephine's emeralds from one Italian duke and an estate in Ireland from an English general and some Russian aristo's oldest daughter.'

'Really?' I froze, my fork halfway to my mouth. 'The aristocracy gambled with their children?'

Leo waggled his hand. 'This child was about forty-one at the time. The good news for us was that Rudolfo was gallant enough to decline the daughter but quite happy to take the jewels and the estate.'

I was privately quite glad I wouldn't be wearing those. 'Are there any that I'm officially supposed to wear?'

A thrill ran through me. Me! Being an official part of the jewel displaying!

'You can have whatever you like, you've got first pick since Mom's wearing the emeralds. So find a dress, then choose which pieces suit you best.' Leo attacked his steak with gusto. 'Has Mom spoken to you about meeting with a designer? I love that blue Zoë Weiss one, but I think for this ball all the dresses have to be a certain color this year, for charity.'

'Sofia didn't mention it,' I said. 'We covered nearly everything else, though.'

He put his cutlery down and reached into his pocket for his iPhone. 'How about you come out with me on Thursday, for the weekend? We can meet with the designers for your therapy garden, and Mom can schedule a consult for the dress, and we can check in with the jeweler, and still have time for ourselves.'

Leo gave me a winning look. Normally I'd have said yes immediately, but this time I couldn't.

'Sorry, I can't get away till Friday night,' I said. 'I've meetings all Friday with the Palace View developers, about the communal meadow area that we're creating. I'm getting some people round from the bee conservation — what?'

Leo was doing that 'as soon as you stop talking I'm going to start' wineglass fidget. It was very off-putting.

'No, go on,' he prompted.

But I'd lost my train of thought. 'Um, yeah, Palace View. I need to make sure everything's on track, because if Ted and I do well on this, then it could be the opening we need to — what?'

'I was just thinking that now you've got so many demands on your time, isn't it time you thought about some sideways management?'

'Sorry?'

'Well, someone's going to have to take over the reins at some point, so why not now? Get them to sit in on the meetings, train them up.'

I tightened my grip on my wineglass. 'But it's my project. And it took me ages to get to this point.'

'It'll still be your project,' he said easily, 'but if you've got a good assistant on the case, you can run it from wherever you happen to be. That's how I deal with office stuff when I'm in Nirona. We all do it.'

'We're not really at the point where we can afford an assistant,' I said. We weren't even at the point where I could borrow five grand from the business to pay off my credit card. Resistance fermented in my stomach.

'Tell you what,' said Leo, returning to his steak. 'Why don't I invest in your eco-friendly landscaping company — right up my portfolio alley — and you can hire someone? You'll be freed up, Ted'll get someone new to boss around, business expands. Everyone's a winner.'

I gazed at him over the table, seeing the banker in him properly for the first time. One half of my brain was saying, *Wow, he wants to invest in my business,* and the other half was saying, quite loudly, *Isn't this just another case of chucking money at a problem so it goes away?*

When I didn't respond, Leo stopped eating and looked at me. 'What?'

'That's not how normal people do business,' I said. 'You haven't even asked to see my accounts.'

'Don't need to. It's a sound proposition. You've got me sold on the global importance of bees,' he added playfully.

Jo's voice was in my ear, warning me that I was coming across as chippy, but I couldn't shake the fact that in one day, Sofia had blown more than the original start-up cost of our business on my appearance, not even including the clothes.

Was *I* a problem she and Leo had been told to chuck money at? My wonky British teeth were one thing but how were they planning on solving the problem of my shyness? And the small matter of me not being a natural performer, like they were? I was good at what I was good at — or didn't that matter anymore?

A tense silence descended over the table. Leo and I hadn't ever really argued but something had been building up inside me for a while. This was the helicopter and the cricket pitch and everything else, rolled up into one big ball. And it was rolling toward me like something from an Indiana Jones film, sped on its way by my own guilt at enjoying my pamper day quite so much.

'What?' he said reasonably, unaware of the boulder of doom behind him.

'My business is my baby,' I said. 'Just like you're proud of having your banking job? I don't know if I want you to buy it, just like that. You wouldn't let your dad buy out your fund to give you more time at home.'

Leo flinched. 'Ouch. Sorry. I just wanted to make things easier for you. I'll organize a PA to handle your admin, take some stress off that way. You'll need one in Nirona—'

'That's not the point!'

'Isn't it?' He frowned at me as if he failed to see what on earth my problem was. 'So what is?'

'Stop trying to solve everything with money!' I yelled. 'It's not the same thing as thinking it through!'

'Amy, you're being irrational.'

The atmosphere sharpened, and I floundered, out of my depth. Uncomfortable questions were jostling for position in my head, but I was scared to unleash them, for fear of where they might drag the conversation.

Leo looked as if he was struggling to speak — or not speak — pressing his lips together coolly. I'd come to recognize that expression lately.

'I'm just normal, Leo,' I said unhappily. 'I'm a completely normal girl. And I'm trying to meet you in the middle, but my middle's miles away from yours. All you have to do is get the bus occasionally. I have to get my head around seeing us referred to as Leomy on the Internet. I *need* my job to remind myself who I am.'

Leo said nothing for a long moment; then he pushed his plate aside and reached for my hands across the table. 'Yes, you're normal,' he said. 'But that's the most amazing thing about you. You're completely normal, and you have no idea how special you are. Wherever you want to make this middle, fine — that's where I'm going to be.'

He smiled, and I smiled weakly back, because my mouth wouldn't do anything else when Leo smiled at me. He stroked my engagement ring with his thumb, inviting me into the private world that sprang up around us even in a busy restaurant, and I felt the awkwardness inside me melt like dew off the summer leaves.

'As long as we're always honest with each other,' he said quietly. 'That's all we can do. Don't ever hide anything from me, Amy. Even if it's hard, or you hate it, you have to tell me, so I can help you.'

'I will,' I said. 'You know what a terrible liar I am.'

The moment passed, but a tiny nugget of awkwardness remained unmelted, like the stone chips that always seemed to end up in my shoes in the rose garden. I hadn't quite said everything I'd meant to. And, more disturbing than that, I wasn't sure either of us was being totally honest about the worlds we were promising to share. And the spotlight of the wedding was getting closer by the day.

# CHAPTER TWENTY-THREE

As the weeks went on, e-mails from Nirona started to come thicker and faster until every morning began with a barrage of communications from Liza's office that Jo had to help me reply to with proper tact and punctuation.

For the engagement photo, for the wedding, for the coronation, everything. And the more Liza e-mailed me about helicopters and security for the Nirona blessing, the more determined I was to keep the Yorkshire wedding ceremony as quiet and simple as I possibly could.

Leo stood by me on that. He had to agree to let Boris's security people handle the security aspect — I was really looking forward to liaising with the vicar about that — but otherwise, it was down to me.

I found it easier to deal with Mum's nerves face-to-face, so one weekend I took Badger up on the train with my file of notes, to try to pin down some details. Leo had given me four dates in November and December that would work for him and most of the rest of the family, so now all I had to do was go and see Reverend Barnaby about where to hide four SAS-trained sniper bodyguards in the Lady Chapel.

I didn't dare give Mum the whole picture for fear of her

going into complete meltdown, so I'd earmarked isolated chunks, like the cake or the flowers. I didn't tell her, for instance, that Liza had already turned down three six-figure offers from magazines to cover the ceremony, or that Zoë Weiss had sent me a huge bunch of all-white flowers with a note in her microscopic handwriting asking if I'd be requiring her couture services for bridesmaids' dresses. (Jo squirreled that away for her 'memory box.')

I knew Mum was baking away some stress when I arrived, because the scent of vanilla was strong from five doors down the street; and lo and behold, when Dad opened the door, he had flour on his mustache, and there were already four racks of sponge drops cooling in the hall. I had to pick Badger up before he inhaled the lot in one pass.

After some warning looks, Dad and I shuffled down the cramped hallway to the kitchen, where Mum was swirling frosting roses onto a tower of ivory cupcakes. When she saw me, her face lit up.

'What do you think?' she asked, gesturing at their delicate snowy magnificence.

'They're better than anything I've seen in any shop in London,' I replied, because they were.

Mum's cheeks dimpled and turned pink. At home she was as cheerful as you like; it was just outside the house that she turned into a nervous, anxious wreck.

'Have a cup of tea, love.' Dad pressed a plate of scones into my hand. There was a lot of cake to get through on the table. 'How's it all going? I hear you were in the magazines again, at some premiere.' He gave it the full French pronunciation.

I'd made a conscious decision to be as matter-of-fact about these things as possible. It seemed to work for Leo. 'Yes, Leo took me and Jo — it was for charity. We went to the drinks reception first in the Savoy, and Jo won a whole pod to herself on the London Eye in the prize draw. She says we can have it for my hen night, if you want?'

Mum looked starstruck. 'Did you see anyone famous?'

'Um, Nicole Kidman and Dame Judi Dench. And Elton John. And that one you like from *Coronation Street*.'

She looked as if she was about to keel over with delight into her Kenwood Chef mixer. 'Ken Barlow!'

'Him.'

'Eat up, love,' said Dad through a mouthful of scone. 'You look like you could do with a good meal. Are you feeling all right? You're all pinched round the nose.'

'It's pre-wedding nerves.' Mum patted my arm and frowned at the unexpected bone she encountered. 'Oh, Amy. You've got to keep your strength up.'

I stared sadly at the scone. According to my diet, I wasn't supposed to be eating white flour. Let alone white flour mixed with rich Yorkshire butter, plump sultanas, freshly laid eggs, homemade strawberry jam, primrose-yellow clotted Devon cream . . .

'We've had a few people ring us up,' Mum went on, brushing flour off her pinny. 'You know, wanting to know about your wedding. Said they were friends of yours from school, wanting your new address—'

'I told your mother to say she'd have to check with you.' Dad's bank managerial security settings had evidently been activated. 'I reckoned if you wanted to be in touch, you would be. And so many folk have been phoning up — well, I don't recall you having that many friends, to be frank, love.'

I smiled weakly. He had a point.

Kelly had been the popular one. She'd been the friend-of-everybody-girl in her gang, whereas what little popularity I had was mainly down to being Kelly's sister — and that wore off fast once she'd left. I had two more years to do at school after her court case, and I spent most of that hiding from the whispers in the library. I certainly didn't go round collecting addresses on Leavers' Day.

'Mum, don't tell anyone anything. They're probably journalists,' I said. 'I don't really speak to anyone from school.'

'That's what I said.' Dad looked pleased and cut himself another slice of cake. 'I've got my old football whistle next to the phone for next time.'

Mum was still fussing with the teapot. 'Di Overend was round too, wanting to know if you'd set a date. She's booking her cruise in advance and she wanted to be sure she didn't miss it.'

Di Overend had a nerve. She clearly had no idea that fourteen fairly senior European royals had been cut that morning from Liza's guest list, on grounds of space.

I adjusted my face to Tact Setting: High. 'Did you tell Di it was going to be a very, very small wedding?'

'Of course I did. She said, good, much more exclusive for those who do come. She's already got a hat. She says you ought to specify a maximum hat size so you don't get monstrosities like Princess Beatrice's blocking the view for everyone.'

I blanched. That was all I needed, Di Overend shoving Princess Charlene of Monaco out of the way to get a better view.

I got out my planner. 'I need to talk to you about the date. Boris's coronation is set for the beginning of October in the cathedral, and Liza thinks if we can do the blessing there before Christmas, it'll mean the cathedral will still be decorated for the public to enjoy over the — what?'

Mum and Dad were both staring at me, scones halfway to their mouths.

'What?' I frowned, then looked down at my papers. The words *coronation* and *cathedral* and *the public* looked pretty normal in the context of Liza's e-mails, but hearing them in my parents' kitchen did make them sound a bit . . . different.

'It's okay,' I said hurriedly. 'You won't have to do a thing about that. Liza's got a team of event planners on the case. I'm in charge of everything here, and it's going to be small and simple. I just need to give her the date.'

'Never mind about small and simple. You must have the wedding you want, love.' Dad coughed and looked embarrassed. 'We've a bit put by, so don't think you've to scrimp on the necessities.'

I went red. 'Dad, that's not why it's going to be small. I want a quiet service in St. Cuthbert's, where it's just about me and Leo, and our families. Before we have to go through it all again in front of —'

I nearly said 'millions of people,' but then I saw Mum's aghast expression and realized — DUR! — that she'd have to be there too. I was effectively describing her ultimate phobia: not only going out in public, but being just left of the center of attention as the mother of the bride. Oh, and having to stand next to Liza Bachmann while she did it.

'Don't think about that,' I said, slapping the file shut. 'Just think about who you want to invite, and bear in mind that there's only room for about forty people in the church. And fifteen of them will be from Leo's family.'

'And what about afterward? We can't have the reception here.' Mum looked panicky. 'We've only one lavatory! And where would everyone sit?'

Dad tried to look jovial. 'Leo's mum's a model, isn't she? She won't take up much space. And there's always the yard — I can get the barbecue set up.'

I laughed, but none of us said what we were thinking: that even by royal standards, our Hadley Green house would have been ideal for an intimate reception, with the long velvety lawn stretching down to the stream and Dad's flowers blooming, no matter what time of year . . .

I leaped in before anyone could mention it. 'I thought the church hall would be the best place to have the reception. It's so pretty — do you remember when Leigh Sullivan had her Christmas wedding, and the Gardeners' Club covered all the beams in holly and ivy and put candles all round the walls? It looked amazing.'

'We can stand you the Stanley Arms,' insisted Dad. 'Never let it be said that you didn't get a sit-down reception with chicken or beef.'

'I'd rather have the church hall,' I insisted. 'It's a listed building — Leo loves the history! And it's where I always wanted to have my reception when I was little. Do you remember? How

I'd got it all planned, with me as Snow White and Kelly as Rose Red?'

As soon as I'd said it, I wished I could rewind and get the words back.

Mum's lip quivered, and I knew she was fighting not to say something. I could almost see the words banging their tiny fists against her lips in an effort to get out.

Dad glanced across and noticed too. He swiftly offered me the plate of scones. 'Come on, love, can we not tempt you to a scone? Baked this morning. Strawberries from the backyard too. Jam's a touch sharp this year but I'm thinking of blending in some Elsantas with the—'

'IjustwishKellywasheretobeyourbridesmaid!' Mum burst out, and put a hand over her mouth. Her rings were digging into her plump pink hands.

The words, once out, hung like toxic gas and filled the space around us.

'She would have loved all this so much,' Mum wailed. 'Choosing the dresses and talking about the flowers and helping you with everything!'

I swallowed. I'd known this was going to be difficult. It was awkward enough negotiating the Kelly obstacle course at the best of times, but Mum was moving the goalposts here. Her imaginary Kelly might be eager to help with the table favors, but the Kelly I remembered would almost certainly have upstaged me by dyeing her hair black the night before or shortening her dress by about two feet.

'I always wanted her to be my bridesmaid too,' I said carefully, 'but I'm not sure she'd have found it easy to keep quiet about some of the details. I mean, it's all very high security—'

'Are you saying she wouldn't have been good enough?' Mum demanded.

Dad and I exchanged weary glances.

'No, Pamela,' said Dad. 'Amy's saying that copping off with the best man and telling the groom about the bride's hen night shenanigans won't go down so well if half the crowned heads of Europe are at the reception.'

'Oh, for pity's sake, Stan! Debbie's wedding was ten years ago! Are you ever going to let it go?'

I wanted to point out that none of us had had more than a birthday card from Kelly in the last ten years, so God only knew in what outlandish ways she'd been wrecking weddings in the meantime, but I kept my mouth shut.

Dad turned to me, appealing for me to pour oil on troubled waters, as only I could. 'If Kelly wants to be at Amy's wedding, I'm sure she'd be very welcome, won't she, love?'

They both looked at me, their honest faces full of hope that at least I could be relied upon to do the decent thing. I'd seen that look so many times over the years it didn't need any explanation. Amy, our reliable sensible daughter. Amy, who will not let us down.

I wanted to say Kelly would be welcome, I really did.

But even though it was purely theoretical, my brain was still saying no. *NO. NO. NO.*

'Of course,' I lied.

Mum insisted on doing the washing-up herself — family code for 'I need to pull myself together' — so Dad and I took our tea into the yard.

He was keen to show me his latest hive he'd got from a beekeeper up in Scarborough, and we had a good natter about my latest kitchen garden in Fulham and how Ted and I were getting on with sourcing a London-based beekeeper to help us with honey collection. It was almost like old times, and we'd have been there for hours if Badger hadn't reminded me that part of the sitting-on-the-train deal was that he got to go for a good sniff round his old haunts.

'I won't come with you,' Dad said, eyeing Badger, who eyed him beadily back. 'Best to keep an eye on your mum.'

He grimaced in his sad-sweet fashion, and I knew what he was trying to say.

'Is she . . . is she going to be okay with this?' I glanced at the kitchen window. 'I've tried to make it as easy as I can for her, with the church and the small do. She doesn't have to come to the big blessing circus in Nirona if she doesn't want to — I'm sure we can think of a way round it.'

'I know.' Dad looked down at his hands, rough where he'd been digging. 'She wants to be there, Amy. She's so proud of you, we both are. And she really likes Leo. He's a sound chap.'

That was the ultimate Dad accolade: the badge of sound chap-ness. Leo had won more Brownie points than I'd thought possible by sending Mum a whole crate of lemons grown in the family's citrus orchards, after she'd mentioned that she'd read about them in a recipe book. He'd got even more points from Dad for sending them first class and with all the duty and what-have-you paid, plus some seeds for him to try them out himself.

For a second, I thought about telling my dad what Leo had

said about investing in my business so I could spend more time in Nirona with him, to see if Dad would say I'd been daft to turn it down. But then I didn't. I didn't know which answer I wanted to hear.

'Kelly hasn't been in touch at all?' I said instead. I'd wondered if maybe she'd Googled me, and been stunned to see me in my new incarnation as half of Leomy. If she had, it hadn't prompted any contact.

He shook his head. 'I'd never say it to your mum, love, but maybe it's for the best. I wouldn't want your mother to think she'd only bothered to get in touch again because . . . well. You know what I mean.'

'Dad,' I said, with real passion since Mum was out of earshot, 'if our Kelly turned up now just because she thought she could have a go at Leo's brother and get some free stuff, I'd be the first one barring her from the church. Wedding dress or not, I'm not afraid to rugby-tackle her.'

He laughed, and some of the tension lines disappeared round his forehead. 'You get that dog walked before he destroys any more of my borders. We'll still be here when you get back.'

I didn't say anything, and hugged him instead. My dad was the only man I knew who could make someone cry or laugh just with a twitch of his silvery eyebrows, and a well-timed silence.

While Badger reacquainted himself with lampposts in the park, I tried to calculate which members of my family would accept an invitation to my wedding. There weren't many; we'd fallen out quite badly with most of them, thanks to Kelly.

I wanted to give Mum plenty of time to get herself together, so I called by the café on the corner where I'd had a Saturday job during my A levels. Someone had obviously taken it over since then, because now there was a pair of metal tables and chairs outside, plus a stripy awning. I ordered a coffee for me and a bowl of water for Badger, put on my shades, and started flicking through my instructions from Liza.

'Amy? Amy Wilde?'

I looked up. A woman about my age with very black hair cut in a bob was hovering over my table.

'It is, isn't it!' As she smiled in triumph, the top lip curled back to reveal a pair of rabbity front teeth, and I knew exactly who it was: Jennifer Wainwright.

I slapped the file shut as a long-forgotten panic gripped my guts. Much in the same way that Jennifer Wainwright had gripped me in the girls' loos at Rothery Senior School.

'Hello,' I said, and went to take my shades off, then decided not to.

'Aw! I knew it was you from your lovely hair!' Jennifer sounded much friendlier than she'd done back in the days when she'd run through various loud descriptions of my hair, starting with 'troll head' and ending with 'albino pube-fro.' 'I hear you're moving in much more exciting circles these days!'

'Um . . .' Why was she being so matey?

Before I could answer, she reached out and touched my wrist. 'Oooh, look at that bracelet! Isn't that gorgeous?' She looked up sharply. 'Was that a present from Leo? Is it from Tiffany's?'

'Um, no, Chaumet.'

Why had I told her that? Was it because it was positively

freaky to hear Jennifer Wainwright referring to Leo in that familiar first-name way?

'Chaumet! Don't even know who they are! Get you!'

Then I had to let her admire my diamond bracelet and explain about the daisies being a private joke about my job, and before I knew it, Jennifer was ensconced in the chair opposite. I could feel Badger retreating under my seat.

'Talk about Prince of Diamonds!' Jennifer leaned forward and patted my arm. 'Have you set a date? You and your' — she pulled air quotes as if she were the first person in Yorkshire to know about them — '"international ski champion banker"?'

'How did you know Leo was—' I began.

'Don't worry, I'm not a stalker!' She giggled, and actually, that was even more unsettling. 'I work for the *Rothery Gazette*. I've got to keep on top of all the national and international stories, for work.' She mimed air typing. 'I follow Liza Bachmann's Twitter feed. She's an inspiration.'

That made sense. After Kelly, Jennifer had taken over as the school's biggest purveyor of semi-accurate gossip and scurrilous rumor. No one dared not be friends with her for fear of what might leak out. I could imagine her these days on a doorstep, demanding to see the fatal scene of the chip-pan fire, asking if they had home insurance, would this now put them off chips for life, etc.

'I've tried phoning your mum and dad a few times,' she went on chummily, 'but they don't seem to know anything, which is a bit odd, isn't it? Did your mum give you the message, that I'd rung? She said she'd pass on my number.'

I stared at Jennifer Wainwright through my shades (expensive Tom Ford ones; a gift from Leo in duty-free when I'd forgotten mine) and tried to work out how I could possibly exit this conversation without bursting into a run. I *didn't* want to draw attention to myself in the local paper. But at the back of my mind, a little voice was reminding me that I was wearing a diamond bracelet and was about to marry an actual prince, and Jennifer Wainwright was probably still living with her boyfriend, Kian, and definitely still getting her hair done at Kutting Krew on Lowther Street.

'Ooh, are those Tom Fords?' She leaned forward, and for a moment I thought she was going to take them off my face to try them on.

'Yes,' I said. 'Jennifer, please don't phone my parents — they aren't involved in any of this.'

'Aren't they? Why not? But you won't mind if I send the photographers round, will you?' she persisted. 'So they can take some pics of your childhood home — maybe some of your mum and dad. Maybe ask them how they feel about their little girl stepping up into high society. Although . . .'

She paused for effect. 'That's not your childhood home, is it?'

My insides dropped as if I were on one of those terrifying rides at Alton Towers that try to make you lose your lunch in the first ten seconds.

'Didn't you . . . move? Am I right?'

She looked at me, her sharp eyes taking in every detail of my face, even behind the huge shades, and I knew she was already making notes. She knew about Kelly, she knew about us selling our house to pay the debts, she knew everything. And she knew I knew.

And then Leo's voice swam into my head, talking about letting the press have a little, so they'd leave you alone. He was right. I had to start thinking like a media-savvy operator, not a scared teenager. I could nip this in the bud. I just had to think like Giselle, and tell Jennifer what *I* wanted her to know. Not what she wanted. And it was only the *Rothery Gazette*, for crying out loud.

I mustered up all the coolness I could manage.

'Okay,' I said lightly. 'Why don't we have a quick chat now, while I'm here, and then you can stop ringing my family? Yes?'

'Yes.' Jennifer looked triumphant. 'Listen, I'll go and get myself a coffee and something to eat. I could eat a cow through a five-bar gate. You want a bit of cake? They do a good cheesecake here.'

'No, thanks,' I said automatically. 'I'm off dairy this week.'

She stared at me as if I'd lost my mind. 'You're what?'

'Off dairy. Dermatologist's orders. It's a bit of a pain but . . . that's what you've got to do.' I smiled my best princess smile. 'When your future mother-in-law's a top international supermodel, you've got to up your game.'

Jennifer stared at me for a moment, her brain obviously struggling to process the boggling unreality of what she was hearing; then she scooted into the café.

*Yes!* I thought, and quickly slapped on some lip gloss in the reflection of the metal table. I might not be a Sofia-level princess, but I was getting there, baby steps at a time.

# CHAPTER TWENTY-FOUR

I don't know how I managed to get through four weeks of Sofia's ruthless improvement program but I did, and I have to admit that by the time I was ready to fly out for the engagement photo shoot, I barely recognized myself.

I had a proper waist for the first time in my life. I'd managed to drag myself through four sessions a week with Sofia's boot-camp psycho as well as doing extra days for Ted (that credit card bill from Harvey Nichols wasn't paying itself), and since there was nothing else to eat in the flat apart from what arrived daily in the little white boxes, I had no choice but to stick to the diet.

Sofia had arranged for double portions to be delivered; I thought she was being generous in letting Jo act as a diet cheerleader, but Jo pointed out that she was probably just making sure there was no extra food hanging around to tempt me.

'And I'm going to be your bridesmaid,' she added. 'It's even more important for the chief bridesmaid to have a tiny photogenic arse. It's virtually compulsory these days. My arse could be my launchpad to stardom.'

On one sobering occasion we nearly came to blows over the last broccoli stem, and I did seriously contemplate Badger's box of deliciously carby Bonios, but we both lost exactly what

Dr Johnsson had promised we would, and Jo celebrated by walking around the house and garden in her bikini for all of Saturday, something that sent Dickon into spasms of joy through his binoculars.

My hair was looking shiny too, and my nails were getting better, although Ted thought it was ridiculous that I was now wearing gloves inside gloves.

'How long are you going to keep this up?' he grumbled as we sowed seeds into the wildflower area at the back of Richard's Palace View development.

It had been a scrappy lawn, but after mowing and raking and Ted faffing around with soil tests, it was ready to be turned into a butterfly-friendly meadow of foxgloves, cornflowers, chamomile, and hollyhocks. Coupled with the broad balcony planters I'd designed, filled with thick clusters of lavender and poppies and dahlias, the meadow would turn Palace View into a bee paradise in a few months. I was really excited about it, and in his own way, so was Ted.

I pulled off my gloves and wiped my sweaty forehead with the back of my hand. 'Well, the photo shoot's next weekend. I suppose . . . I'll be keeping it up till after the wedding.'

'And then?' Ted gave me a clear look.

'It's about making grooming a way of life,' I blustered. 'I'm getting used to it. And it won't be so hard to maintain, once I'm on top of it. It'll be a routine. Like mowing the lawn once it's all been . . . sown.'

'So are you signed up for these facial acid baths forever?' he inquired, with the sensitivity that had driven two girls out of our college house share. 'What happens after that? Will you have to have Botox? Is it in the job description — must have no wrinkles? Do you get a warning if you can't fit into your royal ensembles?'

'They're not acid baths, it's a glycolic peel,' I said automatically. 'And . . . and . . .'

An endless line of white fat-free food boxes floated before my eyes, and I felt a strong inclination to change the subject. 'Why have we got "Chelsea House Visits" in the diary for this afternoon?'

Ted stopped digging and took a long swig from his water bottle. 'Jo's Callie Whatsit recommended two more friends who want you to design a roof garden.' He paused and looked at me meaningfully. 'I booked them in for you while you were having your eyebrows done.'

'Oh. Good. Thanks.' I'd been trying to keep up with the admin, but I was having to block out time for extra beauty treatments, and the work was backing up.

'Jo says one of them is the editor of a lifestyle magazine,' he added.

'Really?' Now that could be *very* useful. 'Are we giving Jo and Callie Hamilton commission for new clients?'

'Over my dead body.' Ted chucked the empty bottle into his bag and belched freely. 'She said Callie more or less forced the numbers into her hand — she's got Jo doing their loft conversions too. Does she fancy Jo, this Callie woman? She's taking a big interest in her.'

I wasn't sure whether Ted would prefer Callie over Rolf as a potential love rival for Jo's affections. I didn't like to tell him — though he probably knew — that Jo and Rolf were now teetering on the edge of an actual relationship, going by the amount of times she 'missed the last bus' and had to stay over in Rolf Towers.

'She is a bit *Single White Female*.' I opened another packet of wildflower seed mix: linaria and bugloss and verbena for butterflies. 'I think she's lonely. Jo says her boyfriend's never at home, and she keeps pretending he's away on business but it's pretty obvious he's married.'

'How obvious?' Ted looked baffled. 'He's paying for her flat, surely that means . . .'

It was nice hanging round with Ted. He made me feel streetwise.

'He only ever sees her midweek? He lets her do endless building work to the flat so he can't sleep there? She treats her project manager like some kind of guru because she's got no mates of her own?'

Ted's expression curdled. 'I am so glad to be single,' he said.

'Good job.' I put my gloves back on and started scattering the seeds across the raked earth. 'The only wild-oat-sowing you're doing is round the back of Richard Chalmers's posh flats.'

'Oi,' said Ted. 'I could sack you.'

'No, you couldn't, this business is half mine,' I reminded him. 'And who's got the Westminster parking permit for the van?'

Ted started to say Jo, then changed his mind.

I flew out to Nirona with Leo that weekend; I felt as if I'd been completely resurfaced from the toes up, while he had merely had his hair cut.

Liza had decided that the engagement photo shoot should take place in the state ballroom, where the Crown Princess Ball would be held several days before the coronation.

It was a majestic room, with high painted ceilings, full-length windows overlooking the most formal gardens, and elaborate gold sconces along each wall holding tapering ivory candles. When Leo and I walked in, racks of clothes were already waiting in one corner, along with banks of lights, reflectors, a makeup station, and a small army of photographers, stylists, assistants, and palace staff in purple uniforms. Two staff members in dark glasses flanked a table where several morocco boxes were discreetly arranged; they contained some of the state jewelry that I was supposed to wear in the portrait. Quite honestly, I don't think even Queen Elizabeth had diamonds the size of these. Rudolfo must have been some card player.

'Don't panic,' Leo whispered as I hesitated at the double doors, seeing the bustle of activity inside. 'We did this for their wedding anniversary picture last year, and it honestly takes an hour.'

'An hour?'

'Yup. And that was with Sofia demanding two changes of outfit. You'll be fine.'

I smiled up at him, but my stomach was rumbling with both nerves and hunger.

The hairdresser whisked me away to put my hair into rollers while the makeup artist wiped my face and started working on it with a huge palette of concealers and shaders. It took her an age to do my foundation — which made me wonder just how effective my weekly facials actually were — and when she got out a packet of false eyelashes, I knew this wasn't going to be a ten-minute job.

She wouldn't let me look at myself, but every so often Liza would shimmy up and gush, 'Wow, honey! You look fabulous!' and then mutter something to the makeup artist, who would get the big palette out again and respackle my face.

After an eternity the rollers came out, the powder went on, and I was allowed to see myself in a hand mirror.

When I say I didn't recognize my own face, I don't mean that in a vain way. I mean the blond woman staring back at me was a whole league more beautiful than I ever thought I could be. A tiara of silver cobwebs studded with tiny pearls and diamonds sat in my shining updo, and my flawless skin looked peachy smooth. I would have cried if I wasn't so scared of dislodging the sixty-five individual lashes making up my doelike eyes.

'Now for the clothes!' Liza bustled up with the first selection, and that's where things started to come off the rails a bit.

Nothing fitted. I mean, nothing. I'd lost about eight pounds on the white-box diet, but my bones were those of a healthy English gardener, not a model, and all the clothes were designer sample sizes.

'Who called these in?' demanded Liza furiously, when yet another straining Issa dress refused to zip past my ribs. 'Nina? Which stylist was in charge of the wardrobe?'

Nina looked up from her BlackBerry. Unlike the rest of the shoot team, she didn't seem scared of Liza. 'Sofia. She said she'd take care of Amy's clothes while she was calling in her own for that interview she's doing about the book.'

'Well, she must have got the wrong size because nothing fits. These are all fine for Sofia but far too small for Amy. They're making her look *huge*.'

I cringed, but felt annoyed at the same time. Sofia knew what size I was. She'd been checking out the scale when Dr Johnsson got out his sadistic fat calipers. She'd even made that 'really?' face that calipers went up that far.

Everyone was looking at me now but pretending not to, and that made it a million times worse.

'Do you want me to get some more sent over from the mainland?' Nina chirped. 'It'll take a few hours to get them from Milan.'

'No.' Liza rubbed her hands together. 'No. We'll just have to cover up the gaps. Where are the cardigans? Cardigans! Now! And some big pins!'

'Sorry,' I muttered. I suddenly had a painful insight into how Mum felt when she walked down the high street – the makeup artist was staring at me as if she'd never seen a zip that wouldn't do up before. 'I've been following the diet and the exercise and–'

'It's not your fault!' trilled Liza unconvincingly. 'We'll know for next time!'

'She could wear her own clothes,' suggested Leo. 'They look good to me.'

He'd been waiting patiently while we prepared behind one

of the screens, but now he'd reappeared with some jewelry boxes, wearing a perfect dark gray suit. Things always seemed a bit more normal when Leo stepped in, even here.

'This is the formal photograph,' Liza pointed out. 'For the stamps, and then the gallery.'

'Do we have to start with that one? It's not the one I'd like released to the press.'

'What? Of course it's the one.'

'It's not what Amy and I are about. I'd like our engagement photo to be taken in the gardens, in normal clothes, just me and her.'

Liza looked annoyed. 'Do you think I've had the ballroom professionally lit for fun? Leo, it's just not how—'

'Mom.' He pulled off his tie and undid his top button, revealing a flash of tanned neck. 'I'm not that keen on this suit myself. I wear enough suits at work. It's not who I am when I'm here.'

'Leo, this is a formal portrait of the heir to the throne and his fiancée, and it needs to have a certain . . .' Liza dropped her voice discreetly. 'Dignity.'

'I could still wear the tiara.' I turned red as everyone's eyes turned to me. 'I mean, I could wear normal clothes with all the state jewelry, and we could sit in the garden. It would look informal but relaxed . . .'

'Exactly,' said Leo at once. 'That's what I meant. It would be a neat little commentary on how the monarchy's taking a less-formal direction while maintaining our connection with the tradition we love so much. Isn't that what we're meant to be representing? Not some stuffy accountant with his chess set.'

We all knew what he was talking about: the strange gray portrait of Pavlos that had been discreetly moved out of the main reception room, his king held aloft against a backdrop of, well, more gray. For someone declaring checkmate, he'd looked kind of woeful. As if he'd rather be out orienteering or filing a tax return.

'Fine.' Liza's eyes flicked from side to side as she hastily recalibrated the situation. 'Fine. Okay.'

'I think jeans,' said Leo, taking charge. 'Blue jeans and white shirts. Bare feet. Show me your feet, Amy.'

I kicked off my flats quite happily — my feet were size eight, but they were the one part of my body that I could guarantee to display evidence of boniness, and I spent a lot of time on my feet at work, so I'd always been kind to them. Sofia's regime of weekly pedicures had just upgraded what I already did, and today my toes were a glimmery deep green, like beetle shells.

'Perfect!' said Leo. 'What about those emeralds — let's match them to Amy's toes. And you could take your hair down so that tiara doesn't look so stiff . . .' He pulled out some of the rolls that the hairdresser had spent ages pinning in, and smiled at me. 'There, that's so pretty. I love your curls.'

'Leo!'

He turned back with a smile, but kept one hand resting protectively on my shoulder. 'Come on, Mom, it's — what do you call it? Editorial. We're putting an editorial stamp on the new portrait. Your fresh vision for our family. Not anyone else's.'

That seemed to do the trick. Liza's expression changed, and she clapped her hands sharply.

'Okay, people. We're taking this outside. Jenna, Sam, I need two clean white shirts, one from His Highness's wardrobe, one from my own.' She shot me — or rather, my chest — a sidelong glance. 'Um, maybe one from my husband's too . . .'

Leo slid an arm around my waist and squeezed without saying anything.

I squeezed back and trod softly on his toe, and he laughed.

# CHAPTER TWENTY-FIVE

Mum loved my engagement photograph. So did Dad, although he wasn't so impressed by some of the edging plants in the royal gardens.

'You look just like your Auntie Gloria,' she said, flicking through the spread in *Hello!* 'Although you could have brushed your hair.'

'It was meant to be like that,' I said over my shoulder. 'Tousled. And they've airbrushed my double chin out.'

Mum and Jo were in the back of the Range Rover, poring over the new edition of the magazine that I'd collected on the way up, while I sat in front with Billy and tried to persuade him to turn part of his lawn over to wildflowers.

'Shut up about your double chin,' said Jo. 'They didn't airbrush the way Leo's looking at you, did they?'

Someone with Photoshop had worked a bit of magic, but Jo had a point — the blissful smiles Leo and I were both wearing as he rested his head on my shoulder in one of the candid snaps were completely natural. The sun had come out, sparkling off the sapphire-blue sea in the background and warming my bare feet on the grass, and I'd felt like the luckiest girl in the world. It was exactly like a holiday snap, except I was wearing about a million pounds worth of jewelry, and the stately home in the background belonged to my fiancé, not the National Trust.

'Memo to *Tatler*: All tiaras should be worn on tously hair from now on,' Jo went on. 'You look as if you've just stumbled back from a ball the morning after. So in love. You're so gorgeous, the pair of you. If I didn't know you, I'd be eaten up with jealousy.'

'Well, you do know me.' I felt embarrassed, especially since Billy was clearly trying not to smile. 'And you know that underneath that smile is an agonizing invisible brace, and behind the camera are twelve people telling me to suck my tummy in.'

'Stop spoiling the magic!'

'Yes, Amy. It's bad manners not to accept a compliment.' Mum colored up too.

'Where did you read that?'

'Debrett's etiquette guide. Your father and I have been preparing for your wedding — it's very complicated. I don't want to make a faux pas and call someone the wrong kind of highness.'

I was about to tell her not to be so daft, but I had an abrupt vision of the pile of reading matter in my own overnight bag: Sofia's *Illustrated History of Nirona*, *Teach Yourself Italian*, *Ballroom Dancing for Beginners*. I'd only negotiated this time off from the preparations because I'd promised to study and shun carbs while I was in Yorkshire.

'You'll be fine,' said Jo quickly. 'People who matter don't mind, and people who mind don't matter. Just don't name-drop. That's what Earl Spencer once told me. Anyway, which shop are we going to first? I can't wait!'

Jo and Mum and I were in the Range Rover heading for Leeds to choose my wedding dress. I'd wanted to drive myself, but Leo had flown to New York for work, and had thoughtfully insisted that I take Billy and the car while he was away.

'It'll be easier,' he'd said. 'He can whiz you round town to different places and you won't have to worry about parking. And you can have a glass of wine if it all gets too much. Anyway, don't argue, because my assistant's already booked him into the Leeds Hilton for the night, and Billy likes a hotel.'

I couldn't argue with that. And since I wasn't driving, I could concentrate on keeping Mum's anxiety at being out of the house at the lowest possible level. I had my fingers crossed that it might abate once she was out of immediate town gossip range — I knew I certainly felt worlds more relaxed in London than I did in Rothery.

'We're booked in at the Wedding Warehouse,' I said, pulling out the notebook.

'What? Not Selfridges?'

'No. I just want something simple.' I didn't add, *and Dad's paying for the dress.* 'We're going to try to get your bridesmaid's dress sorted out, and something for Mum too. And then we'll go out for tea.'

'Fabulous!'

I glanced in the rearview mirror. Jo looked thrilled. Mum, squashed into a big floral mac that had fitted her last summer but now didn't, looked a lot less so.

Billy dropped us off at the door, and we trooped into the ivory satin wonderland that was the Wedding Warehouse.

Sylvia ('your gown fairy for today!') lost no time in pouring Mum and Jo 'a complimentary glass of bubbly' and hustling me toward the racks of glossy, sparkly, netty whiteness.

'Close your eyes and imagine yourself at the altar,' she instructed with a waft of her French manicure. 'What are you seeing?'

'Her very own handsome prince,' said Jo.

Sylvia covered her throat with her hands and pulled an 'Aw! Kittens!' face. 'That's lovely!'

I glared at Jo. 'I'm seeing something very simple,' I stressed. 'Something unfussy, that won't crease or be too big to sit down in. Something that won't look like a dress walking down the aisle with a woman hidden somewhere inside it.'

'But not too plain,' said Mum from the velvet sofa in the corner. 'You want to make the most of your lovely figure.'

'So, no meringues is what you're saying, Mum,' said Sylvia, and then turned pink.

I turned pink at the same time Mum did. It was something that happened a lot; the more people noted Mum's size, the more their brains seemed to make food references, and the more they drew attention to themselves, the more likely they were to make another one. I did it myself.

Jo leaped in to defuse the embarrassment with the dexterity I wished I could learn from Sofia's reading list. 'She wants to look like a very off-duty princess. Don't you? Ooh, I like this one with the daisies on the neckline — what do you think, Pam? Ivory or cream?'

'I like cream,' said Mum, and blushed again.

'Me too.' I grabbed the dress off the hanger. 'Let's start with this.'

I thought I'd be in and out of the changing room for hours, but with her characteristic good taste, Jo had picked the one wedding gown in the shop that fitted me, suited me, and, most of all, made me look like me, but me in a perfume commercial from 1962.

Unlike most of the Barbie-skirted showstoppers lining the walls, this dress had been hand sewn by a local designer. It was made from soft washed silk, with off-the-shoulder three-quarter sleeves that showed off my collarbones, and decorated with tiny daisies sewn around the edges, scattering down the full, knee-length skirt. It was the sort of dress that made you twirl and pose and then just stare at yourself and smile.

Sylvia zipped me up, and then made an involuntary *awwww* noise. The transformation between the me in jeans who'd arrived and the wedding me was so dramatic that it was almost too rude to draw attention to it.

'This is the one, isn't it?' I said in a small voice. This was exactly how, as a nine-year-old, I'd imagined I'd look on my wedding day. A real country bride, fresh and simple.

Sylvia patted my arm. 'I'm lost for words, love,' she said. 'And that doesn't happen often, I can tell you. You stay there, and I'll prepare them for your big moment.'

She swept out into the main room where Mum and Jo were waiting patiently with pink satin 'suspense masks' over their eyes, so they could really appreciate 'the wow factor.'

'You can remove your masks, ladies,' she said, beckoning

me onto the bridal viewing podium. 'And if you reach for the box of tissues, I think you'll need them, Mum.'

Mum and Jo pulled off the masks, and their mouths dropped into perfect Os.

Mum's eyes filled up immediately, and Jo clasped her own cheeks.

'You look beautiful,' she gasped. 'Your tiny waist! Your hair! Oh, Amy . . . Pam, what do you think? Is that the one?'

Mum was so overcome she couldn't make the words come out. She nodded her head, then shook it, then nodded again. Then reached for the tissues. 'Happy tears,' she managed, which set Jo off properly.

Sylvia darted forward before I even knew I was crying and shoved a wodge of tissues between my watery eyes and the pristine top. 'Let me just pop the finishing touch on.' She grabbed a full-length veil from the stand and pushed the comb into my ponytail.

Then, as an afterthought, she picked up a crystal tiara and shoved that on too.

'If you're going to marry your handsome prince, you want to look like a princess,' she added with an indulgent beam.

Jo's face creased up behind the tissue, and I warned her not to say anything with my eyebrows.

'It's very nice, but I was thinking of having flowers in my hair,' I said, reaching to take it off. 'Some Avalanche roses, with maybe some ivy and mistletoe? It's a winter wedding.'

'Ooh, mind the veil with your ring . . . Now, that's a lovely one!' Sylvia grabbed my hand to examine my engagement ring; engagement rings were like pregnant bumps, I'd come to realize — everyone felt at liberty to have a good look. I felt awkward, like I had when Jennifer Wainwright had nearly wrenched my sunglasses off my head to examine them.

'How much was that? If you don't mind me asking. It looks just like the real thing!'

I really didn't know what to say. I had no idea what it was worth; weren't the sorts of jewels you inherited priceless? 'Um, I wouldn't like to say.'

'Smart lass!' Sylvia winked at me. 'It's what lots of my clients are doing now — getting a big rock from QVC and leaving the real one at home.'

'It's real,' said Jo at the same time that I said, 'Yes, it's Diamonique.'

I didn't want to draw any more attention to myself than I had to. Although I was hypersensitive to my growing Internet celebrity status, fortunately it hadn't yet spread beyond the outer reaches of the social gossip columns, and the people who read them. But Jennifer's article had been in the local paper — Mum had a copy for me — and one of the reasons I'd come to Leeds and avoided our town was so no one would be looking at us and pointing. They might not have seen my horrible candid photos on YoungHot&Royal.com, but they had definitely seen the embarrassing photo of me at Hadley Green Primary School sports day that Jennifer had dug out of her own album.

'Well, that's me sorted,' I said, to change the subject. 'Do you have bridesmaids' dresses we could look at now?'

Sylvia waved at the second room, where the racks were every color of the rainbow but mainly burgundy. 'We most certainly do. What's your color scheme? Do you have a theme, apart from winter? I've had some gorgeous new dresses just come in — lovely shades of chocolate and almond . . .' She glanced sideways at Mum. 'Um, rich brownie colors — um, lots of lovely prom styles!'

Mum busied herself examining a display of white Cinderella shoes.

'Are we not going to Selfri—?' Jo started, aghast.

'Jo, can you come and help me out of this?' I darted my eyes toward the changing room. 'I don't want to get it dirty.'

'Oh, er, right. Of course.' She followed me in and pulled the velvet curtain across.

'Listen,' I hissed before she could start, 'I want to get everything here if we can.'

'Why?' She raised her hands. 'You can't just buy the first dress you try on! You should shop around a bit. And it's not like you're on a budget — you could get me and your mum something really fab from Selfridges that we could both wear again after—'

'I *am* on a budget!' I dropped my voice even further. 'Dad's paying for this wedding, I don't want it to cost a fortune. And Mum's . . .' I hesitated, not sure how much to say, even to Jo. 'Mum's very self-conscious. I don't want her feeling out of place at Selfridges, especially if nothing fits. They don't really cater for the larger lady, whereas there's bound to be something here for her.'

'All the more reason to find her something fabulous! There are plenty of bigger celebrities who shop at—'

'Jo, no, it's not just that.' It was so hard to explain why

Mum was the way she was, not without getting into the whole Kelly thing. 'She's very, very shy. This wedding's already a lot to get her head around — I just want the nice lady to bring Mum all the mother-of-the-bride clothes she has, so we can find her an outfit and she can stop worrying.'

I paused. 'You can get something amazing for the blessing in Nirona. I promise.'

Jo squinted at me. She knew a family cover-up when she heard one. 'Fine,' she said, 'but lay off the red peplums. I'm not standing next to Leo Wolfsburg and his princess bride dressed as a disco strawberry.'

It took fifteen minutes to fit Jo up with a matching leaf-green washed-silk bombshell dress (although to wind her up, I made her try on three burgundy strapless numbers with peplums), but a lot longer to find something for Mum.

'This is very popular with my MOBs,' Sylvia puffed as she hauled at the zip of yet another fitted sheath dress. It was pistachio green with a brocade skirt and cropped jacket and made Mum look like a fun-runner dressed as a pea pod. 'Some of them are much . . . bigger . . . than . . . you. There! What do you think? Pop the bolero on, Mum!'

Mum slipped her plump arms into the metallic bolero and looked at me in the mirror with mortified eyes. If anything was going to pop, it was her skirt. Her freckled pink bosom was bursting out of the straining satin bustier like an overfilled cream puff. She'd tried on six of these, and this was the one that made her look least like a sofa.

'Or maybe a wrap?' Jo suggested, offering her own filmy

cashmere scarf. 'That might be warmer, for the church? It will be December.'

'Mum?' I looked at her anxiously.

Her face had fallen when she thought no one was looking, but now she pulled on a brave smile. 'I like it! It's a very nice color. And maybe I'll lose a few pounds before the wedding.' She tugged at the skirt and frowned at herself.

My heart broke at the anxiety she was trying — and failing — to hide. I couldn't bear it.

'We can try something else?' I suggested. 'We can nip into Leeds and—'

'No,' said Mum, horrified. 'Not Leeds. I've tried on quite enough outfits. I don't want to go anywhere else.'

'All my mums lose weight,' said Sylvia, patting her arm. 'It's the stress. I should market it as the Wedding Diet Plan!'

Not my mum, I thought miserably. Stress would have the opposite effect, and Sylvia didn't even know about the supermodel mother of the groom on the other side of the pews, and the international press outside.

God. This was supposed to be the happiest day of my life, and already it was giving me a stress rash.

'Yes, very nice. I'll take it. Now, will someone help me out of this?' Mum waved her arms, and there was an ominous ripping noise from the bolero sleeve.

'We can fix that,' said Sylvia quickly.

Mum insisted on paying — by check; 'no credit cards in our family!' — and we left the dresses to be adjusted by Sylvia's team of seamstresses. I treated the four of us to tea in a country house hotel on the outskirts of the city, where the scones weren't as light as Mum's, and then Billy drove us home.

It took some determined coaxing from Jo to get Mum out of her introspective mood. I was no help, feeling thoroughly mixed-up myself, but Jo generously ran through her family's catalogue of wedding disasters — how her uncle had set fire to an usher 'not by mistake'; how her cousin had broken down outside the church and confessed she was in love with the bridesmaid; how her grandfather had sliced through the electrics for the Ritz hotel with the ceremonial cake sword — until eventually, by the time we were off the motorway and into the countryside again, Mum was almost back to her normal self.

'How did you face the neighbors?' she kept giggling, to which Jo deadpanned, 'We bought a house on an island.'

I spotted her tensing up again as the GPS steered us through our old village, and realized too late that I should have given Billy different directions. Hadley Green looked idyllic. The Yorkshire in Bloom village competition was in full swing, and every cottage was adorned with cascading hanging baskets and decorative beds in a riot of reds and oranges. I could smell the sweet tang of mown grass even through the Range Rover's air conditioning.

'Ooh, look at that house!' Jo pointed out her window. 'Now, that is what I call an English country cottage! Look at those roses! And the adorable swing on the apple tree!'

'That's where we used to live,' I said quietly from the front.

The whitewashed double front of our old house was bathed in early summer sunshine, and all the ice creams we'd licked on that rolling lawn flashed before my eyes. All the bee stings and daisy chains. All the sunbathing (Kelly) and the ladybird catching (me). There still wasn't a dandelion speckling its bowling-green finish; Dad would be proud.

It was years since I'd been past here, and I wondered if Mum and Dad ever talked about it. I guessed not — our life Before the Kelly Business was never referred to. That was the biggest loss of all, not the money or the gardens. The fact that we'd had such happy times, but they were locked away, never to be spoken of.

'It's like something from a Thomas Hardy novel.' Jo was leaning forward. She couldn't see the warning look on my face. 'Why did you move from such a gorgeous house, Pam? Downsizing?'

'Something like that,' I said hurriedly.

As we drove past, I caught sight of a For Sale board outside, and hoped Mum hadn't seen it too. She'd gone very quiet again.

# CHAPTER TWENTY-SIX

I thought about Mum's outfit constantly once I was back in London. I couldn't forget the expression I'd caught in the mirror — horror mixed with an awful sort of resignation, as if she didn't deserve anything better. I kicked myself; I'd got it wrong, and I should have whisked her round every boutique in Yorkshire till I found her something. Or I should have brought the dresses to her.

The trouble was, I was so busy that I didn't know when I could get home again to fix it. I ran lots of situation-salvaging options through my brain as I followed Ted round the gardens of South London, tidying and pruning from morning till dusk. It was getting hotter and we were well into our peak lawn-nurturing season, as well as our garden-sitting watering service for regulars on holiday. The wild rooftop gardens where I'd planted some meadow beds last year were buzzing with honeybees, and the long grasses gave Badger a shady spot to cool his paws while we sweated away under our cricket hats.

A few days later, I was driving back from a heavy afternoon's pruning in Cheyne Walk, dreaming of a long cool shower and a glass of wine with Leo in his garden, when my mobile rang: it was Sylvia from the Wedding Warehouse.

'Good news!' she caroled. 'I've got your dresses back for the first fitting. When can we book you in?'

'Already? I didn't think it needed any adjusting,' I said, surprised. Zoë Weiss had taken two fittings for a dress that had hugged me like a second skin, but it had draping and a corset. The wedding dress had felt perfect to me.

'Well, normally it would take a lot longer, but as you say, your dress didn't need much doing to it. And of course, we need to have your lovely mum and friend back too, for theirs!'

Mum's dress. That needed to be just right, for her to feel confident. And I had to be there too, to make sure she knew how wonderful I thought she looked.

'Let me get my diary.' I pulled my bag out from underneath Badger, who was curled up on it in the shady footwell of the van. 'Um . . . I'm quite tied up with work until . . .'

My diary had gone from being completely empty apart from Zumba to blocks of 'trainer,' 'dance class,' 'Italian lesson,' 'dinner with Leo?' all the way through to the Coronation Ball in October. Which was only nine ballroom dancing lessons away now. I flipped the pages quickly.

'To be honest, while we're talking about your mum's dress . . .' I could virtually hear Sylvia biting her lip.

'What about it?'

'We might have to think about another color. We can't get another bolero in her size, as they're not making them anymore, and . . .'

Sylvia carried on talking, but my head was filled with the haunting image of my pretty mother, squeezed into a dress that did nothing for her, not objecting because she didn't like to make a fuss. On a day that should be a happy family occasion.

That did it. I had a credit card, didn't I? Mum didn't have to have that outfit. I could get her one that actually suited her.

'Sylvia, let me get back to you with dates,' I said. 'I need to get hold of my bridesmaid and see when we can come up.'

And then I put my Tom Ford sunglasses on and drove to Sloane Street.

It went against the awkward stance I'd taken about chucking money at problems, but if there was one situation where it was worth breaking my own rules, this was it.

I just needed to put my conscience on hold for a bit.

The doorman at the Zoë Weiss shop almost didn't let me in, such was my end-of-day aroma. Admittedly, I didn't look like a classic Zoë Weiss customer, if the two skinny, capri-panted women browsing in the dazzling white shop were anything to go by, but maybe my surge of panicky confidence convinced him.

I walked over to the mirrored counter in the corner, positioned between two dummies wearing Zoë's trademark halter-neck satin evening gowns in scarlet and turquoise, and wished I'd worn at least one of the expensive key pieces Sofia had made me buy. I didn't even have the handbag, just my leather work satchel.

'Is Zoë here, please?'

The assistant looked me up and down and drew her own conclusions.

'No,' she said, patronizingly. 'This is just her shop. Do you go into Armani and expect to see Giorgio in the back running up a little skirt?'

'She does spend some time here,' I insisted. 'She was here a few months ago.'

'Did you read that in *Grazia*?'

'No, I know it because I saw her. Here.'

The assistant stared back at me, twice as hard as I was staring at her. To be fair, she'd achieved a level of precision grooming that even Sofia would applaud, and I was intimidated.

I made myself think of Mum. And the hideous bolero. I couldn't let her try that on again. She'd back out of the wedding.

'Do you have a number for her, then?' I went on. 'I need to speak to her. Tell her . . .' I hated doing this, it really wasn't me, but the assistant was talking over me. I made myself channel Sofia. 'Tell her it's Amy Wilde.'

'I don't think she's—'

I raised my voice. 'Or Amy Wolfsburg?'

'—offering work experience to—'

I hated doing this, but I carried on, louder. 'Liza Bachmann's future daughter-in-law.'

'—students at the moment, and—'

I reached into the inner pocket of my bag and pulled out Liza's business card, the one she'd given me with all her contact details on, and put it on the desk.

Silence. I tingled with a mixture of triumph and embarrassment. Had I really done that? Had I just pulled the 'do you know who I am?' thing? Oh God. That was so . . . Rolf.

But it worked. The assistant's eyes widened, and she gulped visibly.

'One moment, please,' she said, and hurried off.

I pretended to look at some tiny shoes while the two other women in the shop pretended not to look at me.

A long minute passed during which I felt my armpits becoming less fragrant by the second, and eventually the assistant returned with an incredulous look on her face.

'If you would like to follow me,' she said in an undertone, and now the two other shoppers really were gawping.

Zoë was upstairs in the all-white studio above the shop, sitting in a white egg-shaped chair with a tiny white espresso cup in her hand, while three assistants scurried around as she snapped orders and jabbed at things with her tiny red nails.

When she saw me, she shrieked in delight and pointed at me.

'It's my lady gardener!' She wagged the finger. 'I saw you in that magazine with your jeans and your tiara and your handsome prince. What happened to the fabulous evening piece I heard Elie Saab was making for your big shoot? Didn't you like it?'

'It didn't fit me,' I confessed. I didn't know who she was talking about. 'Nothing did. That's why I wore the jeans.'

'What?' Zoë looked surprised. 'But that's extraordinary. Who was supposed to be arranging your wardrobe for that? Liza spoke to Elie and Giorgio and—'

'It doesn't matter,' I said blushing. 'I wore that beautiful ballgown you made me for the formal portrait — which was very special for me, because I wore it the night Leo proposed. That's the one that'll be on the stamps eventually, not the jeans one. I think.'

'Oh, how darling.' Zoë held out her cup to be refilled with coffee and clasped her hands together. 'Have you come to show me?'

'No, I've come to ask you a favor.'

'You want me to make your wedding gown!' Zoë spun round in her egg chair in delight. 'How fabulous! Of course I will!'

'Um, I've already got one,' I said awkwardly. 'But I'd like you to make a dress for my mother.'

I paused, unsure of how to lay it out so Zoë wouldn't laugh me out of her studio. 'She's . . . she's quite a large lady, and I can't find anything that suits her, and I thought maybe if I gave you her measurements and some photographs of her—'

'Darling, bring her down here. Bring her to my studio.' Zoë waved to an assistant for her big desk diary. 'You've put one of my designs on letters going all over the world, it's the least I can do.'

'I can't. She wouldn't come, she's so shy.' I blinked back tears. I wasn't sure what had come over me, but I suddenly felt incredibly emotional.

Zoë looked at me, and sucked her teeth. Then, with a discreet flick of her hand, she dismissed her assistants and patted the white leather sofa next to her egg chair. I sank down with a thump.

'I know it sounds daft,' I gabbled, 'but if you could make something for her, I can pay for it. Me personally, not Liza or

Leo. Please don't let her know how much it costs, but if you can make her feel good about herself on my wedding day, it'll be worth whatever you'd charge. As long as it's not over the limit on my card.'

Oh dear. Had I said that aloud? But I had no idea how much Zoë charged for dresses.

'You made me look like a model in that ballgown,' I pleaded. 'I know you can make my mum look good.'

There was a long pause.

'Of course.' Zoë sounded relatively somber for once. 'My mother is somewhat zaftig, but she is a goddess. She made me want to design better clothes. I like making clothes for real women — we'll make her look like a million dollars.'

'Really? Thank you!' I felt a weight lift from my shoulders for the first time in days. 'That would be so kind.'

'Kind? Darling, I don't think you realize what a favor you're doing for me,' said Zoë. 'You're going to have a lot of cameras on you from now on. Liza Bachmann's daughter-in-law, Prince Leo's wife . . . And you're a beautiful girl, a real girl. Not a skinny Minnie like Duchess Kate. I like breasts, and some junk in the trunk. Makes things hang better! Don't tell Liza I said that, though. She has a junkless trunk.'

I turned red. 'I hope there won't be too many cameras . . . I don't really like having my photo taken.'

Zoë laughed, as if I'd said something funny on purpose. 'Did you miss the royal wedding? Haven't you noticed there's a worldwide shortage of princes getting married? And you, my darling, are such an English rose!'

'No, not really. I get so spotty, and my hands are . . .'

Why was it so hard to take compliments? I wondered. Why did I automatically bat them away?

Dodgy Chris, said a glum voice in my head. Dad, and his dire warnings about people who told gullible girls what they wanted to hear. Kelly was a right sucker for a compliment, and look where it got her.

Zoë picked up a green pencil from the desk and twirled it round her fingers. 'You come back to me in two years' time, when you're on the cover of every magazine with that mermaid hair and those big green eyes, and tell me you don't like having your photo taken. Now, let's talk about your mom . . .'

I smiled, but I had more faith in Zoë's design ability than her fortune-telling.

# CHAPTER TWENTY-SEVEN

When your diary goes from quite busy to packed with appointments like planes stacking up in Heathrow, time passes very quickly. Worryingly quickly.

I was aware of ticking things off my to-do list — booking caterers, finalizing numbers for the Hadley Green ceremony, double-checking with Dad that he and Mum had valid passports for the Nirona blessing — but time was sliding by faster than I realized in my own life. July turned into August turned into September, and I noticed autumn creeping into the leaves and soil, but it barely seemed ten days since my last credit card bill had come and there was another month gone.

Until I saw it on the newsagents' stand by the Sloane Square Underground, I had, for instance, completely forgotten that Grace Wright's rooftop garden was going to feature in the October issue of *Gardens Illustrated* — she'd told me that someone was coming to photograph it in July, when the cottage-garden containers and wildflower barrels were at their multicolored, blowsy best.

Well, actually, she'd asked me if I could 'borrow' some extra plants for her, 'just to zhush it up a bit.' Daddy was planning to sell, apparently, now that she was moving in with Richard.

It was very much mission accomplished for both Daddy and Grace.

'Are you not moving in with your fiancé?' she'd asked from her sun lounger. Since I'd got engaged, Grace had spent a lot of time sipping green tea on the balcony and telling me all about her wedding dramas. I'd nodded, pruned, and mentally crossed off a lot of ideas from my own list.

I'd told her that, no, I wasn't.

She'd looked shocked — as far as her Botox would allow. 'Really? Are you ... saving yourself?' Her voice dropped respectfully, but also slightly disbelievingly. 'Is it part of the deal about marrying the heir to the throne?' She mouthed, 'No bedding before the wedding?'

I'd laughed at that point, because it definitely was not; but I didn't know how to explain why I hadn't moved in with Leo in terms Grace would understand.

The truth was, I loved sharing a flat with Jo. Leominster Place was more and more like a comfort blanket for me, the safe place between Leo's super-high-class world of jewels and assistants, and the small, net-curtained world of Rothery that I'd almost forgotten how to live in after three years in London. Jo helped me smooth out the problems in both, putting Sofia's curt e-mails about my measurements and Mum's anxious phone calls about the church choir into perspective. She'd even shelved her plans to take *Chicago-a-go-go* up to the Edinburgh Festival so she could keep me sane while the decisions mounted up for both ceremonies, and every time we went out, she left the house first, so she could check for lurking paparazzi.

I'd never had a friend like her before. I'd been shy at school, and then a pariah; spending time with funny, confident Jo, who dragged me along to all her parties and then gossiped about them over a fry-up afterward, was something I would miss more than I could say. The summer had gone by too fast as it was, and I only had a few more weeks of flat-sharing — with her, and Dickon and Mrs Mainwaring, and Badger — and I wanted to enjoy them as much as I wanted to keep moving in with Leo as a special moment in a relationship that was already going at a million miles an hour.

Jo and I were heading up to the King's Road to get some lunch, since we were working on the same house in Passmore Street: Jo was making sure the electricians didn't leave before the carpenters arrived, and I was sketching out a plan to overhaul the neglected garden.

I stopped as soon as I saw Grace's balcony on the magazine stand. The main heading was 'Country Heaven in the London Sky,' and I was bursting with pride. I'd made that.

'Wow!' said Jo in a loud voice over my shoulder. 'Is that garden, on the front cover of that national magazine, designed by Amy Wilde of Botham & Wilde Gardens? Is it? And is the magazine only four pounds? I'll have ten to give to all my friends!'

'Shh!' I nudged her. People were turning round to see what the fuss was about as they left the Tube station.

'No, this is not a *shh*ing situation. This is a trumpet moment!' Jo reached into her bag for her purse and bought the two copies that were there. 'You should send one to your mum and dad! They'll be so proud of you.'

I smiled, but at the same time I wondered if, somewhere, Kelly would see it. I mean, it was unlikely — she always said gardening was dead boring — but you never knew, she might be in a dentist's waiting room. Getting her teeth whitened, knowing Kelly.

I'd been thinking about Kelly quite a lot lately, because the invitations had arrived from the printers in Harrogate, and we were on a countdown to post them exactly six weeks before the ceremony on December 7. Mum still had Kelly down on her list of invitees from our side, but with no flicker of contact from her, despite me and Leo appearing on the lower slopes of the *Daily Mail* website's Sidebar of Celebrity, and no forwarding address, I didn't know where Mum was planning on sending it. Maybe Santa could forward it on from the North Pole.

I looked down and grinned at the magazine in my hands. Excitement mingled with pride at what this exposure might mean for my design consultancy dreams. Ted and I had a friend who'd had her copper water features spotlit in a magazine, and she'd sold her entire shedful almost overnight and been commissioned by Heal's to design a line.

'We should go out tonight to celebrate,' Jo went on, linking her arm through mine and shepherding me across the road. 'After dancing class. Rolf says he's found a great new restaurant in Ebury Street, and I'm trying to encourage him into tasteful ways. Which means restaurants with fully clad staff and no theme other than food.'

'You're spending a lot of time with Rolf,' I observed. 'Have you changed your mind about the whole marrying-into-royalty ban?'

Jo shot me a sideways glance. 'I'll see how you get on with it first.'

'Ah-ha! That's not what I asked!'

I'd noticed that Jo's merciless criticism of Rolf had changed over the past few weeks. It was no longer the disparaging tone she'd always used in the beginning, but had softened into the pointy banter she and Ted cheerfully slapped each other with.

'I just see it as my duty to do what I can to save you from a brother-in-law who opens champagne bottles as if he's just won a Grand Prix,' she said. 'If I can knock some manners into Rolf before it's too late, you never know, you might invite me to your principality. I could oversee work on your nursery.'

I ignored that. 'Last time I saw Rolf, he was wearing a plain blue shirt. Was that down to you as well?'

Jo seemed pleased. 'Perhaps. Listen, knocking men into shape is a family tradition. My dear mother Marigold's grand-mama was the same. She went out with a personage we cannot name as a sort of learner girlfriend. Taught him all she knew, and then was retired to a teensy little château in the Isle of Wight.'

'So she didn't listen to her father when it came to royalty either.'

'No rings were involved. And . . .' Jo arched her eyebrow. 'It depends who you mean by her father.'

This was the sort of conversation I would really miss. I hugged my magazines to my chest and made a mental note to ask Leo to sort out a permanent guest room for Jo in the east wing.

*

Jo and I were enjoying a smoothie and the air con in Pret a Manger when my phone rang. It was Leo.

'Amy, is this a good time to talk?'

'Just having lunch with Jo,' I said happily. 'I've got something to show you later.'

I was hoping he might respond to the sauciness in my voice, but he didn't.

'That's great,' he said in a strained tone. 'Listen, I need you to come and meet me and Mom in her suite at Claridge's. There's something we need to discuss.'

The smile slid from my face. 'That sounds ... ominous. What does she want to discuss?'

I guessed it was about my dress for the blessing. Zoë Weiss had been asking, but I wasn't allowed to choose a designer before Liza had squared off her complicated series of favors owed between various international celebrity types. It was awkward, since Zoë had shown me the nearly finished dress she'd made for Mum, and it was so beautiful it nearly made me cry. (I had a feeling the finished invoice would make me cry too, having done some research, but I'd cross that bridge later.)

'It's a press thing,' said Leo. He sounded guarded.

'Is this about Rolf?' I glanced at Jo. 'Has he done—'

'No. Look, I'd rather not discuss it over the phone. How soon can you get here?'

I pushed my unfinished smoothie toward Jo. 'Well, I've got to finish up in Passmore Street, and then I said I'd go round to—'

'No, there's no time for that. Can you get in a taxi right now?'

'Okay,' I said, bewildered.

It couldn't be the dress. Maybe they'd found out Di Overend's nephew Ryan was penciled in to take the Hadley Green wedding photos.

I borrowed twenty quid from Jo and hailed a black cab, which got me to Claridge's in seventeen minutes, during which time I'd run through all possible options and decided it had to be something to do with my proposed therapy garden in Nirona. I'd worked through the night all weekend, and given the organizers a very detailed plan of the sensory stimulation areas I wanted to create — maybe it was too specific?

Leo was waiting for me in the tiled lobby. His face was strained, as if he'd been listening without speaking for a long time.

'Hi, Leo,' I said, reaching up for a kiss. 'What's happened? Are you all right?'

He grabbed my arms. 'Amy,' he said, 'I just want you to know that I—'

'Amy!'

We spun round to see Liza at the bottom of the sweeping staircase. She was wearing a coral sleeveless shift with bare legs, and I marveled anew at her perfectly golden tan and the effortless way her mane was today swept into a messy updo, held in place by huge sunglasses.

But while her clothes said warm, her expression said cold. Very cold indeed.

Behind her was Giselle, the press officer. Giselle was the embodiment of that expression 'she looked like a bulldog

chewing a wasp' (or the less polite variants), but in navy sep-
arates.

'Shall we go up to my suite?' said Liza, and it wasn't really
a question.

Liza had taken the Brook Penthouse, which was, as far as I
could see without craning my neck into all the rooms, a complete Art Deco flat at the top of the hotel.

She steered me into the soft lilac sitting room, which had
a lavish panoramic view of London over the private roof terrace, and then pointedly positioned me on the sofa facing the
fireplace, not the distracting window.

Leo sat down next to me, and Liza and Giselle faced us.

I took a deep breath and tried to smile. I'd been sitting in
a garden all morning moving plant pots around, and I wasn't
even well dressed enough to be a staff member here.

Liza did not return my tentative smile. 'I won't beat about
the bush. We have a problem, Amy.'

A million terrible thoughts flashed through my mind. Well,
a couple of headline ones and several thousand minor ones.

What had I done? What had she found out about me? Had
Leo been involved in one of those big banking crises?
Had Dr Johnsson told her I'd been cheating on the diet in
Pret a Manger? Had Martin Ecclestone sold his story to
YoungHot&Royal?

The pause stretched out across the glass coffee table.

'Don't play mind games, Mom,' snapped Leo. 'This isn't *CSI:
Mayfair*. There's going to be something in the paper, Amy,' he
said, turning to me. 'Something about you.'

I actually thought I was going to be sick.

Liza looked at us both. Her immaculately lined eyes had the furious gleam of a woman whose elaborate plans have been derailed by a loose paper clip. 'Giselle keeps close tabs on all news outlets, as you know, and she's brought it to my attention that two newspapers are intending to run with this. Giselle?'

Giselle pursed her lips and pushed her black-rimmed glasses farther up her small nose. She took a leather portfolio out of her bag, unzipped it, and pushed a piece of paper across the glass toward Leo.

I felt a shameful rush of relief that Leo seemed to be the one who needed to deal with it.

Then she removed another and pushed it toward me.

Slowly, and with Liza's eyes burning twin holes in the top of my head, I began to read.

As my eyes moved down the page, a furious buzzing noise started up in my ears like a swarm of angry hornets, and my tongue suddenly seemed too big for my mouth.

The headline was 'How to Marrow a Millionaire!' and beneath it was a photograph of me at Hadley Green Agricultural Show, aged about six, going by the missing front teeth. I was standing next to Dad and his prize marrow for that year, which was about the same size as me. Dad had been en route to the Gardeners' Club comedy dancing display, and was sporting a flat cap with his fancy dress trousers belted with twine — something that was not explained in the caption.

Next to that was a photo of Leo at a premiere in black tie, and then a long-lens paparazzi shot of me leaning against the Botham & Wilde Gardens van, swigging from a bottle of water.

The photographer had managed to make it look as if it wasn't necessarily water, and had also captured Badger apparently peeing against someone else's hedge.

'I would never let Badger do that,' I gasped. 'And my dad was a bank manager! He was in a costume in that photo!'

Leo and Liza said nothing.

Well. They were embarrassing photos, sure, but did they warrant this level of drama?

I looked up, and Giselle snapped, 'Read the copy.'

My eyes skimmed over the text, but I couldn't make them engage with the words. Phrases were familiar — *'Amy is a jobbing gardener in London . . . parents live in an ex-council house in the down-at-heel former mining town of Rothery . . . Prince Leo, banker and millionaire heir to the principality of Nirona, met at a no-holds-barred party thrown by society actress the Hon. Jo de Verais, former on-off girlfriend of Leo's brother Rolf . . .'* — but other parts were so weird I couldn't believe they were talking about me. Like the things I'd allegedly said.

*Living up to royal standards is a nightmare,* confesses Amy, 26. *I haven't eaten for days and I'm going mad. But when your mum-in-law's a supermodel, you can't expect anything to be normal!*

'I never said that!' I protested. 'I mean, I said I was *starving,* but it was a manner of speaking.'

'So we'll sue for fabrication,' said Leo. 'Giselle, get on the phone right now, tell them we've got lawyers on the case. We'll want to see tapes.'

I raised my eyes very slowly from the page. Liza was staring at me, and I felt her eyes burning my face.

'Amy?' she said. 'Don't even think about lying to me. Have you been speaking to the press?'

I opened my mouth, but then closed it. There was no point. I already looked guiltier than Badger next to an empty packet of biscuits.

*Amy, who only achieved average results at her local compre-hensive, now sports diamond bracelets worth more than fifty thousand pounds from exclusive jewelers-to-royalty Chaumet and high-end designer sunglasses when she returns to slum it in her former home . . .*

'I did —' My voice cracked. 'I did do a very informal interview with my local paper. I think that's where that photograph has come from.'

'What?'

'I knew it,' said Giselle. 'It'll be on tape. We can't sue for fabrication. Shit.'

'I don't understand — it ran weeks ago,' I spluttered. 'I didn't even think it was worth mentioning. I mean, it was just with a girl I knew from school.' I was babbling now. 'It didn't say any of those things! It was just "Amy works in London, she's really excited about marrying a prince, she's met Keira Knightley at a premiere." It didn't even make the front page — they probably thought Jennifer was making it up.'

'So who is the "close friend of the princess-to-be" who's supplied these quotes?' demanded Liza. 'The ones about you being terrified of offending me because I'm so high-maintenance? And how you're being crushed by the responsibility of what you'll have to take on as a "top international princess"?'

She sounded concerned, but I honestly couldn't tell if she felt sorry for me or wanted to murder me now. Her politeness was like a suit of armor.

'I have no idea — I don't have any close friends apart from . . .'

Jo wouldn't. Jo just . . . wouldn't.

Leo was staring at me now. Or he was, until he put his head in his hands and groaned.

'Jo would hardly describe *herself* as a society actress,' I protested. 'And she wouldn't get her own name wrong!'

'It's probably the original journalist,' said Giselle through gritted teeth. 'I bet she's tried to sell them the story, and they've done a deal for the pictures, interviewed her, then airbrushed her out of the picture.'

'Liza, I'm really sorry.' I was mortified. 'I never said anything like that. Yes, I might have said it was a strain not eating carbs — we met at a café! — but I was just making conversation. I certainly didn't say you were high-maintenance or that I didn't want to take on any responsibilities . . .'

*. . . except when you were showing off to Jennifer about how many staff your mother-in-law had, and telling her how you had to come up with a list of four charities to take on as your personal mission . . .*

I was struggling to breathe now. Was this it? Was this where I had to break off the engagement for real this time? I glanced across at Leo, but his face was a steely mask too. I hadn't felt so sick with shame and panic in a long time. The thought of everyone reading that and thinking I'd said those things — here in London, and up at home — was so monumentally humiliating that my brain wouldn't let me contemplate it all at once. It was an iceberg of embarrassment.

*Although,* said a little voice, right at the back of all the white noise, *there's no mention of Kelly and what she did.* I'd take being called a gold-digger over some of the other possible options.

I kept my eyes glued to the pale oak flooring in case Giselle and Liza could read my mind.

'Can we stop them running it?' Leo directed his question to Giselle.

She shook her head. 'I had to call in every favor I had to stop that photo of Rolf in the tank last year. If we try to spike this, they'll only try to run it again with new stuff.' She cast a beady eye at me. 'Didn't I make it clear enough, Amy, that all press communication has to be run past me, and I will run it past Liza and Boris?'

I nodded meekly. 'I didn't think the *Rothery Gazette* counted as . . . press.'

'Everything counts with the Internet,' said Liza.

She put her hands to her head and let out a yowl of frustration. 'I have been working so hard recently. *So hard*, just to get the family on message for the coronation. I've flown back and forth from New York to Washington to London to Italy pushing the Be an Everyday Princess campaign, I've written all Boris's speeches for the next six months, I've even hired a press agent for Rolf. But I do not expect to have to deal with being called a control-freak anorexic in the pages of the British gutter press, by the real-life princess I'm supposed to be coaching myself! Do you have any idea how this will play in the US?'

'But I didn't—!' I began.

'And what the hell is a *top* international princess?' she demanded crazily. 'Is there any other kind? Your journalists are so sloppy!'

'We can handle this.' Leo shifted forward on the sofa and started to count off his fingers, as if he were in a business meeting. 'Amy, this is a great moment to launch your therapy garden. We can do a photo call, you and me, planting vegetables with kids. Say you've always loved getting your hands dirty, play up your normal-girl roots. They're nothing to be ashamed of. In fact, let's get your mum to send us more photos of you with your dad.'

He glared at Giselle, who paused and then, under the weight of his stare, began writing.

Leo turned to Liza. 'Mom, I'm sure you and Amy can do a little shopping this afternoon together? There should be plenty of photographers in town today — there's a garden party at Buckingham Palace. Maybe you two could pop into Ladurée for macaroons — that ought to kill the anorexia and the animosity in one go.'

'We need more than that,' said Giselle. 'We need a bigger statement.'

Liza had been thinking, moving her diamond rings up and down her fingers, alternately pouting and squinching her glossy apricot lips. Finally she looked up and stared straight at me.

'The Coronation Ball,' she said.

I nodded. It was only a few weeks away now, and to be honest, I wasn't massively looking forward to everyone staring at me, commenting on my outfit, my ability to waltz, my fitness to marry Prince Charming, and now my apparent obsession with marrows. I was secretly hoping that Sofia would demand to take center stage in all the available diamonds. I fully intended to let her.

Liza's gaze didn't waver from my face. 'Amy will recite the grace at dinner,' she said. 'And she can be the girl who brings in the golden slipper.'

I heard a sharp intake of breath to my left.

'Mom—' Leo began, as Giselle failed to speak, and Liza raised a hand to silence him without looking.

Then I heard a voice say, 'I'll do it. Of course I'll do it,' and to my absolute horror, I realized it was mine.

The stroppy Yorkshire voices in my head had finally taken control. And they seemed to be making a point.

# CHAPTER TWENTY-EIGHT

Of course, I found out soon enough that while being asked to read the grace and present the golden slipper that started the Coronation Ball was a significant honor, it was also a significant honor that had originally been earmarked for Sofia, as the eldest daughter of the soon-to-be-crowned Sovereign Prince.

It also meant being the center of attention not once but twice, and being expected to fulfill both tasks without slipping up or saying the wrong thing, but I didn't let myself think about that.

I was relieved — and a bit surprised — when the note the courier delivered from Sofia was cordiality itself. She was very busy with a landmark ruling involving a sizable estate in Geneva, said the monogrammed card clipped to the manila file of instructions, so she was more than pleased to hand over the duty to me. And the slipper ceremony, the note went on in her firm handwriting, had always felt rather degrading to women, with its patriarchal Cinderella overtones, and when many women in the third world had no shoes at all, it was obscene to have one made of gold studded with Swarovski crystals.

Rolf, though, was positively gleeful about the possibility of a giant catfight between me and Sofia. He rubbed his hands when I told him and Leo about the Swarovski crystal comment.

'I'd watch your coffee if I were you,' he said. 'Sofie's got form in the area of sabotage.'

'As have you,' Jo pointed out.

His thick brown eyebrows shot up. 'I have no idea what you mean.'

'Yes, you do,' said Leo. 'And let's let it drop.'

'That's what all the girls say,' Rolf replied with a smug grin, and then yelped as Jo kicked him under the table.

We were sitting in the Wolseley on Piccadilly after another dancing lesson. It was a compromise venue, in that it was flashy enough for Rolf to be seen in, but far too noisy for even his conversation to be particularly audible. Our table was in the mezzanine balcony, with a great view of all the other diners, and the food looked delicious, but I had no appetite for my scallops.

On top of the stress now filling my head at the thought of having to dance in an actual spotlight at the ball when I still couldn't turn without stamping on Leo's foot, another picture of me had popped up on the Internet that morning. I was pushing a wheelbarrow under the heading 'Her Royal Thighness.' It also referred to me as 'blooming,' which everyone knows is code for 'is she fat or pregnant?' I wasn't even fat. I'd lost another four pounds, but there wasn't much I could do with my thighs. They were just muscular.

Jo saw me frowning and gave me a kick too, for good measure.

'This grace sounds like an honor,' she said brightly. 'Is it a tradition, Leo?'

He nodded. 'It's supposed to reflect the family supper held after the first coronation. That's why it's usually read by a junior member of the family.'

'Although it's bollocks, because the first coronation was a huge affair with half the crowned heads of Europe squashed into the cathedral.' Rolf leaned over with a confidential tap of the nose. 'We just like to pretend that the family's been around since "ooh, let's break focaccia over this campfire" times. We haven't. The Wolfsburgs are a medium-old family that other royal families marry their reserve children into. And we're German, not Italian.'

Leo glared at him, but Rolf grinned back. 'It's true. And now we're half American.'

'And the shoe?' Jo went on, as if Rolf hadn't spoken.

'The shoe tradition comes from a coronation ball in 1790 when the princess lost her slipper before the dancing,' said Leo, before Rolf could say whatever he was going to. Leo had clearly spent a lot of his school holidays following the tour guide around the palace. 'The night was almost ruined, it looked like an awful omen, and she was about to leave when a page found the slipper under a table.'

'Someone's lapdog had run off with it, according to legend,' Rolf interrupted. 'What kind of lapdog not specified. So maybe you should bring Badger and reenact the whole—'

'No!' said Jo and I at the same time.

'It's honestly nothing to worry about.' Leo topped up my wineglass. 'It won't take more than a few moments. A page from the household will bring you a cushion with a fancy gold shoe on it, you give it to Mom, she'll thank you, you'll curtsy, she'll put it on, and then she and Dad will do a demonstration waltz and we'll all clap.'

'And then we'll all get drunk. Wa-hey.' Rolf waved at the waiter for more wine. Jo ignored him. She was using the 'ignore the bad, reward the good' training method I'd used on Badger, with about the same success.

'And then when you've got a lovely smiley photo of Amy and your mother, the papers will stop printing all that nonsense about how there's a War of the Princesses on?' she asked.

'Oh. So you saw the papers?' Leo frowned.

''Fraid so,' said Jo. Giselle had biked an early edition of another paper round to our flat this morning; I was *at loggerheads with fashion icon Liza Bachmann about the double wedding snub.*' And we weren't allowed to engage — for which read, I wasn't allowed to go back to Rothery and beat up Jennifer Wainwright. Who was probably thrilled to be singled out in the newsroom by a royal writ.

'Our legal team is on the case,' said Leo. 'We've given one newspaper exclusive access to the ball and a seat at the coronation in return for an assurance that they'll lay off Amy, and the rest are on a warning.'

'And that's definite?' I asked.

'We have very good lawyers,' said Leo.

Next to him, Rolf nodded, like a man who knew. 'Serge and Guillermo have been out in town every night this week, wearing the most tasteless jeans and snogging anything that moves,' he said. 'And no one's said a word.'

'Quite,' said Jo. 'Decadence is so last year. Charity work and gardening is where it's all happening now.'

A look of sheer horror flashed across Rolf's face, but he didn't say anything. Maybe Jo was kicking him very hard.

My parents, of course, were mortified about the newspaper stories, and had rung me immediately to assure me they'd had nothing to do with it.

I knew they hadn't, and told them so, but nothing I said could assuage their guilt. I offered to send them off on holiday for a week, to ride out the sniggers in the high street, but Dad refused, on the grounds that it would make it look more true.

He was right, and I was proud of his dignity in the face of the twine-belt trousers pic, but a dark cloud now hung over the Yorkshire wedding plans. Even taking Mum's beautiful Zoë Weiss dress up the following weekend didn't entirely wipe out the strange feeling of déjà vu in the house.

'Is that my frock from the shop?' Mum said when I carried the box in from the car. Her whole body was braced for disappointment, and she shut the door quickly in case anyone was looking.

'It is.' Despite my low-level gloom, excitement bubbled inside me at the surprise I was about to give her. I knew Zoë wouldn't let me down. I'd sent photos of Mum and the measurements from the other dress, and Zoë'd presented me with a ribbon-tied box and a promise that if Mum didn't like it, she'd wear the thing herself to my wedding.

I'd tried to pay her with my credit card, but she'd waved it away with a horrified expression. 'Pay me later,' she said. 'In column inches, when you're on the best-dressed lists. And your mom's my new poster girl for royal bridal mothers.'

I smiled encouragingly at Mum. 'Want to try it on? Show Dad?'

She gritted her teeth.

'Pop it on, Pam,' said Dad. 'I'm looking forward to seeing the knockout I'll be escorting to the reception.' Dad had never ever made a reference to Mum's ballooning weight, despite his spade/spade attitude to most things. It was the only area in his life where he managed to exercise some tact, out of sheer love.

She looked at us both and sighed, then turned toward the stairs.

My old bedroom had the biggest mirror, so we went in there. Mum removed the blouse and wide-leg trousers she always wore, and I tied my scarf round her eyes so she'd get the 'wow factor' like in the shop.

'Maybe you need to hand those out to the rest of the congregation,' she said awkwardly.

I said nothing and lifted the pool of holly-green silk jersey from the tissue paper and slipped it over her head, pulling all the folds and pleats into place until it hung as Zoë had meant it to. Then I stood back and felt my throat choke up with emotion.

Zoë wasn't a dress designer, she was an artist. A sculptress. The luxuriant fabric fitted and draped as if it had been precision-cut to Mum's marble curves, and the color, a rich Christmassy green, made her skin glow and her baby-blond hair gleam. Mum's best bits — her unlined neck and her strong shoulders — were framed by the swooping design, and any lumps vanished into the draping.

'This doesn't feel like the dress I tried on,' said Mum, worried. 'Have they sent the right one?'

I didn't say anything — I couldn't, not without a telltale sniff — but I pulled the scarf off her eyes.

The instant Mum saw herself in the mirror, her hands went to her mouth and her eyes filled with tears. Neither of us spoke. Slowly, she shook her head from side to side, as if she couldn't believe what she was seeing. She moved her hips a little, this way and that, marveling that every angle was more flattering than the last.

Zoë hadn't tried to hide her size, but she'd made her statuesque, in the real sense of the word. Mum looked like a Greek goddess of plenty, ample and magnificent; and as I watched, her spine seemed to straighten and her chin lifted unconsciously.

Her eyes met mine in the mirror, and though her mouth formed words, they wouldn't come out.

'What's going on up there?' Dad was waiting at the bottom of the stairs. 'Can I see? Are you decent?'

Mum turned to me and clutched my hands. She couldn't speak. I couldn't speak. Her expression, though, said everything her heart couldn't — gratitude and delight and surprise and a touch of pride. It was the pride that finished me off.

'Do you like it?' I croaked.

She nodded, and laughed at her own daftness.

'It's my wedding present to you,' I blubbed. 'For being such a wonderful mum. I wanted you to look as special outside as you are inside.'

'Oh, Amy,' she wept. 'You needn't have. You needn't have.'

'I'm coming up,' announced Dad, ready with his usual brave encouragement; but when he got to the top of the stairs, he stopped, dumbfounded by what he saw.

'Pamela,' he said simply, his face awestruck with adoration. He couldn't manage any more.

I watched them communicating silently in that instant, all the happiness and sadness of their long marriage swirling between them in a torrent of love. I wished with all my heart that Leo and I would have a bond that lasted like that. It was magical and real at the same time.

I crept downstairs, and left them to it.

What felt like a week but was really three weeks later, Leo, Rolf, Jo, and I were at Heathrow Airport waiting for our flight to Naples for the Crown Princess Ball.

We were flying business class, mainly because that meant we could hide out in the VIP lounge out of reach of the photographers who'd followed us to the airport. Liza had ramped up her publicity efforts in the run-up to the coronation, and her latest stop in her Be an Everyday Princess campaign was the White House, where 'Princess Eliza of Nirona' had conducted an exclusive interview with the First Lady for the *Times*, about how the correct underwear and a wide range of intelligent conversational openers could improve the quality of life for you and everyone around you.

Leo was reading it while we waited. Rolf was scrolling through his e-mails on the phone. Jo was over by the complimentary coffee facilities, trying to talk Callie Hamilton down from her latest episode. I was mainly preoccupied with not staring at our fellow business-class travelers and working out if I should know them or not.

Leo glanced up from the double-page spread of Liza standing next to a fireplace looking imperial. 'Okay?' he mouthed.

I nodded and stifled a yawn. It was very early, and I was knackered. I'd been gardening nonstop all week, and had finished a makeover for a garden in Pimlico that even Ted said was the best I'd done. Following the feature in the magazine, I'd been contacted by someone from English Heritage about wildflower meadows, and they'd asked if I wanted to get involved with their community project to transform various unloved bits of London scrubland into butterfly and bee meadows.

I'd said yes, obviously — making up wildflower mixes like a gardening cocktail-maker was my idea of heaven, not a paid consultancy role.

'Got everything?' Leo mouthed, and I nodded again.

In my bag was my ballgown — couture Vivienne Westwood this time, fitted in her Mayfair atelier with Liza commenting via Skype — and the folder of official info about the grace/shoe ceremony that Sofia had forwarded, where I'd have to stand, what I'd have to do, etc. The grace was only a few lines long, but it was in German, which I didn't speak. Even before it arrived, Leo had suggested hiring a speech coach/drama teacher to help me, but I'd pointed out that I lived with a drama coach. Jo had introduced me to one of her German clients, and I'd practiced it with her until I was pretty confident my accent wasn't unwittingly turning the words into filthy swearing.

Leo winked, and I managed a smile. He seemed to think my grace-giving and shoe-presenting was an honor I'd pull off with aplomb; but even though I now knew it off by heart, I was still worried that what I could do perfectly well in the privacy of my own flat would feel very different with thousands of eyes on me.

I was determined to overcome my nerves, though, because I wanted to show him that I was trying to meet him halfway with this whole mad deal. The assistant/investing in the business hadn't been mentioned again, but I knew he'd been biting his lip about the amount of time I'd spent working when he'd wanted me to be in Nirona with him. We hadn't rowed — we just hadn't talked about it. I hated having things we didn't talk about, when we were so open about everything else. But then, I hated rows more than anything.

Leo winked again, more flirtily, and I reminded myself that once the ordeal was over, I'd be dancing, in a palace, with the man who'd now shot up to number two in the hot European prince rankings, thanks to some candid beach holiday shots of us on our recent two-night Saint-Tropez minibreak. No one looked as good as Leo did in a pair of swimming trunks. Absolutely no one.

And a matter of weeks after that? I'd be married to him.

I sank into my leather armchair, and winked back at Leo.

The palace was overflowing with organizers when we disembarked from the royal helicopter from the mainland, and while Rolf and Leo went off to check in with the palace officials, Jo and I were swept off to our rooms in the main part of the house, where Boris and Liza were now installed.

There was no sign of Pavlos, and as we followed the maids down the main hall, I noted that the gloomy chess portrait had been moved to the other end of the portrait gallery and replaced with a full-length Mario Testino photograph of Liza in a tiara and fur coat.

Jo was ushered off to the guest wing, and I was taken to Leo's new suite, which overlooked the Mediterranean gardens. It was a huge room with full-length windows, decorated in a tasteful palette of cream and gold with bright splashes of color in the modern art that filled the walls. (I should have known what the modern art was, clearly, but I didn't.)

When the maid had left, I spotted two leather folders on the desk, each containing a timetable of events for me and for Leo, and I opened mine with relief — I liked to know exactly what was going on.

It was nearly 11 a.m. now, I noted, and the hairdresser and makeup artist would be arriving in my room to beautify me at 4 p.m. There would be drinks with Boris and Liza at 6 p.m., official drinks with the guests at 6:30 p.m.; dinner would commence with the grace at 8 p.m. and then the first dance of the Coronation Ball would take place at 10:30 p.m.

Carriages — or in our case, a piggyback up the stairs — would be at 2 a.m.

I took out my phone and took a photo of the timetable to send to Mum. It was quite surreal. The unsettling sensation of floating through a dream was getting stronger all the time, along with the butterflies in my stomach.

The best person to settle those was Jo, but as I stepped out of my room to find hers, I bumped straight into Sofia.

Her hair was wet and she was wearing a gray tracksuit that looked very designer, and she didn't look thrilled to see me, possibly because she wasn't wearing any makeup and her eyes were a lot smaller without her usual swooping liner.

'Hello!' I said. 'Have you been swimming?'

Sofia looked at me — as if I might have meant something more interesting — and then nodded. 'The pool's right outside your window. Didn't you notice?'

'No. No, I didn't.'

She smiled tightly. 'Leo's got the second-best room in the whole palace. Lucky him.'

I didn't want to go down that whole penis-and-luck road, thanks. 'Are you looking forward to tonight? Least you can relax!'

*Hmm. That might not have been very tactful, Amy.*

Sofia ran a hand through her damp hair, as if I was holding her up from drying it. 'It'll be nice to relax after the week I've had. Litigation is very draining. Especially when you're dealing with some of the richest families in Switzerland.'

'It must be. Wow. Um, I've got the timetable of events . . .' I wasn't sure how to put this, but I didn't want to bother Liza. '. . . and there isn't a time on it for me to do a run-through of the grace? Or the shoe ceremony. Have I got the wrong copy?'

Sofia shook her head. 'No, it wouldn't be on the timetable, because it depends on how Mom and Dad are running. One of the chamberlains will come and find you, don't worry.'

'Oh, good,' I said. I still didn't feel relieved. If anything, the butterflies were doubling. 'Do I have to carry one of those bleepers like you get in Itsu, for when your table's ready?'

She just stared at me, and I squirmed. It wasn't even lunch and I already felt like opening the nearest bottle of wine.

'No,' said Sofia. 'You don't.'

I found Jo in her room, and we went for a walk around the gardens. I showed her the rose gardens, and pointed out some of the more unusual plants; then, with no sign of Rolf or Leo, and Jo's interest in plants more or less exhausted, we went back to our rooms for a refreshing power nap before all the dressing-up began.

Just looking at the enormous emperor-size bed with an antique carved headboard made me feel sleepy. Six soft pillows were stacked at the head, and a satin bedspread had been thrown over the foot, in case the autumn chill nipped at us in the night. (Unlikely, given the sort of state-of-the-art central heating that seemed to read body temperature and adjust accordingly.)

I checked my watch. It was five past three. No one had come to find me for the dinner rehearsal yet, but they knew where Leo's room was. If I could get a half-hour nap before the hairdresser arrived, I'd be so much more alert . . .

I was asleep before the goose down settled in the feathery quilt.

Some time later, I was woken by the sound of Leo's voice as he entered the suite.

'Amy? Are you in here?'

I opened my bleary eyes. What time was it? I grabbed my phone off the bedside table.

Oh, my God, it was *quarter to five*.

'Amy?' Leo strode into the bedroom and seemed surprised to find me under the satin quilt. 'You're in here!'

'Yes, I was having a nap. I lost track of time.' I sat up, but my fuzzy brain was clinging to snooze mode.

He made an effort not to look stressed, but failed. 'The stylist's been waiting outside for nearly an hour. We've been searching everywhere for you — the rehearsal's nearly done. Come on, if we hurry, we can probably still catch everyone in the hall.'

I had a metallic taste in my mouth, the taste of *sheer panic*. I hunted for my shoes and tried to straighten my creased clothes. 'But I've been here since three. Why didn't anyone knock?'

Leo was frowning. 'I don't know. Look, it doesn't matter, here's your folder, come on.'

I followed him down the corridor at a trot, and we practically ran down the sweeping staircase to the main hall. The palace had been closed to visitors all day, and already the massive banks of white flowers and long red carpets were in place for the evening's entertainment. I had to swerve past caterers and lighting equipment and maids carrying trays of glasses; my coordination wasn't great at the best of times, but when I was half-awake it bordered on dangerous.

'It's okay, I've found her!' Leo announced as we burst through the doors of the banqueting hall, making the crowd of people around the top table stop what they were doing.

I came to a shuddering halt behind him. The hall was like something from a film. The gilt-touched walls were hung with flags between the painted sections depicting bright angels and soldiers and dancing girls, stretching up toward the vaulted ceiling. Long tables covered with white cloths and shining glasses ran the length of the room, with a raised platform at one end where the top table stood beneath an intricate medieval tapestry.

I'd been shown round the room on previous visits, but not when it was dressed for a state occasion like this. The gilded majesty of the architecture and decoration knocked the breath out of me — as, I guessed, it had originally been intended to. I was silent with awe. I felt like a tourist at Buckingham Palace, except I was being allowed behind the velvet rope. More than that, I was being invited to sit at that top table.

I felt a bit faint.

'Ah, Amy, we thought you'd run off again!' Boris got up from his seat at the top table. He was wearing — I'm not joking — a plastic replica of a crown.

'We've been looking for you,' said Liza pointedly. Her hair was already in rollers but was wrapped in a glamorous silk scarf. 'We're running very late now.'

I started to explain and apologize, but she clapped her hands together to get the attention of everyone in the room. Now that I looked, there really were a lot of people there. My nerves jangled and I tried to calm myself with deep breaths, as Jo had coached me.

They didn't work.

'Amy, we need to get your level for the speech.' She pointed to a microphone placed on the top table. 'This is what will happen.'

She nodded toward Nina, bearing a clipboard and head-phones, who dutifully recited, 'Fanfare from royal trumpeters. Their Serene Highnesses the Prince Boris and Princess Eliza will enter the hall from the east door.' Air-steward gesture to hidden door. 'The rest of the royal party, see notes, will enter from the west door.' Another gesture. 'Trumpets to stop. Miss Amelia Wilde to stand and give the formal grace from her position at seat ten at the top table.'

She pointed to my empty space.

'What? Do you want me to do it now?' I asked stupidly.

'Yes, please,' said Liza.

Leo squeezed my arm, and I set off self-consciously toward the raised platform with my folder. I went up the steps, trying to keep my head up, sat down at the place indicated, and then got up again. The microphone made a loud scrapy noise, and someone rushed forward to adjust it.

The tables looked very long from up here. How many place settings? Two hundred? Three hundred?

My knees wobbled; I blinked hard and told myself I could do this. I'd practiced. It was only four sentences and I knew them by heart.

Someone coughed impatiently.

'*Wir danken Dir,*' I began, '*O Christus, unser Gott, das Du . . .*'

A sharp intake of breath ran around the hall, and the sea of faces beneath me looked horrified.

The words died in my mouth. Had I pronounced it wrong? Had I just told them their aunts were fat, or worse? I looked at Leo, but even his expression was a mixture of surprise and dismay.

'What?' I squeaked. 'What have I done?'

Boris removed the plastic crown from his head with a sigh and looked at me. 'Oh dear,' he said. 'You've just brought two hundred years' bad luck on the whole family.'

# CHAPTER TWENTY-NINE

In the commotion that ensued after my mortifying faux pas, I clung desperately to the one silver lining available: at least this was only happening in front of forty or so really important people, and not the four hundred and seventy-three (it turned out) who would be there that night.

'Ignore Dad,' Leo said urgently when I stumbled off the platform. 'It's not bad luck, it's just a silly tradition. We don't speak German in the palace — it's a rule our ancestors set to make themselves fit in with the Italian families.'

'I didn't know!' I wailed. I wanted a trapdoor to open beneath me. I'd been doing guttural German flourishes and everything! 'This was what I was sent to learn, I swear.'

'The grace is in Latin!' Liza had stormed over with Nina and Giselle in her wake. 'It's always in Latin, who on earth does grace in German?'

'If that's what Amy was sent, then clearly someone's made an error.' Leo's expression was steely. 'Nina, can we get Amy the right version to prepare?'

I turned to him, all my confidence gone. My face felt ashen; I had no idea what it looked like. 'Maybe you should read it. Or Sofia should.'

'No,' said Leo. 'That's probably exactly what Sofia wants. She sent you the documents, didn't she?'

'They would have come from the central palace office.' Liza glared at him. 'We can check with Nina. But I imagine that Sofia only forwarded what she was sent herself. She's been working flat-out on this Agnetto estate case, Leo. I hardly think she has time to devote to ridiculous schemes to upset people. It's just one of those things. Amy reading the grace is in the official order, and there's plenty of time left to prepare.'

There was not. There was just over an hour. And I'd be in makeup for most of that!

'Amy, do you still want to do it?' Leo looked at me, his eyes filled with concern.

I took a deep breath. Deep down, I wanted him to say he'd do it — but if I said no, I'd look hopeless. I heard Dad's voice in my head: *Don't run away from problems, Amy.*

And I thought of Pavlos. You could be removed at a stroke round here for not quite coming up to the mark. Could they do that to me?

I shook myself. *Don't be stupid.*

But they had. They'd sacked Pavlos's entire family.

I nodded, and the pride on Leo's face touched me.

'Nina!' roared Liza. 'Nina, can we get this grace?'

Nina scurried off as Liza checked her watch.

'What about the shoe?' I asked in a small voice. 'Do we need to rehearse that?'

'We should, but we're out of time. A page will pass you the shoe on a cushion — just bring it to me, I'll put it on, and we'll take it from there.' And with that, Liza steamed away, checking the clipboard Giselle was holding out to her. Her head bounced up as if her radar had gone off. 'Is that photographer accredited?'

Every head spun to see a burly photographer in the back of the hall, snapping away. Giselle started to march over, but he raised his paw and waved at us.

'Mick Morris, freelance for the *Mail*?'

'He's accredited,' growled Liza. 'Giselle, just go and check what he's got. I said they could have all-access, but I didn't specify picture control.'

So some outsider had been watching my embarrassing performance? I didn't think my heart could sink any further at that point, but it did.

Leo saw my shoulders slump and put his arm around me. 'It'll be fine,' he whispered, then in a louder voice added, 'Come on, we need to get you to the stylist. Nina, please have the right grace sent to our room as soon as possible.'

And he swept me away. I was pretty sure that as soon as we passed through the massive stone arch, the whispering began.

I didn't speak as Leo led me down the frescoed corridors and out into the main hall again. My brain was too busy replaying the horror on everyone's faces. I wished we could go and sit in the gardens, now illuminated with flaming torches and hidden spotlights, just to get my pulse rate down, but there was no time. The evening was sweeping us along like a ruthless conveyor belt.

Back in our rooms, my ballgown was hanging ready on a stand, and the hairstylist was impatiently lining up rollers along the marble sideboard while the makeup artist chatted on her phone in Japanese. They both stopped when they saw Leo and visibly swooned.

'I'll leave you in the hands of these capable ladies,' he said, kissing my forehead. 'Call me when you're ready and I'll bring the jewelry along.'

The stylist and the makeup girl immediately started working on me, as if I were a car in Kwik Fit having a speed service. Hair washed, rollers in, face cleaned and primed and under-coated, nails wiped and polished . . . Their hands moved at lightning pace.

At some point, Nina appeared with a piece of paper with the grace on it — and it was in Latin. I hadn't done Latin at school, though it wasn't completely unfamiliar, thanks to all the plant names I'd learned off by heart. I started to mouth the words to myself, but it was no use, my nerves were shot to bits, and they blurred into meaningless clumps of letters.

It felt weird, letting these two strangers touch me without even talking, so I asked halting questions about what products they were using, to distract myself from the panic festering inside me; and by the time my hair was set, we were on friendly enough terms for them to help me on with my silvery ballgown.

I needed an extra pair of hands to handle the corsetry inside, but once I was winched into it, my bosom teetering at the very edge of the bodice like a perfect cappuccino, the transformation was nearly complete. The stylist pinned up my hair, then sprayed it with a whole can of Elnett; the makeup artist gave me a lipstick; and as they left I called Leo, and held my breath.

The expression on his face when he walked in made everything else stop. His eyes widened, then softened, and a slow, delighted smile spread across his handsome face, as if I were the most wonderful thing he'd ever seen.

He put down the jewel cases he was carrying on the sideboard and walked around me, saying nothing but letting the smile widen until his whole face was wreathed in a blissful sort of glow.

'You know,' he said, touching my powdered chin with his finger, 'I almost don't want to put any of these diamonds on you, because they couldn't make you look more beautiful than you already do. You're like the most beautiful daisy, all fresh and golden. Perfect.'

I smiled back. He looked pretty stunning too in his white tie and tails, with glass-shined shoes and diamond studs.

'Oh, go on. I need to give them all something to look at while I mess up the grace.'

Leo looked serious for a moment. 'I can do that, you know. I want you to enjoy tonight, not feel like it's a big test.'

'It's fine.' *It's nothing, after all, compared with the number of people who'll watch us get married.* I pushed the thought away. 'Just tell me how to pronounce the words.'

'I will. But first, jewels. I brought you my favorites — this is the set that my grandmother wore when she hosted the ball for Granddad's coronation in 1964. Even Liz Taylor was blown away by these.' He picked up the first box and opened it with a snap to reveal a glittering drop diamond necklace on a bed of blue velvet.

Blimey.

'You might want to retouch your lipstick,' said Jo, with a very un-Jo-like smirk.

'Your Royal Hotness,' added Rolf.

Leo and I missed most of the drinks reception while he speed-coached me through the Latin grace in a deserted side room.

He marked up the paper with pauses, and made me read it several times, until the words sounded familiar; but I still wasn't convinced that I'd be able to do it without stumbling, not with all those eyes on me.

'Leo,' I said, because I couldn't stop myself. 'Did Sofia do this on purpose?'

'No.' He said it too quickly, and I didn't believe him.

'She must have. She wants me to screw this up, doesn't she? She wants me to look stupid, just like she deliberately didn't get me anything I could wear at the photo shoot!'

Leo looked grim. 'I can only imagine that was a mistake.'

'I can't do it,' I said suddenly. Wasn't it better to bail out than prove to everyone that I wasn't up to a public role? 'Let Sofia read the grace, she clearly wants to. It's not like I can't do this, but I need preparation and—'

Leo leaned forward and looked — well, not angry, but impatient. 'Amy, I don't want to patronize you, but this kind of change of plan — it happens all the time. You've got to get over it. Mom *needs* you to do this to counterbalance that press business. And if Sofia is shit-stirring, you can't give her the satisfaction! That's what the real world's like. I know plants are easier to handle, but this is what it is.'

I stared at him mutely, too scared to open my mouth in case something came out that I couldn't take back.

He looked at me, then looked at his watch. 'So, what's it to be?'

'You're used to this!' I hissed. 'I'm not. I can't just—'

'Then *don't* do it,' he hissed back. 'Give it here.'

He made to snatch the paper from me, but some inner stubbornness made me keep hold of it.

'Fine,' he said, his eyes hardening. 'I'm not going to make you do something you don't want to. But I've got to tell someone that—'

'I'll do it,' I said, furious. 'I'll . . . bloody do it.'

Leo relaxed slightly, but I didn't dial down my glare. I wasn't sure where this was going. But it felt like something had shifted.

The instant we walked into the drinks reception, two things happened — conversation near the door stopped as everyone stared at me, and then Liza swooped on Leo, and carried him off to talk to various European royal relations.

I was left on my own, and if Jo hadn't rescued me with a cry of delight, I'd have stayed by the door until dinner. Jo was in her element, swimming between different conversations like a beautiful orange fish in a sea of penguins. I was never great about introducing myself, so she did it for me with the same ease as if we'd been at a house party in Fulham; but the conversation flashed back and forth so fast I couldn't keep up in my adrenaline-ragged state.

I can't tell you how blank my mind went every time someone asked me a question. Utterly blank. The more they stared at me, waiting for some witticism to fall from my lips, the louder my nerves jangled in my head, and the more I sipped from the drink in my hand to fill the silence. For once, it wasn't Party Paralysis to blame — it was so much more complicated than that.

I knew Leo was glancing at me, but he filled in my silences manfully, and I carried on smiling, more and more glassily as the panic took hold. Was it always going to be like this? His family tripping me up? Him mainly on my side . . . but not quite?

I was relieved when a trumpet sounded and chamberlains appeared to gather the top-table stars to one side, for their separate entrance. But the second the relief hit me, it was drained away by the thought that my grace was now minutes away.

Leo, Rolf, and I were taken to an anteroom behind the main hall where Liza and Boris were being tidied by assistants while Pavlos and his family looked on. Pavlos seemed happy not to have the fuss, but his wife, Mathilde, was wearing a lemon-sucking expression and what I assumed was the number-four tiara. The boys, I noted, looked very hungover.

If Liza had been incredible before, now she was like a queen multiplied by the power of international supermodel. Her angular face was flawless, and her spun-gold hair was held in place by a dazzling tiara that put anything I'd seen on the British royals to shame. Next to her, Sofia was also having her eyeliner retouched by two artists, while her clinging black gown was spot-checked for dust. The photographer I'd seen before was snapping away, getting 'behind-the-scenes' shots, but Liza had left nothing to chance: they were already perfect.

Boris, meanwhile, wasn't wearing his plastic crown, but his jacket was covered with a rainbow of medals, and another assistant was pressing powder onto his forehead. When he saw us, he grinned amiably.

'Ah, there you are,' he said. 'All set?'

I nodded dumbly and tightened my grip on my evening bag.

'Your Highness, if you're ready . . .' murmured a chamberlain, and suddenly everything began to move very fast.

I heard a muted trumpet sound in the hall; then Liza and Boris disappeared through a doorway, triggering a distant wave of applause in the hall.

Leo, Rolf, and I glanced at each other. I wondered if I looked as sick as I felt. Sofia dismissed her makeup artist with a wave, and I cast a thinly veiled glare in her direction, but she didn't respond; and then we were being lined up and marched in a line through the opposite door.

It was like stepping onto a West End stage. The lights were focused on the top table, and I blinked as the sea of faces turned toward us, watching, whispering, assessing. We sat, and the toasts began in Italian, more trumpeting, a speech from Boris in three languages, and then, far too soon, my name was announced and an expectant silence fell in the hall.

I pushed back my chair and stood up, sure that the microphone would pick up the thudding in my chest. My heart was beating so hard I was surprised my pushed-up cleavage wasn't wobbling like a jelly.

My hand shook, and the Latin words on the paper in my hand blurred.

I made myself think of Leo. And of my mum and dad.

But I couldn't read them. The letters jumbled up before my eyes, and I felt light-headed.

'Benedic . . .' I started from memory, but my voice croaked.

I could feel Leo beside me, willing me to get it right. I knew he'd stand up and read it too, if I asked him, but I didn't want to. I really didn't want him to.

The silence stretched out, and I heard some nervous coughing and rattling of china below.

From the depths of my memory, Mum's voice popped up in my head, saying grace before our Sunday roast round at Gran's. Roast beef, Yorkshire puddings, cabbage, the grace she said the nuns had taught her at school . . .

'Without thy presence, naught, O Lord, is sweet,' said a voice somewhere miles above me. It was my voice, but it sounded very Yorkshire in the hall. It also sounded very loud. 'No pleasure to our lips can aught supply, whether this wine we drink or food we eat, till Grace divine and Faith shall sanctify.'

And then I sat down, only just making my chair, which a steward had pulled out for me.

There was a brief pause, and then Leo on one side and Rolf on the other began their pistol-shot clapping, and soon everyone in the hall followed suit, until a trumpet blew again, and everyone dived into their starters.

I grabbed the glass of water with a trembling hand and tried to quell the rising sickness in my stomach. I'd done it. But I felt as if I'd just walked a tightrope.

'Well done.' Rolf leaned over. 'What language was that? Did you learn it on your gap year or something?'

Under the table, Leo squeezed my knee, and as I glanced

at him with a mixture of crossness and relief, I saw the photographer capture our private moment.

I hoped he hadn't caught Leo's almost imperceptible flinch backward at my unexpectedly fierce response.

I barely ate any of the exquisite food placed in front of me, but at least being between Leo and Rolf meant that the conversation flowed without much effort required on my part.

Plate after crested plate was swept away and replaced, and then the silver pots of coffee had been and gone; another steward arrived to lead us from the table and out to the ballroom where the dancing would commence in about fifteen minutes.

I took advantage of the chaos to slip away to a quiet corner to retouch my makeup, but I lost sight of Leo in the crowd and panicked, because I wasn't sure where I was supposed to be for the shoe ceremony. I'd assumed that such a formal ceremony would be rigidly organized, but everyone else seemed to know what they were doing, as if they'd done it so many times before.

Time slithered past alarmingly as I struggled through the crowds of identical jackets and tanned skin, looking for a familiar face, but I seemed to be going round the corridors in circles. Panic began to creep over my chest, tightening my lungs, and I was sure people stopped talking as I approached. Were they discussing me? The tiara was pinching my head now, but I didn't dare take it off in case I lost it too.

I needed some space, I told myself. If I could just stop for a minute, I could recover.

To my immense relief, I suddenly saw Leo and Liza up ahead of me; they were talking to some dignitaries, nodding and smiling as if this evening were just a normal gathering. As I watched, Leo tapped his Rolex and they moved away, presumably to get into position for the opening ceremony.

I hurried after them; they were heading toward the anteroom between the ballroom and the main corridor, where I'd changed into my jeans for the engagement photo. They seemed to be deep in conversation, so I hung back, waiting for a natural break so I could butt in without looking rude. The surging crowds pushed me nearer; I lost them, and when I looked again they'd disappeared.

They must have gone into the anteroom. I reached the door and slipped discreetly inside, and waited for the right moment to announce myself and ask if Liza's shoe was ready for collection.

I wasn't eavesdropping. I couldn't help hearing. Liza wasn't exactly keeping her voice down.

'Leo,' she was saying, 'you've got to speak to Amy about how she's coming across. She's very aloof. Infanta Elena of Spain told me she didn't ask her a single question, not even who she was.'

*Who?*

'Amy's shy, Mom. She's not used to big events like this, but she'll get used to it.'

'Will she, though? I thought you were going to talk to her after my charity ball in London — did she even know she'd blanked Carla Bruni? You did talk to her about that, didn't you, Leo?'

I felt chilly. Carla Bruni? She'd been at the Make Up for Therapy Ball? I'd *thought* it was her, but hadn't liked to say in case it wasn't. And what were you supposed to say to Carla Bruni — 'Do you mind wearing flats?'

More to the point, what was Leo supposed to have said to me? Because he hadn't said a *thing*.

Then Liza spoke again, and she sounded exasperated. 'This is the life she's going to have to lead with you, Leo. She doesn't seem to get any of it. Like tonight — that was supposed to be damage limitation, not more cannon fodder. All she had to do was read a simple grace. If Amy can't handle public events, if she can't give you the support you need, you're going to have a rough time. Both of you.'

I knew Leo would be pushing his hand into his thick hair. I knew he would be frowning, hunting for tactful words. 'She's great at talking to people individually, Mom. Just not at big events. Amy's natural, she's down-to-earth, I mean, I thought doing the grace in English was a clever—'

Liza snapped, 'So you're going to abandon state dinners in favor of individual kitchen suppers? Don't be ridiculous. Options, Leo. There are always options. You don't have to dump her in front of the whole world. There are ways of managing this so both of you can have a good exit.'

There was an even longer pause, and I felt sick.

*Say something, Leo!* I thought fiercely. *Say something!*

I wasn't prepared for the resignation in Leo's voice. 'I don't want to make her do something she doesn't want to do . . .'

I didn't catch any more because the door behind me opened and Boris appeared, rearranging the medals on his dinner jacket. When he saw me, a cheerful grin spread across his pink face.

'Amy!' he said, doing his boxy-pointy thing. 'Are you running away or hiding?'

I swallowed my distress as best I could and tried to look normal.

'I'm preparing for the shoe ceremony,' I said with as much dignity as I could muster. 'I'm not running away, I'm early.'

Boris's smile intensified, and I realized he was, (a) a bit drunk, and (b) having the best night ever.

Willi had known exactly how this whole princely deal worked, I realized. Boris's charming bonhomie was precisely the sort of secret ingredient a really popular monarch needed. You either had it, or you didn't. Pavlos didn't, and neither did I. And look what had happened to Pavlos.

I pulled on a bright smile despite the leaden sensation in my chest, and said, 'I think Liza and Leo are through here. Shall we?'

I offered my hand, and Boris gallantly offered his arm for me to take.

And when Leo and Liza saw us appear from the other room, only the faintest flicker of unease crossed Leo's handsome face. Liza's showed no sign of flickering at all.

# CHAPTER THIRTY

What can I say about the shoe ceremony? I was on autopilot for the whole thing.

I managed to bring the right (Louboutin stiletto) shoe to Liza at the right time, and I smiled in the right direction for the cameras as she pretended to try it on, and I waited the right length of time while Liza and Boris sailed around the dance floor to tumultuous applause, and then I shuffled through the right steps with Leo, who seemed more focused than I'd ever seen him as he whirled me around beneath the spectacular glittering chandeliers, to the orchestra playing in the gallery above us.

It was over quickly, and I had one dance with Rolf, which he spent telling me what a 'game-changing girl' Jo was. The photographer got some nice photos of that too, although I don't know whether I managed to keep my face in a suitable arrangement the whole time.

But it all felt too late. If I hadn't heard that conversation between Liza and Leo, I might have convinced myself that I'd pulled it back — but I hadn't. When Leo told me how charming everyone had found my English grace, it sounded as if he was convincing himself as much as me; but I couldn't let my face drop in case someone snapped me looking miserable.

I went through the rest of the ball in a sort of trance, my cheeks aching from smiling, asking inane questions so no one could accuse me of being aloof. It was a relief when Leo found me at half one, and murmured that Boris and Liza had left, and so now we could too.

Jo and Rolf were still dancing a wild quickstep on the slowly emptying floor, their feet flashing in split-second unison as their flirty glances burned up the air around them. Again, I thought, you could either do that or you couldn't. Jo was so much more fitted to this sort of life than me. Performance and sociability ran somewhere in her blood, whereas my blood ran with tea and fertilizer. And that was fine. That was just the way it was. Frankly, I didn't think any amount of diamonds could compensate for a lifetime of evenings like that, especially with the additional delights of Sofia for Christmas, for the foreseeable future.

Leo was quiet as he escorted me up the sweeping staircase to the family apartments. He didn't make any reference to the conversation he'd had with his mother, and I didn't have the energy to fight about it. Instead he asked me if I'd enjoyed the evening, and seemed to take my wooden responses for tiredness. I couldn't believe any of the compliments he passed on, even though I knew I was being churlish; and when he carefully removed the gorgeous diamond necklace, and unclipped the diamond cuff, and pulled the heavy tiara out of my hair, instead of falling into his arms and making love on the huge bed, I pretended to slump with weariness as soon as my head touched the pillow.

Leo curled himself round behind me, tucking the throw

around my blistered feet, and soon I heard him breathing drowsily, and I knew he was asleep.

I didn't sleep. I lay there replaying the events of the night over and over, but my mind wouldn't let me edit and improve the version the way it usually did — it made me face up to the blunt reality. It wasn't my fault. It wasn't Leo's fault. It wasn't anyone's fault.

I loved Leo, but was I really going to be able to do this?

I often felt better after a shower, but not even a cloudburst showerhead the size of a serving plate could wash away the ashy grayness of the previous night.

It was just six thirty, so I pulled on jeans and a cashmere sweater and went through to the sitting room of our suite. The long arched windows looked out over the pool and the gardens, which were dappled with early-morning sunlight, and the organic confusion of the flowers was strangely comforting to my raw soul.

As I passed, I glanced at my mobile, charging on the desk, and noted that I had four missed calls, all from home. I frowned and picked up my messages.

First, Dad. That was unusual — he never rang unless Mum was unable to hold a telephone (i.e., never).

*'Amy, love, I expect you'll be in Nirona now, at your ball. Hope you're having a nice time. Could you give us a ring, when you've a moment? Thanks. It's Dad, by the way.'* That was at four yesterday.

*'Amy, it's Dad again. Can you ring? Thanks.'*

My throat tightened. He sounded anxious.

The seven o'clock call was downright worried. *'Amy, it's Dad.*

*I don't know if you've seen, but there's been something in the news-paper that's upset your mum, and I was wondering if there was anything you could do about it. Maybe you could call me?'*

The eight o'clock call was only three seconds long, but I caught the distinct sound of crying in the background. Mum crying.

Awful thoughts dive-bombed my mind. What had the paper got hold of? Kelly? The court case? An old boyfriend of mine with some cringy story?

I grabbed Leo's iPad from the desk and turned it on, flicking through the newspaper websites. Dad hadn't said what it was, or where . . .

'Shedding for the Wedding?' ran the headline.

Last night's champagne burned the back of my throat like acid.

There, in all our glory, were me, Jo, and Mum outside Wed-ding Warehouse, lining up to get into the Range Rover with our bags. I looked bad enough, but the angle they'd got of Mum was very cruel. It made her seem twice the size she really was, and the strain on her face — caused by that awful dress — looked like peevishness, not self-loathing.

To make matters worse, they'd put a photo of Liza and the First Lady next to it, ostensibly to illustrate the other mother-in-law but really so everyone could have a good gawp at the chasm between Leo's skinny, chic mother and my lovely normal mum.

The headline referred to more paparazzi shots they'd got of me and the psycho personal trainer as I puffed my way round Hyde Park like a walrus in a tracksuit, but I didn't even care. The comments beneath were so horrible I could barely bring myself to read them, but I did, because I knew Mum would have winced over each stupid one.

'*Like mother, like daughter, watch out, Leo!*'

'*OMG, it's the new Princess of Whales LOL!*'

And on and on.

I closed my eyes, but the images were burned on my brain. I'd done this to Mum. She'd be distraught right now, and Dad twice as distressed, and it was my fault.

I couldn't think there, surrounded by the discarded clothes of the previous night, so I slipped out, down to the gardens to call Dad out of earshot. It was early, but Mum never slept when she was upset and Dad would be sitting there with her.

The morning air had an autumnal nip, and the gardens were empty, apart from a few seagulls. I just stared at the phone, paralyzed.

What could I say? 'Sorry'? 'I'll make it up to you'? 'Just ignore it — they'll get bored after a couple of years'? I was signing them up to this sort of invasion of privacy for life.

Even Liza's so-called media strategy hadn't protected me — this was presumably revenge from the other papers for not getting access to the ball.

I stared blindly at the stone wall, and listened to the distant hush of the sea and the swish of the automatic water sprays. I don't know how long I sat there, but eventually I heard footsteps on the stone path.

'What are you doing down here?'

Jo was standing on the grass in front of me, wearing a pair

of shades that hid her face. She was dressed in the sort of weekend casual look I'd spent five thousand pounds acquiring in Harvey Nichols, except the cashmere draped over her shoulders was vintage and authentically moth-eaten.

'Why are you up?' I demanded. 'Not even the gardeners are out!'

She sat down on the bench next to me with a wince. 'My flight's at midday and I've got to get back to the mainland to catch it. Callie's off on holiday, and I said I'd drop in this afternoon to make sure everything was on track with the wet room.'

'You're leaving me here? For Callie?' I pretended to sound wounded, but actually I was wounded. The thought of Jo leaving felt like my last ally melting away.

'Listen, her bonus paid for last night's dress, don't knock it.'

'She's in love with you,' I said glumly. 'The boyfriend's just a cover. She'll get you to move in next, and Ted and Rolf will have to throw themselves off the London Eye.'

Jo dug an elbow in my ribs. 'What's with you? I thought you'd still be tucked up with Prince Gorgeous. Especially after your big triumph last night.'

I turned to her with pleading eyes. 'Do you have to go home? Can't you stay for the coronation? Surely Rolf can get you in.'

'Darling, I need to get back.' I couldn't see Jo's face properly behind her shades, but her smile was touched with a sort of resignation. 'And if I stay, it'll just give Rolf the wrong idea, so—'

'The wrong idea? Was that the wrong idea you were giving

him last night? He seemed to think it was a very right idea, from where I was standing.'

She sighed and stretched out her legs. Jo had the perfect legs for cropped trousers; her ankles were finely chiseled. 'I had a wonderful time last night. But that's as far as it goes with me and Rolf. It was a grand finale.'

'Does he know that?'

'I think so.'

'Can you take your shades off, please? You're not the only one with a hangover.'

Jo pushed the sunglasses onto her head with a sigh, and I saw her eyes were purple-ringed, like mine, and red. I wondered if she'd been crying, or if she hadn't actually been to bed at all. Her own bed, I mean.

She patted my knee. 'Don't worry, I've told Rolf exactly the sort of girlfriend he needs to find. And I'll find her for him, if he wants, but it's not me, darling.'

'Why?' I couldn't believe I was hearing this. Well, I could. But after what I'd seen last night . . .

'Oh, so many reasons! Because my family is just one PR disaster after another? There's so much dirt on them Liza would have to hire another Giselle to fight the fires. And I couldn't carry on acting. What if I got a great part, or what if I were only given parts because of who I was with? I mean, Rolf's fun, underneath the big act, but . . . it's not the life for me.'

'But I've got a job,' I said, my brain starting to race. Leo had been a bit cagey about how much time I'd have to spend doing charity work; he'd been less enthusiastic about the English

Heritage wildflower consultancy than I'd expected. 'And my family isn't—'

I stopped myself. Jo didn't know the whole story about my family.

'Your family is delightful!' she protested, nudging me play-fully. 'Okay, the marrow photo was a bit embarrassing but—'

'Jo, it's got much worse than that,' I said, and told her about the pictures of Mum, and Dad's calls. Her face tightened with sympathy.

'You need to get Leo's lawyers right on that,' she said, grab-bing my hand. 'Right this morning. How vile!'

I didn't say anything, but as my brain slowly woke up, a terrible sense of foreboding was settling on me. How long would the celeb press take to start digging around properly? News fed news in the shallow pools of celebrity stories; I wasn't famous, not really, but it would only take a few more photos before a strange Kardashian-like fascination would stick. And there was much worse out there about us. Much worse. And worst of all, when would Kelly decide the time — or, more likely, the *price* — was right to reappear, salacious story ready to go?

Jo squeezed my hand, and I considered throwing myself at her feet and begging her not to go.

'Come on, let's get Leo onto this right away,' she said. 'He'd do anything for you, you know that.' She hugged me. 'Be brave and ride this out, Amy. It's just a nine-day wonder. You and Leo — you're a match made in heaven.'

I managed a smile, but I didn't feel like smiling. I had another five days of this, five days of intensive preparation for the coronation, which would no doubt involve Liza giving me spot checks on every head of state in the known world, and demanding three conversational openers for each.

We went in for breakfast, and as we picked at the fruits and pastries on the buffet table, Leo arrived, hair damp from the shower. His face was shocked and drawn, and he took me to one side, away from the curious gazes of Rolf and Sofia.

'I've just looked on my iPad,' he muttered. 'I'm absolutely livid. I'm going to get the lawyers onto this at once. What can we do for your mother? Would she like us to take legal action?'

'I don't think that's going to be much help in the post office,' I said.

Leo's eyes were full of apology. 'I wish I could say you get used to it, but —' He broke off as Sofia approached, her hair wet from her morning swim. 'Good morning,' he said stiffly.

'Did I hear the words *legal action*?' She cupped a hand to her ear.

'Yes,' said Leo at the same time that I said, 'No.'

Oh, what was the point? They'd all know soon enough; what else was Giselle for?

Leo filled Sofia in while my appetite dwindled from nothing to whatever negative appetite was. Her eyes widened in disgust, then her nose flared, and to my surprise, she took my arm.

'Amy, I'm *appalled*,' she said. 'It's so sexist — when Rolf went through his blubber phase, no one even mentioned it. If we don't come down hard on these repellent people, this'll just be the start.'

I blinked in surprise. This wasn't the reaction I'd expected.

I'd anticipated a brisk 'get with the program' and a note for Mum from Dr Johnsson.

'Let's go and talk to Giselle,' said Sofia. 'I'll take you. I need to check a few things with her myself.'

Leo made to come with us, but Sofia waved him away. 'No need. We don't always have to have the big man around. We girls are perfectly capable of dealing with problems.'

'It's fine,' I said hurriedly. 'I wanted to talk to Giselle about the dogs' home.' I'd agreed to take on that patronage, as well as the therapy garden, 'to make sure the kids and dogs angle is covered.' (Giselle's words, not mine.) 'She wanted to know if Badger and I would do a photo shoot in London when we get back. I don't mind.'

Leo's face brightened at that, and he touched my arm. 'Tell me exactly what's happening,' he said. 'I'll either be here or in the cathedral with the event organizers, okay?'

I smiled, nervously, because Sofia had just taken my other arm. 'Okay.'

She ushered me down the corridors to the admin area of the palace, where the oil paintings were more martial; but when we were on our own, she suddenly did a double take to check we were unobserved, and pulled me into a room.

A vast library, I think. I didn't have time to inspect it.

'Listen,' Sofia said, fixing me with her sharp eyes, 'I'm going to lay it on the line for you, since everyone else seems to be pussyfooting around. This is just the beginning. Your life with Leo is going to be like this all the time from now on. All you have to be is sociable, not blindingly intelligent, but if you're not up to it, do him a favor, do yourself a favor, do Giselle a favor, and call it a day.'

She said it in such a matter-of-fact tone that I was annoyed rather than mortified. It wasn't as if I hadn't noticed the photographers up till now.

'Is this about the grace? Because that was pretty amateur,' I said.

'I have no idea what you mean.'

I had so little left to lose now that my tongue seemed to be operating on its own. That, or Jo really had started to control me remotely. 'You're saying you could do a better job of everything, I suppose?'

'Yes.' Sofia stared at me as if I were mad. 'Of course I could. But not your job — Leo's. You're just the set dressing. In any other country in the entire world, I'd be doing Leo's job *and* yours now. It's just here that this outrageous insult to me and you exists.'

'Sorry, I should be insulted?'

She clutched her forehead as if she couldn't comprehend my slowness. 'Instead of writing about what I'm doing to, I don't know, protect women's rights in inheritance cases, they'll be writing about the size of your butt. You prefer that kind of feminism? You want to be picked over by the fashion blogs every day? Are you pregnant? Are you fatter than Kate Middleton? Is your mom on a diet?'

That struck home like a slap. I wondered exactly how much Sofia knew about those pap shots. Just like I wondered how much she really knew about my folder of ball-prep information, and my engagement photo wardrobe.

'I can put up with newspapers criticizing me,' I said, looking her square in the face. 'I'll learn. I'll get better. But not my family. They are *not* part of the bargain.'

A smile curled the corner of Sofia's nude lip. 'That's not up to you. And that's what I wanted to talk to you about, on your own.'

My throat clenched.

She tipped her head to one side and fixed me with an unflinching gaze. 'We need to talk about Kelly.'

# CHAPTER THIRTY-ONE

I said nothing, but the thoughts wouldn't stay still in my head. Panic was making them fly round like loose papers in a breeze. If I'd ever wanted to go back in time and do something differently, it was now.

Sofia inspected her nails. 'I've been told — can't say by whom — that a certain American magazine, assisted by a certain British tabloid, has tracked down your sister. Kelly, isn't it?'

She knew it was. I nodded dumbly.

'And there are some good reasons, I understand, why you wouldn't want Kelly to be dragged through the press.'

Of course I didn't! Mum had nearly died under the stress the first time round. And it had only been in the *Rothery Gazette*. What if it was on the front of every tabloid? Kelly telling all on *Loose Women*? Mum would never leave the house again.

I felt nauseated, and weirdly hurt. How come strangers had found Kelly when we couldn't?

'Now, we can stop that,' said Sofia. 'I can stop that. I can probably nip it in the bud so tightly that even Mom and Dad, even Leo, don't have to know about it.' She paused, to watch my reaction. 'You did tell Leo about your sister — and the jail time?'

'There was no jail time,' I snapped, 'it was a suspended

sentence.' I realized my error the second the words were out of my mouth.

Sofia pursed her lips in courtroom triumph. How she'd remained unpunched in her career was a mystery to me.

'That kind of thing doesn't stay secret forever, Amy. As long as you're in the spotlight here, there'll be a reporter who'll persuade her. A producer with enough money to make a documentary.' She rubbed her fingers together. 'You can't blame a girl like Kelly for wanting a little of her sister's good fortune. It doesn't sound as if she's had much of her own lately.'

I gripped the table with both hands. Was she bluffing? What did Sofia know? What had Kelly done now?

Sofia saw my horror and shrugged. 'Look, it might seem harsh, but I'm trying to help you. This is what it's like when you're in a high-profile family, Amy. You can't have any secrets. You can't even fib to your dietician in case he decides to write a book. I'm not expecting an instant decision — it's a lot to take in, I know. But you need to think fast — aren't the invitations to the cathedral blessing here due to go out on Monday?'

I nodded dumbly.

She made an 'oh dear' face, then smiled sympathetically. Like a viper. 'In the meantime,' she went on, 'why don't we go see Giselle, and see if we can't negotiate a nice lump sum for your mother, to compensate her for that offensive photograph they printed? That might take some of the sting out of it.'

I wanted to tell Sofia that money wouldn't even touch the sides of the agonies my mother would be suffering right now, but what was the point? Money was the answer to everything in the Wolfsburg scheme of things.

I followed her back out into the corridor. My brain was spinning so fast I could hardly focus, but one thing stood out.

I had to get back to England. I had to warn Mum and Dad, not on the phone, in person, and I had to try to find Kelly myself first. I had no idea how I could do that, but waiting here for the bomb to drop wasn't even an option. And I didn't want Leo to know.

The cogs in my brain spun and spun and finally stopped, like a slot machine coming up with three lemons.

*How could I marry Leo? Really. How could this ever work?*

'Sofia,' I said, as if a thought had just occurred to me, 'I've left my phone in my room — I should go and get it, in case you need details of . . . stuff.'

I was the world's worst spontaneous fibber. Even my ears felt red.

'Sure.' Sofia was checking her BlackBerry; now that she'd finished with me, I was off her radar. 'We'll be in the press center. Get one of the staff to bring you down if you can't find it.'

'Okay. See you in a sec.'

I shot Sofia the most poisonous look I'd ever shot anyone, and spun on my heel. Jo would be leaving for the airport in fifteen minutes, which didn't give me much time.

I threw a few things into my handbag — not much, so as not to draw attention to the fact I'd gone — and tried not to look at Leo's cuff links on the table, the ones I'd given him, the ones he wore more than all his expensive ones. A pain was piercing my chest, and I had to concentrate on the logistics of getting home, or else it would swamp me.

I took a piece of paper from the morocco leather writing set on the desk and scribbled him a short note, writing the first thing that came into my head.

*Dear Leo,*

*I love you and the time we've had together, but this isn't a life I can share with you. You once said you loved me because I'm normal — well, I am. But I don't think a normal wife is right for you, and one day you'd wake up and realize you needed an orchid, not a daisy – even a diamond one.*

*Love, Amy*

I pulled the engagement ring from my finger and left it on top of the folded paper, along with my diamond daisy chain. I didn't want Sofia coming after me, accusing me of nicking the family silver.

And then without looking back at the rumpled bed or Leo's discarded white shirt on the chair, I grabbed my bag and ran down the stairs to find Jo.

Jo's bags were being loaded into the back of a purple palace Range Rover when I ran down to the private entrance to the state apartments. She seemed pleased to see me.

'Come to say goodbye?' she asked. 'Aw, I'll miss you. Still, you'll have a great week, recovering before the—'

'No,' I said brightly, avoiding her hug and grabbing the car door handle. 'I'm coming with you to the airport. I'll say goodbye there.'

'Really?' Jo frowned. 'Aren't you supposed to be going to the cathedral for a rehearsal?'

'They don't need me, just Leo.' I jumped into the back of the car and clamped my handbag between my knees so she wouldn't see how full it was.

'Come on,' I added, 'we don't want to be late! We've got to set off right now — apparently there are delays on the motorway. Leo says sorry not to say goodbye in person, but they're in some family meeting. About, um, Rolf.'

Jo gave me a funny look, but she got in, and then to my intense relief we were purring down the winding mountain road from the palace to the small harbor on the other side of the island, where the ferry took tourists back and forth throughout the day.

Jo chatted about the ball and the other dresses and how Callie would probably demand every single detail, and I answered as best I could while keeping one anxious eye on the rearview mirror in case a purple palace car appeared with a furious Leo at the wheel.

But nothing followed us. We boarded the ferry, and I watched the white castle recede into the sparkling blue of the sea, turning my gaze away before I had time to register a 'last look.' And then we were on the Italian mainland, speeding down the motorway to the airport, and the magnitude of what I'd done slowly broke over me like the worst hangover known to man.

I'd done it again. I'd run away. I'd done the thing Dad had told us never to do. But, I argued, I had to be true to the person I knew I was when all the diamonds were packed away. And that person wanted to put things right at home before any-thing else.

'Are you okay?' asked Jo. 'You're going to break your phone, gripping it that hard.'

'Just thinking about Dad,' I said. He hadn't picked up when I called; I guessed the phone was off the hook. I'd left a mes-sage telling them not to panic, that I was on my way, but it wasn't enough. I didn't have the right words for more; it was a hug that was needed now, a silent reassurance.

Jo squeezed my knee sympathetically, and we said nothing until the driver signaled to turn off for the airport.

'Jo,' I said as we drove toward departures, 'put your shades on, and my hat, and get out first. I'll get the driver to drop me at the side. But don't go anywhere, okay? I'll see you by the British Airways first-class desk.'

'But I'm not flying first class, Princess Amy.'

'Do it. Please.'

Again she looked at me strangely, but nodded, and pulled my hat low over her eyes. It looked a lot better on her.

As she got out, three photographers loitering by the entrance followed her, shouting, 'Amy! Amy! Over here! Over the shoulder!' as I'd guessed they would, so when I slipped out of the car round the corner, I was able to walk in un-noticed.

Jo was waiting by the BA VIP check-in desk, looking flushed. A crew member was guarding her.

'What was that in aid of?' she said. 'Did you want me to have a taste of the VIP lifestyle before I go home?'

'Something like that.' I fumbled in my bag for my purse,

and looked at the BA rep. 'Are there any seats left on this flight? In first?'

I couldn't go and ask in economy. Too many people looking.

'I'll check for you, madam,' he said, and began rattling away at the computer.

'What?' Jo hissed.

'I'm coming with you.' I glanced across the airport concourse, still paranoid that Leo would arrive, or Sofia, or some minion I wouldn't even recognize until it was too late.

'But they need you here, for interviews and stuff. Rolf said you and Leo were launching your gardening for therapy charity tomorrow?'

'I've got to get home.' I pried my credit card out of my purse and prayed it had enough credit left on it.

'I have two seats in first class, madam,' announced the steward.

'I'll take them,' I said, without even bothering to ask the price. 'She's upgrading. Give them your ticket, Jo.'

She slid it over the counter without taking her bewildered eyes off me. 'What's happened?'

'I can't tell you now. When we get home.'

'Passports?' The BA steward had seen it all before; he didn't even register our frantic whispering.

'Is it something to do with those photos of your mum?' Jo asked, then her face clouded. 'Leo doesn't know you're here, does he? What's going on?'

The steward coughed. 'I'm sorry, madam, the card's been declined. Do you have an alternative method of payment?'

'You're kidding!' Black spots danced before my eyes. I'd been paying it off! Had someone blocked my cards? Had Leo realized I'd gone, and pulled strings to stop me leaving the country?

'Here.' Jo shoved a card at him. 'My emergency card,' she explained. 'Dad gave it to me. I was to use it only if I was about to be deported. This had better be a very good reason.'

I was on pins through passport control, and it was only when we were safely on board and taxiing down the runway that my legs stopped shaking and I sank into my seat.

Jo kept glancing at me, but I was trying to order everything in my head and I couldn't. I kept seeing hideous visions of Kelly chatting to a couple of seedy journalists, wringing her hands and pretending to look ashamed. Eventually Jo gave up and concentrated on getting full value from her upgrade; there wasn't a lot of time on the flight to work through a mini bag of toiletries, but she did it.

My butterflies of guilt returned as we went through UK customs; I half-expected to see someone in dark glasses holding up a sign saying Amy Wilde: Runaway Princess among the bored taxi drivers or maybe a gaggle of tipped-off paparazzi, but the only familiar face in the crowd was Ted's below his shock of dark curls. He was holding a sarcastic sign reading The Duchess of de Vere's Chauffeur.

'What's he doing here?' I asked nervily.

'He's giving me a lift home.'

'In the van?'

'Well, yes. Unless he's been out and bought that Ferrari while we were away. Is that a problem? It seats three.'

'No, just that I'll be driving around in a big van marked

Amy Wilde Is in Here!' I squeaked. I was too stressed to add my usual concerns: that Ted didn't use his mirrors enough for my liking and barely understood roundabouts.

Jo pulled me to one side and grabbed my arms. 'I don't know what you've done, but can you at least keep the hysterical paranoia down until we're out of here? Because right now you're asking to get our bags – and very possibly our digestive tracts – searched by the nice men in plastic gloves.'

She had a point. I tried to get a grip. I didn't want Ted asking questions too.

'Fine,' I said, breathing through my nose. 'Fine.'

Ted seemed surprised to see me, but gallantly shouldered my bag as well as Jo's. 'We are honored,' he said. 'A duchess and a princess. I should have got a flag to put on the front of the van.'

'Hello, Ted,' I said. My voice was very high. 'How've you been?'

'Busy. I've found a bee bloke in Clapham who wants to talk to you, and we need to fill in that sunken garden thing you designed in Eaton Place – it's a magnet for urban fox orgies, apparently.'

'Lovely,' I squeaked.

Jo shot me a sidelong look and took over the conversation until we were in the car park, telling Ted all about the ball and the dinner, and how much she'd liked the palace gardens. If I was quiet, he didn't seem to notice; he was more interested in whether Rolf had 'made an arse of himself' and what sort of loo paper an actual palace supplied.

We were pulling into Leominster Place when I caught sight

of the photographer, drinking a coffee and making a call by the postbox opposite our flat. I saw the sun glint off his lens, and it went through me like a knife.

'Can you drop me here?' I asked, grabbing Ted's arm.

'Get off!' The van screeched to a halt. 'I've told you a million times before, you do not interfere with the . . .'

But I wasn't listening. I grabbed my bag from the footwell and slipped out, using the van as cover as I crouched down. I'd seen that guy before — he was probably the sod who'd got the photos of me wobbling around the park.

I made a mental note to get a water pistol. How powerful would it need to be to wreck a digital camera from an upstairs balcony?

Jo's window buzzed down. 'I've got to see Callie before she goes, but I'll be back ASAP,' she said. 'Do you need anything?'

I shook my head, then walked as fast as I could without drawing attention to myself round the back of the house, where I climbed up the fire escape, just as Leo had done the night we met, and knocked on the kitchen window of a very surprised Mrs Mainwaring.

Badger, at least, was pleased to see me home.

# CHAPTER THIRTY-TWO

Jo came back from Callie Hamilton's in under two hours, which, considering she'd had to get to Knightsbridge and back, was possibly the shortest appointment she'd ever had with her.

She found me and Badger curled up on the sofa together like a woman and her dog from Pompeii, except I was whimpering involuntarily every so often, and Badger was snoring. He perked up when Jo arrived, though.

'Right,' she said, dumping her bag on the coffee table. 'That's Callie packed off to Paris for three nights. Now you can tell me everything. And it had better be good, because I have nine — count 'em — nine missed calls from Rolf on my phone. That's nine more than I'd normally expect.'

That was nothing. I'd had so many missed calls from Leo I'd buried my phone at the bottom of my bag hours ago.

I looked up from the sofa. 'It's obvious, isn't it? I've called off the wedding.'

Jo threw her hands in the air in mime-confusion. 'Why? Because one newspaper prints some embarrassing photos of your poor mum?'

'No, it's more than that.'

She rubbed her eyes. 'Have you had any tea?'

'Not yet.'

'Well, I'm going to make you a pot of tea, and you're going to start from the beginning, and we are going to work this out.'

As Jo spoke, her phone rang, and my stomach lurched. Without saying anything, she turned it off, then went over to the big black old-fashioned telephone by the door and took it off its hook. It made a satisfyingly Hollywood clunk.

Then she marched over to the window, swished the curtains shut, and locked the door.

'Anything else? Badger, come here.' He trotted over obligingly, and Jo picked him up and pretended to talk into his furry white stomach. 'Hello, journalists. Have you bugged this dog? Because the noises you can hear are mainly his gippy guts.'

I managed a weak smile, and curled up on the sofa, hugging my knees to my chest. Badger jumped up next to me, and the familiar smell of his biscuity coat made me want to cry again.

'You've got to tell me everything,' Jo called over the sound of the boiling kettle. 'I know you're a secret squirrel, but if we're going to sort this out, I need to know all the gory details.'

I flinched. Why was I so worried about telling Jo the truth? It wasn't as if everyone in the whole world wasn't about to know.

It was because Kelly had the knack of wiping out my friendships, even now, even from a distance of God knew how many miles.

'So, come on, out with it.' Jo put the tea tray down next to me and pulled the padded satin top off another of Rolf's enormous boxes of chocolates. Tea and chocolate: Jo's prescription for everything. 'Unless,' she added, 'Leo has some kind of weird sexual deviancy thing. You can mime that if you'd prefer.'

I took a deep breath. 'Sofia tipped me off that a couple of big newspapers have hired journalists to track down my sister, Kelly.'

'I didn't know you had a sister!' Jo's eyes bulged.

'Well, I do. I haven't seen her for eight years. She left home under a big cloud and we haven't seen her since.'

'Why didn't you say?'

I could tell Jo was reining in her natural instinct to revel in the scandal, seeing how much it was upsetting me.

'Because I didn't want you to know! Kelly put our family through a living hell. She forced my mum and dad to sell the house we grew up in, she shamed my dad into taking early retirement. And then she vanished and left us to sort out her mess, and we never talk about her but she's there every time I go home and . . .' I was aware my voice was rising and getting more and more thickly northern with each word.

I stopped and covered my mouth with my hand. Where was this anger coming from? I'd never felt so angry about Kelly before.

'So what did she do?'

I pressed my tongue against the back of my front teeth. 'It was awful.'

'More awful than both parents remarrying spouses younger than you?' asked Jo seriously. 'Worse than one uncle going to prison for setting fire to a different uncle's collection of price-less Roman sex toys for the insurance money? I don't think so.'

'Yes, but it's all right for you,' I protested. 'You don't *care* what people think! You don't have to go to corner shops and know that conversations stop when you walk in, and hear the neighbors joking about nailing down their stuff when the Wildes come round!'

Jo's expression softened, and she pushed the sweet tea into my hands. 'Whatever your sister did has no bearing on you. Every family has a black sheep or two.'

My phone rang in my bag, and I cringed. I knew it would be Leo. We stared as it rang and rang, and then it stopped.

'Start from the beginning,' said Jo. 'And let me get a pencil and paper — family stuff is really complicated. I know.'

So I told her. Once I started, I couldn't stop, and as the words spilled out of my mouth, the undermining little voice in the back of my head noted that it was the first time I'd actually told someone else. I'd rehearsed plenty — editing different bits in and out — but I'd never had a friend I'd wanted to trust with the whole unvarnished truth.

'Kelly was the popular one at school,' I said into my mug of tea, 'and she always had older boyfriends. Boys her own age were scared of her. She had that magnetic thing that cool girls have — you know, always wanting the next thing up, and getting it. She didn't go to university like Mum and Dad hoped, because she messed up her exams, but Dad got her a sales job with a friend of his who ran a garage, and she met Chris there. He was buying a top-of-the-range BMW, for cash.'

I remembered that detail. Kelly had told me so many times: 'A *cherry-red M6! I knew he had class, Amy. That car smelled of money . . .'*

'Well, they started going out, even though Chris was nearly thirty. He was into property, doing up cheap terraced houses in Leeds and York, and renting them out to students. Even Dad was impressed with him — he wasn't a spivvy type, he spoke nicely and he'd been to uni. And he was loaded — well, for round our way, he was. Kelly was living the dream: designer handbags, posh shoes, drinks bought for her everywhere they went. Chris even got her her own sports car, personalized plates and everything.'

'Oh dear,' murmured Jo.

'Anyway.' My face was flushing just thinking about it. 'One day Kelly came home and said that Chris had been tipped off about a whole terrace up for sale near the university in Leeds. He'd come up with a business plan that investors could put money into an individual house in the row, so their return could be based on rental income — I don't know exactly how it worked, but she wanted Mum and Dad to get in on it. And it looked great on paper, a good long-term investment.'

Jo's face said what I was feeling.

'Yeah, I know. But it did. This was ten years ago, remember? Anyway, Kelly was a great saleswoman, and she persuaded Dad to invest a lump sum, and Gran, and a couple of our neighbors, and the guy she worked for . . . lots of people, it turned out later. Hundreds of thousands of pounds.'

'And it didn't work out? The market crashed?' said Jo, obviously trying to spare me the pain of saying it.

I half-laughed. 'No. I wish. There were no houses. It turned out that Chris was using all the money they were investing to pay off some other investments he'd made that had lost money. He'd done all right at first, but he got cocky and thought he could play the stock market, but he was taking bigger and bigger losses, and he couldn't stop. One of our neighbors, Roy, started asking questions and tipped off the police, and it turned out the Inland Revenue had had their eye on Chris for a while as part of a big fraud sting, and of course that was linked to other stuff. Worse stuff. I think that was what finished Dad off.'

I fell silent. There were some things I couldn't say. I'd had nightmares for years about the police raiding our cottage at six in the morning with sniffer dogs, looking for evidence of tax fraud. Kelly had hidden forged deeds in our house for Chris, without telling Dad. I'd never forget the sight of Mum hysterical in her nightie, Dad angry but powerless to do anything — both of them lifelong upstanding citizens and supporters of the police, being treated like criminals.

'The worst thing was' — I didn't mean to say it, but I couldn't stop it coming out — 'that the police or a journalist found some dirty photos of Kelly that Chris had taken. One of them was her naked on a bed covered in fifty-pound notes. Grinning like a basketful of chips, covered in other people's hard-earned cash. Of course, it was in every single paper. That was so typical of Kelly. She never *thought*. She never thought about anything.'

Jo covered her mouth with her hands. 'Oh my God. But was she involved? Did she know what was going on?'

I shook my head. 'She isn't the questioning type. As long as the champagne was flowing and all her mates were envying her tacky car, she wouldn't care.' I knew I sounded bitter, but I was. 'It went to court, and she pleaded guilty to some of the lesser charges and got off with a suspended sentence and community service, in return for giving evidence for the prosecution.'

'And Chris?'

'He got seven years for various frauds, but he was bankrupt — no one could recover anything from him. You know our old house that you saw, when we got the wedding dress?'

Jo nodded.

'Mum and Dad sold it to try to pay back some of the people Kelly had persuaded to invest. Dad said he couldn't face seeing people he'd known all his life in hardship because of our family. He took early retirement — well, he had to, he worked for a bank — and Mum developed anxiety disorders, and put on all that weight.'

I was shocked at the vividness of the memories. It was all coming back, not in mental images, but in the tightness in my chest, the acid taste of shame in my throat. 'The trial was in all the local papers for weeks. I couldn't move schools, because there was no room for me anywhere else. Dad and I dug up a whole allotment that summer, just to get away from everyone talking about us. Probably spoke about two words to each other, but our blisters were massive.'

'Oh, Amy.' Jo's eyes were wet with tears. 'You poor things.'

'We got through it. Mum and Dad blamed themselves for not spotting the signs, or not protecting Kelly — you know what parents are like. I wasn't allowed boyfriends, even if I'd wanted one, which I didn't. I found it really hard to trust anyone. I still do.' I swallowed. 'Apart from you.'

Jo leaned across and took my hand without speaking.

I rubbed my eyes angrily with my spare hand. 'But what makes it worse is that Kelly didn't even have the guts to stick around. She just took off one night and left a self-pitying note about how everyone was better off without her. We were the ones who had to deal with the whispers and the crummy new house. She's twenty-eight now, and still hasn't grown up enough to come back and help Mum and Dad.'

But that was exactly what I'd just done to Leo. Left a note. Vanished. Left him to pick up the pieces. I pushed it away.

'And you don't know where she is?'

'No idea. We get a Christmas card and birthday cards, and her writing's just the same, but she manages to post them from really vague places so the postmark's no help. Some are from London. That's what's so scary — maybe Sofia's telling the truth and those reporters have found her. They know how to track down missing persons.'

'Well, if she's carried on her life of crime, she shouldn't be that hard to find.' Jo slapped her thighs and reached for her trusty laptop. 'My friend Dennis works for the Met Police, I'm sure he could do a quick check through their various systems. And there's always prison?'

I lifted my wet eyes to her. 'Don't.'

She pulled an apologetic expression, then looked remorseful. 'Oh, Amy, I'm mortified that I pointed out your house when I saw it. I told Rolf about it, what a gorgeous place you'd grown up in, how lucky Leo was to have a real English rose from a real English rose garden. I wish you'd said. It wouldn't have made the *slightest* difference to me.'

I squirmed. 'I can't bear the thought of Leo finding out — and don't say, why didn't I tell him. There was never a good time. And now it's like a double whammy — not just the Kelly thing, but the fact I didn't tell him.'

'Would you believe me if I told you that, honestly, no one will care? Worse stuff goes on all the time.'

I looked Jo in the eye, and wished I could make her understand what small village life was like. Static and judgmental and suffocating. 'I know that. But my mum and dad will care. They'll care very much when it all gets raked over again back home.'

She gazed at me very sadly, then rubbed her hands together. 'Then we need to find Kelly ourselves. I need details: birth date, description — anything you can think of. Have you got a photo? Does she look like you?'

I shook my head. 'No. You wouldn't take us for sisters; she looks more like my gran. Hang on. I've got an album.'

I went into my room, pulling open the divan drawer underneath my bed. Right at the back was my box of valuables, including my own collection of photos that had escaped Mum's cull. I picked out the slim album and went back to the sitting room to give it to Jo.

'Here,' I said. 'She's not a criminal. She's just daft. You can tell by looking at her.'

I opened it to a photograph of me and Kelly on prize-giving day at school; Mum had wrestled my hair into plaits and Kelly was sporting her ill-advised perm, which ironically gave her frizz just like mine. She was also sporting a red, swollen forehead and penciled-on eyebrows, caused by her 'wondering' if her leg wax would also work on her brows, the night before the ceremony. The end result was half Frankenstein's monster and half Bette Davis, yet she still looked like the sort of girl who could start a party in a damp tent. She was mugging for the camera as if auditioning for some reality television show; I was looking embarrassed. I was fourteen years old.

Anger and sadness and something else, something more painful, swilled around inside me as Jo turned the page to a shot of the four of us on a beach with our old dog, Jolly Roger. There had been a time when we'd been a really happy nuclear family. Deep down (a long way down right now), I missed feckless, selfish Kelly exactly as much as I was glad she'd effed off out of our lives.

'Dear God,' said Jo, and I knew she was winding up for one of her killer character assassinations.

'I know. But she's still my sister,' I said. 'So go easy on the eyebrow thing. They're my genes too.'

Jo stared at the photographs for a long time, and then looked at me. 'So let me get this straight. You're telling me that you've given up the man you love and a lifetime of white-tie balls, and all because you want to stop the *National Enquirer* finding your sister and shaming your mum?'

'Yes.' I paused. 'Well, that and the constant earache from Sofia about Leo inheriting instead of her. And having to leave the business I've built up here. And having to be on a bloody diet all the time.'

Jo pushed the chocolates toward me again, and I took three, because for the first time in weeks there was no reason not to.

'And if we could find Kelly first?' she asked. 'What would you do?'

I considered that through a mouthful of rose cream. 'I suppose,' I said slowly, 'I'd make her go home and apologize to Mum and Dad. Then something good might have come out of this.'

'And if you did that? You'd think about making up with Leo?' Jo seemed hopeful, but I wasn't.

I didn't want to answer her.

She waited a long time, then said, with a straight face, 'If there's one thing my ludicrous family has taught me, it's never ever ignore your heart. It's so much wiser than your head in the long run.'

There were times when I thought Jo's family should run their own fancy embroidered pillow shop.

Jo made more tea and listened to Leo's frantic messages — I couldn't bear to hear his voice — then summarized them in a way that I could stand.

He was bewildered. Everyone was asking questions. What had he done wrong? He loved me. Whatever it was, we could fix it.

She stood over me while I texted him to say that I needed time to think about the enormity of what I was taking on, and that I hadn't realized until the ball the true extent of the job that meant so much to him. I also had to consider the impact on my family, since my parents were in a state of shock.

Within the hour, I got an e-mail from Leo's office address, with Giselle and the press center copied in. It contained an attached press release from Prince Leopold, stating that Miss Amy Wilde had had, with deep regret, to withdraw from the state coronation of Crown Prince Boris of Nirona and Svetland on Saturday, due to a family illness. No further details were supplied as it was a private matter.

He then texted me to say that he would be in touch in a week's time, and that he hoped very much that he'd be able to return the gifts I'd left behind.

My heart broke at that, and I gave up and spent the rest of the day crying, and in the brief pauses when I wasn't crying, shoving Charbonnel et Walker chocolates into my mouth.

I don't remember much about the next few days because they blurred into one soggy mass of achy misery. It felt like I had the flu, not a broken heart.

I spent hours on the phone to my parents, but I couldn't leave the house because by now the story of the gardening princess's mysterious bunk from the coronation had reached the rumor mill, and there was a gaggle of photographers lounging outside, leaving Starbucks cups everywhere. Mrs Mainwaring had taken to wearing her best clothes every time she went in and out; since they weren't getting any shots of me, the press pack amused themselves by snapping away at her. Her bridge club had never had so much attention. It was like a geriatric version of *Britain's Next Top Model* out there most days.

The photographers also staked out Ted for a while, until he threatened to get his rugby club round to clear them off. Grace's balcony got another airing in the press, captioned with her name spelled wrong. To my horror, they even pitched up on my parents' doorstep, until Jo arranged for Mum and Dad to be taken to a hotel in the Lake District for a few days until the fuss calmed down. I wanted to go and see them, but I didn't want to create more opportunities for prurient comments, and that made me feel even worse.

There was also the small matter of the fifty thousand pounds that materialized in Dad's bank account. It seemed to make everything worse, as far as he was concerned.

'It's from the newspaper,' he said. 'Is it a bribe? Because we haven't sold them anything. Love, it's not what you think. I didn't want to bother you when you've clearly got enough on your plate, but I had to tell you. Your mother's worried sick.'

'It's compensation, Dad,' I explained. 'For that photo of Mum outside the wedding shop. Leo's lawyers have put the frighteners on the paper — they were threatening to sue on your behalf.'

'I don't want their money!' Dad's honest disgust couldn't have been clearer if he'd been in the room. 'As if any amount of cash could make up for the humiliation your mother's been through! I'd rather have an apology for upsetting a fine, decent woman for no reason whatsoever, and that costs nothing.'

He was right. Of course he was right. I thought guiltily of Mum's expensive dress, and how I'd thrown money at the airline tickets to get away from Nirona. And I didn't feel any better.

*

On Thursday morning, Jo had gone out as normal — normal was now down the fire escape, over next door's garden wall, and out via their alley — and I had settled down to another day of daytime telly, toast, and not looking on YoungHot&Royal to check up on their current analysis of the 'unfolding runaway-bride drama in Nirona.'

Our phone was still unplugged unless we wanted to make a call ourselves, and I'd let my mobile go flat, so the knock on the door nearly made me jump out of my skin.

I peered through the security peephole. It was Dickon. His nose looked freakishly huge from that angle.

'I'm not in the mood,' I said. 'And neither's Badger.'

'No, I've got a message for you, from Jo.'

I opened the door a fraction. I was still in my toast-crumbed pajamas, and I didn't want to give him ideas.

'She wants you to meet Ted in the delivery bay behind Peter Jones in one hour.' He was reading from a hastily scribbled note. 'You have to climb out over the—'

'Yes, yes, I know, the fire escape, next door's garden.'

'And you've got to get dressed. Don't look at me like that, it's what she said.' He showed me the notes he'd scribbled down. 'She's pretty bossy, isn't she?'

'It's her job.'

I started to close the door, but Dickon shoved his foot in the crack. Bold, since he was wearing velvet carpet slippers. 'Amy?'

'Dickon?' I braced myself for the inquiry.

'I just wanted you to know . . .' He looked at me, and for the first time I realized what nice eyes Dickon had. Kind eyes.

Bloodshot, but kind. 'Some of those snappers asked me and Mrs Mainwaring if we'd give them inside info on you and Jo. You know, any stories we had. Photos.'

My heart sank. 'You didn't give them photos of the heaven and hell party?'

Maybe Dad would lend me some of that money to buy them back.

Dickon looked horrified. 'No! No, we didn't. We told them to sod off.' He frowned. 'I'm really sorry this is happening. Let me know if Badger ever needs a walk, yeah?'

I felt an uncontrollable urge to cry. Now even Dickon felt sorry for me. 'Thank you.'

He wagged a finger. 'Now, give me the dog, get dressed, and get out. I can't take another phone call like that.'

# CHAPTER THIRTY-THREE

I got a taxi to Sloane Square rather than walking, on the assumption that the cabbie would spend the entire journey ranting about how shocking the traffic was south of the river and wouldn't notice if Madonna herself got in the back of his cab, and I was right.

My van was parked in the loading bay, blending in with the scenery, and I jumped in before anyone noticed. Ted slammed the engine into gear as if he were starring in a gangster film and roared off down Sloane Avenue, a dramatic gesture only slightly spoiled by his getting stuck behind a bus for most of the way and having to stay in second gear.

'Where are we going?' I demanded. 'And can you take more care with the gears, please?'

'Can't say. And I am taking care.'

I looked across at him. He was wearing shades and a poloneck. Ted never wore anything smart for work.

'Are you dressed up?' I asked him.

'No, I've run out of clean clothes.'

I didn't believe that. It had to have something to do with Jo.

'Are we meeting Jo?' I narrowed my eyes.

Ted looked foxed. 'How did you know?'

'I can smell aftershave.' I turned round to inspect the back of the van. 'And you've cleaned the van out. Look, no mud! Or seed catalogues. It's spotless.'

'Well, I haven't been able to work, have I, what with your newfound notoriety. Can't go anywhere without someone asking if you've lost a glass slipper.'

We drove in silence for a couple of blocks, and then I said, 'Ted, you know, our business is really important to me. It's one of the reasons I decided I couldn't—'

'If this is about your relationship crisis, I don't need to know,' he said quickly, warding off the confession with a palm. 'I'm not Jo. No daytime television carry-on, please.'

'Fine.' I sank back.

A couple of blocks later, he said, 'I know. I mean, I know how much you care about the business. For what it's worth . . .' He coughed. 'It wouldn't be much without you. I'd still be on lawns. Not getting letters from the conservation charities.'

'Thanks.' In my permanently overemotional state, I didn't dare say more for fear of setting off the tears again.

He grunted, and we drove round Hyde Park Corner, down Park Lane, and through town, until I realized we'd gone past Lord's Cricket Ground and were heading out toward the M1.

'Don't ask,' said Ted before I could, and put on his Robert Palmer CD.

After an hour of having to endure Ted whistling guitar solos through his teeth, we finally turned into Toddington Services on the M1. Ted drove round the car park, missing lots of perfectly good spaces, before swerving into the area designated for caravans and pulling up next to a brand-new Porsche Cayenne with blacked-out windows.

My heart leaped into my mouth. Was it Leo? Or had Liza come to get me? I was amazed she hadn't tried to call, but maybe she thought kidnapping me was the easiest option.

I turned to give Ted a piece of my mind, but he was out of the van already. I jumped out after him, on red alert for any burly security guards, but he opened the back door of the Porsche and more or less shoved me inside, then climbed into the front passenger seat.

'Hello!' said Jo from the driver's seat. She too was wearing shades and a polo-neck. Great. I'd been kidnapped by a pair of French jazz musicians. 'Sorry to be so cloak-and-dagger, but it's exciting, isn't it?'

I barely heard her. I was too busy staring at the person on the backseat next to me: a woman who looked very, very like my sister, Kelly.

Kelly, if she'd found a hairdresser even more expensive than the one Sofia had marched me to. Kelly, if she'd had her teeth done. Kelly, if she'd taken the pale Yorkshire skin she'd been born with and flown it off on two Caribbean holidays a year since 2002, with a ski tan top-up in between. The round cow-eyes, the pointy nose, the sly mouth — exactly the same, but with a grown-up edge.

It *was* Kelly.

I'd often wondered how I'd feel if I ever saw my sister again, but I'd never guessed that my initial overriding feeling would be of intense irritation that she looked so bloody well.

She ought to be in tears, I thought irrationally. With bad skin and black roots and a hangdog expression. Instead of which, she looked snootily furious. When I blundered into the backseat, though, that soon changed to shock.

We said nothing. We just stared at each other. Then, because clearly someone had to say something, I looked at Jo and said, 'Would you mind telling me what's going on?'

Jo nodded at Kelly. 'Why don't you ask Callie? I mean, Kelly. Sorry. That's going to take some getting used to.'

'What?' I stared at my big sister. 'You're Callie Hamilton? You're Jo's nightmare client? Since when have you . . . ?' It was too much to take in. I couldn't even start.

'There's no law to say you can't change your name,' huffed Kelly. Her new accent matched her new look; if I'd heard her ordering sushi in Nobu, I'd never have guessed she was from Hadley Green. 'And the surname's mine, I got married. And divorced. Vis-à-vis the name, I fancied a fresh start.'

'You got married?' This got worse. 'And you didn't tell Mum and Dad?'

A shadow passed across Kelly's pretty face. 'Well, I was going to. It was very spur-of-the-moment, me and Greg. We did it in Vegas, but to be fair, by the time we got back from the honeymoon we'd realized we loved each other but we couldn't live with each other, so there didn't seem any point in telling Mum. He was very generous regarding alimony, though.'

That was so Kelly. That was Kelly all over.

Her face brightened again. 'But when me and *Harry* get married, when his divorce comes through, then I'm definitely telling Mum and Dad. I want you all to be there for that. I've been telling Jo, I've got it all planned — I reckon we can get Westminster Abbey! Well, one of the side chapels . . .'

Behind her, Jo drew small circles around her left ear and rolled her eyes. As previously discussed at great length over our kitchen table, Harry the slippery financier/fiancé was about as likely to get divorced as I was to swim the Channel — i.e., possible but extremely unlikely, due to lack of enthusiasm.

She leaned forward, with the 'aw, bless' intimacy she'd always been so good at. 'You know what? Can I tell you something, hon? You haven't changed a bit,' she said.

'Neither have you,' I said icily.

Kelly looked disappointed.

'I recognized her at once from your photo album,' Jo explained from the front seat. 'That photo of her with no eyebrows sealed it — it was one of the first things I noticed about Callie. Her weird skimpy eyebrows.'

'Thanks,' sniffed Kelly.

'No offense,' said Jo, 'but you can always tell an eye pencil.'

'So, can we get a move on?' Ted demanded. 'Are you done? Can I go?'

'Yes. Thanks, Ted, you've been a real star.' Jo leaned over and gave him a big kiss on the cheek, which made him flush. 'I'll give you a ring when we get to where we're meeting Pam and Stan—'

'Hang on, hang on.' Kelly suddenly sounded much more Rothery than before. 'You're not driving this up to Yorkshire, lady.'

'Why not?'

'Because . . .' She looked annoyed with herself. 'Because Harry doesn't know I've got the Cayenne today. He'll check the mileage.'

Jo wrinkled her brow. 'He'll what?'

'It's on a mileage package thing.' Kelly waved her hand airily.

'Fine, let's go in the van,' I said. 'The longer we stay here, the more we look like we're up to no good.'

My words hung in the air, but I wasn't going to apologize. A weird recklessness had overwhelmed me — it wasn't as if my life could get any more surreal. I thought Kelly flinched, but it might just have been the sudden October chill as I yanked open the car door and got out.

Ted refused to drive Kelly's Porsche back to London in case Harry had reported it stolen. Jo refused to drive the van with Ted giving her passive driving instruction from the passenger seat. So I ended up in the back of the van with Kelly, with Ted at the wheel and Jo in the front watching out for any photographers and arguing with Ted over the music choices.

I sat on the bench bit where we normally stored tools and glared at Kelly.

Kelly, free from Jo's supervision, glared back at me. It was just like being back in Dad's caravan, but with less Formica.

'You know, this is just as embarrassing for me as it is for you,' she informed me over the rattle of gardening implements. 'Do you think I want Harry finding out about things that are very much part of my past?'

'You didn't tell him about the six-month suspended sentence?' I rounded my own eyes in pretend shock. 'What sort of fiancé is he?'

'Did you tell your fiancé about it?' she flashed back. 'Clearly not, or I wouldn't have had reporters banging on my door offering me a small fortune for the true story of Prince Leo's so-called squeaky-clean bride-to-be!'

'I didn't put my family through hell!' I snarled. 'And for your information, Kelly, it might be part of your past, but it's very much still part of my and Mum and Dad's present! They live with the consequences of your selfishness every day! And do you have any idea what I've had to give up, just to stop them being dragged through the mud again?'

'It's always poor little you, you, you, isn't it?' sneered Kelly, and if Jo hadn't turned round and banged on the panel, I think I would have clattered her.

'Save it till we get there,' she yelled. 'I don't want to miss any of this, thank you. It would be like coming in halfway through a really good television drama.'

'Fine with me,' said Kelly, and folded her arms.

I folded mine, and we stared at the bags of Gro-Rite for the rest of the journey, and listened to Ted and Jo bicker about the right way to overtake an Eddie Stobart lorry.

Just like old times.


If I'd ever doubted Jo's organizational abilities — and her gentle but firm touch — I had the ultimate confirmation of them when we arrived in Rothery.

She'd guessed that Mum's house would be surrounded by prying eyes, so she'd somehow got word to Dad and had arranged to meet them in a place they'd feel safe and private. After what felt like an eternity, we finally pulled up at the Wilde Family Summit location: the allotments where Dad grew his prizewinning vegetables, just beyond the crematorium.

Ted parked, and we trailed through the various patches to reach Dad's rows. It was a bleak Yorkshire autumn day, but I was impressed by the foliage on show — lots of veg, and some splashes of orange and yellow where enthusiasts were training chrysanthemums up canes. The handful of retired men in flat caps digging their potatoes barely registered our presence, apart from a few sniffs at Jo and Kelly's lack of suitable footwear.

Just before we got to the shed, Ted stopped and looked awkward. 'I'll wait here,' he said, sitting down on the nearest bench. 'I'll, er, let you know if I see anyone coming.'

He tapped the phone in his jacket.

Jo's curiosity was fighting an open battle with her English reserve, all over her face. 'I should too. It's a family moment.'

Kelly started to agree with her, but I cut in.

'No,' I said suddenly. 'Jo, I'd really like you to come in.'

I didn't trust Kelly not to start refashioning her London life to suit the new reality. Not lying, just missing bits out. And I also needed Jo to referee things, in case I really did clatter Kelly.

'Okay,' said Jo very quickly, and with a deep breath I pushed open the door to the shed.

Mum and Dad were wedged on the two chairs inside, next to the potting table. It was the biggest shed on the allotments, but even so, it was a squash for five of us, especially since Dad stored his beekeeping stuff in there. When Kelly squeezed in behind me, Mum let out a gasp as if she'd seen a ghost, and her eyes widened so much I thought she might be having a heart attack.

The earthy air hummed with tension, and then Mum held out her arms, and Kelly let out a loud sob and flung herself into them. Dad hovered next to them for a second, and then threw his arms round the pair of them, and they all howled together.

I could hear Mum sobbing, 'Kelly, oh Kelly, my baby girl,' and Dad patting them both rather awkwardly, and Kelly sobbing, 'I'm sorry, I'm sorry, I'm sorry,' over and over again.

It was like I wasn't even there.

I looked at Jo, dumbfounded. She shrugged, embarrassed, as if she hadn't foreseen anything else happening.

I'm ashamed to say this, but a hot wave of fury swept over me. I was the one who'd supported Mum and Dad for the last ten years! I was the one whose relationship with the most amazing man in the world had been jeopardized because of this! All the pain and shame of the past week bubbled up inside me and burst out at the best available weak spot: Kelly.

'Hello?' I yelled furiously. 'She ruins our lives and gets the prodigal welcome? How about, "Are you all right, Amy, I hear you just broke off your engagement"?'

Kelly kept her head buried in Mum's bosom, but Dad and Mum looked up at once. Mum's face was red and suffused with guilt. Dad reached out his arm and smiled at me. I couldn't remember the last time I'd seen him so happy. How could he be so happy? I was *heartbroken*!

'Come on, love,' he said. 'Plenty of room for you too.'

But that wasn't enough. There was a very angry sixteen-year-old in me, determined to get out after years of being pushed down.

'No! I want her to apologize first. I want her to explain to us where she's been for the past ten years and why she's never shown any interest in anyone but herself. Until now, when she's got her own skin to save.'

Kelly withdrew her tearstained face at that and looked balefully at me. 'That's so unfair. I've been looking out for you all this time I've been in London.' Her dignity was being compromised by that hiccupy sobbing, so she pointed at Jo by way of explanation. 'Why do you think she's been working on my house for so long? You think anyone needs three wet rooms?'

'What?'

'It was my only way of keeping in touch. Jo was the project manager for a friend a few years ago, and she mentioned this young gardener from Yorkshire who was looking for work. I put two and two together, and then when I hired Jo, bingo.' She wiped her eyes, smearing her heavy makeup. 'It was really hard sometimes, hearing what a great time you were having, you two,' she whined. 'Your parties, and the interesting people in your house. You always did fall on your feet, Amy.'

'I wondered why she kept making all her friends hire you and Ted,' Jo pointed out. 'I mean, you're good, but it was a bit weird that she didn't want you to do her own garden.' She sighed. 'And I thought it was for my benefit. Never mind.'

If she was trying to lighten the mood, she was wasting her time.

'Back up there, Kelly,' I snapped. 'I always fell on my feet? Hello? Did you miss the part where I worked my arse off for three years at college to get my degree? And then dug gardens till my nails went black to get my business going?'

Kelly screwed up her face. She looked a lot less polished now. 'But you were clever. It was easy for you, it wasn't like you had a social life to distract you.'

'I had no social life because you made me a total outcast!' I roared.

Mum and Dad were doing a Wimbledon-worthy back-and-forth head swivel.

'Oh, you were always a swot.' Kelly waved a hand. 'Yes, I messed up my A levels, get over it. That's why I wanted to believe all the stuff Chris told me about the investment — I wanted to do something to make Mum and Dad proud of me too, instead of having them remind me how much homework you did.'

'Oh, *Kelly*,' said Mum, but Dad was looking stern.

'And then when I realized how stupid I'd been, I thought leaving was the best thing to do. I didn't want to hear about how I'd messed up again.' Kelly wiped her nose with the back of her hand. 'I had this big plan to go away and get a great job, then come back and show you I wasn't the letdown everyone thought I was.'

'But look at you, love!' Mum stroked Kelly's cashmere-clad and gym-toned bicep. 'In your lovely clothes with that dear handbag. You're obviously doing well for yourself.'

Kelly opened her mouth to lie, but caught me and Jo glaring at her. 'It's not really my money, Mum,' she admitted. 'I got married to a guy who was a bit older than me —'

Oh, it was all coming out now.

'— but it didn't work out and, um, Greg gave me a generous settlement when we separated. I was going to use the money to retrain at something,' she added very quickly, in Dad's direction, 'and then I met Harry, and he wanted me to stay in London and then he proposed . . .'

'You're getting married too!' Mum's face lit up; then the happiness extinguished almost as quickly when Kelly said, 'When his divorce comes through.'

'Oh,' said Mum. Dad didn't say anything.

Kelly looked down at her feet. 'I don't know if that's going to happen now, though. Some journalists have been pestering me, and if I don't give them a story, they're bound to get hold of Chris . . . I don't think Harry's going to want to be married to someone with a criminal record.'

'He's a barrister,' Jo supplied helpfully.

'Dear me,' said Dad under his breath. 'What a pair.'

Silence descended over the shed as the dust settled around us. (Metaphorically. Dad kept a spotless shed.)

Eventually, Kelly reached out to me. I didn't want to take her hand, but everyone was looking at me, so I had to.

'I'm really sorry for doing this to you, Amy,' she said, in a humble voice I'd never heard from her before. 'I didn't want to think about what was going on at home, I was just focused on the future and everything being okay somehow. I was so happy for you when I saw you'd started dating Leo. It made me think maybe I'd get a miracle in my life too, something good so I could come back and not feel like scum. Honestly, you looked beautiful in that Zoë Weiss ballgown. I showed everyone I knew, all my friends . . .'

My eyes filled up. Jo reckoned Kelly — Callie — didn't have many friends. She always said she reckoned the ladies who lunched tolerated Callie because Harry was rich and she had a house near Harrods.

'Do you want me to talk to Leo?' Kelly sounded pathetically eager. 'I'll tell him everything, if it would make him see that you had nothing to do with it. I'll do an interview or something. Whatever you need.'

'Actually,' Jo murmured, 'that's not a bad idea.'

Mum and Dad looked at her in horror.

'No, really,' she went on. 'It's going to come out anyway, much better to be in control of the story.'

'But Liza's got a press agent like a rottweiler,' I pointed out, 'and they still printed . . .' I didn't want to mention Whalegate in front of Mum.

'But if we went to them direct, with Kelly and a tame writer and some exclusive photos . . .'

Light dawned. 'You mean one of those girls who covered your show?'

She nodded. 'Everyone loves a reformed sinner and a royal wedding. Imagine the two together!'

Except there would be no wedding.

The longer I spent at home, the farther away Leo's world felt. Press agents. Ballgowns worth more than cars. For heaven's sake. That wasn't my life. It was Amelia's. Amelia, the made-up princess.

I felt my lip wobble, even though I was trying to hold myself together with every last shred of energy I had.

Dad stretched out his arm to me, and I got a faint whiff of that familiar smell that took me back to the long wordless summer we'd spent together. Washing powder, and a bit of honest sweat; the smell of a man who'd worn suits for work for twenty-five years, and then found himself in shirtsleeves all day, with just his spade and what remained of his pride. My heart ran back to him, like a little girl stumbling over a lawn speckled with daisies.

'If nothing else comes of it,' he said, his gray eyes shining with very un-Yorkshire-man tears, 'you've brought our family together again, Amy. And that's the most wonderful thing you could ever have given your mother and me.'

'Stop it,' I said, but in another second I was enfolded in Dad's arms, my head against Mum's ample bosom, and even Kelly — who still reeked of Joy by Jean Patou, nothing bloody changed — was squeezing me as if we were in a storm and the shed was about to be whisked away.

It didn't feel right to be so happy when my heart was ripped to bits, but weirdly I was. Somewhere, a clock was starting to turn backward, one slow second at a time.

# CHAPTER THIRTY-FOUR

Jo and I said we wouldn't watch the live streaming of Boris's coronation on the Internet, but obviously we did.

'Better to know,' she said, as we parked ourselves in front of the laptop with the last of Rolf's ridiculous bottles of champagne, and a fish pie that Mrs Mainwaring had thoughtfully made for us.

Mrs Mainwaring owed me and Jo, in a roundabout way. She'd seen off a particularly persistent snapper with her handbag, and then a rival paper with very little news to print that day had paid her two thousand pounds to talk about her 'paparazzi hell,' with Dickon in the background, looking suspiciously like a boy toy.

The Saturday of the coronation, the photographers weren't even bothering to hide behind bushes, because of course I was still supposed to be supporting an unnamed member of my family through an illness, and they were desperate to get a glimpse of me not ill, and not in Yorkshire. At least Mum and Dad were safe. They were up in Scotland at the remote hunting-lodge hotel belonging to a friend of Jo's mother, where Kelly would be joining them, accompanied by Sukey the writer, just as soon as she'd finished bringing Harry the barrister up to speed.

'The rule is, we can watch the coronation, but with no sound.' Jo passed me a glass and topped up her own. 'I don't want to know what they're saying.'

'You wouldn't, it's in Italian,' I said, as the TV news station live feed from Nirona flickered into life. The island was quite small, but it seemed everyone had turned out to see the pageantry. Cheering crowds lined the narrow cobbled streets around the cathedral, and the camera was panning along the various dignitaries arriving at the Gothic entrance. I recognized some famous model friends of Liza's, and a couple of royal princes, and some prime ministers and, blimey, that was the American First Lady, wasn't it? And that was definitely Elton John. Elton John never missed a good royal do.

'There are some really famous people there,' I said, surprised.

'Yeah.' Jo looked up from her phone. 'It seems you were the last person to realize that the Wolfsburgs are kind of a big deal.'

'Maybe.' I searched for Leo's face but couldn't see him. I spotted Giselle, though, and Nina, Liza's assistant, in a mad green hat that looked like an alien frying pan. It was weird to see such familiar faces on television like this. In a parallel universe, I was there too. I wondered what I'd have been wearing.

Something hideous, if it had been down to Sofia.

'Oh, look out for Sofia's hat,' said Jo. 'Apparently looks like she got her head stuck in a ceiling tile but came along anyway.'

'Don't read Twitter!' I tried to grab the phone off her. 'I don't want to know what they're saying about —'

I stopped as a subtitle went across the screen. I didn't speak Italian, but I guessed *fuggitiva* and *principessa* meant what I thought they did.

'At least they care,' said Jo, with a pretend solemn look on her face.

The camera spun back to a parade of horse-drawn carriages and cars arriving, and suddenly, getting out of a shining Daimler was Leo.

My heart expanded in my chest at the sight of him. He looked so handsome. So clearly the sum total of a supermodel and a prince, with his broad shoulders and winning smile and the modest wave he did to the crowds. Rolf was behind him, playing up to them a bit more with a bigger wave, but even he had toned things down. His hair was a little shorter, and his suit a little quieter.

'Leo looks good,' said Jo kindly. 'But tired.'

'He looks *affranto*, apparently,' I said, reading the subtitles. 'What's that?'

There was a pause while Jo checked online. 'Heartbroken. I thought you started an Italian course.'

'I only had time for a few lessons.' I couldn't tear my eyes off the screen as Leo walked into the cathedral with Rolf, pausing to speak to the officials who beamed at him as he passed.

*I'd have to be doing that,* said the little voice in my head, and I shrank inside. What would they be scrolling across the screen if I were there? What mean things would they be saying about my hat?

Half of me longed to be by Leo's side, feeling the tender pressure of his hand resting protectively in the hollow of my back, as I had done at the glittering gala nights we'd attended. But half of me was beyond relieved not to be there.

As the ceremony carried on, and I saw the banked cameras and the sea of faces in the cathedral, and then Boris and Liza arriving like the starriest Hollywood stars of all time, decked out in velvet robes and proper crowns, the half dwindled to a quarter, and finally, when Jo was telling me that Sofia's hat had gone viral and already people were linking to satirical web pages devoted to how she was keeping it on her head with magnets, I had to acknowledge that I'd done the right thing.

If I'd been there, I'd have slipped on some horse dung, or blanked the bishop from nerves. Not like Liza, who sailed through the whole thing as if she'd been born to it, all the while casting tiny, camera-friendly, admiring glances Boris's way. The perfect princess wife. Not normal. Not in the least bit normal.

I felt sadly envious of whoever Leo found to fit that role. She was going to be the luckiest woman in the world, as well as one of the most nervous.

I had arranged to meet Leo Monday at lunchtime, as agreed in his e-mail, and I didn't sleep at all on Saturday night or Sunday.

I owed him an explanation, but I didn't really have one. Well, not one that really covered everything in a way I felt did any justice to the soul-searching that had been keeping me hollow-eyed and sleepless.

Instead I worried about where we could meet without anyone seeing us, but as ever he had everything under control;

he texted me early on Monday morning to say he'd be in the summerhouse of the private garden in Trinity Square at 1 p.m. Leo kept such a low profile in London that I didn't even think the press knew where his house was.

There was a burly protection officer lingering by the gate when I arrived; he was dressed as a normal passerby, but most locals near Trinity Square didn't look as if they'd recently been discharged from the marines.

With a nod, he let me in, and I walked down the gravel path that led to the summerhouse. Even on an autumn day like today, the lawns were immaculate, without a single leaf lying around to mess up the green velvet, and the glossy box hedges were dark and still fragrant. Nostalgia swept through me along with the familiar smells, as I remembered all the chatty picnic lunches, and drinks, and sweet, soul-exploring moments we'd had here, with my bare feet up on Leo's lap on the bench, or his head resting near mine as we lay near the rose beds, breathing in the scents of the flowers and the warmed summer air.

This was the last time. This was the very last time I'd be able to wander in this hidden garden where Wolfsburgs fell in love. That broke my heart almost as much as what I knew I had to do.

Leo was waiting in the summerhouse. The table was spread with a white cloth, and three silver domes were arranged on top, just as it had been on our first date. I smiled weakly.

'Lunch?' he said.

He seemed thinner, and though he smiled back at me, I could see deep shadows under his eyes. I'd never seen Leo with stubble, but he had a very fine crop of it on his chin, and it rather suited him.

I sat down, and he whisked the domes away to reveal two club sandwiches and two packets of crisps.

'Good-quality ones,' he added, and the crack in my heart deepened another notch.

I asked him about the coronation, how it had gone, and he told me, describing the events with his usual mix of courteous and dry wit. Now it just reminded me of something he'd once said, about being trained to chat, to put people at ease. It was more of an effort for me to begin with, but his manner coaxed me into almost normal conversation. I confessed that Jo and I had watched it, and played Fashion Police Bingo on the guests, and he looked tickled.

'You'll have seen Sofia's hat, then?' he added with a raised eyebrow.

'I did. Was it a bet?'

'It was her way of making sure no one looked at me and Rolf.' He popped a crisp into his mouth. 'For which I'm actually grateful. There was enough of that already.'

I looked down at my plate. It had the Wolfsburg crest on it: two lions rampant, gold ribbons, white roses. White roses, like the white rose of Yorkshire. 'I'm sorry.'

'The official line is that you're still with your sick relative,' he said, his tone deceptively light. 'That's why the palace hasn't sent out the invitations to the wedding yet. Are you . . . ?' The pause seemed to stretch out forever.

I couldn't say anything. I didn't know what to say.

When Leo spoke again, there was a distinct crack in his voice. 'Are you coming back with me?'

A tear dropped onto my plate, and I shook my head.

Leo said nothing. Then he said, a little stiffly, 'Can I ask why?'

Haltingly, I began to tell him the whole story about Kelly, and my family. About my childhood and why I cared so much about what people thought of me, and how I'd tried to be true to my old life *and* my new one. Why my parents deserved a life too, after giving up so much of theirs to put right Kelly's mistake. And more than that, why he deserved someone outgoing to fit the job he'd been born to do, instead of a lifetime apologizing for me.

I went on for ages. I didn't want to miss anything out. Leo didn't say anything when I'd finished, and I struggled to find a way of explaining what was trying to burst through my chest, and in the end, as usual, I could only find one way of doing it.

'The thing is, Leo,' I said, waving a hand toward the garden outside, 'this place is you. It's elegant and measured, and every bed blooms at the right time because someone's planned the flowering seasons. It's lovely, but I couldn't live in it. I love those wildflower meadows I plant because that's what I feel like inside — I look at meadow banks and I see butterflies and bees and all the rhythms of the seasons, but with a freedom that there just isn't here. And you could never combine the two. It would spoil what someone's taken years to create.'

Leo looked up, and his gaze moved slowly around my face, as if he was trying to print my eyes, my lips, my cheekbones, on his memory. We were both nearly in tears. He reached into his pocket and brought something out, sliding it across the table.

I thought it was my diamond bracelet or the diamond ring, and was about to refuse it, but it wasn't either. It was a Yale key.

'Guess this is the wrong time to give you a present,' he said.

'What is it?'

'I bought us a house.'

'A house?'

He nodded, wretchedly. 'A house up in Yorkshire. One with a mature cottage garden, and an apple tree with a swing in it. A lovely place to bring kids, to see their grandparents.' He didn't need to say it, but he did anyway. 'In Hadley Green.'

The breath choked in my throat. He'd bought our old house, as a surprise for me. It was the sweetest thing to do; but in that instant I realized how little Leo understood me, or my family. I couldn't go back. Dad and Mum . . . they could never go back.

Dad had been right, people like Leo did think that money solved all problems. It had probably been a petty-cash transfer for him, but it was something else entirely to my family.

'But Leo,' I said carefully, 'you know my parents could never ever go back. There are too many memories. Good and bad. Selling it . . .' I gulped. 'Selling it was the only thing that let them keep any dignity after the court case.'

'I realize that now.'

I smiled through my tears. 'And how often would we go there? A garden like that needs constant attention. Mum always used to say it was a full-time job on its own. It's too nice a house to be wasted on a couple who'd only have time to visit twice a year. And I don't want to move back. My life is in London now.'

I pushed the key back over the tablecloth. The tips of our fingers met, and I felt a spark of electricity run up my finger, all the way into my arm. I leaned forward until our foreheads touched, and we sat like that for a while, tears dripping onto the thick tablecloth as all the lost possibilities of our future, the grandchildren, the gardens, the happiness we now wouldn't have, ran through our minds.

And then I knew I had to leave, before my heart gave out completely.

I pushed back my chair and touched his shoulder. 'It's no one's fault, Leo. We're just the right plants in the wrong place. I'll never forget this, though.'

He stood up, pulled me into his arms, and kissed me with a terrible sad hunger, and I kissed him back, trying to fix the taste of him and the feel of his skin against mine in my memory forever.

Then, before I had time to register any 'last anythings,' I grabbed my bag and ran out of the garden.


As October turned into November, I tried to keep as busy as I could. Luckily, Ted and I had more business than we could pack into the working week, to the point where we were even talking about taking on another gardener. Paid for by our own profits.

Well, loud talking. We got as far as defining a job description for a container gardening expert with lawn expertise and 'good legs' (must like small dogs), but no further. But we talked about it a fair bit, since Ted was getting to be a regular visitor round at our flat for dinner. So regular that Dickon was sketching him in a selection of sheets, and Jo was finding it harder to convince me that their bickering wasn't taking on a suspiciously cozy quality.

I planted up Christmas bulbs in our kitchen, and watched the Japanese maples near Leominster Square turn from green to a flaming, luminous orange, while the beeches and oaks in the park dropped their leaves to reveal stark bare branches. That was exactly how I felt inside. As if my life had burst into glorious color, which had suddenly fallen away, leaving nothing but a bare outline of trudging work and sleep and once-a-week Zumba, and a long wait until spring and the hope of new buds.

To be honest, though I pretended to be positive for Jo, I wasn't always sure there would be new buds. Sometimes plants had one bonanza year and were never quite the same. How could any man in the Fox and Anchor match up to Leo? I tried that gloomy metaphor on Jo one evening, and she told me that it depended entirely on the fertilizer you were using.

Jo did her best to cheer me up, as did Ted. Since she and Rolf had amicably parted ways — more amicably on her side than his, I thought — she had more time to spend at home, especially since parties were off the agenda for a while. She tried to get me to work on a new version of *Chicago-a-go-go*, with me as Roxie Hart, and we had some fun evenings hoofing around the flat until Mrs Mainwaring banged on the ceiling.

Only Jo could have persuaded her to give the Mama Morton song a go, and now we only had to get Dickon into tap shoes to have nearly a whole company.

And slowly the date of my abandoned wedding edged closer.

Mum and Dad had told so few family members about the wedding that those who had had a 'save the day' assumed it was just a weirder example of our family instability. And Kelly's second moment in the sun — also in the *Sun* and several other newspapers — had blown my wedding out of the minds of anyone who knew us, what with the stories she hadn't told us about this Greg bloke she'd married.

Kelly apologized well, I had to hand it to her, and I think she was telling the truth about going back to college to study fashion. I only skimmed – I didn't want to read the interview – but Mum seemed okay with it. Sort of. She didn't go into a Victoria sponge baking frenzy afterward, put it that way, and Dad said that a couple of people he hadn't spoken to in years had stopped him in the street to shake his hand in a gruff, sympathetic manner.

And being from Yorkshire, they also commiserated with him on having such a rough time of things with his women-folk, then asked about the marrows.

We were all inching toward feeling normal for the first time in years, and for that I was grateful. Sad, but grateful.

I was at home early one morning at the end of November when the intercom buzzed while I was drying my hair. I yelled at Jo to get it.

She broke off yakking on her phone to shout, 'I'm in the bath! You go!'

I grumbled under my breath — I hadn't heard the hot water pipes clunking, so I knew she wasn't actually in there yet — and went to pick up the intercom.

'The sooner we can train you to do this, the better,' I informed Badger, who was waiting for his morning lap round the block. 'Hello?'

'Hello, miss, it's Billy.'

I frowned. 'Billy with the wisteria?'

'Yes, miss. I've got a parcel for you.'

My belongings had arrived back from Nirona in a suitcase weeks ago — it couldn't be that. (Leo had insisted that I keep the bracelet, but I'd couriered the ring back; it was too precious a part of their family for me to keep.) Was it a plant of some kind? A cutting from Billy's own wisteria?

Scrunching my damp hair into a bun, I pulled on my big sweater and trotted downstairs to open the door.

Billy was at the door, holding a small parcel wrapped in brown paper. When he saw me, he smiled broadly, but wouldn't hand it over. 'I've been told you've to open it in the car,' he said, and gestured toward the Range Rover parked outside the flat.

'What? In the actual car?'

'You might want to get a coat,' he added, with the reluctance of someone spoiling a surprise.

I looked at him for clues, but he was giving nothing else away. I narrowed my eyes in pretend annoyance. 'Hold on,' I said, and yelled up the stairs to Jo, 'I'm nipping out! Don't forget to take Badger out for his pee break!'

I didn't hear what she said, but Mrs Mainwaring banged on her ceiling.

I half-expected to find Leo in the back of the Range Rover, but the seat was empty apart from a jacket and a gray jumper. Were they for me? Or — my heart gave a pang — did they belong to Leo's new girlfriend?

Billy closed the door after me and set off while I stared numbly at the package on my knee. It was beautifully wrapped, the brown paper folded crisply, the flat white ribbon knotted at exactly the right angle.

'Open it, miss,' said Billy over his shoulder, 'or else the timing'll be off.'

I didn't want it to be something I'd have to give back. I didn't want it to be something that would test my pathetic resolve. But I steeled myself and pulled the ribbons off, unfolded the paper, and discovered a plain walnut box.

Plain but perfect, with whorls and loops, and dovetail joints you could run a finger over, polished to a deep sheen. I took a deep breath and pushed open the lid.

The inside was lined with red velvet and contained a single red velvet pouch. I lifted the pouch out — it was very light — and tipped the contents into my hand.

A key on a fine gold chain.

I looked up to ask Billy if he knew what the key was for, and suddenly I saw where we were, and I knew.

He parked directly outside the gate to the private garden in Trinity Square, and leaped out to open my door.

I weighed the key in my hand. It was a nice gesture, but

would I ever want to go in there again, if I couldn't be with Leo? It was like being given the freedom of a city where I couldn't speak the language.

Billy was smiling encouragingly, and I didn't want to upset him since he was clearly in on the whole thing, so I got out and fitted the key into the old Edwardian lock.

The gate swung open, but what I saw when I walked in wasn't what I expected.

The rose garden at the center and its Nironan statue fountain were still there. But the manicured lawns had gone. The beds of regimented bedding plants had gone. In their place were newly dug banks of soil, and sprouting from them like alien flowers were big photographs on bendy wires, as high as my waist.

Wild poppies, cornflowers, vetch, campion, buttercups, sorrel, oxeye daisies, all waving gently in the breeze.

I turned round slowly, taking it in. Beneath the big trees were wobbly photos of crocus drifts and wild daffodils, and long grasses waved where the croquet lawn had once been. Someone had been through the whole garden and turned it into a virtual meadow.

When I'd turned a full circle, I saw Leo standing in front of me. He was dressed in jeans and a peacoat, and though his expression was eager, I could see some jumpiness in his blue eyes.

I had to struggle not to touch him, even now. Seeing him made me feel as if something had clicked into focus.

'They're just sown,' he explained. 'Hence the photos. And you can change things if you want. You're the expert.'

'But your lovely lawns,' I breathed, shocked at what he'd done. 'What would your grandfather think? What about the croquet?'

'Willi would love the idea of long grass to lie in right in the middle of town. No woman would have been safe. And he loathed croquet. As do I.'

Leo took my hands and gazed deeply into my eyes. 'Amy, you've always been so good at seeing what other people can't. You were right — this garden, it was just like my life in Nirona. Planned out by other people. Beautiful, but limited.'

'That wasn't a criticism,' I began, but he shushed me.

'I've been doing a lot of thinking since I saw you. What you said about your parents ... it made me weigh up what was really important to me. What I couldn't live without. There's only one thing I can't live without, and that's you.' His expression softened. 'So I spoke to Dad, and to Sofia, and I told them it was time we overturned that ridiculous male primogeniture business.'

My mouth dropped open. 'What?'

Leo cleared his throat. 'Sofia's overseeing the documents — obviously — but the act should be ratified in the first parliament of Dad's reign. Sofia gets what she always wanted, and she'll be very good at it.'

'But what about you? You won't be the crown prince!'

I knew how much it meant to him. I knew how much he loved being part of a chain reaching back into history. He'd given that up. For me. To make my life more normal.

'I'll still get to be part of it all. I just won't have to make it my entire life. And do you think I could enjoy all that, knowing you hated it? And knowing it was because of that that I'd lost you?' His fingers threaded through mine. 'I'd have ended up hating every minute. This way, I'll keep my job in London, and I'll still have duties and charities, but it'll give me more time to get properly involved with them, like your therapy garden.'

'That's . . .' I didn't know what to say. 'That's a bold step for feminism. Sophia must be thrilled.'

Leo nodded wryly. 'She certainly is. I'll need some help, though. I don't know much about therapy gardens. Or dogs.'

There was a brief pause as we gazed shyly at each other, neither of us wanting to spoil the moment, and then Leo clapped a hand to his pocket. 'Nearly forgot, sorry. Soooo, what I suppose I have to ask you is . . .'

He dropped to his knee and took my left hand, looking up with the most appealing expression I'd ever seen. White noise buzzed in my head like a million bumblebees, and I felt faint with excitement.

'Will you do me the great honor,' said Leo, 'of sharing your life with me?'

I nodded. And then I said, 'Yes. Yes, please.'

I hadn't even looked at the ring Leo was holding, but now he was putting it onto my left hand I realized it wasn't the priceless ring his grandfather had given him to give me: it was a much smaller one, a circlet of perfect rose-red rubies set on a gold band. Smaller but beautiful. More me.

'A poppy,' he said simply. 'For the most precious garden-variety flower in the whole world.'

I didn't have any more words. Instead, I reached out for him, and as Leo's arms wrapped round my waist and mine curled around his neck, I felt as if our souls had clicked into place, like a key in a lock.

We stood there kissing and kissing while the fields of photographic flowers behind us flickered in the wind, and as the breeze passed over the flowerbeds, I wondered if it picked up some of our happiness like the meadow mix Leo had sown, and carried it on the currents to spread all over London.

Little pockets of love and whispered promises like daisies and buttercups springing up in the cracks of pavements. I hoped so. There was more than enough to go round.

# EPILOGUE

FROM THE *ROTHERY GAZETTE*, ANNOUNCEMENTS:

On December 12, in St. Cuthbert's Church, Hadley Green, Amy, younger daughter of Mr and Mrs Stanley Wilde of Station Rise, Rothery, to Leo, elder son of Mr and Mrs Boris Wolfsburg of Nirona and London. The bride was attended by her friend, the Honorable Josephine de Vere, and the best man was the groom's brother, Rolf. The honeymoon will be spent in North Yorkshire and Italy.

FROM *HELLO!* MAGAZINE:

... after the intimate private ceremony in the bride's home village in Yorkshire earlier in the month, the celebrations continued with a blessing in the magnificent surroundings of Nirona Cathedral, where the groom had attended his father's coronation only weeks previously. The blushing bride was the center of attention in a tiara commissioned by Prince Leo and fashioned from diamonds and yellow sapphires, styled to represent a simple daisy chain as a tribute to her career as an in-demand London garden designer.

However, Princess Amy's spotlight was almost stolen by her statuesque mother, Mrs Stanley Wilde, wearing a floor-length Zoë Weiss couture piece in Kelly green silk jersey, which was voted Best Guest Outfit on several Internet sites, including our own . . .

. . . To cheers from the 400 close friends and family, the bride and groom then took to the floor for a brief waltz before being joined by the groom's parents, who performed an exhibition tango to the music of Andrew Lloyd Webber, a tantalizing glimpse, perhaps, of Liza Bachmann's upcoming appearance on Dancing with the Stars . . .

FROM YOUNGHOT&ROYAL.COM:

Tears and confetti all round at the marriage blessing of His Royal Hotness Prince Leo of Nirona — not only is our fave millionaire ski bunny officially off the market now that he's tied the knot with his English rose Amy (okay, so we came round to her . . . ), but his even hotter brother Prince Rolf seems to have found himself a new mystery girlfriend too. Boo! Sources close to the naughty Nironan tell us that not only did he make the entire wedding party cry with his story of how he'd brought the bride and groom together by personally throwing himself off a balcony, but Prince Rude-Olfo apparently spent the last hour of his brother's secret wedding ceremony in Yorkshire tying a hundred cans to the royal getaway car before discovering that he'd accidentally sabotaged his dad's car, not his brother's. Silver *fox Prince Boris was not amused. Especially when it turned out Rolf had forgotten to empty the beer out first. Oops! Still, here are some exclusive photos of Rolf at a polo match later that week (see below) . . .*

the hon. jo de vere
smallest flat, 17 leominster place
pimlico
london sw1v

Dear Jo,

Having a lovely time in [BLANK FOR NEWSPAPER SNOOPING REASONS!!!]. Hope all is okay back in London, and that Dickon and Mrs Mainwaring are over the worst of the hangover now. Also that Badger isn't still wearing the bow tie. Can't wait to see you soon — let me know re: duty-free!!

Lots of love,
Mr & Mrs W xxx

PS We saw you and Ted behind the armor
— do NOT deny! xx

## Acknowledgements

As I am absolutely against the house piglet and/or fancy pants as a substitute for a thank you note, I'll instead say a heartfelt thank you here to my indescribable agent Lizzy Kremer, and also to my new editor Jo Dickinson and her fabulously enthusiastic team at Quercus. You make writing books such fun, and I'm grateful for all the help and inspiration.

And if any princes would like to dispute their rating on YoungHot&Royal.com, do drop me a line at www.hesterbrowne.com . . .

# Book Club Reader's Group Guide

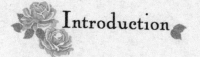

# Introduction

**Amy Wilde**, a young woman with a green thumb, lives in London with her socialite roommate, Jo de Vere. At one of the flamboyant cocktail parties that Jo frequently throws at their flat, Amy meets the tall, blond, and startlingly handsome Leo. They hit it off immediately. After a few romantic dates, Leo reveals that his real name is Leopold — Prince Leopold of Nirona, a wealthy European principality. A whirlwind engagement follows, but is quickly overshadowed by a scandal that makes Leo next in line for the throne — forcing Amy to decide whether or not royalty truly suits her.

# Topics and Questions
## for Discussion

1. Amy makes a distinction between growing up in 'one of Yorkshire's sleepiest villages' (page 7) and living in London. Discuss some of the things Amy thinks and feels about life in London because of her upbringing, and compare Amy's sensibilities with Jo's way of life. Is Amy insecure about or proud of her past?

2. Why do you think Amy doesn't tell Jo about her time with Leo at their party? Do you think Amy would have gone out with Leo had she known he was a prince?

3. When Jo tells Amy a boyfriend would make her working life easier, Amy reacts strongly: 'Are you suggesting that I need a boyfriend to *pay my way*?' (page 57) Amy is proud of her ability to support herself without help from anyone. How does this change after she starts dating Leo? Compare their views and how issues occur in their relationship because of money. For example, how does Leo's habit of using money to solve problems affect Amy's opinion of him?

4. Amy has a habit of practicing for conversations aloud to herself while gardening. Reread one of these passages and

discuss whether this habit is helpful for Amy. Is she able to use her practice dialogue when she finally talks to Leo? Can you relate to this habit at all? If so, discuss times when it has been beneficial for you to practice a conversation beforehand.

5. Jo and Amy immediately Google Leo once they find out he is a prince. Discuss the role of online media throughout the rest of the story. Find other passages where the media — whether its stories are true or false — provokes or triggers something to happen. How does the public invade the private, and how does this affect the characters' lives?

6. During Amy's first foray into Leo's world, at the Royal Opera House fundraiser, she ends up running away during the intermission because a girlfriend of Rolf's accosts her in the bathroom (pages 188–90). Discuss whether you think Amy's disappearance was the best way to handle the situation. How would you have reacted if you had been in Amy's position?

7. Throughout the novel, Amy's sister, Kelly, has a ghostlike presence; Amy thinks about her and what happened, but doesn't share the full story until close to the end. How did this ongoing mystery affect your reading of the novel? Did you have any predictions about what happened, or at what point Kelly would reenter Amy's life?

8. Consider the significance of place in the novel. For example, Amy's parents had to sell their first house due

to Kelly's disgrace, and Amy harbors a sad connection to the old house. How does the new house represent their new family life? Discuss other places in the story and the characters' connections to them — Leominster Place, the Nirona palace, Leo's inherited town house in London — in your response.

9. A main issue in the Wolfsburg family is the line of succession. Minutes before dying, Leo's grandfather (Sovereign Prince Wilhelm) decides that Boris will be the next crown prince, not his twin, Pavlos. Meanwhile, Sofia feels cheated because women are still passed over in the succession. Discuss the politics of succession in the novel. Why does Prince Wilhelm give the crown to Boris over Pavlos at the last minute? Do you think Sofia's anger is justified?

10. As soon as Leo becomes heir to the crown, Amy gets more and more wrapped up in the royal world and she is put under a huge magnifying glass — not only by Leo's family, but also by the media. Sofia arrives to 'begin the princessing process' (page 322) on Amy. What does this process entail? How does Amy handle the demands asked of her? Is she happy with the changes? Do you think becoming a public royal figure warrants a complete makeover for someone like Amy?

11. When Amy's Palace View bee conservation project conflicts with Leo's plans, Amy says, 'I'm just normal, Leo. I'm a completely normal girl. And I'm trying to meet you

in the middle, but my middle's miles away from yours (page 344).' How do Amy and Leo find a happy medium between royalty and normalcy? Discuss how well you think Leo can understand Amy's 'normal,' and vice versa.

12. Amy has a close relationship with her parents. How does she try to help and protect them (especially her mother) as they get pulled into the public eye?

13. How do the other characters react to Amy's new position in the world? Consider her parents, Jo, Ted, Dickon, Mrs Mainwaring, Jennifer Wainwright, and Kelly (aka Callie Hamilton).

14. Why does Sofia purposely sabotage Amy? Reflect on the official photo shoot and the grace at the Crown Princess Ball. Do you think Leo and his family put too much pressure on Amy to perform publicly? Or do you agree it is a necessary part of royal life?

15. When Amy tells Leo she cannot marry him, she uses his private garden as a metaphor. She says, '[T]his place is you. It's elegant and measured, and every bed blooms at the right time because someone's planned the flowering seasons. It's lovely, but I couldn't live in it (page 495).' How does this garden metaphor illustrate Amy and Leo's relationship? Why does Amy feel that wildflower meadows are a better fit for her?

## Enhance Your Book Club

1. Visit www.bbc.co.uk/history/royal_weddings to learn more about the history of royal weddings. Compare these real couples' stories with Amy and Leo's courtship. Can you find any similarities? Differences?

2. The story is written entirely from Amy's perspective. Have each member in your book club select a scene and imagine it from Leo's perspective. How would he see the situation differently than Amy does?

3. Test your own green thumb and plan a garden-planting party with your book club! Gather seeds for your favourite flowers and potting soil and spend the afternoon getting your hands dirty.

4. Imagine you've just got engaged to Prince Harry. What would the press dig up about you and your family? And how would you spin it into a positive story?

5. Would the glamour and prestige of royal life outweigh the duty and scrutiny for you? What would be the best and the worst aspects of a public life like Leo and Amy's?